TODD HERZMAN

ACCIDENTAL CHAMPION

BOOK TWO

aethonbooks.com

ACCIDENTAL CHAMPION 2
©2024 TODD HERZMAN

Aethon Books
www.aethonbooks.com

Print and eBook design and formatting by Kevin G. Summers.

Published by Aethon Books LLC.

Aethon Books is not responsible for websites (or their content) that are not owned by the publisher.

Also by Todd Herzman

Accidental Champion

Accidental Champion 2

Accidental Champion 3

———————

Want to discuss our books with other readers and even the authors?

JOIN THE AETHON DISCORD!

Chapter 1
Why Don't I Just See What I Can Do

THE ARMY OF ENEMY DENIZENS AND BEASTS STRETCHED ON farther than the eye could see, covering the horizon on every side of Queen Alastea's castle. A sight that should strike fear into any warrior's heart. The ranks of the Endless Horde held Denizens of all sorts and manner—some that looked no different to those soldiers standing within the castle. Humans, elves, and men who looked like demons—even lizard men—were among them.

There were other races, too. Ones that weren't contained within the walls. Men and women who looked to be dwarves, carrying wicked-looking axes and hammers, each standing no taller than five feet, the men's beards swaying in the wind. Bestial, humanoid Denizens that looked like orcs, sharp tusks jutting out from either side of their jaws. Their skin was the grey of a dull, overcast sky, and their fangs looked jagged and sharp, jutting out from the top of their mouths to sit over their bottom lips.

Xavier Collins stepped up to the parapet atop the castle's battlements on its forward wall. He wore his dark Shrouded Robes, his hood down, and he knew his silver eyes would be visible for anyone to see. Perhaps those eyes of his were the reason Queen Alastea, with her hair such a dark brown it looked black, wearing a silver glowing gown, staff gripped in a long-fingered hand, golden

1

crown resting atop her head, looked at him differently than she did the others.

Or perhaps it was because he, unlike the other members of his party, had his aura under control—a perfect balance struck within his Spirit Core—showing him to be someone of far greater aptitude and power than any ordinary Level 14 Denizen.

His party stood at his back. Howard, a former cop and current Shield Sentinel, his sword sheathed at his side and his large tower shield still within his Storage Ring. Justin, a swordsman, once an Olympic fencer before all this mess, now an Airborne Duellist with the ability to fly, and all while still being only sixteen. And Siobhan, the red-headed Irishwoman who'd migrated to the States but still had a hint of her old accent, wearing mage robes and gripping her staff loosely. She was a Divine Beacon and the only support class among them, able to heal them and teleport them wherever they needed to go, among other things.

Though his party was formidable, especially considering they were each only Level 11, they would not be fighting by Xavier's side. He didn't need them to. Xavier summoned Soultaker, the staff-scythe he'd carried since attaining the epic class of Soultaker, into his hand. The black, arm-length metal blade reflected the sun's light. Queen Alastea's gaze turned to the blade with a curious expression.

It was strange—meeting the woman again. Xavier and his party had been on this floor once already—the fifth floor of the Tower of Champions—and had faced the first four waves of the Endless Horde. Though he supposed saying they destroyed them, not merely faced them, would be a more apt description of what had happened. He had spoken to the queen. Seen her awe of him after he'd fought in that first wave. They'd spent over four hours in this place, and left it less than an hour ago.

And yet the woman didn't recognise him at all.

"What you ask..." Queen Alastea trailed off. She did not look like a woman who was often lost for words. Her adviser—tall, old, and the image of a scholar with his pointed grey beard—inspected

Xavier and his party closely but did not say a word. Queen Alastea cleared her throat, straightened, full of poise. "Your status as Champions of the Void earns you many freedoms, but asking me and my soldiers to stand down against the Endless Horde, when it is *our* people we wish to protect, flies in the face of wisdom."

Xavier smiled. "I assure you, Queen Alastea, once you see what I can do, it should lessen your fears." He rested a hand on the parapet, looking out at the Horde once more. "There will be time for your people to create a portal and escape through it. I will not let a single enemy in these first five waves reach the moat, let alone the top of the battlements."

He didn't plan on the enemies in the latter waves reaching the battlements either, though he still couldn't help but wonder just how many he would be able to endure.

Queen Alastea blinked. "I hope this confidence you have placed in your prowess is something you are able to prove, Champion."

"Xavier," he said. "My name is Xavier."

He hadn't introduced himself the first time he and his party had been on this floor, not that the queen would have remembered that anyway. At the best of times, Xavier wasn't much of a social animal—which, honestly, was quite the understatement. But they intended to spend a lot longer here this time around, and if their plan of gaining a good rapport with the queen were to work, he would have to make an effort to break out of his shell.

This woman. This castle. He was sure that it would have information about the Greater Universe that Xavier and his party had not been able to access. Coming from a newly integrated world, they were highly constrained by all the things they didn't know.

Spending time on this floor could change everything—besides, they would have to spend a long time on this floor anyway if he were going to have a chance at reaching the top spot on the ladder.

I will reach the top spot. It won't be a game of chance. I will face every wave until I have nothing left in me. Until I can no longer endure another single enemy.

It wasn't about winning. Well... it wasn't *only* about winning.

He *needed* to gain the record for this floor if he were going to get the most out of it he could. The title for being number 1 was simply *better* than the titles beneath it. And he would need every title he could get if he was going to protect Earth from the invasion that was no doubt already underway.

He looked over the notification for the floor once more, as he knew the first wave of the Endless Horde was about to charge.

Welcome to the Fifth Floor of the Tower of Champions.
The Fifth Floor of the Tower of Champions is a test of how much you can endure.
Time is frozen on this floor. Outside of this instance, entering this floor will always take a single hour, whether a Champion leaves the floor within one minute or one year.
This castle will soon be under siege from both Denizens and beasts, experiencing increasing waves of difficulty. Unlike other floors, a record on this floor is not based on how quickly it can be cleared, but rather how many waves of enemies one survives.
Each wave has a floor boss, or "wave boss," and once you have cleared the first five waves— a feat that takes no less than five hours—this floor will be considered cleared.
Know this: the castle will fall. You cannot protect it forever.
The waves are never-ending.

It was that last line that excited Xavier the most. It also sent a small shudder up his spine. He didn't think it was a shudder of *fear*, for he didn't feel afraid. Perhaps it was simply anticipation.

Xavier had faced more than one challenge since the System

had integrated Earth. He'd nearly been killed by goblins, pumas, and a humanoid rat-beast that stood on two legs and called itself a king. He'd faced the challenge of clearing the last floor as quickly and efficiently as possible. But right now, he felt powerful beyond what the Tower of Champions could have expected of him.

The challenges the tower threw at him weren't life-threatening, not anymore—they were about achieving the *best possible* time. Not once, on the last two floors, had he worried for his life. It wasn't as though he *wanted* to be in danger, but he yearned for that sense of adventure. That thrill of the fight.

And there was a pit in his stomach, one that hungered for every single soul among the ranks of the Endless Horde.

This would challenge him. *This* would push his level and his limits higher than anything else he'd faced since the integration of Earth. *This* would prepare him for the armies that would be invading his world even as he stood upon those battlements.

War drums beat outside the walls. A horn was blown. Denizens smashed their weapons on their shields. And the first wave of the Endless Horde whipped back their heads and roared. The first wave was comprised of Level 10 enemies. Wolven. Wolf-like beasts the size of horses, twin horns jutting from either side of their heads. They looked ferocious. Formidable. Yet their auras were dull.

They were like ants facing off against a bear.

Xavier's soulkeeping was at capacity. He held 200 souls within him—200 souls he was ready to unleash upon the enemy. At first, he'd intended to spend this wave practising Soul Block, a spell he'd been neglecting, but seeing the look on Queen Alastea's face, the sheer doubt in her brown eyes, he knew he needed to make a show out of this. Display his prowess so she did not doubt his strength.

That would get her onside faster than blundering around out there, letting wolf-like beasts attack him with their slobbering maws.

Standing at the parapet, he took a deep breath—somewhat regretting it as the wind turned, bringing with it a whole army's worth of sweat—and focused. There were at least three thousand enemies in this first wave. He doubted he could take them all out with the number of souls he held in a single casting.

Why don't I just see what I can do.

He stepped up atop the parapet wall, casting Spiritual Trifecta on himself and Spirit Infusion on his staff-scythe. Xavier and his weapon were both overtaken by a silvery glow, each spell enhancing the power of his magic. He gazed around at the oncoming wave without a hint of worry on his face; he launched his attack, casting Soul Strike infused with every single one of the souls in his reserve.

Two hundred bolts of lightning shot forth from his staff. The pure white bolts arced high in the sky, the ones directed at the enemies coming at the castle from the back—as the Endless Horde encircled the walls from every side—shooting straight over the tall towers. He could sense the auras of the enemies back there even if he couldn't see them from where he stood, his aura-sight piercing through the castle's thick stone.

Apparitions sprang to life, taking the avatars of Denizens and beasts he'd used to fill his reserves, their souls coming back to life one last time before they were extinguished in this attack.

Massive Wolven and formidable-looking elven and human warriors and mages—souls he'd harvested from the fourth wave—materialised at the end of the bolts of lightning, taking translucent form long enough to charge through the enemy beasts, causing massive amounts of soul damage.

As he watched, he realised the spell he'd cast had actually been overkill. A single soul could have perhaps taken down twenty of these beasts.

The entire wave died in one spell.

Remaining on the wall, Xavier reaped the souls of the three thousand enemies he'd just killed. Each soul he harvested that he didn't need for his reserve, he instantly consumed with Soul Harden. He pushed away all of the different kill notifications, focusing only on the last two bits of text that popped into his vision.

Soul Harvest has taken a step forward on the path!
Soul Harvest is now a Rank 7 spell.
One cannot walk backward on the path.

Soul Harden has taken a step forward on the path!
Soul Harden is now a Rank 7 spell.
One cannot walk backward on the path.

Oh, this floor... This is gonna be good.

He didn't gain a level from all of those kills—he needed 16 *million* Mastery Points before reaching Level 15—but that didn't matter. He would get there soon enough. Besides, he'd just added another 10 spots to his soulkeeping threshold. That was enough for him for now.

Xavier tried not to smirk. He wanted to look humble. He lowered Soultaker and stepped back off the wall, walking over to Queen Alastea. The woman's eyes were wide as she looked over the parapet at the thousands of dead. The last time he'd been on this floor, he hadn't stuck around to see how she might react to his use of soul magic.

"You... you are indeed all you say you are, Champion of the Void." Queen Alastea paused. "Xavier." She gave a small, stiff bow of the head.

Xavier smiled. "Well, now that you've seen what I can do, and it will still be almost an hour before the next wave... You don't happen to have a library in that castle of yours, do you?"

Queen Alastea blinked, looking a little confused. "I, ah." It was the most flustered he'd seen her. In fact, before this moment, he couldn't have imagined what the queen would even look like flustered. "Yes, we do." She looked to her adviser. "Kalren, would you show these Champions to the library in the castle's leftmost tower?"

Kalren raised a curious eyebrow. He was staring so intently at Xavier as to look almost creepy. He glanced at the queen and lowered his head. "Certainly, Your Majesty." He stepped forward, motioning a hand to the battlements' switchback stairs. "This way."

Xavier grinned as he followed the adviser. Yes, it was facing the waves of the Endless Horde and the challenge that the latter waves would provide that excited him most about this floor. But going to a library in what was basically a fantasy world? Discovering secrets the System had kept from their newly integrated planet?

That... that was a damned close second.

As Xavier and his party followed the old man to the library, Xavier felt something. A prickle on the back of his neck. He frowned, trying to examine what it was he was feeling. It was... it was similar to what he'd felt before, at the end of the previous floor. That presence that had appeared and made him feel like nothing more than a speck of dust. An ant staring up at a mountain.

But this presence was different. More subtle. Once again, he knew it wasn't the System that was looking at him.

This, far more than the sight of the Endless Horde, made Xavier feel a hint of fear, because he couldn't deny it any longer—the things he was doing in the tower were gaining attention from far, far outside of it. He was being watched. Watched by entities more powerful than he could yet imagine.

And who knew if those entities had good intentions.

By the time they reached the double doors up the castle's steps, the presence was gone. Looking at the other members of his party, it was clear they hadn't felt it.

Xavier sighed to himself. *Another thing to add to the list of worries I can't deal with yet.*

The queen's adviser, Kalren, let them through the castle's large doors—past all the realm's citizens that were huddling in fear inside, waiting for the portal to be opened so it could get them out of this place—and up a set of stairs that curled around a tower, until finally they reached the castle's library. When Kalren opened the library's doors, Xavier held in a gasp.

There were more books within the castle's walls than he'd ever hoped to find.

This floor might just end up being their secret weapon.

Chapter 2
You Want to Explain That Again?

When Xavier stepped inside the tower room, his mouth fell open. All he could do was stare around in awe.

The castle's tower library was like something out of Beauty and the Beast. The room was circular, with ceilings three floors high. Bookshelves lined every inch of the walls, reaching all the way up to the tower's ceiling, which was topped off with thick glass, letting the sun bathe the spines in light. He couldn't help but imagine what the place would be like when there was a light rain pattering on that glass, a mug of warm coffee in one hand and a book open in the other, with flames crackling and dancing in the hearth. Maybe some light music as ambiance.

There were staircases and walkways close to the shelves for the books higher up, along with ladders interspersed throughout the place. Tables lined the middle of the room, with lamps atop them. The lamps gave out a warm light. He gave the closest one a double-take when he realised that it wasn't flames that produced their light, but rather crystals. Crystals that gave off a sense of energy.

Is that Spirit Energy powering those lamps? Xavier wondered. His aura-sight certainly seemed to think so.

Justin released an appreciative whistle. "That's a lot of books."

Howard and Siobhan stepped in after them.

Kalren, Queen Alastea's adviser, looked at the books with great admiration. "This is the royal library. A difficult place to gain access to. As you can see, Queen Alastea's family have collected much knowledge in this place." He lowered his head, forehead creasing. "I only wish her parents were here now. Perhaps..." He drifted off and drew in a breath. "My apologies. You may peruse them at your leisure. I will fetch you all when the next wave is close to charging."

"You need only fetch me," Xavier said. "My party will remain here."

Kalren nodded and was about to walk out of the room when Siobhan took a step forward. She cleared her throat. "Why are the books still here? Isn't this castle to be abandoned? Surely there would be enough Storage Rings to store them within."

Kalren paused, turning to face her. "The queen has entrusted me with some of the family's most beloved tomes, but unfortunately, the queendom does not have enough Storage Rings to spare to transport every book from this library to safety. Such an endeavour is no longer within her means. The queen donated all of the ones she had, barring her personal ring, for usage in"—his face scrunched up—"the final battle. She wished the people of her realm the ability to bring all of their beloved possessions with them." He raised his left hand, wiggling his ring finger. "I gave my own to the cause."

Siobhan bowed her head. "Queen Alastea is very kind to her people."

"They are everything to her." He made to leave again, but Siobhan spoke once more.

"Are you able to show us around these books?"

The man paused. A look of frustration flashed across his face, though it was gone in an instant. "My queen has instructed me to leave when the portal opens, which means I have less than five hours remaining to spend by her side before she sacrifices herself. She is the last of the family that I have devoted my entire life to. I wish to spend these few hours by her side, advising her, as is my duty."

Kalren stepped out of the library, his boots thumping lightly on the winding stone stairs that led to the bottom of the tower.

Siobhan looked conflicted as she stared at the door. Xavier thought he knew what she was thinking. That did not feel like the kind of reaction that the System might simply fabricate. She touched a hand to her chest, and none of her usual excitement was present, despite the library they now had access to. "I didn't mean to offend him."

Howard put a hand on the woman's shoulder. "I'm sure the man knows that. We are here to help him and his people, after all."

"So weird," Justin muttered, eyes on the doorway. "Why would the System create such an intricate backstory for these people? Isn't this level just to test how well we protect against a siege? How well we can defend a fortified area?"

Siobhan's gaze fell to the stone floor. "Video games construct narratives to help a player with immersion. Perhaps that's simply what the System is doing." Her words lacked conviction. She heaved a sigh. "In any event, it looks as though we're on our own in here." She gazed up at the many books lining the wall, that spark returning to her eyes. "I didn't imagine they'd have so many! It's rare for medieval societies to have access to this many books."

"This isn't exactly a medieval society," Howard said, walking over to one of the shelves. "In fact, I don't really know *what* to call it."

Xavier turned his own attention toward the books. Though he was impressed with how many of them there were, he did wish that Kalren had stayed. The sheer volume of books in this place gave him a sense of overwhelm. There was so much that they needed to learn. So much they didn't know about to begin with. He stepped over to the nearest bookcase. The tomes that lined the shelf were hardbacks that looked like they should be in a museum. He reached out, just short of touching one, as though worried he might damage them.

The tower library didn't have labelled sections or any sort of dewy decimal system. There were no computers pointing toward a book with all the information he needed. If there was some sort of directory, he couldn't ascertain its location.

The books did have words on their spines. They were in a script he didn't recognise. For one fateful moment, he worried they wouldn't be able to read any of the books. The System might have translated spoken language to them in the tower—there was no way this queen spoke *English*—but that didn't mean it would translate *written* language.

But even though he'd never seen the script before—even though there was no reason he should be able to read it—as he stared at the words, their meaning became clear to him. "Strange," he muttered. The others glanced over. Xavier picked up the book. "It's in another language, another script, but I can *read* it."

"Well thank god for that," Howard said. "So, what exactly is it we're looking for?" The man looked at Siobhan, then over at Xavier. "I'm sure there's plenty of interesting stuff to find in here..."

"Anything useful we can get our hands on. Class manuals, information on newly integrated planets, how to defend against invasion, training modalities, other races' weaknesses, the creation of defences..." Siobhan trailed off. "We need to know *everything*."

Justin ran his finger along the spine of a few different books, walking beside the wall. "Whatever information is in these books didn't seem to help the people out there."

"We aren't them," Xavier said. "I'd also like to find any information on Spirit Cores and Celestial Energy. Anything that can help me gain and strengthen those skills."

"What about the Endless Horde?" Howard asked.

Xavier nodded. He hadn't thought of that. "If you find anything about it, though I don't think it's a priority." He bit his lip, a thought occurring. "We have no idea if this place is real... Do you think, somehow, it could have information on the Tower of Champions? Or why they call us Champions of the Void?"

"Some of these questions you could just ask the queen," Justin muttered. "I'm sure she wouldn't mind, especially considering what you're doing for her."

Siobhan pursed her lips but nodded. "That's a good idea. Perhaps you should head back out and speak with her. You'll need to be out there for the next wave." As she spoke, she took a book and flicked through its pages. "We'll come get you if we find anything."

Xavier looked at the book in his hands. He hadn't even had a chance to open it yet. He sighed and placed it back on the shelf. He didn't want to walk out of this place, but perhaps she was right. His time might be better spent out there. Queen Alastea might be more forthright with information than Sam had been. But he worried about her level of power.

How much could she *really* know if she couldn't deal with these five waves?

Perhaps he'd get an answer to why she had to stay behind. Though he knew that didn't matter when it came to clearing the floor, he'd been curious about it ever since she'd mentioned it.

With some reluctance, he left the others in the library and headed back the way they'd come, down the winding stairs and past the civilians packing the castle tight. He wondered what types of classes they had. What levels they might be. And why they weren't fighting. He supposed he didn't really know what it was like for integrated worlds out there. How many people become fighters, and how many became crafters?

I've no idea how the Greater Universe even works.

As he walked, he summoned his Sector Travel Key. The item that would take him anywhere he wished within his galaxy. It made him once again wonder *where* he would go, and what types of places there would be to see.

Queen Alastea was exactly where he had left her. She turned and greeted him with a minute bow. "I did not expect you to return so quickly. The next wave is still close to fifty minutes away."

"I was hoping you would be able to answer some questions for me."

The queen raised an eyebrow. "Are you curious about our defences?" She swept her gaze around the battlements, at the soldiers arrayed along the walls. "It does not appear as though you need them, considering how you dealt with that first wave."

I don't, he thought. *At least not yet.* "No, that's not what I was curious about." He paused, wondering how honest he should be. Again, he supposed it didn't matter. This woman wouldn't remember who he was. "The world that I and my party come from has been newly integrated."

Queen Alastea blinked. "Newly integrated?" The woman frowned. "I do not understand. What does that mean?"

Adviser Kalren stood behind the queen, his eyes widening at Xavier's words. "I have heard of this, though I didn't believe it to be true."

"Heard of what, Kalren?"

"There are legends of a time when the System did not rule over the Greater Universe. An integration is what happens when the System comes to a world."

Queen Alastea's frown grew deeper. "A time before the System... but the System is eternal?"

"The System is eternal," Kalren said. It didn't sound like an answer to her question—more like a repeated prayer. "But there was a time before it."

Xavier was intrigued by the conversation they were having. Mostly because they spoke of the Greater Universe *at all.* He'd thought of the floors as... contained instances *outside* the normal universe. Fabricated realities created by the System. All the information he'd found said the Tower of Champions had remained unchanged since the System came. Yet these people spoke as though the System had always been. He bit his lip and asked a question he wasn't sure he was supposed to ask. "Do you know about the Tower of Champions?"

The adviser cocked his head to the side. "Of course we know of the Tower of Champions." He raised his chin, peering down at him. "You really are from a newly integrated world."

15

"You... wait, you've heard of the tower?"

Queen Alastea looked confused. "We know. That is where Champions of the Void *come* from, after all." She stared at him for a moment. "You really did not think we would know? We, who summoned you here?"

Xavier walked over to the parapet and leant against it. "You know that... you know that we came from there?" He put a hand on his head. "That means you know that what's happening now has happened before?"

Queen Alastea turned from him. "An infinite number of times, no doubt. Not that we remember. Admittedly, it is difficult to wrap my head around. We knew what summoning Champions of the Void would do, however. It was... it was the only choice I could make." She shut her eyes. "My people would die if you were not here."

Xavier propped himself up against the parapet, trying to understand what the hell was going on here. *These people* are *real. All of it is real.* "You want to explain that again?"

Chapter 3
What-Ifs and Could-Have-Beens

XAVIER SAT ON THE PARAPET WALL OF QUEEN ALASTEA'S castle. Behind him, the ranks upon ranks of the Endless Horde waited for the next wave to begin. In front, Queen Alastea and her adviser, Kalren, stood. He ran a hand through his hair.

These people are real. There were so many things he didn't understand about that.

"What confuses you?" Kalren asked in the tone of a tutor.

Xavier released a sigh. "I was led to believe that the Tower of Champions had been around for as long as the universe itself—since the very beginning of the System."

Kalren bowed his head in a nod. "That is correct."

Xavier blinked. "Then... the floors in the tower *do* change? The manual we read said they remained static..."

"No." Kalren shook his head. "They do not change. They do, in fact, remain static for all eternity. Each Denizen who enters the tower and becomes a Champion faces the same challenges. And they always have, since the very first Denizen."

Xavier shut his eyes and put his head in his hands. He thought he felt a headache coming along. "Then what is it? Time travel? Did... did the System pull things out of time, out of... the future?

Because clearly you know what the Tower of Champions is *and* you're a part of it *and* it's always been around, but you can't have..."

"Ah," Kalren uttered. "I see where the issue is."

"Well, I'm glad someone does."

"You are under the false assumption that there is only one universe."

Xavier opened his eyes, dropping his hands. He raised his head and looked at the adviser. "Multiverse. I had thought of that."

Kalren walked over to the parapet and leant against it beside Xavier. Where before he had been the epitome of seriousness, now he was a little less reserved. "When you first came here, you thought we weren't real, didn't you?"

"This is actually the second time I've been on this floor."

Kalren nodded. "Indeed. Indeed, that is common."

"And yes... I didn't know. I still don't really understand."

"That is fair, considering you came from a newly integrated world. Our world has been a part of the System for longer than our memories can reach. The people of this queendom—those who still remain—do not know of a time before it, so it is difficult for me to put myself in your shoes."

"So this"—Xavier waved a hand—"is an alternate universe?"

"From your perspective, yes. One of an infinite number, in fact. But I assure you, it is very real."

If not for Xavier's Intelligence attribute, it would probably have taken him a lot longer to wrap his head around what was going on. Even then, it simply went against everything that he believed *could* be true. "And this... this universe is now different to the universe I was in the last time I stepped onto this floor. It's changed, because of my actions." His forehead creased, becoming heavily lined as he pieced the implications of that together. "Which means... you are the same people we met, but you *aren't* the *same* people we met."

"Ah, well, at least you catch on fast," Kalren said. "The multiverse is a difficult concept for people to digest, even those born in societies with knowledge of it. It purports an infinite number of universes. Ones that diverge with every single decision.

Summoning a Champion of the Void made this universe branch off perhaps... trillions of times."

The adviser let out a breath. "It is a lot to swallow. A lot to imagine. Surely, we have died many, many times. But *we* cannot concern ourselves with the goings on of other universes, ones we are not in direct contact with, can we? We would get lost in all of the what-ifs and could-have-beens. All we'd do is sit there and contemplate *possibility* without doing a single thing. There might be universes out there where the System never spread; as blasphemous as that is to say, it is a simple truth. The System is eternal, but it may not be omnipresent."

"If this is true..." Xavier felt like he'd never frowned so much in his life, his face scrunched up in what Siobhan would call stinkface. "Then each floor of the tower is connected with a different universe—a different *starting* point in a thousand different universes." He licked his lips, his thoughts coming together. "They couldn't be connected to just one universe, because everything that happens on each floor, with every Denizen that enters it, would change that universe..." He clutched his head again.

Kalren chuckled. "As I said, it is a lot to swallow." He clapped Xavier on the back with more familiarity than he would have expected. "I'm glad you are the Champion of the Void that ended up here. You are clearly strong enough to deal with these waves. And the fact that we are real people—even if we do not share the same universe—seems to be important to you."

Xavier looked at Kalren. "Why wouldn't it be important?"

"Denizens enter the Tower of Champions in search of power. Most Denizens do not care how they acquire that power. In an instance such as this, they might perform their task, but they would not care about the casualties to our number."

"Many of my soldiers would lose their lives had someone less strong or less caring arrived," Queen Alastea said. "I am sure that... that has happened many times." She got a faraway look, no doubt contemplating the what-ifs and could-have-beens.

Xavier, selfishly, wondered if this knowledge actually changed anything for him. Then he remembered the army he had killed. No, the *two* armies he had killed. On the third floor, he had destroyed *both* the elven army *and* the human army in different instances.

Those were all real people, fighting for a real cause, somewhere. And I don't even know which side was in the right—if either of them even were.

Should he feel guilt for that? Had he been wrong to fight? He *needed* to fight. *Needed* this strength to protect and save Earth. It wasn't as though he could simply turn away from it. Was the fact that the people he'd faced in these places *real* something that needed to change the way he approached each floor?

For the most part, the enemies he'd faced *hadn't* been humans or sapient Denizens from other races. Then again, that Rat King he'd faced had been able to talk...

This doesn't change anything for me. It can't.

But in a way, it *expanded* things. He looked at Kalren, at Queen Alastea and her guards, at all the soldiers standing on the wall, in an entirely new light. He'd wondered what it would be like to travel to different worlds. And here he was, already doing it. *These aren't set pieces. Aren't fabrications made by the System. They're real people, just... from somewhere far, far away.*

Xavier raised his chin. He was now even more glad that he'd told the queen he didn't want her soldiers fighting in this conflict. He wouldn't have to worry about getting *real* people killed. *That will happen, when I return to Earth. I won't be able to save everyone. But it's not something that needs to happen now.* Of course, there *were* real people in the Endless Horde.

But they... they were on the wrong side of this conflict.

He stood. Looked at Queen Alastea. "Your people will be safe." Now that he knew she was real, there was another question he had to ask. "Why will you remain here when the portal opens? Why do you think your fate is sealed?"

Queen Alastea peered over the parapet at the enemy Denizens and beasts. "It was my family who angered the Endless Horde.

They will follow the blood that runs through my veins to the ends of the universe. If I go with my people, I will doom them to this fate." She motioned to the Horde. "Whether in ten years, a hundred, or a thousand. The Endless Horde does not stop."

The waves are never-ending. He remembered reading that, from the System notification about this floor. He turned and looked at the ranks. "The notification I received said the waves would never stop. If this is *real*, how can that be possible? And why... why do they wait? Why do they come in waves? Not that I want them all to move at once."

Kalren, his hands folded behind him, spoke, "The System has told you a half-truth."

Xavier's eyes widened. "The System *lies*?"

"The System does what it wishes," Queen Alastea muttered under her breath. "In this case, it only seems like a lie. The Endless Horde has an army that spreads through half of the sector and the ability to connect different worlds with portals. Portals they can afford to keep open for as long as they wish. In theory, there *is* an end to their waves, but it isn't an end you or I will ever see."

"As for why they do not attack all at once..." Kalren began. "As a stronger force, they are restricted by the rules of engagement within this sector. I do not know if these rules hold true in your universe, or even in other sectors. But in this instance, they cannot simply send their strongest Denizen after us. And if they did, the System would punish them greatly. It is shameful for those of a higher grade to eradicate those of a lower one. That does not mean it doesn't happen, of course."

Xavier latched onto this idea. He knew the System put restrictions on which Denizens could travel to Earth while it was being integrated, only allowing them to be a single level higher than the highest-level Denizen from Earth. Perhaps that also meant there were *other* restrictions he didn't know about.

"The System wants to give you a fighting chance. Or... or a way to escape?"

"Indeed," Kalren replied. "Even if the odds are against us."

"But you." Xavier looked at Queen Alastea. "You're sure you cannot leave?"

"I have accepted my fate. I only wish my ancestors had done the same." She raised her chin. "Had they made such a sacrifice, many lives would have been spared."

Xavier didn't have to ask her to understand what she meant. If the Endless Horde pursued her blood wherever it went... someone in her family's past had taken their ire and escaped from the Horde, only to doom one of their descendants later down the line.

It made him wonder what choice he would make were he in Queen Alastea's shoes. He supposed he could understand her sacrifice now. *I think I would fight. I think I would escape, hide, become strong, and then come back and fight.*

Xavier wasn't sure how long it would be until the next wave came, but he was more eager than ever for it. These people were real, and he had the power to save them. To destroy these waves until their portal was created.

And I abandoned them last time... Those were real people I just left after defeating the fourth wave...

He couldn't think about that. As Kalren had said, he should not lose himself in the what-ifs and could-have-beens, nor concern himself with universes he was no longer connected to.

Xavier cleared his throat. "You say these waves are near infinite. That the Endless Horde covers half your sector... I do not see how I could defeat them all. But I do promise you, Queen Alastea, that I will remain here for as long as I possibly can. Your people will survive. They will pass through the portal. And I will remain, taking down as many waves as I can until fighting for a moment longer would mean losing my life. Though I know that will not save you, it will at least give you a chance to live a little longer than you would have otherwise. I do not ask for anything in return. However, I am new to this... System. To all of it. I have many questions that people such as yourselves might be able to answer, if you're willing."

Queen Alastea still looked as poised as ever, but there was

something new in her gaze as she looked at him, as though she were appraising him. "I will answer whatever I can."

Xavier was almost surprised by how much Kalren and the queen had been able to tell him. When he spoke to Sam, there were all sorts of restrictions imposed upon the bartender—the *care*taker. But here, it had been different. He and his party had hoped they'd found a loophole to learning new information about the System and the Greater Universe, and so far it seemed as though he had.

I'm going to learn as much as possible from this floor. He looked out at the Endless Horde. *And I'm going to eradicate as many of their number as I can.*

That was something he wouldn't feel *any* guilt for.

Chapter 4

Soul Block

Xavier spoke with the queen and her adviser, Kalren, right up until the war drums began to beat once more, the thrum of their consistent thuds announcing the imminence of the next wave.

Has it really been an hour already?

He pushed himself off the cold stone, standing from where he'd been sitting on the parapet. Xavier informed the queen to once again order her soldiers not to interfere with the wave. This time, the woman did not argue. She simply lowered her head in a small nod, then had Kalren issue her orders in a booming voice loud enough to be heard along the walls.

Good. The display of power he'd shown during the first wave, taking it out with the use of a single spell and 200 souls, had clearly shown her he knew what he was doing.

"This wave will take longer than the last," Xavier told her. "It may look as though I am in danger, but there are simply some spells I need to rank up."

"My soldiers will not interfere unless I deem it necessary. Perhaps they will learn something by observing you." Queen Alastea stepped up to the parapet, placing her hands upon the stone, her forehead slightly creased. The woman was usually adept at keeping poised, not betraying her emotions. Now, he could see the worry in that expression.

She knows she will die. Maybe not on this wave, or the fifth, or the fiftieth. But she must be wondering: How long can he truly hold out here?

Xavier took a few steps backward, giving himself a bit of run-up, and cast Spiritual Trifecta on himself. Then he sprinted at the parapet. He leapt, soaring over the wall and the moat beyond, and landed in a smooth roll. He couldn't help but grin as he came back to his feet in a sprint. A jump-and-roll like that would be impossible for a normal human. He hadn't even *needed* to roll to absorb the impact to his knees, he'd simply done it so it wouldn't reduce his momentum.

How good would I be at parkour now?

He shook that thought away as the next wave of the Endless Horde charged. Xavier summoned Soultaker from his Storage Ring. Having it in hand increased his running speed because of the Scythe-Staff Mastery boost. Though the shift wasn't huge, he noticed it instantly.

Come on, Endless Horde. Come straight at me.

The enemy Denizens and beasts opened mouths and maws, shouting battle cries and uttering ear-piercing howls that would have curdled the blood of a normal Level 14 Denizen.

Xavier stopped running and let them come. Gripping Soultaker in both hands, he felt no fear, only excitement. He cast Spirit Infusion into the scythe-staff but did not attack the first enemy. He had 210 souls stored and ready to go. He could have destroyed this entire wave in a matter of minutes—maybe less—if he had truly wished.

This isn't where the challenge comes from.

As fast as he'd run, he was now in range of the mages and archers the enemy had. It was the mages he was most interested in taking attacks from—he would get enough physical attacks from the Wolven and the foot soldiers.

The first of the Wolven leapt straight at him, saliva dripping from its fangs, lips pulled back in a terrifying snarl.

Xavier cast Soul Block for the first time. An apparition of a Wolven appeared—one of the souls he had stored from the first wave—just like it might have had he used Soul Strike. But this apparition looked more... *solid* than the Soul Strike apparitions ever did, as though Xavier could reach out and feel its fur. It leapt, throwing itself in front of the attacker.

It was as though the enemy Wolven hit a brick wall. It slammed into the apparition, trying to tear through it with its claws, but found only resistance. The beast yelped, shrunk back, then raised its hackles.

Interesting, Xavier thought. *I wonder what the cooldown on this spell is.*

He opened the Upgrade Quest the moment he could, reading it rapidly.

Soul Block – Rank 1
Upgrade Quest:
As you have now used this spell, you have begun your first step on the path to upgrading it to Rank 2.
Available paths:
Soul Block (Magical) – Use Soul Block to block against a single magical attack. To upgrade, infuse 100 souls into magical Soul Blocks. Progress: 0/100
Soul Block (Physical) – Use Soul Block to block against a single physical attack. To upgrade, infuse 100 souls into physical Soul Blocks. Progress: 1/100
Soul Block (General) – Allows the user to cast Soul Block against both magical and physical attacks at the cost of one third defence. To

upgrade, infuse 50 souls into magical Soul Blocks and 50 souls into physical Soul Blocks.
Magical – Progress: 0/100
Physical – Progress: 1/100
This spell is bound to your Soul Reaper class. Gaining Rank 2 in this spell will not require you to forget another spell, and this spell cannot be forgotten while you remain in the Reaper line of classes.
One cannot walk backward on the path.

Xavier raised an eyebrow. The Upgrade Quest was almost identical to that of Soul Strike.

As the other enemies closed in, attacking in droves and surrounding him completely, Xavier quickly discovered that Soul Block's cooldown worked in exactly the same way as Soul Strike's cooldown. Considering their other similarities, that didn't surprise him.

This meant the spell had the ability to block an attack every single second. Or, he could infuse sixty souls into the spell and block one really *strong* attack per minute. Either way, it would be a great help to him. But it didn't mean that he could block *everything* that came at him.

Xavier's scythe-staff cleaved through the enemies with ease. Apparitions materialised out of thin air, intercepting attacks left and right. At first, he couldn't direct the blocks at specific attacks—they simply blocked whatever attack came at him next. But eventually, he got the hang of directing which attacks Soul Block would defend against. He prioritised physical attacks, from arrows, claws, swords and spears, until he'd accumulated fifty of them. Then he set his attention on only blocking magical strikes.

It only took a few minutes for another notification to appear.

Soul Block has taken a step forward on the

path, upgrading to the spell: Soul Block (General).
Soul Block (General) is a Rank 2 spell.
One cannot walk backward on the path.

Xavier couldn't help but let out a laugh when the spell ranked up so easily. He didn't stop there, however. While he fought, he kept a close eye on the walls—ensuring no enemies got too close to the moat and taking them out with Soul Strikes, something he was able to do even against the enemies on the other side of the castle. This was only possible because he could see their auras even through the stone walls. During that wave, he managed to rank Soul Block up three more times, bringing it up to Rank 5 before every enemy had been defeated.

On his return to the parapet, the queen's adviser told him he'd taken twenty-five minutes on that wave. Xavier nodded back to the man with a grunt. That wasn't too bad, really, considering all he'd gotten out of it. He'd also gained a rank each in his Physical Defence and Magical Defence skills, and a rank in Scythe-Staff Mastery. Bringing them up to Rank 11, 11, and 9 respectively.

"How strong are you, Champion of the Void?" Queen Alastea paused, seeming to consider something. "Champion Xavier."

Xavier smirked. He couldn't help but enjoy being called that. *I'm in an alternate universe, in a fantasy world, and a beautiful queen just called me "Champion Xavier" while I fight to save her people.* Xavier considered his next words. Considered how much he should tell this woman and her adviser. Not to mention the others nearby that had their ears perked, the Queen's Guard and other soldiers on the wall eavesdropping.

Sam had told him to be wary of how much he revealed about himself. Of his class. Of his titles. But... given everything they'd told him about how the Tower of Champions *really* worked and where each floor came from, he knew for a fact that this was the one and only time his universe would be connected to *this* universe. The Tower of Champions' fifth floor would always be here, but Queen Alastea that other Champions met would be in a branched off reality to the one that Xavier was speaking with now.

He could tell them anything, and—in theory—it would never even be *able* to come back to *his* universe. Xavier bit his lip, then told the queen and her adviser just how strong he really was. That he was a True Progenitor. That he'd ranked first on the fourth floor. That he intended to rank first here. He told them of his epic class and that he knew he'd been observed no less than twice by Denizens powerful enough to glimpse within a tower floor.

Powerful enough to glimpse into an alternate universe, Xavier realised.

When he was done, Queen Alastea's eyes were wide. She opened her mouth, closed it, then opened it again. "It seems that we have encountered a great Denizen at the beginning of their journey." She lowered her head in a shallow bow—though far deeper than she'd ever gone before. She was still a queen after all, and he was in her domain. "I am honoured to have you be our Champion."

"From what you have said... there is still much that we can teach you." Adviser Kalren tilted his head to the side. "I can instruct you on how to unlock the two other skills for your Spirit Core, if you wish?"

Xavier blinked. "You can?" He'd been hoping this would be the case. Unlocking Cultivate Energy and Core Strength was still beyond his knowledge. "You know what Celestial Energy is?"

Kalren chuckled. "Indeed." He ran a hand through his pointed beard. "I can also help you unlock your secondary core." He looked at Queen Alastea. "If my queen would allow me to remain here for more than five waves."

Queen Alastea's posture shifted. She'd relaxed slightly as they spoke and Xavier revealed his strength. Now, she straightened once more and looked sternly at her adviser. "We have already discussed this, Kalren."

"Indeed we have, my queen. However..." Kalren motioned to Xavier. "Circumstances have changed. I promise that I will leave when it is no longer deemed safe to stay, but do you not think this man deserves such a reward?"

Xavier was still wrapping his head around what Kalren had said.

What is a secondary core?

Chapter 5
Journey to E Grade

On the battlements, Xavier looked between Queen Alastea and Adviser Kalren. They spoke politely to each other, but there was an undercurrent to their words. If anything, it looked more like they were bickering with one another. Not like an old married couple—no, definitely not. But it was clear that this man had once been her mentor, and now she was his queen. Their relationship, and the roles they played in each other's lives, had changed much over the years.

Finally, the queen let out a sigh. "Fine, Kalren. You may stay. However, if I perceive that at any point you are in even the smallest amount of danger, I will order you to step through that portal. Or if there is any danger of the Endless Horde getting to that portal and identifying where it leads…"

"I won't let that happen," Xavier said. "Trust me, Queen Alastea, your people will be safe."

Queen Alastea looked over at Xavier, a small smirk forming on her lips. "If I am to call you Xavier, then perhaps you should call me Kiralla."

Kalren's eyebrows shot to the top of his forehead as he peered at his queen, though the flicker of emotion did not last long. His eyebrows were back in a neutral position by the time the queen—Kiralla—was looking at him again.

"Kiralla." Xavier nodded at the woman. "I think I can manage that." Once the words had fallen from his mouth, he knew how foolish they sounded. Of course he could manage to call the woman by her damned name.

Was giving me her first name some form of flirting?

He shook that from his head and looked at the adviser. "What was this you said about a secondary core? I've never heard of that before."

Kalren chuckled. "It is remarkable—the things you are capable of despite your lack of knowledge. Please do not take me seeing the humour in it as offensive."

Xavier gave a thin smile. "Not at all."

Kalren cleared his throat. "A secondary core is the next step you will need to take on your journey to E Grade. However, there is much you will need to accomplish before we can begin that step." He rubbed his hands together. "First, you must cycle Spirit Energy through your core."

Xavier dipped his head, stopping himself from sighing. He wanted the man to tell him more, but he also didn't want to waste time asking questions he would get answers to later. "All right. What do I have to do?"

For the next ten minutes, Kalren had Xavier sitting on the cold stone floor of the battlements, deep in meditation, observing his core. The man had instructed him to expend some of his Spirit Energy, so Xavier created some Lesser Spirit Coins and deposited them into his Storage Ring.

"Now that you have fallen into a deep rhythm of meditation, you should be able to see your core. Notice the Spirit Energy entering it naturally. It will take you some time to see the flow of the energy as it enters through your lines. Do not be ashamed if it takes you a few days—"

"I feel it," Xavier said, tilting his head to the side. His reserve was filling up so rapidly it felt as though it was difficult *not* to see it, though he'd never actually observed it before. *I just didn't know what to look for*.

Kalren was silent for a moment. Then he cleared his throat. "You... you see it? Are you sure?"

Xavier nodded.

"Ah, good. Good."

Kalren's surprise was clear. Xavier didn't need to open his eyes and look at the man to see that. Xavier, on the other hand, wasn't all that surprised that he had discovered it so quickly. He didn't think it was because he was particularly gifted—it was just the fact that his Spirit attribute was almost at 500 points.

How could he *not* be able to do something like this?

"What do I do next?"

"Well, if you indeed are able to see the energy entering you, now you must learn how to manipulate it. The reason I had you expend Spirit Energy from your core was so that it would be easy for you to identify one part of the cycle—the Spirit Energy merging with your reserve. That is always the first step, and usually takes quite a bit longer."

Xavier waited for the man to elaborate, interested to learn exactly how he was supposed to manipulate the energy. He'd already learnt how to do that when he'd learnt the Aura Control skill. Though he supposed that must be different to this. "Cycle" made it sound as though the energy would rotate somehow, and the only thing he was truly able to do was control how quickly the energy was burned in his core, decreasing or increasing the strength of his aura.

"Now that you have seen the way Spirit Energy enters your core, observing the lines that it follows through your body, you must pull it from your core and have it circle back around those lines."

Xavier frowned. He wanted to ask *why*, but from all the mentor-student media he'd ever digested in his life, he knew the answer he received would likely be unsatisfying—something along the lines of *because that is what must be done*. Still, he was curious as to the reason for doing such a thing, but he kept that curiosity inside. The information that the adviser had given him about a secondary core still dangled over his head, and he knew that he would only have so much time to receive the man's instructions.

Xavier was confident he would easily be able to deal with the first ten or twenty waves without really breaking a sweat. He was confident he would be able to wipe out a hell of a lot *more* than that —wave 100 had a nice ring to it. What he *wasn't* confident about was how long those waves would take him to complete.

The queen had informed him that each wave would begin their charge after an hour, whether or not the previous wave had been dealt with. It was inevitable that eventually, as the waves became progressively more difficult, Xavier would reach something that he couldn't deal with.

Though he did know he would be much stronger by then, considering how many levels and rank-ups he was going to gain.

So Xavier kept his questions to himself and listened to the man's instructions as attentively as he could. And though the first part of the exercise had been incredibly easy for him to grasp, this second part—pulling the Spirit Energy back out of his core without the use of a spell or through the creation of Lesser Spirit Coins— was turning out to be incredibly difficult.

Before he knew it, the war drums were beating again, and another wave of Denizens and beasts charged toward Queen Alastea's castle. Horns blew, shouts sounded and howls filled the air. A breeze rolled in, and his nose crinkled, registering the scent of not only sweat, but of blood and viscera that had been dispersed on the battlefield during the last two waves. Xavier had an awfully clinical and practical thought, wondering just how littered the space outside the walls would soon become with the dead, and whether they would need to be cleaning away the corpses. He no longer bothered gathering them into his Storage Ring—it simply wasn't a very good use of his time any longer.

Xavier rose from where he sat cross-legged on the stone and leapt over the parapet once more.

The third wave composed of Level 12 enemies. Again, they posed no difficulty to Xavier. He was tempted to simply blast them with Soul Strike—he could pack 250 souls into a single one now—but he didn't wish to grow complacent. If he were going to last here for the latter waves, he would need to strengthen everything, not just his favourite spell.

So, once more, he plunged himself back into the fray. Using Soul Block liberally, he tore through the nearby enemies with spirit-infused melee attacks. Soultaker's blade sheared through their bodies, leaving the battlefield riddled with beasts and Denizens alike sliced neatly in two. Legs, arms, and heads fell to the dirt as his blade cleaved through the mess of enemies. The annoyance at having to deal with another wave quickly dissipated as the excitement of the fight flowed through him, and he harvested one soul after another.

He felt more fluid than before. His skill with his scythe-staff was increasing tremendously fast. Soul Block didn't seem any stronger for all the ranks it had gained, but he knew that was simply because he wasn't facing enemies strong enough to actually harm him. That could also be why it wasn't growing through the ranks terribly quickly despite his rapid use of the spell.

Once again, Xavier kept a close eye on the enemies at the rear of the castle. When they neared the moat, he fired off a Soul Strike infused with 150 souls and took half the wave out all at once. Though he didn't wish to grow complacent, when he realised the strength—or rather, *weakness*—of the enemies was making it more difficult to acquire ranks in his skills, he figured he could focus on that in the latter waves more effectively.

He waited until the end of the wave to read the skill and spell notifications that had popped up, digesting them all at once, finding Soul Block had gained two more ranks, with Soul Harden, Soul Harvest, and Spirit Infusion each gaining one, and his Scythe-Staff Mastery getting to the next rank as well.

Xavier returned to the battlements to take instruction from Kalren, and sometimes even from the queen herself. Once more, he struggled with the seemingly simple task of manipulating his Spirit Energy. Each minute that passed felt like an entire hour as he was stuck in deep meditation, trying to yank the energy free of his core and drag it through the lines in his body. He was sure it was his Willpower stat that helped him keep focused. If it wasn't so high, he probably would have found himself getting frustrated by his lack of progress, as by the time the fourth wave was readying its charge, he hadn't so much as made the Spirit Energy budge.

This wasn't helped by the fact that Kalren seemed to have a little smirk on his face, apparently taking some pleasure in the knowledge that Xavier was struggling with this task. Though Xavier figured he couldn't blame the man. He'd always been frustrated by people who didn't struggle with a skill. There was a perverse kind of pleasure in watching someone talented deal with difficulty—seeing that they too were merely human.

He tore through the fourth wave with blade and spells equally, gaining a few more ranks here and there but ensuring it didn't take him nearly as long as the other two waves. After fifteen minutes, the wave had been defeated and he'd gained another level.

Xavier grinned when he looked at his stats. He didn't need to contemplate where he would spend his twenty free points.

It was time to see if having 500 points in Spirit would break him through another attribute threshold.

Chapter 6
Core Strength

XAVIER SAT, CROSS-LEGGED, ON THE COLD STONE FLOOR OF THE battlements. He could have applied the twenty free stat points the second he'd levelled up, but he wanted to be able to focus on the shift he felt.

With a smile, Xavier placed all the points into his Spirit attribute.

Spirit increased from 493 → 518!

Something shifted within his mind. No, within his very *soul*. An awareness came over him that was like nothing he had ever felt before. The auras of all the soldiers around him on the wall, and that of the waves and waves of the Endless Horde beyond it, felt more... *solid* than a moment ago, as though his Aura Sight had suddenly become five times stronger.

He leant backward where he sat, taking in everything he felt.

It wasn't just what he could sense outside of himself—it was what he could sense *within* himself. He fell into a deep meditation in less than a second. Observing his Spirit Core was as easy as looking down at his own hand. Seeing the Spirit Energy swirling

around it and the lines in which that energy flowed into his core...
it was as clear as day.

So I guess there is a 500-point threshold for attributes.

He felt more *open-minded* and in touch with the Greater
Universe than he had thought possible, instantly knowing that
insights would come to him more easily now. He plucked at the
Spirit Energy within his core, once more trying to bring it out, to
finally begin cycling it. At first, nothing happened—just like every
other time he had tried. Then it was like instinct took over. Like he
was being guided toward the correct action.

By the Greater Universe itself?

This time, Xavier did not *yank* the Spirit Energy from his core.
Instead, he slowly tried to coax it free. He didn't push his will onto
the energy, merely redirected it. Though this didn't work, knowledge entered his mind as he attempted it, showing him something
that should have been obvious before: Spirit Energy wanted to be
free. His core attracted Spirit Energy like a bug zapper attracted
insects. It had an unnatural pull, drawing it into himself. That pull
increased the stronger Xavier's Spirit attribute became. As he
focused, he could even *feel* that pull, despite the fact that his
reserve was completely full.

His next action became abundantly clear. He couldn't *yank* the
Spirit Energy, because it was trapped within him, but there was
something else he could do. Eyes still closed, locked in a deep
meditation, Xavier cast Spiritual Trifecta on himself. He kept close
attention on his Spirit Core as he did. In his mind's eye, it was like
a bright silver orb of light. When the spell was cast, a small amount
of Spirit Energy flooded out of it—as though a valve had been
opened then shut.

*A valve... the Spirit Energy wants to be free. All I need to do is
open my core.*

Xavier pursed his lips in thought. This wasn't what Kalren had
told him, but Kalren had also told him that a Denizen's core felt...
different for everyone, and so the mechanism by which one used to

pull Spirit Energy from their core was always unique. A fact that Xavier couldn't help but find frustrating.

Still, there *was* promise to his idea. But the last time he'd done something like this, he'd almost burned through his core. When he thought about what the worst thing to happen could be—losing all of his Spirit Energy, then his health, then dying—he knew he would need to be careful.

Open my core... yeah, that sounds like a great idea.

Xavier stopped himself from biting his lip. He supposed he shouldn't be too worried. There was every chance that whatever he tried right now wouldn't even work. If opening his core was something that was dangerous, maybe it wouldn't be possible.

Wishful thinking.

Either way, he had to try. And he was sick of wasting precious time thinking about it.

Turning thoughts to action, Xavier tried to claw open a very small surface area of his Spirit Core with his mind. He assumed this would give him the same outcome of every other one of his attempts so far. That nothing at all would happen. And that if it *was* to work, it certainly wouldn't work the first time that he tried.

What he hadn't expected was for it to work *instantly*.

Xavier's Spirit Core opened a crack—as though he'd stabbed a chicken egg with a needle. Spirit Energy flowed out of it at a rate of 100 units per second. Though that sounded like a fast rate, Xavier's full reserve was currently 48,000. Even after the spell he'd just cast, it would take over seven and a half minutes for all his Spirit Energy to deplete itself.

Though that 100 units per second rate was *after* his Spirit Energy recovery, as he wasn't gaining any of the Spirit Energy *back*.

The Spirit Energy flooded back out through the energy lines in his body, flowing away from his core. He knew where it wished to go—straight out of him—but he wasn't going to let it. Perhaps he should have attempted to close the small crack he'd created in his core before attempting to cycle the Spirit Energy, but it felt as though he'd been waiting a long time to figure this out.

Releasing a long breath, Xavier tried to take control of the Spirit Energy. Tried to drag it back into his core. He spent a full two minutes doing this without any luck. His core should have attracted the energy straight back to it, but that pull that he'd felt before was gone. As though the moment he'd cracked open his core, it simply lost the ability to naturally recover Spirit Energy.

That's not good, Xavier thought. *But I'm sure it's only temporary.*

Xavier kept breathing deeply. The longer he was unable to restore his Spirit Energy, the more his panic was beginning to set in. Four minutes had passed now, and still the energy was flowing out of his core. It had seeped out of him and was now drifting into the air—he felt it out there, like wisps of smoke wafting off a fire or hot sweat on skin turning to steam.

Be calm, he told himself. *Focus. Stop fighting the energy.*

The crack in his core still open, now two-thirds of his reserve gone, Xavier turned his attention to the lines in which the energy flowed. Perhaps it wasn't the energy itself that he needed to control, rather the conduits in which it moved through.

I just need to... change the direction...

His whole mind put itself toward this task. There were people speaking to him—people he was only vaguely aware of. He couldn't pull his focus from what he was doing. It reminded him of the time his core had burned straight through all of his Spirit Energy and he'd collapsed onto the floor of the tavern, unconscious. But he wasn't going to let something like that happen again.

He *couldn't* let something like that happen again. There was simply too much at stake for him to make such mistakes.

For a moment, his mind turned away from the task at hand, drifting to his worries and fears. He thought of his mother. She hadn't been on his mind nearly as much as he'd expected she would be, which only made him feel more guilty. He thought of what she must be going through—what *billions* of people on Earth must be going through.

Those who were still alive.

He thought of those damned goblins that had attacked him at the university. He knew there would be more like that. Knew there would be all types of different races stepping out of portals and attacking the people of Earth. *His* people. That this was something normal in the Greater Universe. That the only way to fight it was to be *strong*.

And so, Xavier *had to* be strong.

I cannot fail.

Someone grabbed his shoulder and shook him. Xavier slapped the hand away. Somewhere in his consciousness he registered a harsh *snapping* sound and a sharp hiss. He didn't pay it any mind. He couldn't. His core was too open. Parts of his mind screamed at him to close it—to stop this madness. That he was forcing this—pushing himself too hard.

He ignored the voices. Pushed on.

When the last wisp of Spirit Energy was almost free of his core, something *clicked*. He was able to nudge some of the Spirit Energy, changing the flow of one of the lines back inward toward his core.

He turned his focus to his available Spirit Energy.

300/48,000
200/48,000
100/48,000

...

200/48,000
500/48,000
1,000/48,000

Xavier blinked as the number increased rapidly. The Spirit Energy that still flowed through his lines was turning around, entering back into his core. The more he did it, the easier it became. He felt himself straighten up where he sat. He hadn't even realised that his back had curved and his shoulders had sagged. Didn't realise that his entire body was stiff. Head splitting in pain from the sheer concentration he'd been putting toward this one task.

More minutes passed. The voices that had spoken before had grown quiet. No one tried to grab him again. All the while, his eyes remained closed. Spirit Energy flowed out of his core. It spread outward to his extremities. Spread up through his chest, to his neck, to his head. Then it came back around, constantly circling around the lines until it did a full circuit and went back to his core.

Again and again he did this, feeling the energy flow around him as though it was the most natural thing in the world. The pain in his head cleared, as did the stiffness in his body. His back was straight, shoulders no longer sagging.

The notification came to him at the same time as the war drums began their insistent beat, once more signalling the immanency of the next wave.

Skill Quest Complete!
You unlocked and learned the skill Core
Strength!
Core Strength – Rank 1
You are a student of the Greater Universe. Your
knowledge is but a seed deep in damp earth,
but soon it will grow roots and break up
through the surface of the ground.
May your knowledge of the Greater Universe
blossom.
+5% Aura strength.
+20% Spirit Energy recovery.
+10% Spirit.

Xavier smiled as he released a long breath. *Progress.*

The 10 percent bonus to his Spirit was felt *immediately,*

instantly adding over 40 points to his effective total. When he looked up, he noticed the queen, arms folded at her chest, peering down at him with clear disapproval in her eyes.

"You broke my adviser's arm."

Xavier winced. He looked over at Kalren. "Sorry."

The man shrugged and shook his head. "It is already healed." His gaze narrowed. "I am not sure what it is you just did, but I am very curious."

"The fifth wave is on its way," Queen Alastea said, her voice sharp. "I am glad you came to before it charged."

Xavier smirked. He cast Spiritual Trifecta on himself and infused Spirit into his staff. But he did not stand. Instead, he took a deep breath, then packed all 320 souls that he was now able to contain into a single Soul Strike.

Bolts of lightning shot forth from him in every single direction, sailing in wide arcs toward the enemies in the oncoming wave. He couldn't see the apparitions from here, but he could *feel* them. He felt the souls as they sprang forth, materialising into fierce Denizens and beasts that utterly destroyed the wave.

The war drums ceased.

The horns stopped blaring.

The howls and shouts disappeared to nothing.

The fifth wave of the fifth floor of the Tower of Champions had been cleared in a single spell.

Xavier turned to Adviser Kalren. "Now, teach me how to cultivate Celestial Energy. And... tell me what it is?"

Chapter 7
Legends

Xavier found he couldn't resist watching the castle's exodus.

He'd destroyed the fifth wave in almost an instant, dismissing the notification that came up saying he'd cleared the floor, eager to learn about Celestial Energy. But the queen had to see to her people moving through the portal, and he wasn't selfish enough to keep the adviser from joining her on that.

Queen Kiralla Alastea stood by the portal. They were in a large throne room—the largest hall within the castle. Kiralla was flanked by her Queen's Guard along with two female mages in white robes. If their robes indicated their class, Xavier would assume they were support of some sort. That assumption was reinforced by the fact that they had been the ones to activate the portal.

The portal looked startlingly familiar. It glowed yellow, sparks flying from it as though it were made from liquid lightning.

It brought him right back to standing at the window of his university class, the lecturer droning on as a portal formed outside in the courtyard, a *bloody goblin* stepping out of it. He shuddered at the memory. He may have dealt with all the goblins on campus—almost dying in the process—but he knew there would be countless more roaming Earth's streets.

He blinked, turning his attention back to the present moment. One of the soldiers from the wall had fetched Howard, Siobhan, and Justin from the library. Siobhan had a book clutched in her hands, which wasn't much of a surprise, but she had the courtesy not to read it during the proceedings.

"Kiralla is about to address her people," Xavier said, leaning in as the others came to stand around them.

"Kiralla?" Justin asked.

Howard peered over at the portal. "I think he's talking about the queen."

"Ohh." Siobhan grinned over at him. "You're on a first-name basis with the queen, are you?" The redhead waggled her eyebrows.

"Uh," Xavier uttered. "I suppose."

"Playing it cool, I see," Howard said in a flat tone, the tiniest hint of a smirk touching the sides of his lips.

"On the other side of this portal," Queen Alastea said, speaking in a loud, clear voice, "the rest of our people await. They will welcome you with open arms." She lowered her head. Xavier could have sworn he saw shame flicker in her eyes. "I wish that I could have done more for you all. I wish that I could be the queen that you all deserve. But the fate of the Queendom of Arala has been written in the stars for centuries. The arrogance of my ancestors is what led us here. I do not share their arrogance, and as such, I will not be following."

Gasps sounded in the crowd and chatter began. Some shouted refusals of what she said, others begged for her to come along. Many were silent, however, stoic looks on their faces. These people were to be the last to leave their world. They knew what the Endless Horde was. Knew what it would mean if it were to break through their walls.

One thing he noticed about those gathered was their age. Most of them were older—though who knew what their actual age was, given what he'd learnt about lifespan for Denizens in the Greater Universe. These would all be noncombat, support classes.

There were no children.

All of these people... They probably volunteered for the last portal, knowing it might never come, knowing they might never leave this world.

Queen Alastea raised a hand. It silenced the room. "There is nowhere in this sector that I can hide from the Endless Horde indefinitely. Even if I were to find somewhere and live out the rest of my days in peace, it would come for my family eventually, just as it has now. I will *not* put that risk on my people, or my descendants. I have already made many speeches to you all over the last few days—you know what awaits you when you leave here, the deals I have made. One part of that deal is that I remain. No other world wants us bringing my problem with me, and I refused to lie about why I was leaving."

It still looked as though some citizens in the room wanted to complain, but they did not. They would understand the realities of the situation, the harshness of living in the Greater Universe. Xavier was more surprised that people weren't angry with her. He imagined people back on Earth would be *furious* to discover that their leader's family was responsible for the downfall of their queendom.

The people walked through the portal without much ceremony. Queen Alastea stood in front of it. They touched hands to hers as they passed, one by one.

"She seems well loved," Howard said.

"She does." Justin was full-on staring at Kiralla in a way that only a clueless teenage boy can.

Not that I'm one to speak about women and having a clue, Xavier thought.

As the procession through the portal looked as though it would take a little while, he decided it was about time he told the others about what he'd learnt—about the fact that these people were *real* and that they were in an alternate universe.

That every single time a Champion entered a floor in the Tower of Champions, they created *another* alternate universe.

The three remained silent as he spoke. Their expressions varying. Justin's eyes perpetually became wider, his mouth falling open. Howard's forehead creased, then creased some more, until he had what Siobhan would call stink-face. Siobhan, however, looked *excited*.

"Oh... my... god! Alternate universes? Are you kidding me?" she asked enthusiastically. Then she stopped, her face falling. "So those armies we faced..."

"They were real people," Howard said in a dark voice. "And we killed them."

Xavier rubbed the back of his neck. "The System didn't give us a choice."

"We always have a choice," Howard muttered. "But this damned System just makes it so none of them are good."

Justin's gaze fell to the ground. "I suppose we always knew we would have to kill. This invasion... there will be humans coming to Earth too, won't there?"

"Probably," Xavier said. "Though human, elf, or otherwise... they're all sapient."

"Just hits different when it's..." Howard sighed. "Suppose that's not the right way to think of things. We have to deal with what's in front of us." He looked over at the portal. "I'm glad we helped these people, though I don't know that learning this changes anything."

"Are you kidding?" Siobhan said. "It changes *everything*!"

Xavier frowned. "Because these people are real?"

"No. I mean, yes, that's important. But it means this *place* is real. It means the Endless Horde has an end, as you said."

"That doesn't mean we'll ever see it," Xavier said carefully.

Siobhan crossed her arms at her chest. She smirked. "You don't think you're up to the challenge? Remember, we don't have to worry about how long we spend on this floor. Only an hour will pass back..." She trailed off, shook her head, and let out a chuckle. "Back in our *universe*."

Xavier considered his next words carefully. He looked at

each of them in turn. "I think you think I'm stronger than I truly am." He motioned at himself. "I'm F Grade. The Endless Horde covers half of this sector." He waved out toward the castle doors. "Those Denizens and beasts out there are *nothing* compared with what they'll throw at me later." He remembered, clearly, what it felt like to have something stronger than himself observing him. Feeling like a damned speck of dust—like *nothing*. Xavier might be strong for his level, but how was he supposed to fight... what? Half a galaxy? "It's insane to think I'll be able to defeat them all."

Siobhan tapped a finger to her nose, the book she had with her held in her other hand by her side. "Maybe." She leant forward. "But... you've noticed how weak these people are, haven't you?"

Xavier bit his lip. "Queen Alastea told us the soldiers here are all new recruits. That her mother was the fighter."

Siobhan raised the book she'd brought. "I didn't bring this along just because I like carrying books. I mean, I *do* like carrying books, but..." She shook her head. "I'm getting off track." She tapped the hard cover. "I don't know what things are like in our sector, but here, in this universe..." She tilted her head to the side. "According to this book, there's no one stronger than D Grade."

Xavier shut his eyes. He gripped the bridge of his nose with thumb and forefinger. "I. Am. F. Grade. How am I supposed to defeat a *D Grade Denizen*?"

"We've been talking," Justin said.

"You're F Grade *now*," Howard added. "But that doesn't mean you can't break through to E Grade here."

Xavier raised an eyebrow at the man. He hadn't thought quite that far ahead, but... that was awfully tempting.

"And there are records of E Grades defeating D Grades in the library," Siobhan said excitedly.

Howard looked sideways at her. "Records is perhaps putting it optimistically. They were more like legends."

"Myths," Justin added. "Fables. Stories."

Siobhan raised a hand. "I choose to believe the *records*."

"Just because you believe something doesn't make it true," Howard said with a sigh.

Xavier glanced at the doors out of the hall, contemplating the waves upon waves of the Endless Horde. "Half a sector. Do you understand how insanely *large* a galaxy is?"

"Ah!" Siobhan opened the book, stabbing her finger at something. "This sector—Alrari... Alrayrir..."

"Alrararian," Howard stated confidently.

"Right! This—what he said—sector is apparently what's called an *infant* sector. This infancy doesn't refer to the sector's age, it's actually been integrated for just shy of a million years."

Xavier blinked at that. *A million years.* He could barely even contemplate that kind of time frame.

"But, even though it's been around for a while, it's a *small* galaxy, and therefore a small sector. The sector doesn't have all that much to offer. Whenever someone becomes strong enough to leave it for greener pastures..." She shrugged. "The powerful flee this place. That's what created a power vacuum that the Endless Horde were able to fill. The book says that in the Greater Universe, they're actually considered to be a very weak force."

"Is this a history book?" Xavier asked.

Siobhan nodded.

"But you only just discovered this place was real, so you were reading it before thinking it was... fiction?"

"I thought the knowledge might come in handy," Siobhan said.

Howard grunted. "Especially when we discovered the Endless Horde isn't as endless as we thought."

"We were going to tell you; we just wanted to gather more information first," Siobhan said. "Now, as I was saying, apparently almost the entire sector was destroyed, or rather consumed by something called a..." She paused, running a finger along the page, tapping a line when she found it. "Galaxy Eater. Man, those sound bad."

"Really bad," Justin said. "Anything that eats galaxies..." He shuddered.

Xavier released a breath. He had thought a galaxy would hold millions, maybe billions, of worlds. Though he supposed he didn't know how many would be inhabited. "How many worlds does this sector have?"

"It contains a thousand inhabited worlds, with varying levels of population," Siobhan said. "*Small* populations. An infant sector, remember?"

"When you say small?" Xavier was still sceptical.

"The System causes a lot of upheaval and death, and not everyone is a soldier," Howard said. "There's no telling how *accurate* this book is, but it puts the population of this sector at three billion Denizens."

Xavier frowned. "That can't be right. We have more than twice as many people on Earth."

"Do we?" Siobhan whispered. "We've no idea how many people died while we were gone." She closed the book, held it in her left, placing her right hand over it. "It might seem like... like we're stronger now, with the System. And we are, in a way. But... there are a lot of dangers out there. More than there ever were before. Things like the Endless Horde aren't the only things. Almost every world is in constant conflict and war. And not only with *other* worlds, but with their own. And apparently there's something called *cosmic diseases*, epidemics on the scale of multiple worlds that kill weaker denizens in droves. Without a Denizen of at least C Grade to protect a sector from threats or to keep some semblance of peace... it's difficult for a sector to grow strong."

Xavier shook his head, taking it all in. *Galaxy eaters? Cosmic diseases? What the hell has Earth gotten into...* "That still puts the Endless Horde in the many millions. Maybe even at a billion. If the waves are all three thousand strong..."

"The waves will increase in number." Adviser Kalren suddenly appeared beside them, the queen to his left. Xavier hadn't even noticed him walk over. The throne room was clear of people. Everyone but those in his party, the adviser, and the queen had left through the portal—which remained open. "Not just in the level of their Denizens and beasts, but in the number of them they will throw at you. The System will soon adapt to your strength. So far, you have dealt with waves of three thousand enemies. Soon, there will undoubtedly be waves with far more than that."

"How many more?"

Kalren lowered his head. "I don't know."

"But we heard what you were saying, about our sector," the queen said. "It's true. We are a weak sector. But to do something like this, defeat the Endless Horde... It would indeed be a thing of legend. If it were to be done, the System would reward you more greatly than you could ever imagine."

Chapter 8
Celestial Energy

On the first day, the sun shone bright over a battlefield stained with blood. Thousands of corpses littered the ground. All of them died by scythe or soul. All of them by Xavier's hand.

Every hour, he fought. Every hour, he won. The levels came consistently at first. Every three or four waves, the notification would pop up into his vision, bringing a stab of dopamine that fuelled his energy more than the strength from the added stats. His skill and spell rank-ups came steadily as well, until eventually they became harder and harder to acquire.

The pit inside him never filled. He had thought he'd gained a semblance of control over it. Had thought his strong Willpower attribute helped him deal with it. But the more souls he took, the deeper the pit became, until the hole in him felt as endless as the horde outside the castle's walls.

On the second day, dull clouds covered the sky. The Denizens and beasts both became more fierce, their spells more varied and deadly. It started to take longer for Xavier to take down a wave. No longer could he simply throw out a single Soul Strike and take them down.

They had not become truly difficult—not yet. He was beyond

these enemies in so many ways. But he could see them becoming tougher. Could *feel* their strength growing even as his own did. Knew what it foretold in the days to come.

On the third day, he stood on the parapet, the hood of his Shrouded Robes draped over his head. The Endless Horde did not bury their dead—they burned them. Powerful fire mages of a demonic race Kalren called the Amondi walked up from far back in the ranks, stepping out in front of the army. Before the exodus, there had been several of these Amondi in the Queen's Guard.

But these were different. More powerful than any other Denizen Xavier had laid eyes on. He couldn't feel their aura, but there was something about the way they held themselves. Xavier could not scan them from this distance. Even the queen and Kalren were unable to tell him their levels.

At the end of each wave, these Amondi fire mages obliterated the dead, turning them to ash. They did not bother scavenging their corpses or weapons—they just discarded them completely.

On the fourth day, the clouds became darker. The rain started, spitting down on them in constant sheets, washing away the ash from the battlefield and mixing in with the blood.

Each day, the levels came less frequently. He needed to take down more and more waves to make any difference. His ranks had stalled, too. He'd been trying to keep them as balanced as possible, though there were some he still hadn't figured out—like Assimilate Properties, a skill they hadn't been able to find any information about in the library.

He added points into his other attributes, but for the most part, he kept pumping up his Spirit attribute more and more. Eventually, it pushed over 1,000, putting him over the edge of another threshold.

The level of power he could summon felt absolutely insane. The apparitions he brought to life obliterated the stronger wave bosses with ease, even as the enemies' levels rose over 50, he could still take out an entire wave within half an hour. Every now and then, he noticed that Howard, Siobhan or Justin found themselves at the battlements, watching him destroy the Endless Horde from the sidelines. Observing the sheer devastation he was able to dish out.

He brought his Intelligence and Willpower attributes over 500, smashing through two more thresholds of power. When his Willpower hit 500, he could breathe a little easier. The hunger inside of him dimmed. Not as much as he wished it to—but enough that he could deal with it again.

I guess it does help.

Lightning cracked in the sky, thunder rolling. The rain pelted ever harder. The battlefield had been a muddied, ash-ridden mess for the last few days without the rain—enough blood soaked the ground to make every inch of it soft—but now, it was even worse. There wasn't an inch of solid ground out there.

After he had destroyed the hundredth wave, Xavier returned to the wall. All he wanted to do was rest. He hadn't slept for over four days straight. He wasn't exactly sure if he *needed* sleep anymore, but he sure would appreciate some. The closest he got to sleeping was the deep meditation he experienced, which always helped rejuvenate his body and mind.

But it didn't quite feel like *enough.*

The tiredness didn't make his reactions slower. It didn't dim his power. It just... settled somewhere in his mind, bringing a small pain behind his eyes that never seemed to dull no matter how many levels he gained. It was a pain that appeared to be increasing the longer he remained awake. It made him wonder just how long he could do this for.

And the levels, too, were beginning to stall. It wasn't just that he needed more and more Mastery Points every level that he gained. Something else was happening—he wasn't gaining as many Mastery Points per kill as he used to. At first, he hadn't even noticed. He never looked at the kill notifications anymore. If he did, they'd be the only things he would ever see. He'd be reading them until the end of time.

"The System adjusts," Adviser Kalren had told him when

Xavier had asked the man about this. "I've heard of this happening with Denizens of legend. Progenitors who gain immense power through titles. The System knows they are stronger, so they scale the number of points they receive."

To Xavier, it seemed exceedingly unfair. But he supposed he shouldn't speak of what was fair and what wasn't, considering how many things he'd benefited from.

The man had been a patient teacher and had actually become easy to talk to. He had guided Xavier through each of the skills he needed to gain from his Spirit Core, teaching him how to sense Celestial Energy in the air.

It turned out Celestial Energy was *everywhere*.

Xavier was honestly unsure how he hadn't noticed it before. Sensing Celestial Energy was a little bit like seeing auras, except it was about a thousand times fainter. But once he knew what to look for... it was like when a shard of sunlight shines on particles drifting in the air.

According to Kalren—and the man had yet to steer him wrong —Celestial Energy was the main power behind all Denizen's abilities. There were countless energy systems. Xavier had known of Spirit Energy, of course. And Toughness Energy, as Howard had gained that when he'd chosen his class at Level 10.

But there was energy for *every* attribute. Strength. Speed. Toughness. Intelligence. Willpower. Each of them had their own core within the body of a Denizen. Simply being able to access the energy that came from those cores—as Howard was able to do for Toughness—didn't actually give one the ability to "unlock" the core that held that energy.

Otherwise, every Denizen would instantly be able to unlock their Spirit Core, as they had access to the energy it held from the very beginning.

"Unlocking your Spirit Core and your secondary core—whatever it ends up being—is a prerequisite to achieving E Grade. And, we assume, unlocking more is required to reaching D Grade, though we do not have access to that knowledge in our humble queendom," Kalren had explained. "It is theorised that the higher grades are able to infuse all six energies into their weapons and armour."

And Celestial Energy was behind it all—it could be cultivated into *every* core, turned into any type of energy. A pure energy source that worked for each of them. Technically, Kalren explained, Xavier already had the ability to cultivate Celestial Energy into his Spirit Core—it happened naturally. It was what Spirit Recovery *did*.

But doing it on purpose was a whole different beast.

Though it hadn't taken him long to reveal the energy that had always been there—to actually see it in the air—two days had passed before he'd finally been able to cultivate enough of the energy into himself manually and unlock the skill.

When he'd finally done it, he couldn't help himself. He'd jumped onto his feet and thrust his fist into the air, an action that had made the always-poised queen burst out into a small fit of giggles, something that took her quite a long time to rein in. He couldn't help but laugh along with her at the ridiculousness of what he'd just done. But he couldn't help himself—every step forward he made in this place would be a win for the people of Earth.

After that hundredth wave on the fourth day, Xavier examined his attributes and stats, marvelling at how far he'd come. Even if he *was* beginning to stall.

XAVIER COLLINS
Age: 20
Race: Human
Grade: F
Moral Faction: World Defender (Planet Earth)
Class: Soul Reaper (Epic)
Level 35
Strength: 280 (342)
Speed: 276 (337)

Toughness: 370 (451)
Intelligence: 417 (626)
Willpower: 412 (503)
Spirit: 626 (1,045)
Mastery Points for this level:
1,035,530/432,000,000
Available Spirit Energy: 105,500/105,500
Available Skill Points: 0
Free stat points remaining: 0
Titles:
Bloodied Hands, Born on a Battlefield, Settlement Defender, Quester, First Defender of Planet Earth, Survivor, All 100, First All 100, 1,000 Stats, First to 1,000 Stats, Greater Butcher, Fourth-Floor Climber, Solo Tower Climber 4, 1st Fourth-Floor Climber, Fourth Floor Ranked 1 – RECORD HOLDER (Completion Time – 4 sec)
Spells List:
Spiritual Trifecta – Rank 15
Heavy Telekinesis – Rank 14
Spirit Break (All) – Rank 14
Spirit Infusion – Rank 16
Soul Harvest – Rank 18
Soul Strike (Ranged) – Rank 20
Soul Block – Rank 15
Soul Harden – Rank 16
Skills List:
Physical Resistance – Rank 20
Magical Potency – Rank 20
Magical Resistance – Rank 20
Physical Damage – Rank 20
Assimilate Properties – Rank 1
Scythe-Staff Mastery – Rank 20
Meditation – Rank 20

Aura Control – Rank 10
Core Strength – Rank 10
Cultivate Energy – Rank 10
Lesser Spirit Coins: 329,289

Level 35. He'd gained over 20 levels since he'd entered this floor four days ago. And back in his universe, only an hour would have passed once he returned. *This is unbelievable.* But it also made him worry. For several reasons. He couldn't have been the only Denizen to take advantage of this—couldn't be the only Denizen to gain all the levels possible on this floor.

Would a hundred waves really be enough to gain the top spot?

And then... then there was Earth.

Their research in the library had been quite fruitful over the last few days. Something Xavier had instantly been worried about when he'd decided to stay on this floor for as long as possible was just how high-level he would become. Yes, he wished to become as *strong* as possible, but, paradoxically, the higher level he became, the more danger Earth would be in.

The invaders that came to Earth were restricted in their level. They could only send people to Earth that were a single level higher than the highest-level Denizen on the planet. As Xavier wasn't currently *on* the planet, and neither were any of the other Champions from Earth, their levels did not yet affect this restriction.

However, the moment they returned, it would.

And though he worried deeply about this, Siobhan had found an ancient tome in the library that spoke of the rules around newly integrated worlds. There had been a *very* interesting detail hidden within the pages: Invaders didn't know what the highest-level Denizen on a world they were invading would be. The only way they could find that out was by scanning people while on the world or by sending different Denizens through portals and hoping they would survive.

It has to be worth the risk. If I don't become strong, Earth won't stand a chance.

When he did return, he would simply have to ensure that none of the enemies ever discovered what level he was.

He looked over at the queen. She stood, hands neatly folded behind her back, staring out at the Endless Horde just as she always did, her golden crown still resting on her head, even though all but one of her subjects were already days gone into a different world. In these moments of quiet, he couldn't help but see the look of loss on her face. His party might have dreamt up the possibility that he could defeat the Endless Horde—something that would no doubt give him a damned *amazing* title—and in turn, free the queen from her fate. But she knew just as well as he did that such a task had to be beyond difficult, if not completely impossible.

Still, the more time he spent here, the longer he got to know the queen... the more he wished it could be true.

The more he hoped he would be able to save her.

Chapter 9
Change the Game

Two weeks had passed since Xavier, Howard, Siobhan, and Justin had entered the fifth floor of the Tower of Champions.

Xavier, sitting upon the cold stone of the battlements, opened his mind to the world. To the universe. Sinking into a deep meditative state, he opened himself up to *everything*. Whenever he did this, the power of the millions of auras outside the walls—those limitless waves of the Endless Horde—threatened to overwhelm his mind.

But it was easy for him to look past them. Easy for him to block them out, or at least dull their existence.

Celestial Energy. It was in the air. Everywhere. It was a difficult thing to describe what it looked like in his mind's eye. Like describing what radiation or gravity waves looked like.

He only knew what they *felt* like.

Taking a deep breath, he drew on the strands of energy, tugging it toward him—toward his core. This task was close to natural for him now. It did not take a great amount of conscious effort for him to maintain. But maintaining it helped him in several ways.

At first, he'd been dubious. Though the three skills around his Spirit Core appeared important, all they really seemed to do was give him a few bonuses to his Spirit attribute and its recovery. All bonuses were welcome, but how useful was it in the grand scheme of his training?

Turns out—*incredibly* so.

The three skills were interconnected. Drawing in Celestial Energy boosted his Spirit Energy's recovery, which was already absurdly high. Having more Spirit Energy enter his core meant he was able to cycle it through his core more effectively—as he found he couldn't cycle the *same* Spirit Energy through his core over and over. Each unit of Spirit Energy could only be cycled a single time.

Xavier was glad he had someone here to explain that to him. Were he training completely on his own, it likely would have taken him an embarrassing amount of time to realise it. Time that would have been wasted.

Then there was his Aura Control. Whenever he gained a new rank in his other two skills, he had to shift the burning of his Spirit Energy to balance it within his core. There was a constant synergy to maintain.

But that synergy wasn't the only reason this was an important path. Each of the skills helped him increase his awareness of not only himself, but the world and universe around him. The skill descriptions said something vague about his knowledge of the Greater Universe only being a seed in damp earth, one that would soon grow roots and break through to the surface. Those descriptions had yet to change the more ranks he gained in each of the three skills, but he was sure they one day would—Kalren had confirmed as much, after all.

And as his awareness of self increased, along with his use of meditation, his journey toward E Grade shortened. The more aware he became, the easier it would be for him to discover what his secondary core would be. When he asked Kalren which attribute his second core would manifest as, the man's forehead had bunched up in a frown. He'd stared off into the distance and thought for a long time, then simply shook his head.

"I have no clue."

Kalren, unfortunately, did not know everything.

The secondary core which Denizens manifested, or discovered —the terminology in the books the other members of his party had shown him seemed to use the words interchangeably—tended to be based on what someone's most powerful attribute was.

If their most powerful attribute was Spirit, then it went to their second most powerful attribute. The only problem with this advice was that it was constantly contradicted. There were many cases cited where someone manifested a core for their weakest attribute —like a mage gaining a Strength Core as their secondary core. This was theorised as a natural way the System helped balance certain classes. Though other Denizens theorised that it was more about *sabotage* than balance.

Xavier didn't know what to believe, and he honestly didn't care which was true. If everything went according to plan, he would one day manifest every core there was to manifest. Considering he was a True Progenitor, he found that to be the most likely scenario.

He also considered it to be his goal: to become one of the strongest Denizens in the Greater Universe. To rise through the different grades until he was strong enough to defend Earth from any threat.

And he felt confident that it was possible. That he could make it happen. Unless, of course, he ended up getting himself killed on this floor or another—or during the invasion of Earth.

Highly unlikely.

As he didn't mind which of his cores he unlocked next, he wasn't focusing on any one particular attribute. He simply searched within himself for the core, waiting for it to manifest itself. Of course, if he *had* to choose, he knew what that choice would be: Intelligence.

He could only imagine how much stronger it would make his spells if he were able to infuse Soultaker with Intelligence Energy. Not only that, he would likely gain more skills that would boost his Intelligence as well.

War drums sounded outside the walls. He'd lost track of what wave this was now, though he knew that Kalren and Queen Alastea had tallied each wave up on a sheaf of parchment. Though Xavier wasn't able to find time to sleep, the queen and her loyal adviser did. They took shifts sitting at the wall, watching and taking note of his achievements.

Howard, Siobhan, and Justin still sifted through the library. Queen Alastea had been kind enough to offer them any books they wished to keep. They were prioritising which ones they took, looking for basic manuals that would be able to help others back at the Tower of Champions on top of any they could use to help Xavier and themselves.

Xavier snapped his eyes open as the war horns began to sound along with the drums. He released a sigh and picked himself up off the stone. He could have snapped to his feet in a split second, but he didn't feel the need. He summoned Soultaker from his Storage Ring, infusing it with Spirit Energy. It thrummed with power, just as he did.

The waves had long ago become monotonous. There wasn't anything *new* about them. The Endless Horde, consuming half of the sector, was surprisingly uniform.

Xavier delivered nothing but death to his enemies, and all he could think of was how *bored* he was doing this. He wanted to push through as many of these waves as he could. Wanted to use this opportunity to push himself as far forward as possible. To gain as many advantages as he could out of this floor, especially as it paused time back in his own universe—an opportunity he didn't know he would ever have again.

And there was still that part of him that wondered if he could defeat the entirety of the Endless Horde.

But something about what he was doing felt... *off*. The Tower of Champions had become too easy for him.

No challenge. That's what it is.

Half an hour, maybe forty minutes, passed before the entirety of the wave was dead around the castle. The waves of enemies *were* increasing in difficulty, but they were increasing too slow.

And getting a nerfed amount of Mastery Points made him wonder how worth it each wave even was. Though the waves took longer for him to clear, he still hadn't needed to use the health potions within his Storage Ring.

In his mind, he saw himself going through all 955 floors after this one and he couldn't believe how he felt about it. Xavier *should* have felt excited. Maybe daunted, by how large the task ahead of him would be.

But it just felt... exhausting.

The System wants to control my every move. Wants to push me on a singular path, from one floor to the next. Though he was taking full advantage of that path, trying to squeeze out everything from it he could, he still didn't feel in *control*.

He wanted *more*. And that feeling of wanting more seized his heart, clenching it. He remembered feeling this exact same way before the System had come—always moving through life wanting *more*. And hadn't he gotten exactly what he wished for? Not only was he on another world, he was in another *universe*, fighting an endless wave of enemies. Humans, beasts, and fantasy races of all kinds that were no longer mere fantasies but realities.

And here he was, still wanting more?

A challenge.

That's what he was missing. *That's* why it was boring.

When he returned to the battlements and sat cross-legged on the stone, he pulled out the Sector Travel Key from his Storage Ring. A frown creased his forehead as he had an absurd thought.

Could this work here?

He glanced behind him. He couldn't see through the wall to the castle, where inside the portal still remained open, awaiting Kalren eventually stepping through it. But holding that Sector Travel Key in his hand, and thinking about that portal, made him wonder how long the System would allow him to stay in this universe.

The floor has already been cleared. I cleared the fifth wave on the first day. The only way this floor ends is if I die or return through the door to the Staging Room from the Safe Zone.

At least, so he thought.

He clutched the key, wondering if it would even work. He was sure Sam had said something about it *not* being able to work while in the tower. But did that rule apply here?

Besides, I don't even need to use this. I could simply step through that portal in the castle. I could live free in this universe, for as long as I wished. For years. Decades. Hell, I could remain here for centuries if the System let me. And when I returned from my adventures, I could step into that Safe Zone and return home—and only an hour would have passed in my universe.

Xavier shook his head and sighed. He deposited the Sector Travel Key back into his Storage Ring. No. Abandoning this floor wasn't the answer. Abandoning his plan wasn't the answer. Whether he'd made the choice to follow this path or the System had steered him toward it, he didn't know.

But he couldn't simply run off while Earth was in peril. He couldn't put pause on everything that was happening—even if he technically *could*, he'd never truly be able to relax while Earth was in danger.

Instead of falling back into a deep meditation, Xavier stood. He stepped back over to the parapet and looked over at those endless waves.

"What is it?" Kiralla asked. She looked up from the parchment with a yawn.

Xavier motioned at the enemy with a dismissive wave. "I hate how they just stand there."

The queen raised an eyebrow. "You wish they would all attack at once?"

He crossed his arms, wondering how selfish he might sound. "It's the stop-and-start nature of this floor... It's starting to get to me." He rubbed the back of his neck. "I'm wondering if there's another way to deal with the enemy." He looked over at her. "How far away do you think I am from reaching E Grade?"

Queen Alastea ran a hand through her hair. After the first week he'd been here, she'd taken off her golden crown. Now, her hair was no longer intricately braided atop her head. She let it hang down and frame her face. She didn't sit quite as straight either. It wasn't that she'd grown lazy, or even weary—which she had every right to be—it simply felt as though she'd grown more comfortable around him. "I've never heard of anyone reaching E Grade until they gained Level 100, Xavier. You should be proud of yourself for being halfway there after such a short time."

He lowered his head. That was exactly what Kalren had told him. And he supposed she was right. He *should* be proud of what he'd achieved. These last few weeks on this floor had brought his level all the way up to 50 now.

But still, it never felt like enough.

And the insights Xavier gained from his meditation were telling him a very different story about reaching E Grade. Not the *full* story. He just had a feeling—an inkling—that he could reach it much earlier than Level 100.

The *facts* that Kalren had told him were that a Denizen needed to unlock both his Spirit Core and his secondary core—whatever core that ended up being—before they were able to reach E Grade. And that this tended to happen after the Denizen had attained Level 100.

He also told Xavier that people usually didn't unlock their Spirit Core until they were well over Level 60, 70, and sometimes even Level 80. And there were even some Denizens who didn't achieve E Grade until they were Level 120—even higher, if they had gotten a particularly poor class.

Xavier had discovered his Spirit Core at Level 10.

"Siobhan told me of some legends in your books," Xavier said softly, "of great Denizens achieving E Grade before Level 100."

Queen Alastea looked at the enemy waves. "I've never found much comfort in legends. Legends are outliers, and it is the legends who get to write their own history, for they are always the victors. The strongest. No one can see their level. No one knows when they achieved something. They could simply be lying to bolster their reputation."

Xavier didn't think she was right. If they were the strongest, why would they *need* to bolster their reputation? But instead of *telling* her she was wrong, he would simply prove it was possible. Because the moment he achieved E Grade rank, he was going to turn things on this floor around. He wasn't simply going to sit on this damned wall and wait for the next wave to come to him. He was going to change the game. Walk down a path the System *hadn't* set out for him. Walk down a path that no other Denizen had ever walked before him.

He was going to take the fight to the enemy.

And he wasn't going to wait until Level 100 to make that happen.

Chapter 10
Wave One Thousand

"Wave 1,000," Adviser Kalren said. The man sat at a small table on the battlements, one that had been brought up from the inn weeks ago. He held a quill in his hand, poised over a long scroll. It was an odd sight, like seeing an accountant working next to a battlefield.

"What?" Xavier asked, sure he couldn't have heard that right. "Wave... that's the *thousandth* wave?"

Kalren pointed toward a number on the left-hand side of the scroll, hovering his quill's nib just above it. "You have been here for six weeks. Almost forty-three days. The waves have come hourly without ceasing." He nodded curtly. "Yes. This next wave is wave 1,000."

Xavier sighed. He was sitting on the parapet, his legs dangling over the side. "Feels more like a million," he muttered. But he couldn't help but smile at the knowledge.

Six weeks.

They'd spent longer here than they had back in the Tower of Champions proper. He knew sometimes it *could* take upwards of a week, even two, for denizens to clear each of the first ten floors, but he'd never expected to spend so long on one.

Xavier still felt the monotony. The incessant *grind* of the floor.

Each of the waves became successively more difficult, while at the same time, what he gained from them diminished. Though he was fortunate that he hadn't needed to deal with any enemies of a higher grade than his own yet.

After so long at it, he'd begun to find a rhythm. The pain in his head from lack of sleep was still there, but he was far better able to deal with it now. The pain hadn't lessened—if anything, it worsened—but his tolerance had improved tremendously.

When he'd spoken to Adviser Kalren about this, the man had said he'd heard Denizens of higher grades didn't need sleep. That they could go without for hundreds of years if they needed to.

Xavier wondered if reaching E Grade would take the pain away.

As time had passed and Xavier had taken down progressively more waves of the Endless Horde, he'd come across ever more limitations. The Mastery Points he received were the first thing that became limited, something he'd simply had to accept. This floor of the Tower of Champions, these waves... they hadn't been chosen with someone like him in mind.

The other limitations felt more severe.

He'd been progressively increasing the ranks of his spells and skills while fighting the waves of the Endless Horde, repeating the same tactics over and over until he moved onto different ones to advance different abilities.

Some waves, he focused entirely upon Heavy Telekinesis. His skill with the spell had grown tremendously. It lacked the precision another path of telekinesis would have given him, but the more focus he'd given the spell, the more versatile he'd been able to make it.

It had been Adviser Kalren's prompting that had made him push the ability further. Initially, while Xavier had been fighting goblins back on Earth and clearing the first few Tower of Champions floors, he'd focused purely on brute force with the spell's application, as that was its highlighted strength.

Now, after hours and hours, days and days, and many waves,

Xavier could do far more than simply fling an enemy into a wall, floor, or ceiling. He couldn't levitate a sword and launch it at someone—such applied control was too precise—but he could levitate his enemy and crush their bones where they hovered in the air.

The first time he'd broken through and managed such a feat, it looked like the beast he'd used the spell on had been put into a car crusher.

First, he could do that with only a single enemy. At the time, it hadn't seemed like a terribly useful application of the spell. He'd been focusing so hard on his Soul Strike spell—which was dramatically more effective, especially in such a large-scale battle—but as he progressed with the Heavy Telekinesis spell, he was able to crush multiple enemies at once. He could even pick up enemies—or allies—and move them in the air without simply giving them a heavy *push*. Such an application wasn't much use to him right now, but he could see how it could come in handy in the future.

Besides, even though his soulkeeping threshold had expanded an incredible amount over the last few weeks, not every floor would be like this—with waves and waves of enemies for him to reap. Not every encounter outside of the tower would be like this, either. He needed to prepare for situations where he was fighting *without* a full reserve of souls, and without any means of gaining any more.

As useful as all of his soul-based spells were, Xavier didn't want to only be reliant on them. Especially with all the research that the others had been doing in the library. On the second week of their being there, Justin had brought a book up to the battlements. The book detailed an entire society of golems—*constructs*, much like Siobhan's Divine Guardian, but of a more permanent nature.

It wasn't entirely clear, but it seemed as though these constructs didn't have souls.

Then there were armies of the undead. He had no idea if he could harvest *undead* souls, or if they even had any. And while he had his melee abilities—which he'd also been strengthening to a high degree—he wanted to be more versatile.

But that was when he'd been hit by his limitations. Advancing his spells and skills, he'd run straight into an immovable wall, unable to push any of them past the rank of 50. He'd been made aware of this limitation already. According to Kalren, while there appeared to be no limits to how many attributes an F Grade Denizen could possess, there were hard limits on how strong their skills and spells could *become*.

This had honestly taken Xavier by surprise. Mostly because if there were limits to how much he could rank up these things... he hadn't expected to reach them so *quickly*. So when he told Kalren of trying to break past those limits, the man had looked at him with a deeply furrowed brow.

"You, of all people, should not be surprised coming up against these barriers." The man had stood from his small table, then walked to the parapets. He rested a hand on the wall and motioned toward the Endless Horde with the other one. "Sometimes I wonder if you are truly aware of the position you are in. This situation... is entirely unique. If you were a *normal* Denizen, one who had entered the Tower of Champions at the proving age with prior knowledge of what you would face but lacking the titles you have access to as a True Progenitor... you would be able to farm the different floors for levels, yes. But this?" He shook his head in slight disbelief, his gaze drifting over the ranks and ranks of soldiers and beasts. "This isn't a once-in-a-lifetime opportunity, Xavier. This isn't even a once-in-a-*billion*-lifetimes opportunity. The Greater Universe is more vast than any of us can truly imagine, and though I would not wager my life on it, I would say that the position you are in is entirely unique to *you*. A normal Denizen would not be able to progress their skills and spells at the rate you have. The amount of Mastery Points they would receive from these enemies would be significantly higher. They would have reached Level 100 —or *more*—before being able to rank up that many spells and skills."

Xavier thought about what the man had said once more as he surveyed the enemy. *Entirely unique to you.* That appeared to be true, but he couldn't bet on it. Once again, he recalled being visited upon by that presence that made him feel like an ant in the face of a supernova. Out of so many Denizens, could he truly be the first to get this far?

It boggled his mind trying to think about who else could have been in this position. All he knew was that he needed to keep going —needed to keep pushing.

But Adviser Kalren's point was clear. Other Denizens simply wouldn't have been able to gain as many ranks as him by his level— which had stalled out at Level 60 and was now growing at a snail's pace.

There were some skills he *hadn't* been able to rank up quite as quickly, however. Assimilate Properties was one of them. He had tried a myriad of different, slightly crazy things to spur the skill into activating over the last few weeks. Kiralla had observed him, a single eyebrow raised high, as he'd dug gashes into his arm and rubbed rocks into the wounds.

"What in the Greater Universe are you doing?" Her level of bafflement had been amusing, so he hadn't stopped there. He'd tried all sorts of different materials. It was a bit of a gruesome procedure. The skin healing over the rocks, trapping them inside. But he hadn't been able to imagine another way of doing it.

Unfortunately, it simply hadn't worked, even though when he'd originally gained the skill, it had been when he'd broken through the 100-point Toughness threshold while arrowheads had been lodged into him. His skin had healed over them, and his body had tried to "purge" the impurities.

This was a process he hadn't managed to repeat, which baffled him. It didn't appear to work like other skills, and his party hadn't been able to find information about it within the library. That didn't mean there *wasn't* information about it. No doubt it was hidden within one of the myriad of volumes in the tower library, but just because they'd been there for some time didn't mean they'd had a chance to go through them all—even with their accelerated reading speed.

Identify was another skill that hadn't ranked up as swiftly as others. Admittedly, Xavier hadn't been using it as heavily as things like Physical and Mental Resistance. He was often too busy working on uncovering his secondary core or fighting waves to bother with using the skill.

Still, it had proven useful. Though speaking of limitations, Identify has its share. When he'd first used it, the skill had had a cooldown of *ten minutes*—which, incidentally, was the first time he'd encountered a *skill* with a cooldown. That was usually reserved for spells.

The skill could only give him extra information on enemies that were within a certain level limitation. It could only properly identify enemies with levels twice as high as the skill's rank. So, if the skill was Rank 20, he could identify enemies at Level 40.

Considering the level of the enemies he'd faced had progressed far faster than his Identify skill had, he'd never gotten a chance to use it on them, which meant he had to rank it up from Identifying items alone—a very lengthy process when the skill had such a long cooldown.

Still, he diligently identified each of the flagstones that made up the battlements walls—which were all sandstone—along with other items he could find that were of a low enough level to allow him to do so.

It wasn't his favourite skill to advance.

Adviser Kalren cleared his throat, bringing him out of his reverie. "You still have seventeen minutes before the next wave charges toward the walls. You had best make good use of them."

Xavier released a sigh. He settled down onto the cold flagstone floor of the battlements and closed his eyes. *One thousand waves.* When he'd discovered what this floor entailed, he hadn't known how far he would get, only that he would go as far as he could. One thousand was definitely a good number. *Enough to get the top spot?*

He shoved those thoughts away and focused on his breath, looking inside himself and sinking into a deep meditation. Since he'd discovered his Spirit Core at Level 10, and his Spirit attribute was now well over 1,000, he'd assumed it would be far, *far* easier to discover his secondary core.

But no matter how much he "searched inside" himself, using his now–Rank 50 Meditation skill, the discovery alluded him.

It was growing incredibly frustrating. There was supposed to be a core for each attribute within a Denizen, with different energies associated with them. A Spirit Core was everyone's first discovery. He still found it difficult to imagine that there were *five other* cores within his body somewhere he simply couldn't feel. Now that he'd found and developed his Spirit Core, and the three skills associated with it, it was impossible to imagine *not* being able to feel it.

He'd told this to Kalren on several occasions. The man had only shrugged. "I was never blessed with the opportunity to advance beyond F Grade. I wish I could instruct you from more than the knowledge I have gained from books, but I unfortunately cannot."

That was another thing that surprised Xavier. The fact that this man had grown to his age without growing his level and grade very high. The man possessed some sort of administrative, knowledge-based support class that helped him retain memories easier and teach others more easily, but his level could only grow based on the level of those he taught.

Right now, he was Level 62. And it had taken his entire life to get to this point.

This world, even before Kiralla's mother had been killed by the Endless Horde, had always been a weak one.

How did a world like this survive for so long? It felt like an insensitive question to ask, but Queen Alastea had provided him with an answer without his prompting.

This world was millions of years old and had been stripped completely of all its natural resources. Like many worlds in the sector, it was what was considered a "dead" world. The beasts of this world did not thrive, for they had been decimated long ago. For a world to retain its strength, it needed to maintain a *balance*.

When a strong entity ripped it off its resources, its beasts, materials —everything—it was rare it ever came back from it.

And so, such a world wasn't sought-after like Earth was, being a newly integrated world with resources ripe for the taking. If Alastea's family had not gained the ire of the Endless Horde, it might have stood for many more centuries. Those lack of resources also helped explain how weak those in the world were.

Xavier breathed deeply. Even now, with Meditation at Rank 50, it was still difficult for him to quiet his thoughts. He let them drift away and followed the lines in his body—his Spirit Lines— that led to his primary core.

He had done this same exercise countless times with no luck. But this time... this time, he sensed something different.

Chapter 11
Metaphysical Manifestations of Power

Sitting on the flagstone floor of the castle's battlements, deep in concentration, Xavier sharpened his focus to a point and aimed it toward what he'd just sensed.

As he'd followed the Spirit Lines within him that led to his primary core, he'd noticed a discrepancy. The energy he could sense all around him—the energy that entered his body and flowed through the Spirit Lines all the way to his Spirit Core, was Celestial Energy. A pure energy that could theoretically be put toward *any* of the six cores within a Denizen's body. Now that Xavier's awareness over his body and mind had improved, he could easily feel when that energy entered him. Could easily feel its journey. With his Core Strength and Cultivate Energy skills he'd even learnt how to *control* that energy. What he felt wasn't strictly quantifiable. He couldn't see the exact *number* of points of energy that entered into him—he could simply sense a vague amount. But as he was examining these Spirit Lines, he felt some of that energy being siphoned off.

Interesting.

The moment he'd first sensed this, he'd lost it again. It was such a minute amount—probably one hundredth of a single point of

Celestial Energy—that he was surprised he'd managed to feel it at all.

But now that he'd sensed it *once*, he was sure he would be able to sense it again.

"Ten minutes," Adviser Kalren said.

Xavier's brow furrowed at the interruption, even though he'd instructed the man to announce time warnings so he was always aware of when the next wave would arrive. Usually, the short warning, said with a soft voice, wouldn't be enough to knock his concentration. This particular task felt more delicate than other tasks in the past, however. A few more minutes passed before Xavier felt the discrepancy a second time. The moment he did, he seized his mind upon it. The energy was like a single grain of sand on a beach that stretched for a hundred miles, and the only thing extinguishing it from the other grains was that it was a shade darker than the rest.

Xavier managed to follow it through his body for a full six seconds before Adviser Kalren spoke again.

"Five minutes."

Xavier muttered a curse under his breath. *This.* This was why he'd had so much trouble finding his secondary core. Adviser Kalren told him it was because his level wasn't high enough to unlock it. Xavier believed otherwise—he thought it was simply because he hadn't gained enough time meditating in this particular manner. He *was* able to meditate while in combat now. Doing so provided him with unique, combat-related insights that helped his fighting ability in the long term, but it had the shortcoming of slowing his effectiveness in battle even *with* those insights, as it slowed his reaction time.

Still, at least it had given him the chance to rank the skill up.

But the time he had between waves? When he wasn't eating, resting, or seeing to personal hygiene needs—those didn't just *stop* because one was in a never-ending battle—he rarely had more than a few minutes to sink into this state.

For a third time, Xavier homed in on a tiny fraction of the

Celestial Energy he was bringing into his body. Once more, he followed the energy, hoping to find its destination—he was sure it must be feeding one of his other cores, though he still had a very limited understanding of how that all worked.

"One minute," Adviser Kalren announced, in a louder voice than before.

Xavier, knowing the interruption would be coming, didn't let it knock him out of his concentration. He kept following the speck. It appeared to be headed toward his heart. Kalren had quoted a passage to him about the locations of each of the cores. Apparently, their locations within a Denizen's body held little to no meaning. Cores were metaphysical manifestations of power, ones that could not be observed with the naked eye. One could not slay a Denizen and fish out their cores with a knife—it simply didn't work like that. Once a Denizen was slain, the energy within their cores dissipated back into the Greater Universe.

And so, one couldn't simply look for the cores within their heart or their brain, as the placement was symbolic. They did not *technically* reside within the physical plane.

The whole explanation had given Xavier a headache, even after the third time Adviser Kalren had gone over it. Finally, Xavier figured he didn't need to have a full grasp on the theory for him to put things into practice—hopefully he would gain insights along the way that would make everything clearer as he went.

"Ten seconds."

If Xavier wasn't deep in concentration, he would have muttered a curse. The speck of Celestial Energy was travelling through his body tremendously slowly, as though something were blocking it from moving. As it wasn't travelling through one of his Spirit Lines, Xavier had difficulty discerning what could be slowing it down.

Horns blared. War drums sounded. Roars and shouts were unleashed from the thousands of soldiers and beasts that made up the thousandth wave of the Endless Horde. Xavier ignored it all for as long as he could, knowing the seconds he had were dwindling by.

"One second," Adviser Kalren said.

"There!" Xavier said at the same time. He sensed a weak knot of energy. To his mind's eye, it appeared to be inside his heart. He got a *sense* of what the energy was and found it to be familiar. "Willpower."

Xavier opened his eyes as the notification popped up in his vision.

You have gained +10 Willpower!

You have discovered your Willpower Core.

Spell Quest Unlocked: Willpower Infusion
To unlock Willpower Infusion, you must:
1. Cultivate 1,000 points of Celestial Energy into your Willpower Core, turning it into Willpower Energy.
2. Successfully cycle 1,000 points of Willpower Energy through your Willpower Core.
Progress:
1. 0/1,000
2. 0/1,000

He couldn't help but release a laugh as he sprang to his feet. Adviser Kalren had an eyebrow raised and a worried look on his face. The enemy wave began its approach, their stampeding charge like rumbling thunder. Xavier turned to Kalren. "I unlocked my secondary core," he said before sprinting to the parapet and leaping over it.

Xavier ran toward the enemy, summoning Soultaker to his hand, a great big grin on his face. It had been a while since he'd felt this level of excitement. He'd quickly scanned the notification the moment it came up, but as he had less than a second by that point, he hadn't taken in all the details even with his speed-reading abilities.

He went over those now as he sent off a powerful Soul Strike toward the ranks of the Endless Horde surrounding Queen Alastea's castle. He infused every soul in his soulkeeping reserve into the strike, and since he'd gained Rank 50 in each of his Soul Reaping spells, that threshold had stalled out at 1,000, which meant it would be 16 minutes and 40 seconds until he was able to use the spell again.

That was another reason he'd trained Heavy Telekinesis up. His Soul Reaper spells were incredible, but their cooldowns were as limited as the spells were strong. Despite the fact that he'd gained a *huge* number of points in both Spirit and Intelligence since gaining Soul Strike and Soul Block, the spells' cooldowns were still limited—one second per soul infused. That had not budged, and Xavier didn't see it doing so any time soon. Which meant if he were one day able to cast a Soul Strike with 10,000 infused souls, it would take close to three hours before he'd be able to use the spell again.

And long gone were the days when Xavier could send out a Soul Strike and take out an entire wave. The enemies had been growing in strength faster than he was—something he hoped to remedy by evolving to E Grade.

As the Soul Strike arced toward the enemies, powerful apparitions of beasts and soldiers coming to life, Xavier went over the notification again. If this wave was like the last dozen he'd dealt with, the Soul Strike should be able to deal with roughly a quarter of the enemies. The rest would come straight for him, completely ignoring the castle itself. Considering how many waves had come for him—and how many he'd taken down—it often made him wonder about the leader of the Endless Horde, and why they didn't simply pull out of this world. The Endless Horde was forced to come at him in waves by the System—something that still didn't make much of any sense to Xavier—but did that mean they *couldn't* surrender?

The words, said by Sergeant Bradley on the third floor, ran through his mind: *The System doesn't stand for cowards.*

Maybe the leader of the Endless Horde would incur the System's wrath if they were to turn back. He pushed those thoughts out of his mind as he looked at the notification he'd received for discovering his Spirit Core.

A frown lined his forehead. Discovering his Willpower Core hadn't done nearly as much as he'd expected. For one, there weren't any Skill Quests. He'd expected to gain the equivalent skills that he had from the Spirit Core. Interestingly, though, discovering the core *had* unlocked a Spell Quest. His first Spell Quest. *Willpower Infusion.* Xavier could imagine what infusing Willpower Energy into himself might gain him, and the requirements to gain the spell looked awfully similar to what he'd needed to do for some of the Spirit Core's Skill Quests.

What made his grin fall straight from his face, however, was that he couldn't see any mention of evolving to E Grade. He'd thought all he would need to do was discover his secondary core and some sort of quest would reveal itself—or perhaps a "Would you like to evolve?" notification prompt...

Perhaps that had been wishful thinking.

Xavier turned his focus toward the approaching enemies. He couldn't let whatever was going through his mind affect his ability to fight off this wave.

I just gained my secondary core. I will figure out how to get to E Grade.

Chapter 12
Wave Boss

Hundreds of Level 90 Giant Wolven leapt at Xavier. The beasts were each the size of buses and seemed to be carved almost entirely from muscle. Their fur was dark grey and spiked. Their eyes glowed a fierce red. Even when darkness fell upon this world, as it had now, those eyes were visible. As the waves of the Endless Horde had become progressively stronger over those first few days, Xavier had wondered if they would just continue to grow larger and larger. He'd had this absurd image of Wolven the size of mountains bounding toward him. An image that he was glad hadn't become a reality.

Xavier pulsed a Heavy Telekinesis behind him. The spell felt so much more natural and versatile now that he'd gained some skill in it. Roars, yelps, and bones cracking sounded after his attack. He pulsed a five-infused Soul Block every five seconds, blocking the enemies he wasn't actively engaging. Soul apparitions materialised, soaking up strikes left and right. Fighting these beasts, the size that they were, he didn't have to worry too much about them ganging up on him—they were simply too large—but that didn't mean he could fight one of them at a time.

His staff-scythe effortlessly carved into their flesh, gouging long, deep wounds up their sides and through their necks—when he was able to avoid their outstretched claws.

One of the beasts got past his defences and crashed into him. No matter how strong and tough Xavier's body had become since he'd been integrated into the System, and with Spiritual Trifecta glowing silver over his skin, it didn't stop a massive weight crashing into him from knocking him backward.

Unlike Howard, he didn't have any skill or spell that would help him keep rooted to the ground. And even with the density of his muscles, he didn't way a tenth of what these beasts did.

Xavier was flung through the air and crashed into a beast behind him. Straight into the damned thing's slavering jaws. Despite the fact that his most powerful attacks were ranged, Xavier often found there was simply no way to stay out of the fray if he wanted to defeat his enemies in a timely manner. He could no longer deal with a wave from afar. If he did, the next wave would be on its way before he'd killed the first. Letting that happen would mean the end of him being on this floor.

And that was why he kept finding himself in these damned situations. Fangs digging deep into his skin. Saliva falling into his eyes and mouth—not matter how hard he tried to clamp it shut. Acrid, warm breath like a storm's gale in his face.

It almost made him want to leave this floor early.

I haven't reached E Grade yet. I can't leave this floor.

He was more determined than ever to reach E Grade. More determined than ever to defeat the entirety of the Endless Horde, assuming that a thing were even *possible*—especially now he'd unlocked his secondary core.

But that wasn't the only reason he wanted to remain here. And it certainly wasn't because of the Mastery Points—he barely got *any* Mastery Points from these enemies now, as the System had adjusted to his power level.

When I move onto the next few floors, I doubt I'll gain any levels at all.

The other reason he wanted to remain was because of Queen Alastea—Kiralla.

Xavier, Howard, Siobhan, and Justin could leave this floor at any time. Once they returned to the Staging Room, the fifth floor would be complete, and the Endless Horde would never be able to touch them. Adviser Kalren could step through that portal still open in the castle's throne room. He, too, would be free of the Endless Horde.

But Kiralla? She could never leave this place. And that would mean her death.

The Giant Wolven clamped its fangs around his body. Xavier didn't scream at the pain, no matter how intense it was. When he'd been flung through the air, he'd summoned his scythe-staff back into his Storage Ring—the last thing he wanted to do was accidentally lose that thing in the middle of all this chaos. The beasts fangs sliced through his robes and dug into his skin. A *crack* sounded and for once it wasn't an enemy's bones being broken—it was his own.

Okay, *that* made a yelp escape his mouth. Once he'd gained his bearings, he cast Heavy Telekinesis.

The spell slammed into the top of the beast's massive jaw and tore its head clean in half. The scope of the damage looked more like a cannonball had been shot through the roof of the thing's mouth.

He manoeuvred himself out of the beast's jaws—or, well, *one* jaw. Though manoeuvre was probably too fancy a word for what he did, considering he fell face-first onto the blood-soaked, muddied ground of the battlefield. You would think that after having gained so many points in Speed and Strength, Xavier would have gotten a little more graceful than that.

He let out a sigh as he picked himself up off the ground. Not his finest moment. He looked at the cooldown for Soul Strike.

Soul Strike currently has a cooldown of 16 minutes and 40 seconds. It cannot be used for another 3 minutes and 2 seconds.

Dammit, he thought. *That feels like an eternity.*

This was by far his least favourite part of the waves. With Soul Block, Xavier could defend against incredibly powerful strikes. With Soul Strike, he could take down thousands of enemies—at this level—all at once. But he wasn't being struck by a *single* powerful strike. Soul Block was nothing like Howard's Bulwark attack. And Xavier had no movement spells—he wasn't able to get the hell out of the way of this many enemies even if he wanted to.

He had to simply fight in the middle of a mess of thousands of attackers all out for his blood.

He gritted his teeth and ploughed forward. Soultaker carved through one enemy after another. Heavy Telekinesis crushed whole groups of enemies. With each death he wrought, another soul became his, fuelling his blocks. He would have put them toward Soul Harden, but the spell had long stalled at Rank 50 just like his others.

Xavier had restricted kill notifications altogether; otherwise, they would be the only thing he could see, bombarding his vision practically every second.

No matter how many enemies he killed, they simply kept coming. He couldn't get them out of the way fast enough. And with the size of these damned things, he felt like a mouse being attacked by a pack of cats.

Is it a pack of cats? he wondered, then discarded the thought.

His mind always went to strange places while in the middle of battle.

He checked the cooldown for Soul Strike again. *One minute.* Technically, he could have kept the cooldown for Soul Strike visible on the side of his vision at all times, but he didn't like doing that. It was like staring at the time when you were waiting for class to end. It always seemed to make it take far, far longer. Then again, when he didn't have it visible he would bring the damned thing up every minute anyway.

By the time the cooldown finally came up, he'd managed to avoid being chomped by another of the beasts. The *click* in his mind as the cooldown hit zero sent a rush of relief through him. He cast another 1,000-infused Soul Strike at the enemies, focusing on those around him so he could get a little bit of breathing room. The apparitions filled the night with a brilliant light. The beasts didn't even have time to roar before they died.

He took a deep breath as the enemies fell.

Which, of course—given where he was—was a complete mistake. The battlefield had an absolutely awful smell to it. One he still wasn't accustomed to, despite how long he'd spent in this place. The fire mages of the Endless Horde burned their dead, turning them to ashes between waves, and the dust of his slain enemies filled the air as much as anything else.

Xavier's moment of relief didn't last long. Soon, it was once more supplanted by tension. For the first couple of weeks and few hundred waves, Xavier hadn't felt afraid. He hadn't felt a hint of fear from what he'd been experiencing—the waves had simply been too easy to demolish. The way he'd smashed through them made feeling fear a difficult thing, no matter how many enemies he had to face.

He wasn't sure when that had changed. When the fear he'd experienced in the first few hours and days of being thrown into the System had returned.

Now, in these waves, he felt a constant pressure—not just the pressure that settled at the back of his mind from lack of sleep. This was far more intense, and it wasn't something he could simply ignore. As strong as he was, as many of the enemies' attacks as he could shrug off, if he made a wrong move, it could very well end up being his last.

Xavier leapt into the air and landed on one of the Giant Wolven's corpses. He glanced around, trying to see how many enemies remained. He'd cast Soul Strike twice, which meant he'd been in the battle for a little over thirty-three minutes.

Instantly, he knew he'd been a little bit foolish for using 1,000 souls in his last strike. He'd long ago learnt that he needed to be more strategic after his first Soul Strike of a wave. Now he wouldn't be able to use his third Soul Strike until quite late in the wave. Had he used 700, or even 800, that would have reduced the time between strikes by a few minutes.

Which would have let him take out more of the enemies in less time.

Can't dwell on mistakes already made.

He likely wouldn't have acted so brashly if he hadn't almost been eaten by one of these damned Wolven. Or maybe it was because his mind was elsewhere. All he wanted was to get to the end of the wave and see how quickly he could gain that Willpower Infusion spell. Discovering his secondary core was something he'd been trying to do for weeks. Finally, he'd gotten there, and there was no time to enjoy the achievement.

Moments like this made him wish he wasn't fighting these battles alone. Made him wish he could have the others with him. That they could have progressed at the same rate as him. But even though he'd gained a ton of levels on this floor, he wasn't about to give up the solo title. Besides, it was far too late to throw Howard, Siobhan, and Justin into the mix. They would be far too weak to handle enemies like this.

Xavier tore through the rest of the enemies. There was perhaps less than a quarter left. He'd stopped counting the number of enemies in a wave, but from a glance, he could generally get a good estimate. This wave was comprised entirely of high-level Giant Wolven and must have been ten thousand strong, which meant there were still over two thousand of them left.

Fool, he chastised himself. Yes, he'd just told himself he wouldn't dwell on his mistakes, but it looked like he wouldn't be able to clear these bastards until Soul Strike recovered again. *Then I had better be careful how many I infuse in that Soul Strike, or I'll leave the spell in cooldown when the next wave starts.*

By the time Soul Strike met its cooldown, there were still a few hundred enemies left. He infused 200 souls into the spell and took them all down in one swift move.

Then a massive roar sounded. Xavier frowned. *That* shouldn't have happened. The Endless Horde tended to remain quiet until a wave charged forth. *I should still have almost ten minutes until then.*

But this wasn't the next wave. It was the wave boss. Most of the time, Xavier didn't even notice the wave boss—he tended to take it down with one of his massive, area-of-effect Soul Strikes—but this one had been hanging back, at the front of the enemy's ranks. As though waiting for this moment.

It looked an awful lot like a Wolven. Except for the fact that it stood on two legs.

And Xavier wasn't able to scan it.

It's... it's E Grade!

Chapter 13
Cheesy Movie Villains

THE THOUSANDTH WAVE BOSS LOOKED LIKE SOMETHING FROM a nightmare.

It stood maybe twelve feet tall, nowhere near as large as the Giant Wolven, but terrifying nonetheless.

God, it looks like a bloody werewolf. And, considering Xavier wasn't able to scan the damned thing, for all he knew it *could* be a werewolf. Xavier glanced up at the dark sky. Only one of this world's two moons was full. Would a werewolf need them both?

He shook his head.

I can't scan the beast. That must *mean it's E Grade.*

Xavier had never encountered an E Grade beast before. He took a hesitating step back, gripped his scythe-staff tight, feeling foolish.

None of the other wave bosses had even come close to being a challenge for him. He gritted his teeth. He should deal with this beast quickly, else he would barely have a couple of minutes before the next wave came. As he'd just used a 200-infused Soul Strike, it would still be another three minutes until he could use the spell again.

I intend to kill this beast before then.

The range on Xavier's spells had increased dramatically as he'd ranked them up, so he didn't need to be closer than he already was. He took a step forward and grinned as something came to mind.

Maybe I'll get a title for this. The first person from my world to defeat an E Grade. Yeah, that could definitely happen.

The werewolf-looking beast lurched forward and began bounding across the battlefield. Though it could stand on two legs, it ran on all four, leaping over the bodies of the fallen, kicking up ash as it went. Xavier didn't hesitate. He cast Spirit Break.

The E Grade monster paused in its run. No... pause wasn't the right word. A single one of its steps faltered, like one of its limbs couldn't hold its weight, then it kept coming at him, showing no other signs of damage.

What? Xavier thought. This spell had *always* worked for him.

How could it be failing him now? It must have something to do with the fact that the enemy was E Grade.

Even when I've faced wave bosses with strong magical resistance, I've been able to defeat them easily...

In the first few hundred waves, he'd used the wave-bosses as opportunities to practice Spirit Break. That was how he'd ranked it up all the way to 50. How could it not be strong enough to work on this enemy?

He released a breath. He needn't worry about this. He had other ways to defeat it.

Xavier cast Heavy Telekinesis on the werewolf beast, aiming to pick it up and crush its body. Energy flowed from Xavier's staff, and the wave boss rose into the air. Xavier took a step forward, brow furrowed, eyes narrowed, jaw set. He tilted his head to the side and peered at his enemy, then *crushed* it.

Except... the enemy wasn't crushed. The werewolf-like beast simply howled. It didn't even sound like a howl of pain—more like a howl of anger. Xavier's spell wore off, and it fell to the ground, bounding toward him once more as though he hadn't just cast two spells that should have taken the damned thing out of commission.

What the hell is going on here? Xavier thought. *Are E Grades really that much stronger than F Grades?*

Maybe the enemy simply had some sort of super-strong magical defence. If so, then it couldn't last for long.

Xavier cast Heavy Telekinesis on the beast once more.

The beast had closed much of the distance quite effectively with its long, leaping bounds. Xavier sprinted forward as his spell raised it into the air once more. Just because the spell wasn't able to harm the wave boss didn't mean it wasn't helpful. Xavier could keep it in the air and slash his staff-scythe into it without risking any harm to himself—not that he expected this thing to be able to hurt him. Still, he'd be lying if he said he wasn't a little bit worried. This was the first time his spells had been so... ineffective against a beast since he'd been on the second floor facing the Rat King.

It also made him worry about what might come next. If he was facing E Grade wave bosses in this wave, the next waves would have them too. He didn't doubt he'd be able to take them out, but if his spells weren't as effective—or effective at all as the bosses grew even stronger—it would take him much longer and longer.

Which meant he would have even less time between waves than he already did.

And soon, that time will shrink. Then I'll be facing enemies from two different waves at once because I won't have cleared the enemies from the previous wave.

He pushed those worries from his mind. He had to focus on what was in front of him.

Once again, the beast rose into the air. Except this time, it didn't remain there for long.

The beast cocked its head and grinned wickedly. It shrugged, and then fell straight back to the ground. The force of its landing caused an ash cloud form up from the ground. Standing on two legs, the beast cracked its neck, threw its head back, and laughed. Xavier was still running toward it, tightly gripping Soultaker. He halted, skidded in the ash, and stared at the beast.

Did... did it just shrug off one of my attacks?

"Foolish human." The beast walked forward. "Do you really expect to defeat me?"

It was perhaps twenty feet away from him now. It didn't hold any weapons, nor did it wear any armour. Xavier hadn't expected it to be able to talk. He wasn't sure why. The Puma Prime and the Rat King had both been able to communicate with him. Not that they'd said anything important.

But despite how many enemies he'd faced during the past hundreds of waves, none of the humanoid denizens had tried talking to him. There had been humans, elves, demons—all sorts of different Denizens.

Maybe I never gave them a chance to speak before I, you know, killed them.

Xavier stared at the wolf-beast and raised an eyebrow. "What is it with you guys," he said. "Do you all have to talk like cheesy movie villains?"

The wolf frowned. It opened its mouth, baring sharp teeth. "What is... a *cheesy movie*?"

Xavier sighed. Soultaker was already infused with Spirit, and Spiritual Trifecta glowed about him. He was still confident he could win this encounter. He just hoped it wouldn't take long. As much as he would have loved exchanging insults with a beast who didn't understand his references, he needed to move. Though another thing that worried him was the level of confidence this beast held in itself. It didn't seem the least bit worried about the fact that Xavier had just destroyed an entire wave with ease. Or how many other waves he'd decimated before it. It had just stood there, watching him do it the entire time.

Xavier lunged forward, slashing at his enemy with the staff-scythe. The werewolf beast was fast. Faster than Xavier expected—faster than it had been when bounding toward him. A green glow suddenly surrounded it.

Wait, is that... Speed Infusion?

The beast moved in to attack. Its claws elongated as it did.

The damned things looked like they were made from metal. The claws were long, ten-inch blades. Xavier cast Soul Block. He infused a single soul into the spell. He wanted to ensure he could cast it once per second, though from how fast this thing moved he doubted that would be quick enough.

The beast's claws slammed into the soul apparition that appeared—a bus-sized Giant Wolven.

Then something insane happened. Something he'd never seen before.

The beast's claws weren't stopped as though they'd hit a brick wall, like other attacks that hit Soul Block always were. No, instead, its claws slashed through the apparition. The beast's arms were slowed, but its attack wasn't stopped completely. Xavier, not expecting such a thing to happen, stumbled back and barely avoided a swipe to his neck. He swung his staff-scythe at the beast, three times in quick succession, sweeping it toward the werewolf beast's side, down at its head, then at its legs.

His swings were easily dodged. The beast's wicked grin returned. It looked like the big bad wolf from Red Riding Hood with that grin, as though it were playing a joke and he was the foolish granddaughter.

Xavier took three rapid steps back, creating some distance. His eyes widened as he stared at the beast he couldn't scan. It shouldn't have been so much faster than him. Did that Speed Infusion spell really make such a strong difference? Or was it the fact that the beast was E Grade? Both?

Xavier had assumed he would be strong enough to defeat an enemy at the low end of E Grade easily enough, considering how many titles he'd gained, but now he was beginning to worry he'd underestimated them.

But my attributes are so high, and I just discovered my secondary core. I'm on the peak of reaching E Grade. I'm a True Progenitor *on the peak of reaching E Grade.*

And this is just some random E Grade enemy.

It has to be over Level 100. But how many levels over?

His future plans of destroying the entire E Grade horde crumbled each second this damned beast remained alive.

Adapt, he thought. *Persevere and adapt.*

Xavier gritted his teeth. Spirit Break and Heavy Telekinesis had each been barely effective, and a one-infused Soul Block had barely slowed down the beast's strike.

But that didn't mean he couldn't use those spells to his advantage. There would still be a couple of minutes until he could use Soul Strike again, and though he was sure he could kill this damned thing with a single 1,000 infused Soul Strike, he didn't want to risk being without the spell when the next wave arrived.

After Xavier had taken those steps back, the grin on the beast had widened—something he hadn't even realised was possible. It lurched forward and slashed at him once more with its elongated claws. It closed the distance he'd created far too swiftly.

Xavier cast Spirit Break as it lunged. The spell might not have much effect, but it *did* make the beast falter slightly. Then, before the strike could hit, he cast Heavy Telekinesis. He didn't try and pick up the beast this time. He simply aimed downward.

It didn't have the effect he truly wanted—crushing the beast straight into the ground and breaking all its bones—but it did make it stumble.

Which Xavier took full advantage of. He swept his blade toward the enemy's neck. The strike hit dead on. A large gash opened up and blood spilled from the wound. The beast stumbled back two steps, put a hand to its neck. When its hand came away bloody, the beast didn't widen its eyes in fear.

It laughed.

The wound healed, knitting itself back together.

"It looks as though you might pose a challenge after all," the beast said.

Chapter 14

Once More Into the Breach

XAVIER TOOK A STEP BACK AND SWALLOWED. THE WEREWOLF beast didn't seem phased by the strike he'd just landed on its neck. The gash already looked fully healed. The green glow about the beast from what must have been a Speed Infusion was still present —if anything, it seemed to glow brighter than before. But maybe that was his imagination.

I need to act. Need to kill this thing. Fast.

Xavier didn't have a timer telling him when the next wave would come, but he knew it was only minutes away from how many times he'd used his Soul Strike and how long the cooldowns had been.

Can't let this fight go on for much longer.

The cooldown for Soul Strike was still going. He would have to use it on the beast—he was sure of that now.

The werewolf beast bared its teeth in a large smile that made it look even more terrifying. There was something about facing a beast that had no hint of fear in its eyes after seeing what Xavier was capable of. A beast that had no desire to speed things up. That spoke to him almost casually. In fact...

It's stalling! That's *why it was hanging back.*

The waves of the Endless Horde, as far as he could tell, were compelled to fight him. Not once had he seen any of them hang back. Yet this beast had done so. There had been plenty of sapient Denizens among the other waves, yet none of them had done the same thing. It would have been seen as cowardly by the system. But this beast? It wasn't being a coward. It was being tactical.

It's trying to draw out the wave, so I get attacked by the next one while it's still alive.

Xavier gritted his teeth and slammed a Heavy Telekinesis into the bastard beast as he sprinted forward. Melee fighting might not be his specialty, but he'd done his fair share.

Time to end this.

Xavier needed to disorientate the beast. Needed to send a barrage of attacks at it so fierce and unyielding that it couldn't regain its bearings. If it healed so quickly from a deep gash to its neck, it would need to take a lot of punishment.

Then he would hit it with a Soul Strike, the second he could.

The beast slashed at him. Xavier slipped out of its reach. It might be tall, with a massive reach and elongated claws, but Xavier's scythe-staff still had more reach. An instinct told him to avoid blocking that thing's claws with Soultaker's shaft. The weapon he wielded was only for an F Grade Denizen, and though Xavier loved the weapon, he'd probably already outgrown it.

An E Grade's claws might slice straight through it.

Maybe that was why the wound had healed so easily. It might have looked like a deep gash, but that didn't mean he'd actually caused a great deal of damage.

Xavier slammed one Heavy Telekinesis at the beast after another. It was getting even faster at shrugging off the spell. But that didn't matter. The cooldown on the spell was practically non-existent now. He could keep barraging it against his enemy, over and over.

Slice.

Soultaker's blade slashed the beast's leg.

Slice.

Soultaker's blade slashed the beast's shoulder.

Slice. Slice. Slice.

Xavier inflicted one wound after another on the werewolf beast. A few minutes must have passed since he'd engaged the E Grade enemy, as he felt Soul Strike renew.

Finally.

He went to cast the spell.

Nothing happened.

What the hell? Xavier thought. *Why hadn't the spell worked?*

He backed away a few steps, trying to gain his bearings. The spell *should have worked*. He'd attempted to infuse 100 souls into the spell and... nothing had happened.

I have more than enough souls to spare. He hadn't used too many when he'd been using Soul Block—

Oh. The reason became instantly clear. It almost knocked him off his feet. How could he not have noticed? How could he have been such a fool? His Spirit Energy was incredibly high. *Far* higher than anyone else of his own level ever would have been. The limit he could hold was nearing 200,000 *points*, for god's sake.

And yet, as his spells had ranked up and up and up all the way to 50, so had the cost of each of those spells. Even with his Spirit Recovery being so powerful...

Xavier had exhausted all of his Spirit Energy.

Not good. Not good at all.

He brought up his Spirit Energy.

Available Spirit Energy: 1,200/182,600

Crap, crap, crap, Xavier thought. Once upon a time, 1,200 Spirit Energy would have been a great deal. Now? Most of his spells cost 5,000 Spirit Energy, with Spiritual Trifecta costing 10,000.

It was recovering fast. But he couldn't cast a single spell until it reached 5,000.

Then he'd have to wait again.

Xavier had become so used to gaining Spirit Energy from killing countless enemies that he hadn't needed to worry about running out of the stuff since the first floor of the tower.

The werewolf beast tilted its head to the side with that same fearsome grin that it had had before. It took a step backward. The beast, he realised, had barely even tried to attack him. It hadn't even shown Xavier what spells it had—for it *definitely* had some powerful spells it wasn't utilising.

Why is it backing away? Xavier thought.

Horns blared. War drums thundered, their sound even louder than usual as Xavier was far closer to the Endless Horde's frontline than he usually might be.

Wave 1,001 was about to begin.

Xavier released a long sigh. He'd miscalculated, and for the first time since he'd come to this floor, he hadn't killed every enemy in a wave before the next one arrived. He wouldn't have time to learn the new Willpower Infusion spell. Wouldn't have time to learn what he needed to advance to the rank of E Grade.

And this wave would be harder than the last.

The E Grade wave boss disappeared back into the lines of the next wave. Xavier wanted to pursue it. To *kill* it. Leaving that thing alive just meant he would now have *two* E Grades to deal with, as the next wave boss would now be in play.

He gritted his teeth, wishing he had some sort of teleportation spell, or that he could be summoned back to the wall by Siobhan— though the woman would likely be sleeping by now. Besides, she *couldn't* use her Summon spell on him. Not if he wanted to gain the solo title for this floor.

Still, he wanted to confer with the others back on the wall. But there simply wasn't time for that.

Once more into the breach.

His Spirit Energy was back over 5,000 points. In the grand scheme, it hadn't taken long to recover that much. In fact, it had only taken seconds.

Just long enough for him not to have it when he really needed it.

Xavier had to find a new plan, facing this wave. He couldn't simply do what he'd done on the last wave, or the hundreds before that. It may have worked for him in the past, but he wasn't gaining - power while his enemy was.

How do I get stronger?

He couldn't rank up his skills. Couldn't rank up his spells. Though he *did* gain Mastery Points, they were coming in so damned slowly that he wasn't about to reach the next level any time soon.

The new wave charged forward. This wave was composed of human, elven, and demonic Denizens. These waves were usually more difficult for him to face than the ones purely made from Wolven or other beasts. They wore armour. Had more varied spells. Used clever tactics. They tended to take him longer to clear.

I can't let this one take longer. I need to clear it faster than ever.

Not wishing to wait for Soul Strike to refresh that long again, Xavier decided to use 100-infused Soul Strikes instead of 1,000 infused Soul Strikes. He didn't know if it would be more efficient than what he'd been doing in the past, but he did know he would have access to the spell every minute and twenty seconds.

Which meant if he came across another E Grade, he'd be able to use the spell on them.

He cast Soul Strike, clearing enemies farther away from him so he wouldn't need to move as far to engage the front line of this wave. Usually, it would take him longer to engage in melee at the beginning of a wave. But this time, he wasn't far back on the wall.

Every second counts.

As Soultaker slashed through one foe after another, taking them down with an ease that felt comforting after he'd faced—and not defeated—the E Grade wave boss, Xavier considered his options.

I can't expect to defeat this wave faster than I did the last. Not if

I haven't gained more power. And the only way for him to gain power...

It clicked, and Xavier knew what he had to do.

But it wasn't going to be easy.

Chapter 15
To Be Challenged

As Xavier tore through one foe after another, fighting wave 1,001 of the Endless Horde on the fifth floor of the Tower of Champions, he fell into a deep meditative state. Meditation was possible while fighting—it helped him gain new insights into battle strategy—but at the same time, it tended to slow his effectiveness.

It was difficult for him to split his mind too many ways, and no matter how much combat he'd experienced these weeks since Earth's integration, it wasn't as though he could simply go into auto-pilot.

But he needed to use his Meditation skill if he was going to do what he wished to do.

Xavier decapitated an elf with his scythe-staff, sending the thing's head and body falling to the ground. At the same time, he used Soul Block on his left flank, preventing the enemy from hitting him in the side. He flung a good twenty enemies straight into their comrades and they were impaled on their fellow soldiers' spears. Every soul was harvested at the moment of their death.

While doing this, he examined the lines in his body. Examined the Celestial Energy that was entering into him. Unlike the last time he'd done this, he could now feel his Willpower Core. In his mind's eye, it sat at the centre of his heart. The lines the Celestial Energy flowed through toward the core were still fuzzy. It had taken him some time to identify the equivalent lines for his Spirit Core.

He couldn't take that long this time around. He had to gain this spell *now*. He doubted Willpower Infusion would help him a great deal in combat—he imagined it would mostly add to his mental defence and magical defence—but if he was going to become more powerful, getting to E Grade was still the only way.

Whether the advancement would give him an instant boost to his attributes or an upgraded class choice, he honestly didn't know. Though the tower library had a massive number of books, the weakness of this world showed in what it lacked. There simply wasn't enough information about those at E Grade.

That had taken him by surprise. Another thing that had taken him by surprise was the fact that they didn't have access to the System Shop here. Once he and his party had found out that this place was *real*, they'd eventually asked about how they might be able to access System Shop—a loophole they were hoping to take advantage of. If they could access the shop *within* a floor of the tower, especially a time-locked floor like this one...

But Adviser Kalren and Queen Alastea had shaken their heads. The System Shop apparently wasn't something they could afford to give their queendom access to, which made Xavier realise just how much of a backwater planet this floor they'd been put upon was. Though at least he'd learnt something—System Shop's cost money to gain access to when outside the Tower of Champions.

Perhaps we'll be able to do some sort of quest to attain one back on Earth. Maybe someone already has.

Xavier might not know what gaining the rank of E Grade would give him, but at least he would be able to continue ranking up his skills when he reached it.

All I need to do is stay alive long enough during these waves, unlock this spell, and figure out the next step. He sighed. *Yeah, that doesn't sound all that hard.*

As Xavier fought, he looked at the Spell Quest for Willpower Infusion.

Spell Quest Unlocked: Willpower Infusion
To unlock Willpower Infusion, you must:
1. Cultivate 1,000 points of Celestial Energy into your Willpower Core, turning it into Willpower Energy.
2. Successfully cycle 1,000 points of Willpower Energy through your Willpower Core.
Progress:
1. 0/1,000
2. 0/1,000

All right, he thought. It looked as though he would have to cultivate Celestial Energy first. When he'd discovered the Willpower Core, it had barely had any energy within it at all. He'd found the core by sensing energy that had flowed into it, but that energy had only been a fraction of a single point of Celestial Energy.

Now, he would need to drag 1,000 points of Celestial Energy into that core, then cycle it out through the lines within his body, then back in. All while in the middle of fighting the most difficult wave of the Endless Horde he'd yet to face.

Not to mention two E Grade wave bosses.

He'd been keeping his eyes open, trying to spot the next wave boss—and the last wave boss—but they'd yet to make their presence known. *They're hanging back. Waiting for me to deal with the weaker enemies. Hoping to get me caught by another wave.* Usually, he would have time to recover between waves—even if it was only a few minutes. If the enemies weren't the things to kill him, then after enough waves of this, exhaustion just might be...

He tossed out all the thoughts he didn't need; getting stuck in a cycle of negativity simply wouldn't help him. If worse came to worst, he could get out of this place. *Even if Kiralla can't.*

Xavier slashed his scythe-staff in a wide arc, sweeping five heads off their bodies. He summoned a Soul Strike, killing hundreds of enemies. He breathed in and out, as slowly and deeply as he could manage.

His focus sharpened to a knife's edge. He drew Celestial Energy into his body, but every time he did, it went straight for his Spirit Core. When he actively cultivated Celestial Energy, it was a faster, more effective way of recovering his Spirit Energy. His body and mind had developed habits to reinforce these pathways over and over again as he'd ranked up the skill. But now, he needed to use his Cultivate Energy skill to transfer energy into his new core. He had to fight the instincts he'd developed. Break the pathways. Stop them before they started.

It was a difficult thing, stopping yourself from doing something that had become incredibly natural.

Especially when you were in the middle of fighting thousands of enemy soldiers.

This is what I was hoping for, wasn't it? he thought to himself. *I wanted this. I wanted to be challenged.* He hadn't *felt* challenged in the Tower of Champions. Not truly.

And now, he felt like he was facing something he might not be strong enough to endure.

But he *would* endure. He *would* face this. He gritted his teeth and pushed on. Soultaker brought death wherever he swept it, the souls of his enemies streaming toward him, filling the pit deep inside him, satiating his hunger like nothing else could. Apparitions sprang into life. Human, elven, and demon warriors of light, their glowing bodies transparent, tearing through the soldiers all around him with incredible ease.

He was death incarnate. A Soul Reaper. He could do this.

He *would* do this.

Xavier gritted his teeth and *broke* the pathway of his solidified habit, stopping it before it started. He drew in more Celestial

Energy, cultivating it into his body. He focused, as hard as he possibly could in the middle of a battle, on his Willpower Core and sending that energy toward it. When he'd learnt how to do this for his Spirit Core, he'd been able to feel the Spirit Energy moving through his body whenever he cast a spell. He didn't have such a benefit this time around.

Howard would have probably had a much easier time of it when he discovered his Toughness Core, considering he already *had* access to Toughness Energy.

Once more, Xavier followed the fraction of Celestial Energy that he *could* feel heading toward his Willpower Core—what he'd followed to discover the core in the first place. Though the amount of Celestial Energy was incredibly miniscule, it was heading there in a constant flow. And so he followed it, again and again, until the line was obvious in his mind. It wasn't *defined* in his mind's eye. Not yet, at least. Where his Spirit Lines were deep drenches in the ground, this was drawn in the faintest of pencils with the softest of hands.

Still, it was progress.

Now that he could identify one of the Willpower Lines, he drew the Celestial Energy he'd cultivated from the air into it.

Or, at least, he tried to.

It took him six attempts until finally he managed to trace a small amount of energy down the line. When it reached his Willpower Core, he felt the energy inside it glow with a slight warmth—nothing like the raging fire of his Spirit Core, but it was definitely a start.

He looked at the Spell Quest again, bringing up only the progress for the first step.

1/1,000

Seeing it made a laugh loose from his lips. It wasn't much—only a single point—but it was a *start*.

The rest of the wave continued in this way. Xavier had, unfortunately, lost track of how long the wave had lasted. Usually, he could keep a far better eye on the time a wave lasted from his Soul Strike cooldown, but as he was casting the spell every minute and forty seconds and putting the majority of his focus toward his Willpower Core, it simply wasn't possible for him.

The enemy soldiers didn't appear to be thinning a great deal yet, however, so he mustn't have been all that far into the wave.

As he fought, he dragged more Celestial Energy through the Willpower Line. Again and again, he did this, always watching the points tick up and up. It felt like it was going far too slowly, but the fact he was making any progress at all given the circumstances made this a win.

When the Willpower Core hit 500 points of Celestial Energy, Xavier felt like pumping his fist in the air in triumph. It might have only been halfway, but progress was progress.

After the halfway mark, his speed at drawing it into his core seemed to improve faster and faster. It was beginning to feel... well, not *natural*, but definitely *achievable*.

As the technique become more and more practised, he turned his mind toward the E Grade wave boss he'd faced. He hadn't seen it again—nor had he seen the wave boss for *this* wave, which he was sure would also be E Grade and likely a little bit stronger than the last.

If I have to face them both at once...

He checked his progress again.

978/1,000

So close!

He placed the number up in the corner of his vision to keep an eye on it as he fought, watching for when it ticked over the thousand mark. When it did, he let out a whoop which confused and terrified the enemies directly around him.

He hadn't gained the spell yet, but he was getting so much closer—

A horn blared. War drums thundered.
The next wave was already on its way.

Chapter 16
And I Will Be Their Destruction

No, HE THOUGHT. IT CAN'T BE. NOT YET!

Had the wave come faster than the others? Had... had the System changed the rules on him?

Xavier gripped his scythe-staff tightly in both hands as he clenched his jaw, struggling to believe what was happening.

It *couldn't* already be the next wave! He still had perhaps a quarter of *this* wave left. Had the enemies really grown that much stronger that he'd slowed down *that much*?

Or was it because he'd spent so much time meditating?

Whatever the reason, I have to deal with it. I have to keep pushing.

He'd succeeded in achieving the first step of unlocking the Willpower Infusion spell, but that had taken him—apparently—an entire hour!

I'm still standing. Still able to fight, Xavier thought, but he realised that he would seriously have to consider retreating from this floor—even if it meant Queen Alastea's death.

No. I'm not going to let that happen. Not if I can help it.

He would fight until he couldn't anymore. Anything less... anything less wouldn't be good enough. He was still trying to prove that he was worthy of what he'd gained. He, by chance, or skill, or both, had fallen into being the Progenitor of Earth. He couldn't back down from something just because it was *hard*.

A hero wouldn't just get up and walk away from this. A hero would keep pushing. A hero would figure out a way.

Or they would die trying. Xavier figured he could stop short of dying if it really came down to that.

Cycling Willpower out and then back into his core proved to be twice as hard as cultivating it into his core had been in the first place. But though the process was difficult—and required more of his brain space to achieve—it hadn't taken nearly as long for him to get started.

The skills I have in these areas from doing this with the Spirit Core must be helping a great deal.

A consistent *roar* sounded from near the front of the enemy lines—the next wave. Thousands of beasts, throwing their maws wide, creating a cacophony of noise loud enough to be heard over the fighting.

Probably more Wolven. You'd think a galaxy-spanning organisation called "the Endless Horde" would have more variety among its warriors, he thought, not that that was something he needed to be worrying about right now.

The roar reminded him of something else—he would now have *three* wave bosses on the field. *Three* E Grade enemies.

Sweat dotted Xavier's brow. His muscles were tired, tense. This was something he hadn't needed to worry about much. He'd always been able to regain his freshness between waves. His health wasn't lowering too much, and his regeneration was enough to keep it in check even when it did—he could withstand far more damage than he'd ever imagined possible.

Yet he was starting to feel a deep fatigue. A weariness that had nothing to do with his Spirit Energy or his health. And no matter how much he pushed his self-doubt away, it kept assailing his mind. Kept pushing at him.

This spell won't help me. It won't be enough to turn the tide.

An Elven Duellist—Level 91—slashed at his head with one of

its two curved long swords. The pointy-eared bastard had somehow slipped past his Soul Block and was trying to lay into him. Xavier's scythe-staff was in the middle of separating heads from bodies, and he wasn't able to bring it up to block.

The sword slammed into his forehead. He felt it break the skin. Blood dripped into Xavier's left eye, and he blinked it away as he crushed the bastard thing's neck with a Heavy Telekinesis—he should have targeted multiple enemies with that spell, but his anger had made him misstep.

Sloppy.

The wound wasn't a big one—it healed rapidly, but the blood remained, sticking his eyelashes together and blurring his vision. He couldn't clear the enemies around him fast enough to even wipe his face. They were too packed in. Every time he took down one, another would pop up. Again and again, they came. Never ending.

Endless.

And still, he cycled energy through his secondary core. Still he pushed. He looked at his health.

Your health is at 67%.

Xavier cursed. He didn't bother doing it under his breath. Instead, he shouted it in the face of one of the halberd-wielding demons in front of him before burying Soultaker into its chest, straight through its full-plate armour.

His health was falling. Steadily. It was going down slowly, but it *was* going down. That's something he simply couldn't abide. In all his time here, he'd never even needed to take a health potion.

I'm stronger than this. I should be able to deal with this.

Had he been overestimating himself? The others told him that the legends they'd read about in books from the tower library spoke about mighty Denizens that had been able to defeat opponents above their own grade. The head of the Endless Horde was D Grade.

Somehow, the others thought he might be able to defeat them when he was E Grade. *Assuming I'm able to become E Grade before these damned waves overwhelm me.* But he'd had trouble defeating *one* E Grade enemy as an F Grade Denizen. And that was with him being at what he considered to be the peak of E Grade, even if he was "only" Level 60.

At the rate I'm levelling—or rather not *levelling, I might make it to E Grade, but I certainly won't make it to the peak. How could I possibly defeat a D Grade enemy?*

He pushed those thoughts aside.

Focus, focus, focus.

Xavier whirled. He sent a Heavy Telekinesis behind him, trying to clear some space and pushing the enemies back. Again and again. He took a step, cast the spell, took another step. With each casting he killed more enemies—gained more Spirit Energy—he wasn't going to run out of it. Not this time.

I'll never let that happen again if I can help it.

At the same time, he sent Soul Blocks behind him, trying to cover his back. He needed to get out of the fray. Somehow. He was worried about the other members of his party. Things had never gotten this out of hand before, and though the enemy waves had never made for the walls while he was on the battlefield, he didn't know how long that would hold.

Especially now.

That E Grade wave boss was clever, staying back. And now there are three of them.

He could easily imagine them going for the walls, especially considering that was where they would find the queen they were after. The one whose family had angered the Endless Horde in the first place, all those years ago.

He'd wondered if there would somehow be a way to take the woman back with them, through the door in the Safe Zone, back to the Staging Room and the Tower of Champions.

The woman didn't wish to run from her problems, worrying it

would put others in danger. But she'd allowed him to see if she could step into the Safe Zone.

She couldn't even see the door. To her, it had looked like a solid wall of stone. Exactly what it had been before they'd come to this floor.

Xavier made a hole through the enemies, climbing over their corpses. It wasn't just teleportation magic he wished he had right now. He also wished he had the ability to fly—even if it meant having duckling wings like Justin. Though the Airborne Duellist's wings had grown somewhat since they'd made it here.

Eventually, the wall was in view. He sighed in relief—the enemy still weren't making for it.

No. They were all simply coming for him.

But he did notice that everyone was watching him. Not just Adviser Kalren, who'd been there when he'd left the wall. All of them. Queen Alastea. Howard. Siobhan. Justin. They stood there, gazing out at the carnage. Gazing out at him.

He wondered if it was time for the others to return to the Staging Room, what with the battle taking a turn for the worst.

But there wasn't time to talk to them.

At least I know they're still safe. They'll flee if they have to.

His back against the moat and the wall, Xavier whirled and faced the encroaching army. Each and every enemy he could see was barrelling straight toward him, ready to sacrifice their lives to try and bring his demise.

Who benefits from all this death? Why put them all through it?

A part of Xavier was excited about this new reality he'd found when the System integrated Earth into the Greater Universe. He'd embraced it. It wasn't as though he'd had a choice in the matter. He might as well do everything he could to enjoy how things had changed. He loved fantasy. Loved magic. Wanted to explore new worlds. The System had brought all of that.

That, and considering the advantages he'd gained, it hadn't been too difficult to embrace.

Even with all the worries on his mind about Earth...

But he also felt deep anger. A rage against the System for doing this not just to his world, but to countless worlds—worlds not only in his universe, but in *every* universe.

And right now, to him, the Endless Horde represented the System. They represented the needless slaughter it wished for. The conflict and chaos it championed in the Greater Universe.

Right now, they were its avatar.

And I will be their destruction.

That thought started a fire inside of him, and a new idea entered his mind...

The System was the reason for all this carnage, and though it had brought him great power, and perhaps even a longer lifespan, in that moment he hated it for what it did.

People should not have to fight, he thought. *If this System is so powerful that it can change worlds, solar systems, galaxies, even other* universes, *then why must it cause such havoc? Such death?*

The idea was only a seed, and he did not know if he would feel it beyond this moment, but if that seed grew, his aspirations would expand well beyond the protection of Earth.

What if I can change things? What if I grow powerful enough to stop such needless death?

He plunged himself back into the fray. In the minutes he'd fought to make it back to the wall, and the precious seconds he'd stood there, casting Soul Block to prevent ranged spells and projectiles from causing him damage, his health had shot back up a good 10 percent and he'd been able to take a health potion. Though that health potion—being of the lesser variety—had only brought his health up by an extra 6 percent.

That, and he'd also almost finished cycling 1,000 points of Willpower Energy through his core.

He was only 50 points away.

As the Spell Quest ended, and a notification popped up in his vision, Xavier's idea came to the forefront of his mind:

What if I can change the System?

Chapter 17
That's Kinda Creepy

Congratulations, you have completed your Spell Quest and gained the spell Willpower Infusion!

As Xavier read the notification's text, he sent a 300-infused Soul Strike all around him, clearing his immediate area, and gulped down another Lesser Health Potion. He would have to start doing that more often, and he would surely run out soon enough.

He then read the full description of the spell.

Willpower Infusion – Rank 1
Willpower Infusion is a rare spell that is only available to those with a strong Willpower. Willpower Infusion has two paths: the path of defence, and the path of offence.
The path of defence allows the user to imbue Willpower Energy into themselves and their armour. Denizens and armour infused with defensive Willpower Energy gain stronger mental and magical resistance. Denizens imbued with defensive Willpower Energy are also able

to shrug off pain and exhaustion much more easily.
Denizens will also be infused with a sense of confi-
dence. However, if this confidence is left unchecked, it
can get the user into dangerous situations.
The path of offense allows the user to imbue Willpower
Energy into their weapons. When an enemy is struck
with a Willpower-infused weapon, it can shake their
mental fortitude or even strike fear into them. The user
can also infuse offensive Willpower Energy directly into
an enemy, giving the user a limited ability to influence
an enemy's thoughts and behaviour.
Unlike other spells, there is no way to generalise with
Willpower Infusion. The user must choose which path
they wish to follow.
This spell is bound to your secondary core and cannot
be forgotten.
One cannot walk backward on the path.

Whoa, Xavier thought as he read through the description.

Both of those options sounded incredible. Considering what he was going through right now—feeling absolutely exhausted and being bombarded with constant strikes—not to mention second-guessing himself far too much, he could see the value of the first option.

He also imagined it could become incredibly valuable in the future, when he was facing Denizens with strong mental powers—something he'd yet to encounter.

The second option, however, was the one that piqued his interest the most. In a way, it made him think of Spirit Break. If he were able to use Spirit Break to "soften" an enemy's mind, then influence that enemy's mind with Willpower Infusion... perhaps he would be able to *control* an enemy, especially as Willpower Infusion grew in strength.

This made him curious about something. He'd gained Spirit

Infusion not when he'd unlocked his Spirit Core, but when he'd chosen the class of Soul Reaper. It hadn't had anything to do with him discovering the core or unlocking any of the skills.

So why had he unlocked the Spell Quest for Willpower Infusion when discovering his core?

Curious.

Howard, too, had unlocked Toughness Infusion through a class choice.

From the information that he'd gathered, he'd thought that any Denizen could gain these spells. He'd imagined himself with the ability to infuse each of the different attributes' energy into himself and his equipment. But, recalling the Spirit Infusion's description, it had said it was a *rare* spell that was *rarely* learnt by humans.

It had even said it was specifically a Mage spell.

That made it seem as though it would preclude others from learning it. *And would every Denizen really possess Willpower Infusion, giving themselves the ability to control other people's minds or defend against such acts? Especially since it had been defined as a "rare" spell, though it hadn't specified a base class.*

Further study in this area was definitely required. When he'd first come here, he'd thought they'd discovered a treasure trove of information. And in a way, they had—he wouldn't have known anything at all about his secondary core if not for this place.

And yet, the more he learnt the more he realised how very *limited* the knowledge he could gain here truly was.

So much knowledge is locked out by the System. Why would it guard information so much? Why would it prevent new worlds and weak worlds from knowing what others knew? That would just keep them from getting stronger.

Another item for his list of reasons to be angry at the System, which brought him back to that seedling of an idea—an idea that was surely crazy...

What if he could change the System? Could such a thing even be possible? There were things he'd assumed shouldn't be possible that he'd already proven were.

For instance, he was sure that he'd been observed not once, but *twice*, by two different powerful Denizens whilst he was within the tower. And not just within the tower, but while on floors of the tower—which he'd discovered were on entirely different *universes* to his own.

He'd assumed such a thing would be impossible. The Tower of Champions was locked off from the rest of the Greater Universe. A Sector Key, according to Sam, wouldn't even work. And there was no way for them to return to Earth until they'd completed the first ten floors—a task that was taking him considerably longer than he'd expected now that he'd gone on this little side quest on the fifth floor.

So how could those powerful Denizens have observed him?

Even if they did break the System's rules, that didn't mean they were able to change the System. Something like that...

Was absolutely crazy.

And yet, the idea stuck with him. The idea-seedling grew roots that hooked into the back of his mind. It wasn't exactly as though it would be something he could act on. Not as an F Grade Denizen— not as an E Grade Denizen—but if being a True Progenitor was as rare as he expected it to be, then maybe he would one day be capable of such a thing.

As long as I survive the tower, and the invasion of Earth, I could live for a very, very long time.

There was no telling what he might find in his future, especially if he went looking for it.

Xavier clenched his jaw. The enemies around him felt even more numerous than before. There were simply far too many of them. *Something* needed to change. He glanced at the description of the Willpower Infusion spell once more. It definitely didn't feel like it was enough for him to change the tide. Being able to influence an enemy's mind... that could help him against the E Grade wave bosses, assuming they weren't in some way immune to the spell, but it wouldn't help him against the normal ranks of enemies—

Unless...

Xavier smiled, a plan forming in his mind. For the last wave and a half, he'd seriously suspected that he'd been doomed to abandon this floor—that there was no coming back from what he was currently facing.

But if his plan could work...

Xavier cast Willpower Infusion for the first time. He was still in a meditative state, as he'd been since he'd started trying to unlock the spell. Perhaps that was why the insight had come to him so swiftly—and why he gained an intuitive sense of how the spell might work.

He didn't have a great deal of Willpower Energy within his core, and he knew he would need to start actively cultivating it if he wanted to perform this spell more than once. Howard had explained to him that though he possessed Toughness Energy, it didn't flow into him as fast as Spirit Energy did. His recovery was completely different. Far slower, and the spell worked differently than any other spell he possessed, locking up the energy he used.

Xavier didn't think this spell would work in the same way—it would have said so in the spell description if that were the case—but looking at his Willpower Energy, which now displayed in his attributes or whenever he willed it, he would definitely run out if he wasn't careful.

Available Willpower Energy: 1,000/1,000

Only 1,000 points, he thought. *That... that's barely anything.*

A purple-tinged energy flowed through his body. He felt it come from inside of his core—in the place where he'd discovered the Willpower Core. It flowed down his Willpower Lines, through his arms, and into his scythe-staff, just like other spells he cast whilst wielding the weapon.

Then the energy shot out from Soultaker. Instantly, he found that he could direct the energy toward different sources.

This had an inherent disadvantage. It wasn't a typical area-of-effect spell that dealt the same damage to the enemy no matter whether it hit one enemy or twenty. This was the difference between distributing the force of a strike into a wide area or a narrow area. It reduced the effectiveness of the spell on his enemies, but at the same time allowed him to influence more at once.

If his hunch—his insight—was correct, he should *easily* be able to influence the enemies in front of him. His Willpower attribute was nowhere near as powerful as his Spirit attribute, but that didn't mean it wasn't incredibly strong in comparison to those he fought.

The purple energy flowed from his staff like mist. Xavier hadn't seen anything like it. It quickly moved toward the enemies around him, hitting around twenty of them at once. It seeped into their mouths, noses, eyes, getting sucked in.

That's kinda creepy, Xavier thought, then he considered what the spell actually did. *Okay, maybe it is* actually *creepy.*

As the misted energy seeped into his enemies, Xavier's sense was expanded in a way he'd never experienced before. It was like a connection had opened up between his mind and the minds of the enemies around him. A one-way connection. He could not read their thoughts, but he could *touch* their thoughts.

Now, to give them something to do.

He *pushed* on his enemies' minds, instructing them to turn on their own. He had a great big grin on his face, one that no doubt looked frighteningly sinister to any observer.

Xavier's forehead creased. The enemies paused. He felt resistance. Walls forming between him and their minds. *They're fighting off my influence.* Perhaps he'd diluted the spell too much...

He *pushed* on their minds again, mustering up as much of his mental strength as he could.

The enemies just stood there. They didn't turn on their allies.

But, even though they hadn't done as he'd instructed, they had also stopped attacking *him.*

Interesting.

Xavier carved through the pausing enemies with Soultaker—at

the same time, he was constantly crushing and flinging those around him with Heavy Telekinesis.

Perhaps he'd been a little naive and too ambitious. Though the insight he'd gained had told him doing this would be possible, it probably didn't mean he could turn the tide of the fight, making the enemies fight amongst themselves and therefore evening the playing field, while Willpower Infusion was still only a Rank 1 spell.

Still, I have a plan now, Xavier thought. *All I need to do is survive long enough to implement it.*

Chapter 18
This Will Turn the Tide

Willpower Infusion – Rank 1
Upgrade Quest:
As you have now used this spell, you have begun your first step on the path to upgrading it to Rank 2. Available paths:

Willpower Infusion (Defensive) - Infuse defensive Willpower Energy into armour and oneself to gain magical and mental resistance, physical and mental resilience, and confidence. To upgrade, take 1,000 magical attacks while infused. Progress: 0/1,000

Willpower Infusion (Offensive) - Infuse offensive Willpower Energy into weapons and enemies to weaken mental fortitude, strike fear, and influence and control one's enemies. To upgrade, strike or influence 1,000 enemies with Willpower Energy. Progress: 20/1,000

This spell is bound to your secondary core. Gaining Rank 2 in this spell will not require you to forget another spell, and this spell cannot be forgotten. One cannot walk backward on the path.

INFLUENCE 1,000 ENEMIES... THAT'S NOT GOING TO BE TOO difficult.

Though Xavier knew he should probably try out the defensive nature of the Willpower Infusion spell, he didn't think that defence was his main problem right now. A familiar phrase entered his mind: *The best defence is a good offense.* And though it was certainly oversimplified, in this situation, it was definitely true.

He didn't think more confidence would help, either. Feeling more confident wasn't exactly going to deal damage to his enemies.

All he really needed to do right now was figure out a way to kill these guys faster than they could kill him.

So, he made his decision. Even if he wasn't in a situation like this, if he were honest with himself, he was sure he would have always chosen offensive Willpower Energy. It wasn't that he had a desire to control the actions of others, it was simply that it would be another tool for him to use while in battle. It would add to the variety of options he had to choose from, which would only serve to make him an even more deadly opponent.

And, even if it was a bit creepy, controlling other people's minds... it was also incredibly cool. Yes, it was invasive, but so was trying to *kill* him, and that was exactly what these bastards were doing.

Way to justify yourself there, Xavier, he chided himself.

Xavier pushed forward. The spell had a short cooldown of only five seconds. He assumed this was because he'd already developed his Willpower and Intelligence to such a high degree. Though he did worry that the cooldown might go up when the spell got to its second rank, that had only happened the one time when upgrading Spiritual Guidance to Spiritual Trifecta.

Xavier continued his normal onslaught against the enemies before him. The Wolven that were a part of wave 1002 had begun to join the fray as he'd thinned the enemies of wave 1,001 to the point where he could see very few humanoid Denizens.

I still haven't encountered the three E Grade wave bosses that will be around.

He put that out of his mind.

Xavier cast the spell on ten enemies instead of twenty, distributing the misted Willpower Energy half as much as he had the first time. He grinned, watching as it had the desired effect. Ten Giant Wolven, each the size of a bus, hesitated as they'd been heading toward him. He felt their mental walls come up, but this time he was easily able to blast through them and push his will.

The Wolven turned upon their allies and began to tear into them. They snarled, digging vicious claws into their allies' flesh and snapping powerful jaws around their necks. The other Wolven, though not mindless beasts, reacted in just the way Xavier had hoped—with anger and aggression.

It's working! Xavier had an odd inclination to laugh maniacally and shout, "Muahaha!" at his foes, but he was sure the wild grin on his face made him appear mad enough that he didn't need to add to the picture.

Though controlling ten enemies for a short time wouldn't change the tide of the battle to the degree he needed it, it added to his arsenal and occupied more of the enemies that were in his vicinity than he could before. It didn't take long for the Wolven to kill each other. Those who'd struck first—the ones he'd controlled—had been the victors, as they'd been fighting beasts at the same level of power as themselves.

The mental connection *snapped* rather abruptly when the task he'd given them had been complete. He kept a close eye on the beasts—as close as he could, with Soultaker sweeping around in wide, death-delivering arcs.

At first, the beasts looked highly disorientated. Then they looked angry. A rage overtook them that went beyond what he'd seen in the other beasts. They whirled, turning anger upon him.

Interesting. They're intelligent enough to be aware of what just happened.

Watching these beasts, he'd often wondered what the difference between them and the more sapient bestial enemies he'd faced were—why had they not evolved to be more... intelligent?

A question for another time.

Every five seconds, Xavier cast Willpower Infusion again, all the while cultivating more Willpower Energy into his core. Unfortunately, he could cast it faster than he could recover from it—this definitely seemed like it would be an issue as the spell progressed in rank.

Something that didn't take very long.

Willpower Infusion has taken a step forward on the path, upgrading to the spell: Willpower Infusion (offensive).
Willpower Infusion (offensive) is a Rank 2 spell.
One cannot walk backward on the path.

Yes! Xavier thought. By the time he'd managed this, he'd run out of Willpower Energy twice, but the more he cultivated it, the better he became.

He read Willpower Infusion's Rank 2 description:

Willpower Infusion – Rank 2
Willpower Infusion (offensive) is a rare spell that is only available to those with a strong Willpower.
This spell allows the user to imbue Willpower Energy into their weapons. When an enemy is struck with a Willpower infused weapon, it can shake their mental fortitude or even strike fear into them. The user can also infuse offensive Willpower Energy directly into an enemy, giving the user a limited ability to influence an enemy's thoughts and behaviour.
As this spell grows, so will its influence.
This spell is bound to your secondary core and cannot be forgotten.

One cannot walk backward on the path.

Xavier smiled, focusing on one of the last lines. *This spell's influence will grow...*

That made him wonder just how far he might take it.

Usually, gaining a single rank in a spell wouldn't make a massive difference. But when it came to bringing a spell from Rank 1 to Rank 2, especially when one was *specialising* in a single path... well, he hoped this spell had just become a lot more powerful.

He didn't hesitate to test it and see.

A shield wall had formed on his left flank. Humans, elves, and demon warriors with large tower shields and long spears had summoned a defensive Bulwark around them, a spell that appeared far superior to the one that Howard possessed. Xavier had encountered this spell countless times in the previous waves— it was incredibly resistant to his spells. He'd quickly found that if one of these elite squads, as he thought of them, had this barrier up, he needed to take them on directly, as the barrier prevented any of his ranged attacks from doing any damage.

Even his Soul Strike spell couldn't break the barrier, though he wondered if that was because he was using it with area-of-effect in mind. Either way, it wasn't something he was about to test. Not for these worthless enemies.

There were twenty of them. Their spears had a ranged attack— a pulse-beam that shot at him whenever they thrust their weapons forward, something they would do in unison like a rank of archers releasing arrows in a volley.

Xavier tilted his head to the side, wondering something about the Bulwark spell. It defended specifically against attacks that caused physical, magical, or even soul damage—that last one had taken him by surprise, as he'd yet to encounter an enemy resistant to soul damage—but could it defend against a mental attack?

He shot the spell off, aiming it toward half of the enemies within the barrier. Ten was the highest number of enemies he'd found he could control at once. After having used the spell on a thousand enemies to bring it up to Rank 2, he'd experimented using it on different numbers of enemies.

For instance, when he used the spell on five enemies, the effect was instant. They turned on their allies the moment the spell hit them. And it lasted longer, too, allowing him to control those five enemies for a little bit longer after their first kill. He turned them directly against each other and was able to kill all but one in that process.

Meaning it wasn't as effective as using it against ten enemies, even if the spell worked better on fewer.

He'd also used the spell on a single enemy and found that he could control them for much longer. Though, considering the situation, he hadn't let the test go on for more than a minute, as he'd been recovering as much of his Willpower Energy as he could.

Now, when the Rank 2 spell hit these ten enemies within the Bulwark spell's barrier, its effect was as instantaneous as when he would strike five enemies when it had been a Rank 1 spell.

And the connection he had with their minds felt stronger. He could *feel* the invisible strands that tethered their minds to his own, as though they drifted in the air before him. These strands tugged at his enemies' minds.

Xavier sent his will down the strands of Willpower energy and watched with fascination as they slaughtered their brothers- and sisters-in-arms.

A small part of him felt a stab of guilt for doing this to them, but the guilt dissipated quickly. The soldiers of the Endless Horde were the enemy. If he harboured sympathy for the enemy, then he wouldn't be able to do what he needed.

Xavier released a breath. Even after the ten he controlled killed the others in their unit—taking down the Bulwark spell in the process—the connection remained. Xavier wasn't sure how long it would last.

He had them turn on each other.

This... this will work. This will turn the tide.

He didn't know how long he would be able to do this. Didn't

know how long he would be able to hold his own against multiple waves of enemies in play. But he was sure now that he'd found the answer he needed.

I'll make this spell stronger and stronger. Then I'll turn my enemy's army against itself.

He envisioned the spell's rank growing and growing—envisioned being able to control dozens of enemies, then hundreds of them... He didn't know the extent of the spell's limits.

But he did know it would help get him out of this mess.

All he needed to do now was figure out how to advance to E Grade. There must be *something* he was missing. Must be *something* he needed to do. It could be as simple as not being high-enough level, but if that were the case, he didn't know how he would be able to fix that.

As he cultivated more Willpower Energy into his secondary core, cycling the new points of energy through his lines at the same time, he felt something *click*, and three notifications popped up.

Skill Upgrade Available!
Skill Upgrade Available!
Skill Upgrade Available!

Chapter 19
Finally Come To Meet Your Death, Have You?

SKILL UPGRADES? XAVIER THOUGHT, QUICKLY READING THE two notifications that popped up. Though he was getting used to reading notifications while in the middle of battle, he wondered if a time would ever come when it felt normal.

When will any of this feel normal?

Aura Control skill has been upgraded! Aura Control now incorporates two cores.

Core Strength skill has been upgraded! Core Strength now incorporates two cores.

Cultivate Energy skill has been upgraded! Cultivate Energy now incorporates two cores.

Xavier grinned. He'd been wondering if he would get any skills pertaining to his secondary core, as he had for his Spirit Core. The three skills he'd gained when he'd discovered his Spirit Core had helped his Spirit Attribute a great deal, increasing it by an incredible amount. He'd hoped he would get something similar for his

Willpower Core, especially since his new spell relied on the attribute.

This is going to help me a lot.

The Aura Control skill was something he was curious about. He hadn't even known his new core might produce an aura, but he supposed it made perfect sense that it would. Gaining the skill upgrade made him examine the core and realise something interesting.

Huh, Xavier thought. He'd been subconsciously balancing his secondary core so it wouldn't release any aura.

If all E Grades have two cores, then when Sam showed me his aura, was it energy from two cores?

He read over the descriptions of the three different spells as he activated the upgrades. Though really, he only needed to read one of the descriptions—just as before, each of the descriptions was identical but for the skill name, despite the fact that the skills did different things. It was quite an oddity.

Aura Control – Rank 50
You are a student of the Greater Universe. The seed of your knowledge has gained roots in the earth, and soon it will break through the surface of the ground.
May your knowledge of the Greater Universe blossom.
+30% Aura Strength.
+40% Spirit Energy recovery.
+25% Spirit.
+20% Willpower Energy recovery.
+10% Willpower.

A frown lined his face. He'd hoped to have gained a little more Willpower than that, though he knew it wasn't anything to scoff at. These skills, though they helped him a great deal, increased their percentages rather slowly.

Having three of them compounding, though? That made a *huge* difference. With each skill gaining him 10 percent Willpower, he'd increased his Willpower by 30 percent.

The only issue he had with the skills was that though they'd upgraded, they were still Rank 50, meaning he wouldn't be able to bring them up a rank until he got to E Grade.

And he still didn't know how he was going to do that.

Focus on one issue at a time, he thought.

He took his mind off the different skills he'd just gained, turning his full focus to the enemies in his way. *Thousands and thousands of enemies.* He had no idea how much time had passed since this wave had begun—no idea how long it would be until the next wave started.

The three E Grade wave bosses in play hadn't attacked him directly, not since his fight with the first of them on wave 1,000. He was glad for that—he doubted he'd be able to take them, considering he hadn't been able to take *one.* But now that he had Willpower Infusion, and it had just gained another boost?

The spell might be strong enough for me to control those E Grades, at least to a small degree.

As more minutes passed and Xavier defeated hundreds more enemies, he gained several ranks of Willpower Infusion.

Willpower Infusion has taken a step forward on the path!
Willpower Infusion is now a Rank 6 spell.
One cannot walk backward on the path.

He grinned, glancing at the notification. With each rank, the spell grew in strength, and so did his ability to control the enemy soldiers. What he'd once been able to do to ten enemies, he could now do to twenty, then thirty.

The spell had grown in power faster than he'd even hoped it would be able to. His Willpower Energy recovery had also been boosted a great deal. Now that his Cultivate Energy, Core Strength skills had upgraded, he found cultivating Celestial Energy into his secondary core to be easier than ever, and cycling the energy increased its potency.

That was something he'd only learnt recently. He'd finally asked Adviser Kalren what the skill actually *did*. The man had chuckled, not having realised he didn't know.

"It increases the strength of your core—or cores, when a Denizen has more than one. Some Denizens have access to attacks that can directly target an enemy's core of their energies, either stealing that energy or depleting it. For instance, the spell Energy Diffusion can completely empty an enemy's core, and Energy Drain can take someone else's energy and make it your own.

"It also had a secondary benefit. It can increase the *efficiency* of your energy. This allows you to use less Spirit Energy per spell, but only when using energy already cycled."

The first part had worried him. He would hate to encounter an enemy that could drain his cores completely of their energy, and that more than anything had kept him diligently ranking up the skill. Though the secondary benefit of the skill could be helpful—increasing the potency of the energy he used so he used less of it could only be a *good* thing—it hadn't seemed all that useful to him, considering he never actually *ran out* of Spirit Energy.

But now, for his Willpower Energy, increasing the potency meant he could cast the spell far more frequently.

Xavier began to notice the behaviour of those he faced shift and change. The soldiers and beasts were standing farther apart than they had before. As much as they could, packed close on the battlefield. There were more furtive glances left and right. They weren't forming shield walls or fighting as close as they once had, despite the fact that there was barely any room for them.

They're afraid.

The realisation struck him. He didn't know why he found it strange that they would be afraid, considering he was sure these enemies knew they were likely to die at his hand, but despite how many he'd killed, he'd never seen this level of nervousness in them before.

He had always known these enemies feared him. And it wasn't as though he thought the enemy lines would suddenly break and flee from his scythe-staff. No, as nervous as they looked, they weren't cowards. Nor were they *able* to turn back. Xavier hadn't seen an enemy flee since he'd faced the Level 2 Lesser Goblins back on his university's campus.

That feels like so long ago.

But even though they wouldn't break, their nervousness and distrust of their allies showed that his Willpower Infusion was messing with their morale and battering their mental fortitude, which meant it might be even easier for his Willpower Infusion spell to take root.

Xavier wondered how many enemies were left. He was definitely dealing with them faster than he had in a long while.

Then the war drums sounded, and the horns blared once more, announcing the next wave's imminence.

No. I'm not ready! Xavier swore, then gritted his teeth.

Four E Grade bosses would be in the field now, plus maybe another ten thousand soldiers or beasts. *This is getting far too out of hand!* But what else could he do but fight?

He wasn't going to turn from this.

A moment after the new wave had begun, a notification popped up in his vision.

Willpower Infusion has taken a step forward on the path!
Willpower Infusion is now a Rank 12 spell.
One cannot walk backward on the path.

This made Xavier grin. He'd never ranked up a spell this fast before.

He had an idea. He didn't know if it was a good one, but he

was going to follow through with it anyway. He didn't see another way out of this.

Xavier cleared a path through his enemies, heading toward the other side of them. Soultaker carved through one enemy after the next. Willpower Infusion turned soldier against soldier and beast against beast. Soul Block stopped the enemies on his flank and at his back from getting in too close. And Soul Strike made a few hundred foes fall over dead the moment he cast it.

He downed another health potion whenever he could, finally bringing his health back over 90 percent.

It was time to locate one of the wave bosses.

The enemies did not part for him. He *made* them part. Xavier climbed and clambered over the bodies of the dead. The battlefield was a clamour of metal, of rage and spells. Of roars, of claws and teeth. He barrelled through it all until he finally made it to the other side, where the massive ranks of the Endless Horde stood their watch, awaiting their turn to run forward and die by his hand.

And that was where he found the wave bosses. All four of them. They were easy to spot, standing a little ways forward from the stationary ranks. Their auras didn't show. He couldn't feel their power, but some part of him could *sense* it.

And the fact that he couldn't scan any of them was a massive indication of who they were.

They didn't all stand together. They were half a mile apart from each other. *They're staying out of the fight, waiting for the waves to accumulate, waiting until they can stomp me as easily as possible.*

He was glad they waited, for Xavier didn't know what he would do if they all came at him at once.

His gaze came to rest upon the nearest of them. The werewolf beast, the first of the E Grade wave bosses that he'd encountered.

The werewolf beast stepped forward, tucked its chin close to its furry chest, and snarled. "Finally come to meet your death, have you?"

Xavier tilted his head back and smiled, all but ignoring the enemies still crowding around him, each trying to tear a pound of his flesh. He still sent out Heavy Telekinesis. He still had Soul Block at his back, and Soul Strikes streaking through them, but in this moment, he stilled his blade.

A *click* in his mind signified Willpower Infusion reaching the end of its cooldown. Xavier said one simple word in response to the beastman: "No."

Willpower Energy flowed from his core, through his body, and into Soultaker as he cast Willpower Infusion. The mist flowed through the air. It could not be blocked—could not be dodged. It was too swift. The werewolf beast had time enough to frown as it flew toward him, but nothing more.

The misted energy seeped through the beast's eyes, nostrils, mouth, and ears. The werewolf beast threw its head back, fangs bared, and convulsed. The beastman's walls sprang up as the connection tried to form. Xavier had never encountered such mental strength.

He stepped forward, pushing his mind to its limits. He was sure that when he'd gained this spell, less than an hour ago, the E Grade boss would have been able to shake it off with ease. But as he'd gained those skills and ranked the spell up, it had strengthened considerably.

Xavier *pushed*. He'd grown accustomed to this feeling. He'd found the spell was more effective the more focused he was on it, and so all his focus was bent toward this single task.

Click.

The strand of energy solidified. The connection snapped into place.

Xavier had control of an E Grade wave boss—for how long, he didn't know.

Chapter 20
Quick Work We Will Make of This Swine

An immense pressure filled Xavier's mind, a pressure that he'd never before experienced.

The strand of energy between himself and the E Grade boss he now controlled was more solid than any he'd used yet, but it came at a cost, one he hadn't realised until the spell connected his mind to the beastman's.

Energy streamed out of Xavier's secondary core, and it wasn't the cost of the spell he was feeling, for that had already been paid.

What the hell?

The spell had never used more energy than its initial casting before.

It's taking more energy to maintain the connection!

Xavier gritted his teeth. The enemies crowded in around him. Wolven fangs dug through the fabric of his robes. Swords slashed at his head, stabbed at his side. Axes cleaved into his back. Spears thrust for his chest. His mind was stuck. He'd put all his focus into this one task, and his body had frozen as the connection solidified.

Your health is at 55%.

No. No no no.

His health was falling *way* too fast. It was lower than it had ever been during one of these waves! He'd just gotten it back over 90 percent. A panic settled over his mind. A panic that tensed his entire body.

Stop thinking. Stop thinking and move!

But he couldn't. Something strange was happening to him. It took him mere seconds to realise what that was, but those seconds cost him dearly.

My Willpower... As the energy was being drained, every ounce of his secondary core set upon the task of controlling an E Grade Denizen, it was like he'd lost the attribute altogether—at least the mental aspects of it. Without it, he was clamming up.

No. I can't let this happen!

Xavier clenched his jaw. He finally moved, slashing around him with his staff-scythe, separating heads from bodies all around him in a circle. Pushing other enemies away with Heavy Telekinesis. Defending ever more with Soul Block. A space formed around him, and with that space, his mind got a moment to breathe.

And so he pushed a command toward the E Grade boss.

Kill them all!

The beast had stopped convulsing. Now, it was frozen where it stood.

Xavier sent the mental command two more times before he saw it stick. The beastman moved. Slowly, at first, then green energy infused its entire body, and it was off like a shot, tearing through its own ranks, destroying everything in its path. Green, translucent, glowing claws grew from its normal ones and sliced through the bodies of its own allies.

Xavier fought the enemies around him, regaining more control of his own body and mind with every second that passed, forever keeping an eye on the Willpower Energy within him. He'd paused —without meaning to—cultivating more of it into himself when the connection had been made. He began cultivating it again even as he moved, but it wasn't *enough*.

He couldn't bring in more energy fast enough.

His control over the E Grade boss wavered several times. The beastman would freeze in the middle of one of its attacks. A mental *push* got the thing moving again, but every one of those pushes cost him more energy.

Then, all too fast, he used the last drop of his Willpower Energy. His secondary core had been completely emptied with a single spell. The spell had grown more and more expensive as it had increased its ranks, but his Willpower Core had increased how much energy it could store at the exact same rate—which showed him that somehow the core was connected to the spells along with his Willpower attribute.

Xavier grinned. Despite the mess he was in. Despite his core being empty. Despite another ten thousand enemies and another E Grade boss joining the fray. He grinned because he knew that now, he was the one in control.

A great roar of anger filled the air, which only made Xavier's grin turn into a wide smile. The beastman had regained control of its body and mind.

It's going to come after me.

Xavier let it.

The beastman must have killed a thousand soldiers and beasts of the Endless Horde in the nine seconds that Xavier had been able to control it. *Nine whole seconds.* It might not sound like much, but he knew it was a *massive* amount of time. *When I fight the beast, I'll be able to kill it. I'll take over its mind and it won't be able to fight back.*

At least, that was how he envisioned the fight going.

He drew Willpower Energy back into his core, cultivating it faster and smoother than he ever had before. Another roar sounded, and somehow—over the sound of the thousands of enemies around him—he could hear the *thump, thump, thump,* of the E Grade boss's heavy steps on the ground.

Everything around Xavier blurred as his vision tunnelled, narrowing at the enemy barrelling toward him. His Willpower

Energy was steadily rising, and he felt the influence of the attribute once more.

Losing it had been rather startling. Though he realised he hadn't *actually* lost it, it had just *felt* like he'd lost it—that was why he'd been able to regain control of himself.

Still, he would need to keep that in mind for the next time he cast the spell. It had a cost, but as long as he *knew* that cost, he could ensure it didn't hurt him.

Or, at least, he could do his best to ensure it didn't.

As the beastman neared, Xavier cast the spell again. It wouldn't last for as long as last time, but he didn't need it to. As long as it lasted even a couple of seconds, it would be worth it.

Once again, the pressure entered Xavier's mind. This time, he was ready for it. This time, he didn't let it stop him from striking out at the enemies around him.

The strand of Willpower Energy connected him to the E Grade werewolf beast.

Kill them all, away from me.

Xavier pushed the command three times in quick succession and watched as the beastman turned around and instantly started carving into its allies for a second time. He'd commanded the beast to move away from him, so it would take time for it to come back—assuming it came back a third time.

Xavier grinned. The enemy lines were finally, *finally* thinning.

This is going to work.

If he could clear all the enemies before the next wave began, he'd finally be back on track. He'd be able to get to the wall and figure out what he needed to do in order to reach the next rank.

Then, out of the corner of his eyes, he saw the other three E Grade wave bosses begin to stir. They'd been watching this whole time.

Uthor Golbrack was the mightiest warrior from his planet. Though human, he stood at seven feet because of his class—the Berserker class. He hefted his massive, double-bearded war axe onto his shoulder and sniffed as he watched the Champion of the Void kill more of the Endless Horde's fodder. His instructions told him to stand back. To wait. To let the waves accumulate until the Champion became completely overwhelmed.

But Uthor was growing restless. The Champion was, somehow, managing to turn the tide. He glanced over at his fellows. The E Grade wave bosses from the two waves above his own. They were beginning to stir. Talber, an elven archer, gripped his staff in both hands, while Creledifisda, a Wolven Matriarch, growled softly in her throat.

They're growing just as impatient as I am.

They both glanced his way. The eagerness in their eyes was evident. This farce of a battle had gone on long enough. The System may have forced them to do it this way, but now that their waves had begun, they should be able to do *as they wished*—consequences be damned.

Small nods were sent back and forth between them.

A grin alighted Uthor's face. He gripped his war axe—Tabitha—tightly.

He would greatly enjoy separating that Champion's head from his body.

Talber breathed deeply, then coughed.

Fallen Gods, the smell of this place made him ache for the ancient forests of Yea'ldr.

I shall return there soon, once this fight is over. Once my duty has been fulfilled.

The woman who was their target stood upon the wall's battlements. He could see her, hands clasped and clutched at her breast, fear and worry seeping from her eyes. He could make quick work of the woman—one of his arrows might even be able to reach her from here—but that was not how things went.

Not until the Champion was dead.

Talber did not smile as he stepped forth and nocked an arrow, the Champion of the Void in his sights. He took no joy in battle. He had spent more than a century in the Endless Horde now, and he had only joined so that it would not consume his planet. He did his duty—whatever was needed of him—and when nothing was needed, he was given his peace. It had always seemed a fair trade.

This man's death will bring my peace.

Creledifisda sniffed the air. She'd been twitching and ready to move since the moment those war drums had thudded. Why her orders told her to wait, she didn't know. Uthor and Talber looked as though they would wait no more, and so she figured it was time for her to move as well.

Quick work we will make of this swine, and after his death we shall all dine.

Crel chuckled to herself. It wasn't the best rhyme, but what else could she occupy her mind with while she waited? She'd stepped through the portal three days ago, and all she'd bloody done since then was *stand in a line.*

Stand in a line and try not to whine.

Crel cast Strength Infusion on herself. Energy *thrummed* through her body. Her strength grew. Her muscles enlarged. Legs. Arms. Torso.

Time to ravage, time to kill, and in that I find my only thrill.

Chapter 21
He's Going to Get Through This

Siobhan gripped the parapet, her forehead deeply lined. She'd barely moved from that spot for the past few hours. She didn't know how to.

They'd learnt so much in that damned library, and none of it would actually *help* Xavier. Not out there. Not right now.

All she could bloody well do was stand there and watch. Even if Xavier wanted her and the others in the fight, what possible difference would they be able to make now that he and the enemies were so far ahead of them?

"He's in real trouble," Justin said, biting his lip. It wasn't the first time he'd spoken those words. "What... what do we do?"

Howard gripped his shoulder. "Nothing we can do, kid. This is all up to him. You know that."

Justin lowered his head. He didn't even have a flicker of annoyance at being called "kid." He was glad Howard was here. The man was much older than the rest of them, and he had a protective streak—probably because he was old enough to be their father.

That protective streak is probably how he got his class.

The man must miss his wife and children dearly. Siobhan missed her little sister just as much—maybe that was why she saw Justin as more of a little brother than a party member these days.

"He's going to get through this," Siobhan muttered. Not the first time she'd spoken those words, either.

Queen Alastea released a small gasp. The woman had grown more comfortable with them over the last few weeks. With her people gone, she'd slowly taken off the mask of nobility—of royalty —that she'd worn her entire life. The one that prevented her from showing her true emotions when not in the privacy of her own family or closest advisers.

"What is it?" Siobhan asked.

Her gaze swept back over to where Xavier was laying waste to his enemies. She was constantly surprised that the man was still standing. Part of her wished he would just return to the castle and take them back through to the Staging Room, though she knew that was a selfish thought.

We let Queen Alastea die the last time we entered this floor. Trillions of iterations of her in the multiverse must have died here. That thought stabbed at her. *Every iteration of her died... What Champions could have possibly ever defeated the Endless Horde?*

This woman's life always ends here. Perhaps it's her destiny...

"Something has changed," Queen Alastea whispered. "Don't you see it?"

"What? What's changed?" Siobhan narrowed her focus. It was difficult to see the details of what was happening from this distance. She wished she'd acquired a skill or spell that could improve her vision. It had naturally improved over time as she'd gotten more points in her Strength attribute, but it hadn't improved near enough to see all of what was going on.

"There!" Justin said, pointing.

He wasn't pointing at Xavier.

Is that... the wave boss? she thought, and said: "It's killing its allies. Why is it killing its allies?"

Adviser Kalren, standing at the queen's side, raised his chin. "Willpower."

"What?"

"He unlocked his secondary core. He must have gained the

Willpower Infusion spell. It gives one the ability to influence an enemy, even control them. At least it can, if one chooses that path."

Xavier can control the enemy?

Not long ago, learning something like that would have most certainly frightened her. She'd seen Xavier transform over a surprisingly short period of time, over those first few floors, until he was torturing beasts and reaping souls.

But controlling the minds of others... that sounded terribly sinister.

Yet what she felt wasn't fear or worry for what the man might do when he returned to Earth. No. What she felt was *relief*. If he were able to do that, maybe he *could* turn the tide of these waves.

"He's going to get through this," Siobhan said, louder this time. "He's really going to get through this."

"Perhaps it is too soon to tally his wins." Adviser Kalren nodded toward something. "The other wave bosses are moving."

Siobhan flattened herself against the parapet, leaning over it as far as she could. She wished she could get a better view of what was happening.

But she could see enough.

"They're all E Grade," Queen Alastea muttered. "I fear he may not stand a chance, and so my life finally nears its end."

Uthor Golbrack released a loud battle cry as he sprinted toward his enemy. The Champion of the Void who'd killed millions of the Endless Horde's soldiers and beasts. Uthor didn't much care about the losses. He just wanted to get this over with and get the hell off this stupid rock. He had better things to do than stand around and wait.

A red glow engulfed his entire body as he activated his most treasured spell: Berserk.

He'd had this spell since he'd chosen his class all the way back at Level 10.

Uthor had seen what this Champion of the Void could do. Seen what he was capable of. The fact that he could control that weakling Wolven Patriarch meant nothing to him. Uthor's Willpower would be strong enough to withstand such a thing—he was not a fool. He knew how to distribute his attributes.

And this Champion wasn't even E Grade.

You are truly weak, Dradaldi.

The battle cry he released sent a visible tremor through the army. They heard him coming. He'd always taken a certain amount of pride in being able to frighten even those on his own side.

The Champion of the Void's gaze locked onto his. Uthor grinned, expecting to see fear in those eyes.

There was no fear.

His battle cry cut off in his throat as he saw the Champion's determination. The man's jaw was set, muscles in his cheeks feathering. His dark robes billowed in the wind, whipping up behind him. His scythe, with its dark blade, loomed high above his head.

The Champion of the Void's eyes bore into Uthor.

As though he can see into my soul.

The eyes glowed silver, radiating power.

Then the man released his aura.

The tremor that ran through the army at Uthor's battle cry was nothing compared to the shudder that came now as that man's aura was released. It was as though he were a boulder thrown into a lake, and the soldiers and beasts around him water rippling outward from him.

The Endless Horde never broke. No matter how much death it faced—it *never* broke.

And Uthor never broke either.

But that wave of power made him stumble. He'd felt more power before—far, far more power—but he'd never felt something like *that* from an F Grade Denizen. When he scanned his enemy, it said he was only Level 60.

How... how is this possible?

He released a second battle cry, his strides becoming sure again, and barrelled toward the Champion.

It does not matter. He will be dead in moments.

A purple mist flowed out from the man's staff toward Uthor, and he grunted in response.

That will not work on me.

He didn't bother trying to move away from the mist. He ran straight into it.

And the mist dug into his mind.

Talber frowned as the Champion of the Void's aura unleashed and sent a ripple that ran through the army around him.

The elven archer tilted his head to the side. For a moment, he felt bad for this Champion of the Void. This human had potential far beyond anything he'd ever seen before, and now that potential was about to be snuffed out.

But when it is, I will return home and find my peace once more.

The arrow nocked in Talber's bow glowed a brilliant white. Power built up and up as he pulled the string until his hand touched his ear and the string touched his cheek.

Breathe out, and... release.

The arrow flew true. The man might be able to block it with one of his soul apparitions, but Talber was confident it would break right through—

Uthor, that insane human Berserker, leapt in front of the arrow as though he were trying to headbutt it mid-flight. Talber's eyes widened. The arrow lodged itself straight into Uthor's left eye, and though it didn't kill him, it weakened him incredibly. Talber knew a little something about the man's Berserker skill—it doubled the man's strength and speed, making him incredibly deadly and able to dodge enemy attacks.

But at the same time, it weakened the man's defences.

Uthor stumbled backward, the glowing white arrow sticking

out of his head. The light in the arrow pulsed, causing the man to convulse wildly as it caused its secondary damage, weakening him even more.

Then a long black blade sliced straight through his neck, and his head was came clean off.

Uthor Golbrack was dead.

Such a thing couldn't have happened if Talber's arrow hadn't hit Uthor. Uthor wouldn't have been weak enough to be taken down by an F Grade.

Could he?

Talber stepped back. For the first time since he'd joined the Endless Horde, fear's icy fingers gripped his heart and *squeezed*. When Uthor's head and body fell, it revealed the Champion of the Void in the black robes with the vicious scythe, covered in the blood of thousands, standing behind him.

A sinister grin split his lips.

Foolish human weaklings.

Crel's Strength Infusion thrummed through every muscle in her body. Each of her muscles was close to twice the size as they'd been before. She would be strong enough to rip the head straight off that damned Champion of the Void's body when she got close enough.

How did that Uthor let himself get killed by an F Grade child? The very thought made her grumbling roar turn into a bellowing laugh.

That pointy-eared Talber took a step back in surprise. Crel yelled at the man as she passed him.

"Do not pierce me with those sticks of yours!"

Talber's arm shot out, his hand grasped hers as she ran past. She shrugged it off with a growl.

"Be wary, Creledifisda! He is more dangerous than he looks!" the elven archer called from behind her.

Crel scoffed at the man's words. She need not be wary of a child.

Though as she saw Uthor's head roll along the dirt and thud to a stop against another soldier's corpse, a shiver of worry ran up her spine, the fur on her back no doubt sticking up as though she were some frightened pup.

Arrows flitted past her as she sprinted. Four of them, in quick succession, each glowing white. She did not worry that those arrows would hit her. Talber's accuracy was godlike.

That didn't help Uthor.

Crel activated a spell of mental defence—Fortify Mind—one she'd picked up a long time ago. It was rare for her to need to use the spell. She hadn't encountered a great many opponents able to control other people's minds with the amount of strength this F Grade Denizens had.

Does he have a Legendary class that allows him to do such a thing?

It did not matter. She had to kill this child, and she would do just that.

Something heavy slammed into her exposed upper back. An arrow.

Then another.

And another.

Crel stumbled, turned. A slight purple sheen was visible around Talber, the elven archer. Despair filled his eyes as he loosed a fourth arrow. Crel dodged to the side, but something stopped her —like running into a brick wall. It slammed her straight into the arrow's path.

Telekinesis?

The arrow struck her in the neck.

No, no, no.

Talber's hands trembled. The spell that had taken over him fell away. He was once more in control of his own body.

He'd thrown up every mental defence that he had. The spell... It had only taken over him for *two seconds*. But two seconds was enough.

I killed Creledifisda.

Talber swallowed. Not a single one of his arrows had struck the Champion of the Void. He narrowed his eyes... Where had the Champion gone?

He's disappeared.

Something slammed into Talber's side, sending him careening to the ground. The other beastman. The Wolven Patriarch from the thousandth wave. The beastman dug its claws straight into his neck. Talber pulled a dagger from his belt and fought the Wolven Patriarch with everything he had.

I'm playing into that Champion of the Void's hand. Fighting his battles for him. Weakening us both.

But what could he do?

Then a ghostly apparition slammed into the two of them, and everything went dark.

Chapter 22
Yeah, That Should Be Easy Enough

XAVIER SURVEYED THE BATTLEFIELD. HIS HEART BEATING AS hard and incessantly as the war drums that sounded at the start of each wave. His dark, Shrouded Robes were covered in the blood of his enemies to such a degree that they weighed him down as he walked, as though he'd jumped into a lake of the stuff.

He drew in a deep breath.

The battlefield was clear. For the first time in hours, the battlefield was clear. He'd managed to defeat all four of the E Grade bosses in a way he'd never anticipated in the past—he'd controlled their minds and pitted them against each other. It had worked so perfectly.

More perfectly than he'd imagined.

Then he'd cleared the wave that came after it. In a *half hour*, the fastest he'd managed to clear a wave in weeks. He'd made a path straight toward the E Grade wave boss and set it upon its own. It had been one of the demonkin, with horns long as Xavier's forearms and as sharp as Soultaker's blade. The demonkin had been a swordsman, and it had carved through its own with a ruthless efficiency.

As he strode back to the battlements of Queen Alastea's castle, he kept his focus on his breathing, his mind turning over all that had just happened. There were notifications waiting for him—ones he'd put aside as he'd embraced the thrill of battle. When he got back to the wall, he would finally look at them, though he knew they must be titles, for he'd felt a slight difference to his attributes as he'd been fighting. A difference that certainly hadn't come from gaining a level.

He fed his Shrouded Robes with Spirit Energy, activating their self-repair feature. The feature didn't only repair the robes when they were damaged; they cleaned them as well. Something he was eternally grateful for. Though it did nothing for his body. He was sure his skin was stained red by now.

There's a charming thought.

He shook his head, wondering for a moment what exactly he'd become since the System had integrated Earth. All he had to do was turn and look at the battlefield to find an answer to that, it seemed.

A waft of heat came from behind him. The enemy's fire mages were at it again, disposing of the dead.

Xavier leapt over the moat and swiftly climbed the wall, then pulled himself over the parapet with ease. He couldn't have dreamt about doing such a thing back in his parkour days.

The moment he set foot on the stone of the battlements, his boots silently touching down, something thudded into his chest. Arms wrapped around him, then, after a short moment, the person hastily stepped away. Placing a loose strand of hair behind her ear and looking only slightly sheepish, Siobhan beamed at Xavier.

"You're alive!" she said. "I mean, I knew you'd live. Of course you'd live. But I didn't know you'd be able to defeat those waves!"

"Quite something you pulled out there." Howard gripped his hand and patted him on the shoulder with his other.

Justin smiled. "You did it!"

"Indeed." Queen Alastea stepped to the front of them. "You did very well." She inclined her head. "Thank you. For giving me more time than I thought I would ever have."

"I have to second the queen's appreciation," Adviser Kalren

said. "You have done her a great service, and one to me by extension."

Xavier lowered his head in a small bow. Seemed like the appropriate thing to do. "I'm just doing what I can."

"You are doing far more than that, Xavier of Earth." Queen Alastea smiled. "Though that is something you already know."

Siobhan glanced between Queen Alastea and Xavier with an odd look on her face—one Xavier couldn't identify. Her eyebrow rose ever so slightly.

Xavier ran a hand through his hair, then regretted it instantly as he realised just how horribly matted with dried blood it was. *I must smell absolutely terrible.* But it wasn't exactly as though there was time to bathe, even if this was the most time he'd had between waves in a long while.

He looked to Adviser Kalren. "I discovered my secondary core and unlocked a spell for it," he said. "I even upgraded some of my skills—Cultivate Energy, Core Strength, and Aura Control." He frowned. "But I still don't know how to get to E Grade." He tilted his head to the side. "Do you know what the next steps are?"

Adviser Kalren interlocked his fingers in front of him and bent his head down. He released a deep sigh. "I'm afraid not." The lines in his forehead deepened. "I wish that information were available to me."

Xavier suppressed a sigh of his own. He'd suspected this would be the man's answer, but he'd hoped he was wrong about that. "I guess I'll have to figure out the next step on my own."

Kalren raised a finger. "It could simply be because you haven't reached the requisite level—"

Xavier waved a hand. "That *can't* be the case," he snapped.

Adviser Kalren quickly closed his mouth and gave a curt nod. "As you say."

His party glanced at each other.

Xavier hadn't meant to snap at the man. He was just frustrated. Yes, he'd just achieved something rather amazing, especially after how far behind he'd gotten with wave after wave starting before he'd cleared the one before it, and those damned E Grade wave bosses...

But it still isn't enough.

That thought kept running through his mind.

He sat down on the cold stone of the battlements and read the notifications he'd put aside.

Title Unlocked!
Ahead of the Pack: You are well ahead of those from your world. You have become the first fully integrated person from your world to defeat an E Grade Denizen.
You have received +40 to all stats!

Title Unlocked!
Goliath Killer: You have defeated a Denizen of a grade one above your own. This is a feat few in the Greater Universe ever manage and is often an indication of greatness.
You have received +50 to all stats!

Xavier's lips twisted up into a smile.

He'd been expecting to receive titles like this, though he was surprised by just how many stats he received from them. *Over five hundred stat points.*

That felt kind of insane, but perhaps when he reached the rank of E Grade, such numbers wouldn't be so strange to get from single titles. Then again, considering what he'd achieved, he supposed it made sense for these titles to give him this much.

I didn't just defeat one E Grade either. I defeated five of them.

They didn't seem so scary anymore. But Xavier knew he couldn't become complacent.

He looked at his stats. It had been a while since they'd changed, as the Mastery Points he now received had stalled.

XAVIER COLLINS
Age: 21
Race: Human
Grade: F
Moral Faction: World Defender (Planet Earth)
Class: Soul Reaper (Epic)
Level 60
Strength: 535 (722)
Speed: 524 (707)
Toughness: 545 (736)
Intelligence: 648 (1,199)
Willpower: 671 (1,107)
Spirit: 998 (1,996)
Mastery Points for this level:
400,078,638/850,000,000
Available Spirit Energy: 105,500/200,600
Available Willpower Energy: 5,500/25,000
Available Skill Points: 0
Free stat points remaining: 0
Titles:
Bloodied Hands, Born on a Battlefield, Settlement Defender, Quester, First Defender of Planet Earth, Survivor, All 100, First All 100, 1,000 Stats, First to 1,000 Stats, Greater Butcher, Fourth-Floor Climber, Solo Tower Climber 4, 1st Fourth-Floor Climber, Fourth Floor Ranked 1 – RECORD HOLDER (Completion Time – 4 sec), Ahead of the Pack, Goliath Killer
Spells List:
Spiritual Trifecta – Rank 50
Heavy Telekinesis – Rank 50
Spirit Break (All) – Rank 50
Spirit Infusion – Rank 50
Soul Harvest – Rank 50

Soul Strike (Ranged) – Rank 50
Soul Block – Rank 50
Soul Harden – Rank 50
Willpower Infusion – Rank 16
Skills List:
Physical Resistance – Rank 50
Magical Potency – Rank 50
Magical Resistance – Rank 50
Physical Damage – Rank 50
Assimilate Properties – Rank 1
Scythe-Staff Mastery – Rank 50
Meditation – Rank 50
Aura Control – Rank 50
Core Strength – Rank 50
Cultivate Energy – Rank 50
Identify – Rank 23
Lesser Spirit Coins: 3,942,498

A few things stood out to him.

First, and right at the top, was the fact that he was now twenty-one.

When the hell had that happened?

Only an hour was supposed to pass back in his universe while on this floor. Xavier hadn't put too much thought into the consequences of that. He hadn't even considered that he would keep aging while he was here.

Twenty-one. That seems like a milestone I should be celebrating, right?

He wasn't even sure when his age had ticked over. When in the last few weeks had he turned twenty-one? Did this mean his birthday was different now? He frowned, supposing that, in the grand scheme, it wasn't exactly important.

Especially when his lifespan would soon be far more than he ever imagined it could be.

But it wasn't his age that took him by surprise the most. It was some of his stats.

On the battlefield, after defeating that first E Grade wave boss, he'd noticed the notifications come up—he'd known they must be titles. And he'd certainly felt the shift inside of him that came with gaining stats. However, he'd been far too concentrated on the fight to realise the extent of how much had changed.

I broke through the threshold for Willpower. No wonder I dealt with the rest of them so easily.

With his Willpower attribute above 1,000, it would be tremendously more powerful than it had been before. He had certainly noticed that he could control many more enemies, and his control over the other E Grades had become stronger—even if it was still very short-lived. He'd thought that control was simply from Willpower Infusion having ranked up so much. Clearly, he'd been wrong.

Then there was his Spirit attribute. It was incredibly close to breaking through his next threshold. He shook his head in slight awe, contemplating what over 2,000 points in Spirit would feel like.

Only need six more points.

He tilted his head to the side and looked at his Mastery Points. The massive number required to gain the next level always looked so very daunting.

But they've gone up. A lot.

Since his Mastery Points had been stalled by the System, they'd been ticking up at a snail's pace. But now... He looked through his notifications and almost slapped himself in the face when he realised *why* they'd gone up so much.

Xavier had disabled his kill notifications from popping up in his vision some time ago, so he hadn't looked at them after he'd killed the E Grade enemies.

He looked at them now.

You have defeated a Level 120 Human Berserker!
You have gained 30,000,000 Mastery Points.

You have defeated a Level 115 Wolven Matriarch!
You have gained 25,000,000 Mastery Points.

You have defeated a Level 110 Wolven Patriarch!
You have gained 20,000,000 Mastery Points.

You have defeated a Level 125 Elven Archer!
You have gained 35,000,000 Mastery Points.

You have defeated a Level 125 Demonkin Swordmaster!
You have gained 35,000,000 Mastery Points.

Xavier's eyes widened slightly. He'd known the enemies would be over Level 100, but it still took him by surprise just *how* much higher than 100 some of them were.

They're bringing out the big guns now.

Reading the names of the enemies, he knew they weren't terribly specific. They only gave a vague description of their classes. *Maybe if my Identification skill was more developed, I'd be able to learn more about them.*

Perhaps their levels should have worried him, but after how he'd dealt with them, and the wave that came after... He wasn't feeling quite so worried anymore.

In fact, he was starting to see this as an opportunity.

He hadn't been able to gain any levels for some time, but defeating these E Grades—even if it meant defeating a *lot* of them —could very well get his levels moving again, even if agonisingly slowly.

And looking at his attributes, and the threshold he'd just broken through, made him remember breaking through all six thresholds before gaining his first class.

Doing that let me choose an Epic class. If I hadn't done that, I wouldn't have achieved half as much as I have.

Though he knew it was his titles that had gotten him his advantage in the first place, he very much doubted he would have been able to gain the top spot for the fourth floor if not for his Soul Reaper class. Without Soul Strike being able to take out so many of the Dark Wyverns all at once... It simply wouldn't have been possible.

And that had a flow-on effect that got him to where he was now.

What if he was trying to move too fast? What if it *was* possible for him to advance to E Grade, but it was too soon? Not strictly because of his level, but because of his attributes. If he were to push his attributes all past their 1,000-point threshold, his evolution to E Grade may give him a stronger base.

Now, all he needed to do was figure out how to gain enough levels to bring him 835 attribute points over Strength, Speed, and Toughness.

Not to mention continue to defeat the waves of the Endless Horde.

Yeah, that should be easy enough...

Chapter 23
Think Outside the Box

XAVIER HAD TO FORMULATE A PLAN. HAD TO THINK OUTSIDE the box the System had put him into.

During the break between waves, despite it being the longest break he'd had in a while, he'd struggled to make any *actual* progress. All he'd really done was look at his stats and realise his plan had been a foolish one.

If he sped his way straight to E Grade, he could be missing out on a grand opportunity.

But doing the math? He needed to gain thirty levels before he would be able to break through the thresholds for Strength, Speed, and Toughness.

With the way the waves were, he would only be fighting a single E Grade enemy per hour. Even when he gained 35 million Mastery Points or more, it still wasn't *enough.*

Not until every enemy in a wave is E Grade. And I'm nowhere near ready to face that.

Xavier leant against the parapet. Within the next minute, the war drums would sound. The horns would blare. Yet another wave would come for him. He released a long sigh, feeling the weariness that had settled into his body and mind.

How do I push my level forward faster? Is that even possible here?

Maybe he was thinking about this all wrong. It wasn't specifically his levels that he needed to push forward—it was his *stats*. That was how he'd gotten where he was in the first place. Staring out at the oncoming wave, he wondered what he could do... *differently*.

Titles. He needed more titles.

The two titles he'd just gained were the first titles he'd gotten since coming to this floor. But there must be *other* titles that he could gain during these waves.

Think outside the box... Think outside the box.

He wished he could find a list of titles and what he needed to do to gain them. He knew there were some common titles that everyone could gain—like his survivor and butcher titles. There must be other common titles out there as well.

Xavier tapped his fingers on the parapet's stone.

Think, think, think.

The war drums sounded, and he sighed. Once more, he threw himself over the wall. At least he could vent some of his frustration at the enemy.

Strength, Speed, Toughness...

He was far too strong to simply *train* those attributes now, wasn't he? *Even if I could train them, how long would it take to get a single attribute point?* As he fought, purple mist flowing from his staff to turn enemy against enemy, his mind turned the problem over and over. That was when a thought occurred to him. He'd gained a fair amount of Toughness from his Physical Resistance skill.

Huh.

It was almost like the gears in his mind had finally begun to turn as an idea struck him.

Skills.

He hadn't gained any more skill points since coming to this floor, something that had been rather disappointing. But his skills brought him quite a boost with their percentages. And what skill had he thought about getting several times, but never gotten around to it? *Running.* And if there ever was a skill that he could simply *learn*, well, he had to imagine it was running.

I'm about to look exceedingly foolish, Xavier thought, but he didn't really care. As a plan formulated in his mind, Xavier began to do laps around the castle's moat while in the middle of fighting a wave of the Endless Horde.

Yeah, I definitely look like an idiot.

He was confident he would be able to get through this wave with the use of Willpower Infusion, Soul Strike, and Heavy Telekinesis. It would be better if he were to find the E Grade boss and turn it against its own, but he didn't believe it was necessary.

So he ran, focusing his powerful mind on his running technique. He'd never been much of a runner, even in his parkour days, but he'd learnt a thing or two about running technique on YouTube —he just hoped it would be enough.

Performing proper running technique while holding a massive staff-scythe in the middle of a battlefield with over ten thousand enemies wasn't exactly something he ever imagined doing, but the novelty of it refocused his attention.

It only took ten minutes of continuous running before a Skill Quest popped up.

All that running in the halls of the tower... I must have had really bad form.

Skill Quest Unlocked: Running
To unlock Running, run with good form for 100 miles starting now.
Progress: 0/100

Xavier clapped his hands together. One hundred miles. Considering his Speed attribute was currently sitting at 707, such a feat shouldn't be difficult at all—even in the middle of a battle like this.

Why have I never thought to do this before?

He supposed he'd never felt like he'd had the time or the reason.

And so, that was what Xavier did during wave 1,005 of the fifth floor. With perfect running form, he did laps around Queen Alastea's castle while killing and reaping the souls of his enemies.

By the time he faced the final enemy—the E Grade wave boss —a notification popped up in his vision.

Skill Quest Complete!
You unlocked and learnt the skill Running!
Running – Rank 1
Running is one of the oldest and most basic skills a Denizen can possess. Whether you run for endurance or speed, you are now a student of this most ancient skill.
+5% efficiency of movement while running.
+5% movement speed while running.
+5% Speed.

After reading the notification and checking his stats to find gaining that skill had earned him thirty-four points in Speed, Xavier smiled far too widely.

The E Grade wave boss, seeing his smile, hesitated as it rushed him. It was another elf, though this time it was some sort of elven knight. It wore a set of full plate armour with beautiful patterns worked into the metal, and wielded a great, two-handed sword as long as a short spear. Xavier couldn't see the elven knight's expression through his helmet, but he didn't need to see it to know the elf was afraid.

He knows what I'm capable of. Knows he can't win.

Xavier softened the man's mind with Spirit Break before sending Willpower Infusion's purple mist flowing from Soultaker, and in less than a moment, the elven knight turned that great sword on himself.

Xavier watched in mute fascination. There had been a red glowing energy surrounding the man. *Toughness Infusion?* But a quick command dispelled the energy, dissipating the glow completely.

The kill didn't take very long.

Xavier sent a barrage of attacks—spells and slashes from Soultaker. Within a minute, the E Grade wave boss had been destroyed.

You have defeated a Level 125 Elven Knight!
You have gained 35,000,000 Mastery Points.

I guess I was right about him being a knight.

Xavier released a breath. He wasn't sure how much time remained before the next wave. He'd been focusing solely on gaining the Running skill. Now he'd acquired it, he ran back to the battlements. As he went, he noticed he no longer had to concentrate so intently on his technique. It reminded him of when he'd learnt his first skill upon arriving at the Tower of Champions. Staff Mastery. He no longer had that skill—it had morphed into Scythe-Staff Mastery when he'd gained his epic class.

Still, it was hard to forget how amazing it had felt wielding his staff after having gained proficiency in it in a moment. Like the techniques had been downloaded straight into his brain Matrix-style. For his Running skill, it wasn't quite the same. Perhaps because he'd needed to gain the skill by showing his proficiency. But though it wasn't quite as profound a change as that first skill he'd gained was, running with perfect form had become a habit. His muscle memory had adopted it—at a faster rate than it should have—and now it was second nature.

And this is only at Rank 1.

Gaining that one skill hadn't brought him everything he needed, but it was a step in the right direction.

I just need to keep thinking outside the box.

When he reached the wall and climbed over the parapet, the

others were all still there to greet him. A quick back and forth had him explain what he intended to do. When he was done, Siobhan made a "hmm" noise.

Xavier raised an eyebrow. "What is it?"

"Assimilate Properties," she said.

Xavier crossed his arms. "I think I've exhausted every avenue when it comes to that skill."

"Maybe, maybe not..." Siobhan placed her hand, palm facing up, in front of her. A book appeared atop it. She flipped through the pages, her eyes scanning them until she found what she was after. She nodded. "I think you've been going about the skill all wrong."

Xavier thought about all the things he'd tried. All the *painful* things he'd tried. "How so?"

She pointed to a passage on the page. Though rather than have Xavier read what it was, she was silently reading it out to herself. Siobhan often did this. She was briefly reacquainting herself with the material before she summarised its content.

When she was done, she smiled and bobbed her head in a nod. "Yes." She tapped the page. "I think this will work."

Chapter 24
Winged Bears

XAVIER LEANT BACK AGAINST THE PARAPET, ARMS STILL crossed at his chest, and frowned at Siobhan. He'd tried so hard to get Assimilate Properties to work that he couldn't help but suspect she must be wrong about this. He didn't voice his doubts, however —that would have just been rude.

"What does he have to do?" Justin asked. The teenage duellist stood straight with a hand resting on the pommel of his sword. There was something different about him, as though he'd changed in these last six weeks—come into himself a bit more. *He's comfortable here, confident.* It was nice to see.

"This book talks about a skill called Purge Impurities," Siobhan said.

Xavier raised an eyebrow, leaning forward. When he'd gained the Assimilate Properties skill, it had been just as he'd reached the 100-point threshold for Strength. A notification had come up, saying, "Metal impurities detected during Toughness upgrade. Attempting to purge metal impurities…"

He'd tried to recreate the situation several times without any luck.

"Go on," Xavier prompted.

Siobhan turned the page. "Now, it doesn't say a great deal, but

164

it appears as though Toughness helps the body dispose of different 'impurities.' These impurities aren't explained in great depth, but what *is* explained is that there is a way to control—or rather *guide*—this process." She turned the book to face the others, holding it open with her fingers. There was a two-page spread. A diagram of a humanoid's body, standing with their arms spread at each side. Lines ran through the body.

Spirit Lines? he wondered. Then frowned. *Or are those... Toughness Lines?*

"What is this diagram trying to show?" Xavier asked.

"Impurities being *pushed* out of the body, and the process by which that happens."

"What does it even mean by impurities?" Justin's forehead was creased, making him look older than his sixteen years. "Like, toxins?"

Siobhan shrugged. "I'm really not sure."

Xavier stepped forward and gestured for the book. Siobhan handed it over, only slightly reluctantly—she didn't like relinquishing books. He supposed he could understand that. He had a small collection of his favourite novels back in his apartment on Earth that he would never want to part with. *I wonder if they're still even there.* Those aspects of his old life didn't seem all that important anymore, what with the threat to his world. Still, it would be nice to have those old comforts available to him. Especially if he were going to live for hundreds, even thousands, of years.

He shook those thoughts away and focused on the diagram. The lines spread out from the stomach. There were far more lines than he'd first thought. Hundreds of them, as though they were trying to cover every inch of someone's skin. *Maybe they are.*

Xavier tilted his head to the side. "Is this something I can even do?"

"There's no level restriction on the Purge Impurities skill. At least, none that I can find," Siobhan said. "I'm sure it would be possible."

Xavier turned back to the pages before the diagram. With his Speed and Intelligence as high as they were, it didn't take him long to read through it and commit the words to memory.

The only problem was that the text didn't explain *how* to do the skill. It didn't even name the lines in the body that were drawn in the diagram. This fact made his frown only deepen. Still, this was a step closer than they'd been before. And if he could find a way to gain more ranks of Assimilate Properties and assimilate more materials into himself—if that was indeed how it worked— then he should be able to make good progress toward his goals.

Xavier handed the book back to Siobhan. He now had a better idea of what he needed to do. According to Adviser Kalren—ever the timekeeper—there was now only ten minutes left until the beginning of the next wave.

One day, I'll have more time than this. And more variety. A selfish part of him still craved being done with this fight. With this floor. With the Endless Horde. *I'm sure I must have gone through enough waves to be at the top spot by now.*

But that would leave Kiralla in the lurch. No, not *in the lurch.* It would leave the poor woman dead. Besides, he still had plenty of fight in him.

Xavier sat cross-legged on the stone of the battlements and closed his eyes. He fell into a deep meditation, something he could do at a moment's notice nowadays. As he sat there, he went over what the book had said, and what the System notification had told him.

Metal Impurities detected... Purge Impurities...

He understood how metal could be an impurity, but were there other things within his body that might need dispelling? And as the last thing he wanted to do was actually dispel them, how could he *assimilate* them?

Xavier let out a long breath. He was thinking about this in the wrong way. Something told him he'd been right at the start, when he'd tried to rub pebbles and other things into his wounds. But he'd just gotten a step missed. He opened his eyes and leant over to the parapet. Summoning Soultaker to his hand, he cut a small chunk of stone from the wall.

He stared at the stone chunk for a moment before nodding to himself, then swallowing it.

The stone went down hard. It scraped his throat, though it didn't make him bleed—his insides, like his outsides, were much tougher than they used to be. He made a big *gulp* sound, throat bobbing, wondering if this was a foolish thing to do.

Xavier closed his eyes once more, falling back into that meditation. His awareness of his own body had improved dramatically since he'd been integrated into the System, and he found he was able to *feel* where the stone was. It had made it down to his stomach. He wondered if, with his high stats, his stomach acids would be strong enough to dissolve stone now.

An odd thought.

He pushed the thought away and focused, simply trying to *feel* the stone and what his body was doing to it. Purge Impurities might be a skill, but that didn't mean his body didn't do it naturally —that had been clear enough when he'd tried to progress Assimilate Properties in the past.

Sure enough, the weight in his stomach lessened as the seconds passed. Whatever was inside of him *was* starting to dissolve. It was a very strange feeling. Once the weight was completely gone from his stomach, Xavier could no longer find out where it went—it must have been turned into miniscule fragments.

Remembering the diagram, Xavier looked at his skin. "Huh." Tiny pebbles were pushing themselves out of his pores, breaking to the surface of his skin, creating pinpricks of blood. Wounds that healed the instant they were created. His body, as he suspected, was purging the impurity all by itself.

Now I need to slow that progress down... assuming I can figure out how.

Xavier turned his mind toward this task for the next few minutes, eating chunk of stone after chunk of stone. It reminded him of a disease he'd read about once called pica, where people eat all kinds of things that weren't food. Nails, screws, safety pins. The idea should have made him shudder, but if he were honest, he'd started to wonder what else he could get his hands on.

The more he ate, the more he was able to examine and feel what was happening inside of his body. Just like when he'd identified the Willpower Lines when he'd found his secondary core, he was soon able to follow some of the lines that the dissolved bits of stone followed as they flowed through to the surface of his skin.

The more aware he became, the more he understood what was happening. But ten minutes was hardly enough time to figure the process out. And, unlike running, this wasn't exactly something he would be able to do while on the battlefield.

When the wave started, he knew what his focus—other than defeating the enemies in the wave—would be. Running. Each rank he gained in running would gain him a further percentage increase to his Speed attribute. He quickly got into a rhythm, finding it easier and easier to run while throwing out a myriad of spells and dishing out melee attacks and Soul Blocks to keep nearby enemies at bay.

Over the weeks, he'd become more and more at home on the battlefield. It was strange how comfortable he was out here. How relaxed he managed to be whilst in the heat of battle. Though he knew that was only because the enemies were something he could handle. That relaxed feeling had been cracked when he'd faced multiple waves and E Grade bosses at once—at least until he'd managed to triumph over them.

In fact, now he felt even more confident than he had before. He knew, to a certain degree, what he was able to handle. He could take down E Grade enemies. Hell, he could do more than take them down—he could make them *fight* for him. He could control their minds and have them turn on themselves.

And the stronger he became, the more F Grade enemies he was able to control as well. To the point where, when he ran around the battlefield, purple mist flowing from his staff, the enemies around him were almost like a personal army. An army he could use to fight his own battles.

Then, when that army died, he could feed upon their souls.

During that wave, he gained a few more ranks in running. It was kind of insane just how *fast* he could run. *I must be able to run faster than some cars, considering how quickly I managed to gain the running skill.*

He wasn't at *super-speed* quite yet, however. At least what he considered to be super-speed. He didn't think he'd be anywhere nearly as fast as Flash, for instance. *But maybe one day.* The thought made him chuckle, wondering just how fast he could become.

And all of this while I'm still only F Grade.

He struggled to imagine just how much *stronger* the evolution to E Grade was likely to make him. Would he gain more stats? Would his body transform somehow? The E Grades that he'd fought were certainly a lot stronger than the F Grades. He could take Level 90 soldiers and beasts down with a single strike, and several at once with his spells. Hell, he could take several down with a strike with Soultaker if he swept it around in the perfect arc. Not to mention all the damage he could do when he controlled them.

But he had to put far more effort into killing the E Grade enemies. Of course, part of that *could* be the stats they'd gained as they levelled—but he didn't think so.

I'll find out soon enough.

Xavier worked his way around the castle, running laps over and over again as he continued to thin the enemies in the wave. This wave was a mixed one. It contained beasts he hadn't seen before.

One of those beasts was a Flame Chimera. It was the strangest-looking beast he'd ever seen. It had the head of a lion—and the head of a *goat*. Not the most frightening beast to mix with. On top of that—or rather, behind—its tail was literally a snake.

A three-headed, weird looking beast.

Oh, and it *breathed fire*. Hence the "flame" in the name.

Xavier had read about such beasts before back on Earth. Again, he had to wonder how Earth knew of these creatures and different humanoid races—elves, dwarves, *demons*—that turned out to be real. As though somehow the knowledge of the universe, even before the System, had wheedled its way into humanity's subconscious.

Along with the chimeras, there were other beasts. Such as Giant Spiders—these were easy enough to kill, but they still made his skin crawl whenever he saw them—and massive, elephant beasts called Frozen Mastodons that shot spikes of ice from their tusks.

Then there were *Winged Bears*. The name said it all for these beasts. They were furry and looked positively cuddly until they opened their giant maws and roared.

It was the strangest wave he'd faced yet.

Once he'd dealt with these, the wave boss revealed itself.

When he saw it, Xavier actually took a step back. *Holy crap.* It was a variant of the Winged Bears. Except it wore full plate armour and carried a large halberd.

Xavier cast Willpower Infusion on the beastman.

Nothing happened.

Chapter 25
That Doesn't Bode Well

PURPLE MIST FLOWED FROM XAVIER'S SOULTAKER AND floated through the air. When it hit the fully armoured, E Grade Winged Bear, it just... dissipated. Xavier felt the barest of connections to the beastman's mind. A connection that lasted no more than a split second.

What he felt was a mind built like a fortress. One completely impenetrable to his mind control.

The beastman smiled.

Now, Xavier had never seen a bear *smile* before. He didn't think such an action was possible. And he wasn't embarrassed to say that he took another step back.

He tried to scan the beastman, but even before that failed, he knew it wouldn't work. He hadn't been able to scan any of the other E Grades, and this wave boss was likely even stronger than the last.

And I'm not able to control it.

"This farce of an invasion has gone on too long," the beastman said. Its wings extended, each one larger than a car. "You die today." It launched itself forward, flying low near the ground, building up speed as it closed the distance between them.

No more time for hesitating.

Though Xavier had grown reliant on his Willpower Infusion spell, it was certainly not the only weapon in his arsenal. His scythe-staff was infused with Spirit Energy and Willpower Energy already. He hadn't found much use in the spell when it was infused into his weapon, but that was mostly because he one-hit the normal enemies on a wave. He wondered if it would have any effect on this bear, when direct control hadn't been effective. Spiritual Trifecta was active—it was *always* active.

And all of his other spells were powerful enough.

Xavier, not knowing how strong this beastman's magical resistance would be, sidestepped the oncoming attack. At the same time, he threw a Soul Block and a Heavy Telekinesis at the enemy. He'd just used Soul Strike to take down the last remaining enemies in the wave, so it would be on cooldown for another minute and a half.

I'll keep this winged bastard busy until then.

The Soul Block was infused with twenty souls. The beastman couldn't change direction in the air swiftly enough to hit Xavier after he'd sidestepped. The Soul Block apparition formed. A massive, glowing chimera that silently roared at the rapidly approaching beastman.

The Winged Bear's halberd slammed straight into—and then *through*—the apparition as though it wasn't there at all. The glowing chimera dissipated into nothing, wisps of its soul floating through the air until they faded.

Good thing I tested that.

That was when Xavier's Heavy Telekinesis hit the winged beast. It stopped the E Grade wave boss in its tracks, halting its flight in mid-air. But it didn't push the beastman back. The bear gave a small grunt, then shrugged the spell off, and swiftly changed direction to come at Xavier. It hadn't even fallen to the ground, somehow able to remain in the air even after being hit by Heavy Telekinesis.

All right. This thing is strong. Very strong. That didn't bode well. But at least Heavy Telekinesis *had* stopped it. *It's effective enough for what I need to do.*

The beastman flew straight at him once more. Xavier cast Spirit Break. The bear flinched—like it had gotten a hard slap to the face—but kept flying.

Xavier waited until the last moment. Then he sidestepped the attack, sent a Heavy Telekinesis at the bear, and swung an overhead strike straight down at one of its massive wings. Soultaker's pitch-black blade pierced the feathered wing as the beastman came to an abrupt halt mid-air.

A roar of pain escaped its maw, and... Was that a hint of fear in that roar? Willpower Infusion, when used on one of Xavier's weapons, was supposed to inflict fear onto his opponents when he struck them. It was also supposed to negatively affect their mental resistance.

Xavier had assumed such a thing wouldn't work on this beastman, considering how resistant it had been to a direct cast of the spell.

Perhaps it's different when I break the skin with Soultaker...

Regardless, even with his rapid speed of thought, he didn't have time to think on it. While Soultaker's blade was still lodged inside of the beast's wing, it whirled faster than Xavier knew it could move. Xavier's grip on the staff was strong, else it would have been ripped straight out of his hand.

He held tight, and instead of losing his scythe-staff, he was flung into the air across the battlefield.

Oh, crap.

Xavier had a very, very big weakness—he couldn't manoeuvre in the air. At least not effectively. It had never really been something he'd needed to worry about, as unlike Justin, he wasn't able to fly. An inability to manoeuvre in the air was the exact reason he didn't do fancy leaping jumps when attacking an enemy.

Even if such a thing *would* look totally cool.

A loud *whoosh, whoosh, whoosh* of wings sounded from behind him. Something told Xavier that the beastman could fly faster than he'd been thrown.

Xavier threw his arms about, Soultaker gripped in one hand, trying to turn around in the air. At the last second, he managed to do so.

The halberd was coming down to strike his face.

Xavier raised Soultaker and sent Heavy Telekinesis at the bastard simultaneously. The halberd slammed into Xavier's blade, which only threw Xavier farther back. Then Heavy Telekinesis yanked the bear backward—no, it wasn't *yanked* backward, it just looked that way.

It was stopped in mid-air while Xavier kept flying.

He threw a glance over his shoulder, tried to turn back around —too late. The ground came up to greet him. He fell backward. Unable to slow the fall, Xavier *slammed* into the corpses of the beasts he'd killed during the wave. Their bodies did barely anything to cushion his fall, but that didn't matter. A fall like that couldn't really hurt him.

But it did disorientate him. He got back to his feet and shook his head, trying to gain his bearings.

Whoosh, whoosh.

SLAM!

The full weight of the Winged Bear flying at what must have been over a hundred miles per hour slammed straight into Xavier's side. No, it wasn't just the E Grade wave boss's weight— it was their damned *halberd*. The beastman must have had it pointed out in front of him like a medieval knight jousting on horseback.

Pain blossomed in his side. Sharp pain. The shock. His Willpower and Toughness weren't enough to numb the agony the strike brought him.

How much damage did that bastard do to me?

Your health is at 64%.

174

Xavier read his health's status as he rolled uncontrollably along the ground, in a patch of the battlefield clear from corpses. When he finally made it to his feet, he was completely covered in ash.

He gritted his teeth. His health had been around 95 percent before that attack. *One hit took me down 30 percent!* It mightn't seem like a lot, but it showed him how much he *didn't* want to get hit.

Even if Soul Block wasn't effective, he should have used it—should have infused 100 souls into one. But that damned attack had taken him by surprise.

That doesn't bode well.

Facing this Winged Bear, Xavier wondered—not for the first time—if his confidence had been misplaced. If, perhaps, he was well and truly in over his head.

I suppose the only way to find out that is to keep fighting.

The wound in his side hurt like hell, but it was healing. And it didn't stop him from standing. Xavier glanced this way and that. His ears pricked as he heard a *whoosh* coming from above.

The Winged Bear was flying straight down at him.

Xavier, jaw still clenched, gave a strained grin.

Spirit Break! The bear flinched. *Heavy Telekinesis!* It was halted in mid-air.

And, finally: *Soul Strike!*

Xavier infused 500 souls into the spell, which turned into a giant apparition of death. The beasts he'd just faced—Winged Bears, Giant Spiders, Flame Chimeras—they all materialised.

The attack was eerie in its silence. It always felt as though Soul Strike should be *loud*. That it should boom like thunder, especially considering the brilliance of the white lightning arcing from his scythe-staff before materialising into the apparitions.

Each of the beasts' souls opened their maws and roared, yet they made no sound whatsoever.

The E Grade wave boss, on the other hand, *did* make a sound. One of twisted agony. Of tremendous pain. Fear filled its eyes, its face contorted.

The Heavy Telekinesis only stopped it from moving for a moment. After getting hit by the 500-infused Soul Strike, it fell—not *flew*—to the ground. Its massive weight slammed into the dirt, digging a small crater around from the impact.

Xavier didn't waste a single second. He got into position and swept Soultaker down, slamming the blade into the beastman's back. Once, twice. Four times, five times. A dozen, a hundred. He kept the beastman in place by sending constant Heavy Telekinesis and Spirit Break spells down at it, while at the same time attempting to use Willpower Infusion on it.

Though he knew Willpower Infusion would work, he couldn't help himself.

Xavier cultivated Celestial Energy into his body, turning it to Spirit Energy as he sent it to his main core. The last thing he needed was to run out.

What he was surprised by was the fact that the beastman hadn't been killed by the 500-infused Soul Strike in the first place. *This is the strongest enemy I've ever faced by far.*

And he was laying waste to it with every swing.

Xavier was surprised by how many it took. He'd been able to defeat one of the other E Grade bosses by cutting its head clean off —but he imagined he'd only been able to do that because it was already injured. He'd controlled that elf to loose arrows into it.

Its defences were weakened, leaving it susceptible to my attack.

On strike one hundred and one, the Winged Bear finally died. Breathing heavily, Xavier stood straight and threw his head back, looking up at the sky, a sense of relief coming over him.

He read the kill notification.

You have defeated a Level 130 Bear King (Epic)!
You have gained 100,000,000 Mastery Points.

Xavier's gaze was drawn to the number of Mastery Points he'd received for the kill. Then he saw "**(Epic)**" by the name.

Epic... Is that why it was so damned strong? And why I gained so many more Mastery Points, despite it only being a few levels higher than the last E Grade boss I defeated?

Xavier knelt by the beastman's corpse. He touched a hand to its armour—dented and damaged by his many strikes—and stored the Bear King in his Storage Ring.

Perhaps there's something I can do with this...

Chapter 26
A Slap of Instant Clarity

Xavier dumped the corpse of the Bear King onto the battlements' stone floor. The massive beastman lay on its back, wings splayed, reaching from one wall to the other. Its armour was dented, bloodied, and had massive rents through it where Xavier's blade had cut through.

Kiralla stared at the corpse, then raised an eyebrow at Xavier. "Why, pray tell, did you bring this specimen here?"

Xavier nudged the dead beastman with a foot. He faced Howard. "I know the three of you have not been idle while I've been defeating these waves."

Howard crossed his arms at his chest. "We've kept busy. Not so busy as you."

"Which one of you learnt the Dismantle skill?"

Justin stepped forward. He rubbed the back of his head. "I did. It's a bit gruesome, but it seemed like it might come in handy. I've been practising on some of the Wolven corpses you've brought us."

Xavier motioned toward the dead E Grade wave boss. "Are you able to dismantle this?"

Justin frowned, knelt by the Bear King. His gaze moved up and down the corpse. "I'm not sure. I've never worked on an E Grade before. The skill topped out at Rank 50. I haven't been able to push it beyond that."

"Really?" Xavier asked. "You got a skill to Rank 50?"

"Does that surprise you? Aren't most of your skills at that rank?"

"No, I guess it shouldn't surprise me." To be honest, it *did* surprise him. But he supposed there'd been a lot of corpses for the Airborne Duellist to practise on. He just hadn't realised the teenager had done so much of it.

He's had a lot of spare time over these six weeks.

"Why do you want to dismantle it?" Siobhan asked. "You didn't bring back the corpses of the other E Grades."

Xavier crinkled his nose. "It... didn't feel right. Dismantling humanoid races. Not that all of them were." He scratched at the stubble that had formed on his chin. He hadn't exactly spent a great deal of time shaving over these last few weeks. Just enough so a beard hadn't grown—though he'd contemplated growing one on a few occasions. "Then again, this Bear King could talk..."

"Beasts, even those that have grown into sapience, have different properties in their bodies than humanoid Denizens do," Justin said. "Though a beast can eventually become as intelligent, or more intelligent, than a human, elf, dwarf, demonkin, or any other humanoid Denizen or naturally sapient Denizen, their bodies and minds are fundamentally different because they got there through System evolution."

Xavier frowned. "Are there books about this?"

Siobhan nodded. "Several! It's quite an interesting topic, actually."

Adviser Kalren had an odd look on his face. "It is strange what you and your people worry about." He gestured out to the battlements. The fire mages flames, disposing of the Endless Horde's dead, could be heard from here. "You defend us with all of this slaughter, then worry about gathering resources from those you've slain..."

Xavier shook his head. *Suppose he's right. It is an odd way of looking at things.* He imagined he still had a lot of beliefs and ideas that he'd grown up with back on Earth. Things that would be challenged in this new reality they'd all found themselves in.

"And this tangent meant you didn't answer my question." Siobhan nudged him on the shoulder. "Are you... thinking of getting ingredients to assimilate with that skill of yours?"

Xavier grunted his affirmation—a little habit he'd picked up from Howard. "I've no idea if it will work. But this beastman is... incredibly strong. I wondered if..." He sighed. "It might be a foolish idea."

Adviser Kalren ran a hand through his beard. "It is not a foolish idea at all. In fact, I think this puts you on the right track."

Justin rose to his feet. "I'll do what I can. It might take a while. But, before you try to use anything from the beastman, you could try using other things I've dismantled from all the Wolven you've brought back."

Xavier raised his chin. "Good idea."

Justin raised both his hands, palm up. A dozen Wolven fangs appeared in one hand, a dozen claws in the other.

"And you're planning on... *ingesting* those?" Howard asked.

Xavier took the fangs and claws. "If I have to. Why?"

Howard shuddered. "No reason."

Xavier scrunched his face up, looking at what he'd just taken from Justin. It wasn't as though he *wanted* to swallow these things. It certainly wasn't his first choice. But if he were going to really get this skill to work for him—assuming he could get it to work *at all*—he would need to assimilate more than just metal and stone.

That made him wonder if there was any sort of limit to the amount of things he could use with Assimilate Properties. *I'm getting ahead of myself.*

"You have fifteen minutes remaining before your next wave." Adviser Kalren folded his hands in front of him. "If you wish for time to work on your skill, you should take it."

"Before I do that, I have a question. When I defeated this

beast, the kill notification had 'Epic' at the end of its name. Was it referring to the beast's class?"

"Epic?" The bearded adviser raised both brows. "Well, I have not heard of that happening in a long while. Yes, it does indeed refer to the enemy's class rarity."

"How come it doesn't show other class rarities? I've never seen 'Common,' 'Uncommon,' or 'Rare.'

"As far as I am aware, it only appears when one defeats an Epic class." Kalren frowned. "Though I suppose it could appear for Legendary as well. Now *that* would be quite something."

Epic class. No wonder the Bear King was so much more powerful than the other E Grades. He smiled to himself. *And yet I defeated it.*

"All the more reason to dismantle materials from it," Justin said. "Though my blade may not be strong enough to work on this." He looked at Xavier. "May I borrow Soultaker for a time? That blade certainly did damage against this thing."

Xavier summoned his scythe-staff. He infused Spirit Energy into it, then was about to pass it to Justin when Howard stepped over.

"Let me put Toughness Energy into that. He's needed it for his blade to cut through even the lower-level foot soldiers and beasts. It's defensive Toughness Energy—stops the blade from bending and breaking under strain." Howard said.

"Doesn't help me cut easier, though," Justin muttered.

Xavier nodded. "Infusing Soultaker with Spirit Energy is probably the only reason it's been strong enough to still use." He was honestly surprised the blade hadn't shattered when fighting higher-level enemies. "It's a shame we aren't able to access the System Shop here. We'd all be able to upgrade our equipment."

He'd grown attached to Soultaker. It was by far his favourite weapon so far. But he'd also gotten it a *lot* of levels ago—it didn't really make sense for him to keep using it.

"Were the castle's smith still here, I would have her craft you a weapon fit for a king," Queen Alastea said.

Xavier smiled. "That would have been greatly appreciated," he said, thinking, *fit for a king...*

Honestly, he thought he would make a terrible king. A protector? Maybe. But a king? No. He spent far too much time fighting.

He glanced over at the castle. He could see its grand double doors from here. The portal, the one all Queen Alastea's citizens had left through during the exodus, was still open inside of it.

Not for the first time, he wondered what would happen if he or one of the members of his party were to step through it. They would be able to purchase new equipment and other supplies...

But would the System stop them from doing that? Or would they simply be able to walk straight through it with no consequences?

He shook the thought away. *The System would stop us.*

Besides—it was a one-way portal. Getting *back* here would be very difficult, and *very* expensive. Even if he, say, sent through Adviser Kalren, he'd probably have to empty all the coin from his Storage Ring to get him back here.

Either that, or he'd have to use Xavier's Sector Travel Key to get back. *Assuming it would even work here.*

"Ten minutes," Adviser Kalren said.

The man's words brought Xavier out of his reverie. He walked a little ways away from the others—and Justin, kneeling down with Soultaker, about to carve through the Bear King—and sat with his back against the parapet.

He'd deposited the Wolven claws and fangs into his Storage Ring. He brought a single fang out to rest on his palm, scrunching up his nose as he glared at it. Was he really going to swallow one of these, just for a skill he hadn't even learnt to use yet?

I'm probably going to swallow much more than one of these...

Xavier released a long sigh, then tossed it into his mouth. He pretended it was just like a pill he was swallowing. It couldn't be much worse than swallowing *stone*, could it?

Gulp.

Xavier winced. Gripped his neck. The stone had hurt his

throat a little, but his skin had been more than tough enough to deal with it. This, however, was a fang from a beast of a higher level than his own. And inside his body, his high Toughness didn't seem to make enough of a difference.

He'd swallowed it wrong. The fang had gone down his throat sideways. He tasted the blood flowing from the wound. Though it wouldn't take long to heal, it wasn't the most pleasant feeling.

Ah, the things I do for skills.

Just like the stones he'd ingested, he was able to feel this one inside his stomach. However, somehow, it felt as though it had... more weight. Which, considering it was *lighter*, seemed strange.

Maybe because it has some sort of magical properties. Then again, the stone he'd ingested probably had some sort of magical properties, too. Just like the metal that had assimilated into him in the first place. He doubted they would have made the castle's walls from ordinary stone, after all.

It didn't take long for his body to notice the foreign material inside of him. Just like with the stones, it began to break it down. But again, it was like he could *feel* it more. He could *see* more clearly what was going on. As though before he'd been wearing glasses in a dark room, and now he'd taken them off and turned on a light.

Now all I need to do is control *the process. Slow down the purging of these impurities.*

He remembered the initial notification. It had said it was unable to purge impurities in an F Grade Denizen... yet the stones he'd ingested had been purged easily.

Xavier tilted his head to the side in thought.

The arrowheads must have been more significant than the stone. Either that, or the amount of Toughness I have has made it easier for these materials to be purged.

Though he did notice something. The purging of the fang that he'd ingested wasn't just more noticeable within his mind. It was also taking longer, which he was sure was because it was a more powerful ingredient. If his Toughness attribute was lower, he might not be able to purge it at all...

Would it be forced to assimilate with me, then?

He focused on the process, taking deep belly breaths, trying to control it like he might control the different energies that flowed through him. He could feel more of the different lines that the dissolved fang flowed through, on its way to reaching the surface of his skin.

But this process was nothing like cultivating, or cycling, energy through his Spirit and Willpower Lines. This was something his body wanted to dispel, not keep.

Energy flows toward me, this flows away from me...

That thought made something click within his mind, and he was hit with a slap of instant clarity.

I know what I need to do!

Chapter 27
There's Nothing That Can Stand in My Way

Attempting to assimilate *Wolven Fang* into muscular structure...

PAIN STABBED AT HIS STOMACH. BUT IT WAS NOWHERE NEAR as intense as the pain he'd felt when he'd first done this, as though that first time had eased the way for the second.

A minute or so passed until another notification appeared.

Assimilation in progress...
The material you are assimilating has various properties.
You may only draw from one.
Choose from the following:

1. **Speed enhancement.**
2. **Strength enhancement.**
3. **Piercing damage enhancement.**

Holy crap!

Xavier's epiphany had paid off. Big time. He tapped a finger on the stone floor, looking at the different options.

As he'd been aiming to enhance his Speed—and that happened to be at the top of the list—he almost went for that without thinking. But that would have been foolish. He already had a way to increase his Speed by ranking up the Running skill. In fact, currently, out of the three attributes he needed to get to 1,000 points, Speed was already the highest—if only by a small margin.

Piercing damage he could easily do without. Sure, it would be nice to have his staff-scythe blade cut through enemies even easier, but it was hardly the priority.

No, the choice he needed to make was clear.

Strength, he thought, willing the selection.

Assimilation is complete.
Biological impurities of *Wolven Fang* have been assimilated into muscular structure.
You have gained +10 Strength!

Assimilate Properties has reached Rank 2!

Xavier smiled. He couldn't help himself. He burst up to his feet and pumped his fist in the air. "Finally!" He'd done it. He'd ranked up Assimilate Properties. That bastard of a skill had been giving him nothing but trouble since he'd started trying to improve it, and now he'd made the first step.

Compared to all of his other skills, getting to Rank 2 didn't seem like a big deal. Nor did the measly few points in Strength make a major difference. But when you're pushing at a boulder for weeks without it ever budging and it finally does, it doesn't matter how much easier you pushed other boulders in the past—it feels like way more of an accomplishment than anything else.

Xavier released a long breath and looked at the description for the skill.

Assimilate Properties – Rank 2

This is an epic skill that grants you the ability to assimilate foreign properties into your body, mind, and soul if the perfect conditions are met.
List of Current Assimilated Properties:
Crucible Steel (Muscular Structure) – +12 Toughness
Wolven Fang (Muscular Structure) – +12 Strength

Xavier frowned. Toughness and Strength had only gained an extra two points when the skill reached Rank 2. Assimilate Properties didn't seem nearly as helpful as even his Running skill. Ranks in that skill—and most others—earned him a higher *percentage* modifier, which went a long way when it came to boosting his stats.

Still, he couldn't complain. This was only the beginning, after all. The skill had untapped potential. He would find out just how far it could be pushed.

What else does gaining another rank in this skill give me?

Perhaps it would simply make assimilating the next material easier. He supposed he would find that out soon enough.

Xavier looked over at the others. They were staring at him, curious looks on their faces from his little outburst of joy from his success.

"One minute," Adviser Kalren said. He nodded toward the Endless Horde and their endless waves, pushing Xavier straight back into reality.

Xavier just wanted to sigh. *Not a single moment to celebrate in this place.* But he was used to that. Used to the lack of sleep. Used to be constantly *on*, never able to slow down for more than a few minutes—and even in those minutes, still ensuring he was always working toward *something*.

He forced a smile onto his face as he turned toward the next wave. The Endless Horde. The fifth floor. The Tower of Champions. The *System*. All of these things wanted to break him. Would relish in his being defeated. In him dying or giving up.

But Xavier wasn't going to do either. No, he would keep pushing. He would push until he had nothing left to give.

And that's not something I'm going to let happen.

This fight. These waves. They *weren't* endless. They had an end. One he would reach. And the time that he took doing this—the weeks that had gone by and the months that surely would—would be but a blip in his life. A life he would ensure went on for hundreds—no, *thousands*—of years.

He'd seen the expressions on those E Grade wave bosses when he'd first faced them. Seen their confidence. Their smugness or stony calm. He'd turned the tables around and made them feel true fear before defeating them.

And I'll do that with every foe I face. There's nothing that can stand in my way.

There's nothing that can stand in my way.

The thought crossed Melissa Donavan's mind as she waded through the bog. The damned ground beneath her was like quicksand, pulling her farther and farther down with each step she tried to make. But she wasn't going to simply give up and let it. She was going to keep pushing.

Halfway through the bog, she'd already sunk down to her chest.

There was movement behind her. Swift footsteps. As gentle as those bastard elves were on their feet, the noise still filtered through the trees and reached her ears.

Melissa swore inwardly.

After days of being the hunter, she'd finally become the hunted. The elves weren't foolish. They'd noticed their numbers dwindling. Noticed that whenever one elf stepped into the forest alone, they were unlikely to ever return. So now, the elves never left their camp alone—they went in twos.

As though that's enough to stop me.

Melissa was too good at stalking her prey. Too good at staying out of sight. But now they'd turned her into prey. At their portal— the glowing, pulsing mass that stood at the centre of their camp, protected at all times—one of the elves had sat cross-legged on the ground. His head had been down, his fingers interlaced together before him. He looked as though he were in prayer.

And his prayers had been answered when, roughly an hour later, a beast came through the portal.

Melissa had been in one of the trees nearby. High above the elves, where they couldn't see her. The canopy was thick enough that the only thing they'd be able to spot were her eyes staring back down at them, an eventuality that fortunately hadn't come to pass.

The beast that stepped out of the portal was like nothing she'd ever seen. It acted almost like a dog in the way it moved, but it was more like a giant lizard. It was about the height of a pony, and maybe twice as long. The elf that had been praying on the ground for the past hour threw a chunk of meat to the beast. It opened a mouth riddled with rows of teeth and chomped on the meat excitedly, wagging its massive tail behind it.

Another of the elves brought forth an arrow. It stepped up to the beast, slightly hesitantly—as though wary it would bite his arm off—and held up the arrow in offering.

The lizard—after Melissa had scanned it, she found it was called an Obatri—sniffed the arrow near the fletching.

The arrow had been Melissa's, and the lizard was sniffing for her scent. She must have left the smallest hint of sweat behind on it from holding it. It wouldn't be much. She doubted a normal hound would be able to catch her scent from that alone.

But this Obatri lizard beast caught her scent *instantly*. After it had sniffed, it had looked directly at her up in the tree.

And now she was on the run.

It wasn't just the elves' feet that she could hear coming after her. It was that damned lizard. It wasn't nearly as stealthy and quiet as the elves that were its masters. No, this damned beast trudged through the forest like a bull in a China shop.

Stuck in the bog, Melissa stopped trying to wade through it. She breathed in deeply, then let it out slowly, calming her body and mind. She pulled a rope out of one of her Storage Rings. She smirked, looking at the rings on her fingers. So far, she'd recovered three from the elves she'd killed.

Not all of the elves possessed Storage Rings, but she was glad when they did. Inside each of the rings, she'd found supplies—this rope was one of them. Melissa hastily tied the rope around the shaft of an arrow. The other end she tied around her wrist so it wouldn't go missing.

She nocked the arrow, aimed at a tree, and loosed with an exhalation.

Thunk.

The arrow slammed into the tree so hard that the arrowhead came out the other side. She tugged on the rope, glad that the shafts of those arrows were stronger than they looked.

Melissa deposited her bow into the Storage Ring. Slowly— almost agonisingly so—she dragged herself up the rope, one hand at a time. There was a loud *sucking* sound as she came out of the bog, a sound that made her cringe and scrunch up her face. Not the most pleasant thing she'd ever heard.

The sounds of pursuit grew ever louder. They would be on her soon. The lizard beast would scent her coming through this bog and head straight for it.

Come on. She pulled harder, faster. She needed to get out of that damned bog. *You can do this, Melissa. You have to do this.*

She'd gained what felt like a tremendous amount of Strength since the System integrated Earth, even if Strength hadn't been her main attribute. It was remarkable what she was now able to do.

As the sounds of her pursuers grew nearer and nearer, she finally made it out of the bog. She kept pulling on the rope, letting it take her a little ways up the trunk of the tree until she grabbed onto one of the branches and swung herself up to it, landing atop it in a crouch. She then jumped up to the next one and quickly got into position, summoning her bow back to her hand.

Melissa nocked an arrow, drew the string until it was softly digging into her cheek. Her lips twitched up at the sides as the Obatri padded into the clearing—into what *looked* like a clearing.

At the beginning of the bog, where the trees ended and the "clearing" began, Melissa had covered the soft ground with leaves, grass, and fallen branches to make it look like solid ground. These things were light enough that they often took half a day to sink into the bog, and so it was a task she'd been diligently repeating each morning.

It was her insurance in case the elves ever came after her. She'd only be able to outrun them for so long. Besides, she didn't want to outrun them. That would only have them run her out of this forest.

No, she wanted to *outmanoeuvre* them.

And that was exactly what she'd done.

The massive lizard didn't pause as it broke through the trees. It kept running, in that odd way that lizards ran, coming up on two legs almost comically. The elves—a good ten of them—were directly behind the beast. They, too, were not slowing.

This turned her small smile into a full one. The lizard beast and the elves that followed it fell right into her trap. The bog was deceptive. She herself had almost gotten sucked deep into it the first time she'd encountered it. At first, it simply felt like soft ground, until you began to sink. And by the time you realised what was going on, it was too late to simply turn back.

Then, panic began to settle in. If you could not contain that panic, it turned into swift movements that only made the person sink faster.

Melissa didn't know if the elves had bogs where they'd come from. Frankly, she didn't care—she knew it wouldn't matter either way.

For they'd been snared in her trap. The Obatri and the ten elves were swiftly sinking into the bog. Considering their superhuman levels of Strength, Speed, and Toughness, she was mostly sure they would be able to get themselves out of this mess if they were careful enough.

But that would take *time*.

Melissa loosed the first arrow.

There's nothing that can stand in my way.

Chapter 28
Agony

Xavier's blade brought death all around him. Soultaker carved through armour and necks as though there was no resistance at all. It made him wonder what a stronger weapon would be able to do, for this blade could only do such things because it was infused with his Spirit Energy.

He barely felt the extra points in Strength that he'd gained. Twelve points didn't make a wild-enough difference when you already had over seven hundred.

But returning to the battlefield, facing that next wave, he knew something was different. Knew something had shifted in his mindset.

I'm more determined than ever.

More and more, he was starting to *actually* believe he could do this. The doubt that kept coming up, rearing its ugly head, was now showing itself increasingly rarely. He'd proven, time and again, that he was capable of what was seemingly impossible.

He'd already *done* the impossible. He came from nothing. A world newly integrated. No real fighting experience. No tactical experience. He'd gotten lucky. If that Navy SEAL hadn't put his rifle down, Xavier wouldn't be standing—fighting—right now.

But after he'd gotten lucky? Everything after that he'd *earned*. And he would keep earning it.

I hit the top spot. Out of trillions and trillions of Denizens in the Greater Universe, I hit the top spot. Me. Xavier Collins. No one else.

He threw a Heavy Telekinesis to the left, a Soul Block to the right, a Soul Strike behind him. Purple mist flowed from him. Willpower Energy, seeping into the enemies alive around him. Making them turn and face their own. Making them work for him.

I will see this through to the end.

He couldn't keep giving himself an out. Couldn't keep telling himself that he could turn around, step into the Safe Zone, and go back to the Staging Room. That out, that escape... was holding him back. Holding his mind back. His body back.

The simple option he had of being able to quit... he had to throw that away. He had to believe that he could do this; otherwise, he never would. He had to believe that defeating the Endless Horde wasn't just something he was attempting, but a simple inevitability.

And if I can do this, I can do anything. I'll blast through the next floors. I'll return to Earth and push back the threat. No one in our sector will dare attack my world.

As the wave went by, he pushed himself to new limits. Practising his Running skill as he went, ranking it up twice. He sank into meditation before tossing another Wolven Fang into his mouth and swallowing it, trying to see if he could assimilate the same material twice. That, he found, was too difficult to focus on while fighting. At least, it had been at first.

So he did it again. And again. Back on Earth, before the integration, he'd read articles about multitasking. He knew multitasking wasn't truly possible for the human mind—focusing on one thing at a time was always better.

But his mind was no longer merely that of a normal human. The attributes he'd received had turned him into something else, and he could no longer let his beliefs limit what he was capable of, else he would never reach his full potential.

Besides, it wasn't as though Xavier hadn't split his mind before —but this seemed more difficult than merely meditating and fighting at the same time. This was splitting his mind on an entirely new level.

I keep thinking I've hit my limit. Keep thinking there's no way I can push my level, skills, attributes, or abilities farther. But that's all a lie. I've pushed through every barrier. I discovered my secondary core. I unlocked Willpower Infusion. I gained the Running skill. I assimilated a new material. I've blasted through every single one of these roadblocks. It's only a matter of time before I blast through this one.

And so for every minute that passed during that wave as he was fighting, Xavier was struggling to split his mind. Pushing it harder than he'd previously thought possible—harder than he'd previously *allowed* himself to.

After a time, his head became sore. It ached with a splitting pain that only intensified. As though an E Grade warrior had slammed a battle axe straight into his frontal lobe. The pain was excruciating, and he was surprised to find he'd never experienced agony like this before. Not when the goblins had him on his back. Not when the Black Pumas got his health down to 1 percent.

No, this pain was worse than any of that. And it was pain he was inflicting on himself. Pain that he could take away, if only he gave up on his quest to split his mind.

His thoughts berated him, that negativity and doubt returning. A part of him wished he'd chosen the other path for Willpower Infusion, that he could instil himself with the confidence he needed to get past this obstacle.

Why are you doing this? Why are you here? You could be in the tavern back in the Tower of Champions. You could be eating a warm meal and sipping on whiskey in front of the fire. You've already done enough on this floor. You've probably already hit the number one stop on the leaderboard.

Xavier gritted his teeth. He accepted the thoughts he was having, then let them drift away. He didn't need that self-doubt.

And he didn't need the other path of Willpower Infusion to get him past this.

Not when he could do it on his own.

So he kept pushing his mind. Kept feeling that splitting, aching pain.

Until finally, the pain hit its peak. The world flashed white. He couldn't see the battle raging in front of him. His body became limp. As though his muscles had suddenly turned to jelly. The ground came up and slammed into his knee—

No. He was falling. Straight to the dirt. Blows *thudded* down at his body. Cuts opened over every inch of him. This pain—the pain of being attacked by the enemies that surrounded him—was nothing compared to what was happening to his mind. The rest of him felt numb in contrast to that exquisite agony.

What's happening to me?

For a moment, he thought he might be under attack. Thought perhaps that whoever the E Grade wave boss of this wave was had hit him with a mental attack of some sort.

Then he remembered the pain he'd been putting himself through. Remembered that he'd been trying to split his mind.

Apparently, he'd succeeded. But *this* wasn't exactly what he'd envisioned when he'd hatched this foolish plan. He hadn't known pushing himself like this would put him on the ground. Would make the world around him entirely white. His attackers invisible.

Awareness flooded back to him. He threw spells left and right, attempting to create a circle of space around him. A buffer so he could recover from this. His vision slowly cleared. Just in time to see a massive human warrior wearing golden plate armour, a yellow glow surrounding him, swing down at him with a battle axe that would do more than simply hurt his head.

Xavier threw himself out of the way, only missing the attack by a hairsbreadth. The strike split and cratered the ground where he'd just been lying. Xavier saw the damage as he got to his feet. Though his awareness had returned and his vision was no longer clouded by that flash of white, he still felt a touch disorientated from what had happened to him.

A notification was awaiting his attention.

For a moment, he thought he didn't have time to read the notification. Then he realised his mind truly *was* in two parts. It was perhaps the strangest thing that he'd ever experienced.

But it was most definitely happening.

At the same time as his enemy came toward him, moving with a confidence that could only have been born from experience, and Xavier prepared to defend against the E Grade warrior, he read the notification.

You have learnt the skill Split Mind!
Split Mind − Rank 1
This is an epic skill that grants you the ability
to split your consciousness into multiple parts.
+1% Intelligence.
+1% Willpower.

Though Xavier couldn't say that he was impressed by the percentage modifiers the skill offered, he was surprised he'd gotten the skill at all. The moment the notification popped up, however, the pain that he'd been experiencing dulled.

It didn't disappear completely—it was definitely still there. But that pain was nowhere near as severe as it had been only moments ago.

Xavier turned the axe warrior's attack away with Soultaker. A physical block or parry usually wasn't his first choice—he tended to prefer to use Soul Block or throw a Heavy Telekinesis his enemy's way to stop them in their tracks. But the Heavy Telekinesis he'd sent against this golden-glowing bastard hadn't done a damned thing.

His arm shuddered under the strain of blocking the warrior's attack. Xavier glimpsed the man's eyes through the slit in his helm. They were *glowing*, just as Xavier's eyes sometimes glowed.

Though whereas Xavier eyes glowed silver, this man's glowed yellow.

What attribute is that?

He didn't know. But apparently, this warrior was incredibly resistant to magic.

Fortunately for Xavier, being resistant to magic didn't make one resistant to soul damage.

Xavier took a swift step back, waiting for Soul Strike to reach the end of its cooldown. It was only six seconds away. Six seconds until he could blast this warrior with as many souls as he had left in his reserve.

Only when Xavier stepped back, there was no longer any ground. It dropped away. His reflexes being as fast as they were, he shouldn't have lost his balance. But a rock suddenly jutted out, pushing his front foot *up*, making him fall straight backward.

Earth magic. This bastard has earth magic.

As he fell, Xavier spun so he could face the ground. He held Soultaker with one hand and was going to stop his fall with the other. Only he was falling straight into a hole that was larger than a two-storey house.

Once again, he wished he had some ability to fly like Justin. But he at least managed to reorient himself in the air enough to land in a crouch.

He sprinted for the wall of the hole, ready to leap at it and climb straight out and back up to the battlefield. Then a shadow fell over him. No... that wasn't a shadow.

The hole was closing.

Xavier was being buried alive.

Chapter 29
Buried Alive

First came the darkness. What had once been clear as day turned instantly to the blackest night. Then sound was muffled. The constant clash and rumble of the battlefield drifted away, like it was miles in the distance instead of a few feet above his head.

Though he could still hear low a rumble above him, the contrast made it feel like the deepest silence he'd ever experienced, after being in that battle for so long, wave after wave, for going on six weeks.

Dirt walloped him in the head, falling on all sides of him until he could barely move his limbs even with all the Strength he possessed. It got into his eyes. His ears. Up his nose and into his mouth. He tasted the grit. Smelled what it was.

The thought came unbidden. *It's not all dirt. It's the ashes of all those you've killed.*

He yelled at the top of his lungs but made nary a sound. If he could barely hear the enemy from down here, he doubted they could hear him stuck under the ground.

I'm being buried alive.

It certainly wasn't how he'd thought he'd go out.

The last thing to come was the lack of air. There simply wasn't any room for it. No matter how strong and powerful and tough his body had become, he still needed to breathe. He may have been superhuman, but he still had lungs. It was a weakness he hadn't even realised had been a weakness until that moment.

He breathed as shallowly as he could, spitting out the dirt and ash that gritted between his teeth. He struggled, trying to shove the dirt away or somehow climb out of this mess, but he wasn't able to.

That human warrior, the E Grade wave boss with the yellow glow about his golden armour... How was he able to perform earth magic? Shouldn't that only be something a mage could do?

Xavier shoved the thought aside. Even with his consciousness split as it currently was, he didn't have time for such contemplations. He needed to find a way out of here.

He had no idea how long he'd be able to hold his breath.

Trying to climb out of this wasn't the only thing he'd attempted. He'd thrown Heavy Telekinesis left, right, front, and back. At first, it made a small amount of room for him to move in, but that room didn't last long as more dirt kept falling down from above, filling the holes he'd just created.

All he was doing was making the dirt and ash down here denser, making it more difficult for him to move. He tried to shove the dirt *up* with the spell, but that wasn't working either. Something was blocking him.

The E Grade boss.

Xavier didn't know how much time was passing. Felt like every second was an age. His lungs hadn't started burning yet. That was good. But he knew they would soon. He racked his mind, trying to think of a solution to this mess.

Heavy Telekinesis seemed like the only useful spell to him right now, yet it wasn't doing anything to help. After he'd failed to push the dirt and ash out of the way, he thought to use it downward, to harden the ground beneath his feet in an attempt to push off it. If he could do that, maybe he could climb out of the ground inch by inch.

But it was slow going, and there was a pressure atop him that kept shoving him farther down into the earth, eradicating any progress he made.

His mind turned over all the other spells he possessed.

Soul Strike and Soul Block simply aren't useful. Not here. Soul Strike's apparitions don't interact with matter. They harm the enemy by moving through them. Soul Block won't help either. There are no attacks for me to block.

He even tested the spell, just in case, wondering if the dirt and ash crushing down on him would be considered an attack, as he'd only gotten into this situation because of the E Grade's earth magic.

Unfortunately, his suspicions had been correct—it did nothing to help him.

Spiritual Trifecta makes me stronger, my mind calmer, but it isn't enough to get me out of here. Being stronger doesn't seem to help. And it doesn't matter how calm I am. If I can't breathe, it will still mean my death.

He still used the spell. Helping his mind remain calm would hopefully at least help him come up with a way out of this.

Spirit Break, Spirit Infusion, Soul Harvest, Soul Harden... all of these spells were at Rank 50, yet they were completely useless. To him.

And his last spell: Willpower Infusion...

He hadn't been able to control the E Grade wave boss. The man had simply been too strong. His mental defences were impenetrable—at least, impenetrable to him.

Xavier struggled, angling his head upward. He could no longer see the auras of these enemies. They were high-enough level to have control over their auras. Especially the E Grade wave boss.

He *could* send Soul Strikes through the earth and up at his enemies. If he infused enough souls into the spell, it might be enough to kill the boss—assuming he *hit* the boss without being able to aim.

It could work, but it would also kill all the enemies around the wave boss...

Willpower Infusion.

The spell entered his mind again. It might not be effective against the wave boss, but that didn't mean it wasn't still useful.

What if he used the other enemies in the area to his advantage? He could easily control them, after all. That, in fact, would be child's play.

Xavier, still trying his hardest not to breathe in the dirt and ash, holding his breath, as well as he could, forced a smile onto his face. A plan was forming in his mind. This situation he'd gotten himself into—it felt impossible.

There were parts of his mind that were screaming out at him, begging him to get help from his party members. Even if they weren't strong enough to fight the wave—and they certainly weren't strong enough to fight the wave *boss*—Siobhan could use her Summon spell to teleport him out of danger.

But if Siobhan used a single spell on him, Xavier would no longer be considered soloing the floor. Besides, he didn't *need* help. He could do this on his own.

He shoved those thoughts away. Shoved the fear away. Fear, as natural as it was, wouldn't serve him right now.

Xavier couldn't see the purple mist that flowed out of his staff and seeped through the dirt and ash that was piled above and all around him. But he knew it was pouring out from his staff. He could feel the energy rise. It wasn't stopped by something as simple as the earth. His eyes shut, he imagined it coming off the ground like steam off a hot surface.

It touched several minds. It would have invaded through mouths, noses, ears. Anything it could get through. He felt the energy latch onto at least a dozen of them. Without being able to see what was going on from down there, it was difficult to give them commands.

But there were some things he could tell them to do.

Free me, he willed through the lines connecting him to his enemies—no. Not his enemies. Right now, they were his thralls. *Free me from the ground.*

Almost instantly, the connection to two of the thralls was cut off. His spell hadn't been defeated. He knew this feeling—the thralls had been killed. The human warrior with the earth magic would have seen what they were doing.

The other thralls he was connected to died as well. Their deaths were swift. The abrupt slicing of the connection stabbed at Xavier's mind. The mental anguish became physical, hurting his head. But the pain was nothing like what he'd felt when he'd split his mind in two.

In mere seconds, his plan had failed.

But failure was only something that could stop you if you let it. Xavier was still alive—even if he wasn't breathing. He could feel the sting in his lungs now. It was a dull throb. Nowhere near the most painful thing he'd experienced. But it wasn't a good sign. Lack of oxygen did terrible things to a human's body and mind. He just hoped none of that would happen quick enough to stop him.

He counted down the seconds until Willpower Infusion reached the end of its cooldown. Again, each second passed in an age to him. An eternity under all that dirt and ash—that was what he'd spend down here if he let this kill him. It would truly become his grave.

He wasn't going to let that happen.

Once more, he thought to use Soul Strike. Thought to target the enemy above. But he'd only have one chance at it. If the spell didn't work, the E Grade wave boss wouldn't stick around in the same place to get hit a second time.

Then how would he be able to target it from down here? He wouldn't need to be directly above Xavier to keep him in this damned grave.

Think, think, think.

As calm as he tried to be, Xavier felt panic beginning to set in. Usually, to calm his mind, he would do the breathing exercises associated with his Meditation skill.

That clearly wasn't an option right now.

His body was tense. His chest tight. The thudding of his heart reverberated in his ears.

Focus. Xavier forced his body to relax. His fingers clutched Soultaker's shaft—he couldn't even move the weapon, as densely packed as the earth was around him. He loosened his grip. His other hand was clenched in a fist. He forced the tension away.

Forced it out of every inch of him he could.

His lungs burned. More and more as each second passed.

The pain might not mean much to him compared to other things he'd endured. But the pain was a warning he couldn't ignore.

Willpower Infusion finally reached the end of its cooldown. Xavier almost cast the spell instantly, then thought better of it. His first plan hadn't worked. It had been thwarted almost instantly. If he were going to get out of this—and he *was* going to get out of this —he needed to come up with something better.

The Willpower Infusion spell was still his best bet.

Focus.

Xavier cast the spell again. Purple mist seeped through the dirt and ash and rose through the earth until it came off the ground. It sought the nearest mind and hit a wall—the E Grade boss—but instead of pushing it, Xavier made the mist seek another victim.

A *single* victim.

He could spread out the spell and take control of more minds, but the more minds he controlled the more tenuous his connection to them. Willpower Infusion had gained several ranks since the last time he'd used it to control a single lower-level soldier of the Endless Horde.

His mind was still split. His head throbbed once more with the strain of keeping that going. It wanted to snap back together. Become one. It *begged* to be whole.

Xavier gritted his teeth. Tasted the ash. Then forced his jaw to relax. He had to remain calm. As calm as he could.

The purple mist found its next victim, clutching onto a weak mind. The line between Xavier and his new thrall snapped into place. The strongest connection he'd ever possessed with one of his thralls.

And he was about to make it stronger. At least, that was the plan.

Xavier had no idea if this would work. No idea if the thrall would even *live* long enough for him to try this. He didn't command the thrall to move. He just let it stand there, hoping that would stop the E Grade wave boss from killing it like it had the others.

Then Xavier shoved one half of his split consciousness into the thrall's mind.

Chapter 30
Split Mind

Xavier briefly glimpsed the notification that popped up in his vision. Willpower Infusion had ranked up by *three* the instant one part of his split consciousness had slammed into the thrall he was now controlling.

God, this is weird. Xavier had been through a lot of weird stuff since he'd been integrated into the System. He'd been yanked from his normal life. Taken to the void and judged. He'd killed countless enemies, reaped countless souls, and now he was controlling another being from inside that being's head.

The worst part of what he was doing was the disorientation.

Having his mind split in two when it was inside of his own body was one thing.

Having it split into two different *places*? Well, that was another thing entirely.

Xavier's instinct, which had been long ingrained in him, was to take deep breaths to calm down and deal with what he was going through. But that wasn't an option—not in his own body. His lungs were burning, more and more as each second went by. And there was absolutely no air around him.

Inside the soldier he'd hijacked, it was a different story. As strange as it was, Xavier made the soldier take three deep breaths.

It helped.

His focus grew. And as he released the third breath, he received another notification.

Split Mind has reached Rank 2!

The difference that one rank made—or maybe the calming of his mind—was stark and instantaneous. Xavier moved the soldier's body until he was facing the E Grade wave boss. Laying eyes on the beast of a man with his golden full-plate armour made fear blossom in his chest.

Xavier frowned. No. Fear didn't blossom in *Xavier's* chest—it blossomed in the chest of the soldier he inhabited. Not only was he controlling the man, his consciousness was *inside* the soldier's body —which gave him an insight he'd never had before. It wasn't just that he could see through the man's eyes. He could *feel* what the man was feeling.

And part of that was his unbridled fear at facing the E Grade wave boss.

That fear seeped its way into Xavier's mind, trying to batter at his confidence. Trying to overwhelm his own emotions.

I can't face that E Grade. He's too powerful, and I'm stuck underground, completely defenceless. There's nothing I can do down here.

Xavier gritted his teeth. No, he didn't grit *his own* teeth. He gritted the teeth of the man he inhabited. Another strange sensation, but he was beginning to get the hang of it. He couldn't let the man's fear get to him. Fear, like any emotion, was just that—*an emotion.*

We can't choose the emotions we feel. All we can do is choose how we respond to those emotions.

The first part of that—not being able to choose one's emotions—was more true now for Xavier than it had ever been before.

These emotions aren't even mine.

Now that he had a good view of his enemy, Xavier could cast Soul Strike on the E Grade Wave boss.

Except Xavier could feel that he was slowly losing consciousness. It was hard to tell that the area around him—around *his own* body—back in the ground was dimming, what with it being pitch black. But his mind... *that* was beginning to dim. Spots of white floating about his vision, just about the only damned things he was able to see.

And his lungs. God, his *lungs*. It felt as though someone had jammed a dagger into each one and was wiggling the blades around, trying to make him feel the most amount of pain possible. He was holding his breath, for there was nothing to breathe, but that was getting harder and harder to manage.

Push through it. You didn't come this far to get buried alive and die. You didn't get this far to fail.

He'd blown through every roadblock he'd come to. Gotten passed each obstacle. Each apparent dead end.

He would get through this one.

Xavier cast Soul Strike. He had 821 souls in his reserve, and he used *every single one of them*.

It was everything he had, and it would mean that—even if he managed to reap more souls from underground—he wouldn't be able to recast the spell for almost fourteen minutes.

And he doubted he'd survive that long if this didn't work.

The E Grade wave boss stepped toward the soldier that half of Xavier's consciousness currently controlled. Through the slit in his helm, Xavier could see only anger. The man would have seen the purple mist envelope and enter the soldier.

Xavier didn't move a muscle. All he did was track the E Grade's movement with his eyes as the massive soul apparition materialised and rose up from the ground.

Whenever Xavier used Soul Strike with the souls of different humanoid soldiers or different beasts mixed in against a single target, rather than splitting up the souls to cause area-of-effect damage, the soul apparition would appear as something that looked unholy and terrifying—an amalgamation of the different souls he'd consumed. Extra limbs and heads and muscles in strange places. Wolven teeth and claws and tails.

It was one such apparition that he watched now.

A thought struck him. *What happens if this soldier dies while part of my mind is inside of it?*

It was a question he really didn't want the answer to.

A moment before the E Grade warrior made it to the soldier, the soul apparition soared through him. The power of 821 souls was immense. It wasn't *all* the power Xavier could field—in fact, it was less than *half*—but it was all the power he could field *right now*. It brought the man to his knees. Xavier could practically see the man's health draining before his eyes.

But it wasn't gone completely.

He still lived, and Xavier's reserve of souls had just been depleted. The pit inside of him widened, feeling as empty as it ever had. His lungs felt as though they were being stabbed, over and over and over, the blades twisting.

The world was dimming, even through the eyes of the soldier he possessed.

The E Grade warrior rose to his feet, an intense look of concentration burning in his eyes. A power seemed to overtake the man. The glow about him didn't change—it was the same yellow as before. But that wasn't what Xavier was feeling.

Then it clicked—the E Grade warrior was unleashing its aura.

Xavier felt a weakness in the body he possessed. With that weakness came a compulsion to do whatever the man in front of him wished. He was flooded with the need to *comply*.

Normally, Xavier doubted something like this would impact his ability to control one of his thralls with Willpower Infusion. But this wasn't at all normal. With half of Xavier's conscious mind inside of the thrall, that need to *obey* flooded into him.

This would have been the perfect moment to attach the E Grade warrior. In fact, he'd been about to make the thrall do just that. It was clear, even with the E Grade warrior standing and looking as powerful as he was, that the man had been gravely wounded by the Soul Strike.

But every moment that passed would give him an opportunity to heal.

A potion appeared inside the E Grade warrior's hand, as though from nowhere. Xavier made the thrall blink without even thinking to. The E Grade wore gauntlets. Beneath those gauntlets, however, he must be wearing a Storage Ring.

Xavier had been surprised that none of the enemies he'd faced in the previous waves had possessed Storage Rings—at least none of them that he'd checked. And the Endless Horde didn't seem worried about gathering resources from their own dead. They didn't pick the bodies for coin, weapons, or armour. They simply destroyed them, burning them to ash piles.

Think, think, think.

The E Grade pulled the cork off the health potion with his teeth, spitting it onto the ground, then he brought the bottle up to his lips. It felt as though it were happening in slow motion, despite the speed of the E Grade's movements.

If that bastard warrior drank that potion, that would be the end. Xavier would die, the ground on this alien planet in a whole different universe would become his eternal resting place. His party would return to the Tower of Champions without him. Maybe they, and the other Champions, would be enough to save Earth. Maybe they wouldn't.

Either way, he wouldn't be there to see it.

No. Xavier lungs burned. *I won't die. I could recast Willpower Infusion. Get word to my party...* The world dimmed ever more. *Siobhan... could get me out... use her Summon spell... Couldn't she?*

He didn't know. Maybe the range was too far. Maybe he was kidding himself.

Xavier pushed at the mind of the thrall he inhabited. The aura's compulsion dimmed, then disappeared. He made the man burst forward and thrust his sword right into the E Grade's hand. The E Grade—clearly overconfident—had shut his eyes briefly, probably in anticipation of tasting the health potion that was less than a centimetre from touching his lips.

The E Grade cursed. He also stumbled backward. For an F Grade warrior as weak as the one Xavier was controlling to be able to make an E Grade stumble?

The E Grade must be truly weakened by my Soul Strike. It's only standing through sheer force of will.

But the sword point hadn't even made it through the gauntlet. It had just made a loud metallic clink on impact.

Xavier didn't let up. He pushed the thrall forward. And he wasn't simply commanding the thrall to attack. He *was* the thrall, controlling every single one of its motions, not merely sending it orders.

He made the thrall thrust, slash, and finally *kick* the weakened E Grade warrior in the chest. The warrior stumbled backward and actually fell to the ground—the ground that Xavier was buried beneath.

Suddenly, the pain in Xavier's lungs peaked, then dulled completely.

He could no longer feel himself—only the thrall he inhabited.

The sensation was even stranger than having his consciousness split and being in two places at once.

My body's unconscious. All I have is the thrall I'm in. And Willpower Infusion could end at any moment.

Chapter 31
A Puff for the Fallen

THUMP, THUMP, THUMP.

Xavier felt his heartbeat. It was the only damned thing he could feel from his own body. Not that he knew how that could be possible.

He could also feel that it was slowing.

Thump... thump... thump...

He couldn't access his health, not with his body unconscious. He couldn't use any of his own spells. Couldn't bring up any System notifications at all.

Xavier could still barely believe it. That the thing that was about to do him in had been *dirt* and *ash*. He recalled when he'd been sucked into the ground by the Rat King on the second floor of the Tower of Champions.

That mistake had almost gotten his party killed. This mistake? Was about to get *him* killed.

Kill... kill... kill...

It was the one word that kept repeating in his mind. The part of his mind that was still awake. The line of Willpower Energy that was keeping him connected to the thrall was thinning. And danger was mounting. There were hundreds of soldiers around the thrall and the E Grade. Soldiers that had, up till now, been standing back.

But something told Xavier they wouldn't hesitate for much longer.

His thrall stood over the E Grade warrior, who lay on his back after being kicked to the ground. The sword the thrall held hadn't been able to penetrate the E Grade's armour.

But there was a slit in the man's helm. The slit the man looked through. Xavier could see the E Grade's eyes. He made the thrall flip the sword around into a reverse grip, blade down.

He sank to his knees and slammed the sword's point straight through the helm's slit and into the E Grade warrior's right eye.

Xavier couldn't see the kill notification, but he knew it must have come. The body of the E Grade warrior went completely limp, the life draining from his one remaining eye.

The thrall released his grip on the sword's hilt and leant back. Killing the E Grade... had done nothing. It wasn't as though the wave boss would bring Xavier enough Mastery Points for him to gain a level—and the instant health regeneration that would bring.

Xavier was still unconscious, deep in the ground, unable to free himself.

The soldiers around the thrall finally acted. They sprang forward. A half-dozen blades pierced the thrall's body. A scream died in the thrall's throat as blood gurgled from it.

Xavier felt the thrall's death. He tried to break the connection between himself and the soldier, but it was no use. His conscious mind in his own body was no longer able to *control* it. Just as he couldn't cast any spells, neither could he dispel any.

He'd thought he'd felt pain. Thought he'd felt agony. Splitting his mind had been the worst of it. But this? The death of the soldier, as blades slipped in and out of his body, digging through his armour as though it weren't there, piercing organs and arteries?

God... *This* was pain.

The thrall died, and Xavier felt as though it was his own death. *It will be my death... soon...*

The half of his consciousness that was in the soldier snapped back to his body.

The world went black.

Siobhan gripped the stone parapet. Her hands were clenched so tight that her knuckles had gone white, making the freckles dotting her skin even more prominent. "I need to summon him back," she said, not for the first time. "He's going to die under there."

Adviser Kalren had his hands folded behind his back. His posture was straight, dignified. But Siobhan had spent enough time with the man to know when he was afraid. It was all in his eyes. "I think you are right."

"Do it," Queen Alastea said. It was hard not to hear it as a command. Though her voice, right now, was not that of a royal. It was strained. She, too, was afraid. If Xavier failed, she would soon die.

Though Siobhan didn't think it was only fear for herself that made the woman's voice strain.

She's grown to care for Xavier.

Howard stood at her other side. The tall, broad man's face was that of stone, his expression hard to read. He must have developed quite the poker face in his previous line of work. "Not yet."

"I can feel his health. Even from here." It was a benefit of her healing spell—it let her feel the health of those in her party. Let her know when they were in danger. Xavier's health had been fine, even as he'd been trapped underground. But it was falling fast. *He can't hold his breath anymore. It's been too long. Even for him.* She bit her lip. "I have to do something, Howard."

"Look!" Justin pointed at one of the soldiers. A small ring had formed around where Xavier had been buried alive. Only the E Grade wave boss stood atop the earth.

A nearby soldier was engulfed with Xavier's purple mist.

"He's still conscious," Justin said. "He still has a chance."

"The last time he controlled soldiers, they all met their deaths in seconds," Howard grumbled. "Now he's trying to control a single one? Don't see how *that* will work."

There was something strange about the way this soldier moved. The way it tilted its head and stared at the E Grade warrior. As though Xavier's control of it was more... complete?

It moves like Xavier moves.

Siobhan had no idea what that would mean, though she worried Howard's words would be the truth of things.

Then a Soul Strike rose from the ground. The apparition was a mutated amalgamation of different beasts and humanoid Denizens. It looked terrifying. Horrendous. Powerful.

And there was an odd beauty to it, too. Perhaps that beauty was simply in its sheer power.

He's still in the fight.

Moments later, the E Grade warrior was taken to its knees. The soldier stabbed a sword through the slit in its eyes.

"Yes!" Howard pumped his fist, his expression no longer so stony.

Then the soldier Xavier possessed died, and the battlefield became silent. They stared at the mound for what felt like an eternity, waiting for Xavier to climb out.

All the while, Siobhan felt his health creeping further down by the second.

She willed her staff out of her Storage Ring and clutched it as tightly as she'd just clutched the wall. "Time... time to summon him back."

Howard put a hand on her wrist, nodding to the dirt where Xavier had been buried. "Wait."

Mariad rested his spear on his shoulder and let out a sigh, looking down at the dead wave boss and the fellow soldier he'd just had to help kill. He spat on the ground beside them, then he took a pipe from beneath his armour and sparked a flame inside of it with a small magical device he'd picked up in Deveral.

A puff for the fallen.

He didn't really care about the dead soldier. Or the wave boss, for that matter. But he'd thought he would die today. Having a puff from the pipe seemed the right thing to do.

He brought up the Quest Log they all shared.

Quest Log
Current Quest: Clear this world of all inhabitants so it can be claimed for the Endless Horde.
To receive a bonus reward, secure the death of Queen Kiralla Alastea of Arala.
Before the Endless Horde may breach the castle's walls, all Champions of the Void on the battlefield must be slain. If there are no Champions of the Void on the battlefield, the walls may be breached.
Champions on the battlefield: 1

Mariad frowned, not bothering to read the list of rewards and bonus rewards that followed. He was confused about something.

Why did it still list a Champion of the Void on the battlefield? He should be dead. No one can survive down there... Can they?

He looked down at the ground, his pipe sagging from his mouth. He crouched, touched his free hand to the dirt, and closed his eyes.

Something was shifting beneath the dirt and ash.

Oh, shi—

At first, Xavier thought the darkness he was experiencing was death. It would only make sense, considering he'd just died.

No. I didn't die. That was the thrall I was inhabiting.

It had sure *felt* like his death.

Was he dreaming? About to die, for real this time?

Then pain hit him. The burning in his lungs. His eyes widened.

He was conscious! Still buried underground—that was why it was so damned dark—but *conscious!*

For the moment, his frantic mind didn't worry about *how* he was conscious, he simply took advantage of it. Now that the E Grade warrior was dead, the man would no longer be able to use his earth magic to keep Xavier down here.

Xavier launched a Heavy Telekinesis straight upward. The earth above him shifted.

He did it again.

And again.

And again.

Light fell on his face. He gasped in a breath of air. It tasted awful. Of sweat, death, ash, and blood. And all manner of things that littered a battlefield when bodies died—things he would rather not ponder. But that didn't matter. Even with how awful it was, it was still the sweetest breath he'd ever taken.

With that breath his health began to regenerate once more.

And with the second breath, the pain in his lungs became more bearable.

With each breath, the pain dulled more. With each breath, he clawed his way out of the ground.

Another Heavy Telekinesis pushed more dirt away. Shed more light into his vision. He narrowed his eyes to it, more from reflex than actual need. Soldiers of the Endless Horde crowded around the hole above him. He had no idea how long it would be until the next wave came.

But it didn't matter—he was still alive.

Once more, he'd survived.

That was when it hit him. The *reason* he'd lived. Down in the ground, he'd fallen unconscious—but it had only been *half* of his mind that had done so. He still felt that half, slowly coming to the more he drew breath.

The other half? It had been safe, stowed away in the thrall's head.

If I hadn't split my mind, none of this would have been possible.

And then that made him wonder... What might be possible in the future?

Chapter 32
Just Following Orders

For a moment, Xavier thought he might be hallucinating.

The first enemy he saw as he climbed out of that hole in the ground was a soldier with a scraggly beard smoking... a pipe? The man was backing away, eyes wide, the pipe sagging from his mouth.

The man had a spear resting on his shoulder. He shrugged it up, spinning it until the blade faced Xavier.

Xavier sighed. He tried not to think about the individual soldiers in the mess of the Endless Horde. Tried not to think about what kind of people they might be when they weren't on the battlefield. In a way, these people were just doing their jobs.

Half a sector of people, just doing their jobs.

But he also knew that *just doing their jobs* and *just following orders* were excuses many people had used in Earth's history to commit horrible atrocities and not hold themselves accountable. Each of the soldiers in the Endless Horde had a choice, even if they didn't *believe* they had a choice, they did.

They came here to kill innocent people. Whatever Queen Alastea's ancestors had done to piss them off, they weren't even alive anymore. Their descendants shouldn't be punished for something that wasn't even their fault.

And these soldiers Xavier faced? They were on the wrong side of the conflict.

I shouldn't need to justify why I'm fighting these people—why I'm protecting the queen. I'll need to do far worse than this in the future.

Xavier gripped Soul Reaper tight as the soldier thrust his spear toward him. He sidestepped the strike with ease, and then, with one clean swipe, he cut the man's head off. On its way to the ground, the pipe separated from the head, trailing smoke through the air.

Though it might not be necessary, a part of Xavier was glad he felt the need to justify his actions. And that same part worried about what might happen if he ever *stopped* feeling the need to do so—especially with how many years he was likely to live.

Because however he justified destroying the Endless Horde, he knew for a fact that he wasn't doing it out of simple altruism. He wasn't doing it to save Queen Alastea—at least, that wasn't *the only* reason he was doing it.

He wanted power. Needed it.

The more he gained—the more powerful he became—the more he desired it. In a way, it felt as though it were an addiction. Which was something that should probably worry him. But it didn't.

It emboldened him.

If I'm going to be addicted to anything in the Greater Universe, getting stronger sounds like the smartest thing to choose.

Now he'd defeated the E Grade wave boss, that warrior with the earth magic who'd trapped him deep underground, bringing him the closest to death he'd perhaps ever been since the first floor, it didn't take long for Xavier to deal with the rest of the wave.

He returned to the wall with a plan. His mind was still split. The half that had been unconscious had been fully awake and thinking a mile a minute after he'd climbed free of the ground.

He knew exactly how he was going to tackle the next few waves, and what he was going to do during them.

Strength, Speed, and Toughness. Those were the three attributes that were keeping him from taking the next step. For each one, he would need to develop skills and assimilate into himself different materials if he were going to break the 1000-point attribute threshold, then push to E Grade, and finally destroy the Endless Horde.

Not to mention get himself off this rock and through the next floors.

Earth's waiting for me.

Earth wouldn't be defenceless without its Champions—but it would be close enough.

When Xavier returned to the wall, Siobhan embraced him. The hug came out of nowhere. It took him a moment to hug her back with his free arm, the other holding Soultaker.

She stepped back and gave him a sniff.

Xavier raised an eyebrow at her. The other members of his party, along with Adviser Kalren and Queen Alastea, were arrayed around him in a semi-circle. "Concerned about me, were you?"

"I almost summoned you back a hundred times." Siobhan bit her lip. Her eyes were watery, but no tears fell. "If I waited too long... and you'd died..." She creased her forehead, dropping her gaze to the stone floor. "It would have been my fault."

Xavier put a hand on her shoulder and squeezed. "No. It wouldn't have been your fault." He dropped his hand and looked at the others. "It would have been mine."

Queen Alastea looked as though she wanted to say something. Her lips parted, but no words escaped them.

"Glad you survived that." Howard shook his head. "Don't know how you keep managing it."

Xavier grinned. "I split my mind in half and put part of it into an enemy soldier." He went on to explain the rest of what had happened.

His mind—though aching something fierce—was still split in

two. He knew how to make it whole again. He could feel the mental mechanism. His mind *wanted* to be as one. So really, it would take less effort to bring the two halves back together than it was to keep sustaining them apart.

His mind could use the rest. But rest was something he didn't have the luxury of partaking in.

So, while he spoke to the others, he did what he'd been unable to do on the battlefield. He consumed another Wolven Fang and underwent the process of assimilating the material for a second time.

Though he worried going through this process would do nothing for him, at least there was no harm in trying.

Nothing but a little bit of wasted time and energy.

He tossed the fang into his mouth like it was a piece of popcorn and he was at the movies. He swallowed the fang. Felt it scrape his throat and journey down to his stomach. Like the last times he'd swallowed Wolven Fangs, it didn't go down easy. But he was getting used to the unpleasant sensation.

This was what he'd been trying to do when he first split his mind. Before the E Grade warrior had attacked him and buried him alive.

At least that bastard got what was coming to him.

Xavier frowned at the thought that had just slipped through his mind. It was more... spiteful than he usually felt when fighting against enemies. No. Spiteful wasn't the right word. It was more... *personal.*

He didn't know if that was a good thing or not.

Xavier let the thought and his feelings around it drift away and focused on the task at hand. At least, he focused on the task with one part of his mind. The other was still engaged in conversation.

"If it is time for you and your party to abandon my queendom, I will understand." Queen Alastea lowered her head, her expression hidden in shadow but easy enough for Xavier to read.

She's afraid.

The thought felt like an obvious one. Of course the woman was afraid. Xavier had only just been contemplating his own death, as he'd been buried alive. His lungs in intense agony. And when that thrall he'd been inhabiting had died—that was when it had hit him the most.

Xavier was willing to risk his life for what he was trying to achieve. Both here and when he finally returned to Earth. But death? Death was still as terrifying a prospect as ever.

"I'm not leaving," Xavier said, his voice steel. The determination he'd felt before—to destroy the Endless Horde—hadn't simply disappeared because he'd almost died. If anything, it burned even brighter than it had before.

The woman nodded. She brightened slightly, though there was a tightness around her eyes that showed the fear was still there.

Xavier didn't continue to reassure the woman. He couldn't help but feel a little guilty that his determination to take down the Endless Horde wasn't because he wished to save her. Well, he *did* wish to save her. But, perhaps more than that, he wanted to achieve the impossible. He wanted to grow more powerful. And Earth was his true concern.

Attempting to assimilate *Wolven Fang* into muscular structure...

The material you are assimilating has various properties. However, as you have already assimilated a single property of the Wolven Fang into your muscular structure, you may only draw on that property.

Assimilation is complete.
Biological impurities of *Wolven Fang* have been further assimilated into muscular structure. You have gained +2 Strength!

As the notifications popped up, Xavier blinked. Two Strength didn't seem like a great deal, but it was a whole lot more than nothing, which was exactly what he was "gaining" by not being able to level.

He also noticed that his second assimilation of the Wolven Fang hadn't brought him another rank.

But consuming more of the same material can increase the attribute...

Even if it was only by a little bit, Xavier thought about the possible limitations of the skill. How many different materials would he ultimately be able to assimilate into his body? Would assimilating those things into him change him somehow? Other than only his attributes.

He had a vision of himself consuming thousands of different components that had been dismantled from thousands of different beasts, and finally transforming into some sort of beast himself. As he thought about this, he ran his tongue across his teeth.

Had they become sharper than before? Were they... longer? He was sure that a slight silvery shade had come over his body when he'd assimilated crucible steel, but it was difficult to remember exactly how long and sharp his teeth had been.

The more he thought about it and tested them, the more they felt wrong. But that could have easily been because he was focusing on them to a high degree.

Back when he'd been a teenager, he'd once thought a bump had randomly appeared at the base of his skill. He'd been so focused on it that he'd had the fear that it might be some kind of tumour. Turns out it had always been there, and he just hadn't paid any attention to it.

My teeth are probably exactly as they've always been... But should I measure them? Before assimilating more of these Wolven Fangs?

It felt a little ridiculous to do something like that. He smirked to himself. He'd keep an eye on it, but he doubted his idea had any weight. And he certainly wasn't about to start measuring his teeth.

I suppose I'll find out in time if doing this changes me in unexpected ways...

Chapter 33
Here Goes Nothing

Running has reached Rank 13!
Running has reached Rank 14!
Running has reached Rank 15!

Biological impurities of *Wolven Fang* have been further assimilated into muscular structure.
You have gained +2 Strength!
...
You have gained +2 Strength!
...
You have gained +2 Strength!

Attempting to assimilate *Wolven Claw* into muscular structure...

Assimilation is complete.
Biological impurities of *Wolven Claw* have been assimilated into muscular structure.
You have gained +10 Speed!

Assimilate Properties has reached Rank 3!

Biological impurities of *Wolven Claw* have been further assimilated into muscular structure. You have gained +2 Speed!

...

You have gained +2 Speed!

Attempting to assimilate *Sandstone* into muscular structure...

THE NEXT FEW WAVES WERE SURPRISINGLY UNEVENTFUL. Xavier kept pushing his skills, further and further. As he did, he tried to think of new skills that he could develop—but mostly he was focused on the materials he could use, as that seemed easier to juggle while in combat. Taking a quick moment to swallow something, then guiding the process with half of his mind was easier than developing an entirely new skill, after all.

Justin had dismantled the Bear King, the epic wave boss, after Xavier had lent him his scythe-staff. Once completed, he'd handed Xavier the different materials salvaged from the wave boss's body. But Xavier didn't feel as though he was ready to try assimilating the materials yet. He worried that it would be a waste. If he tried to assimilate them before his skill was a high-enough rank to facilitate it, his body might simply reject the impurities, pushing them out through the pores of his skin.

Or the impurities might be too potent for me to reject.

He didn't know what would happen if *that* ended up being the case, and he'd rather not find out.

So Xavier gritted his teeth and pushed on, finding other ways and other things to build up the skill.

First, he discovered that the most valuable usage of the skill was assimilating a new material. Whenever he assimilated a new material, it would add ten points to whatever attribute that property benefited—and it would gain him a new rank.

Whenever he gained a new rank in Assimilate Properties, he would gain a further two points toward each property he'd assimilated—these two attribute points, he found, weren't mentioned when he assimilated a new property. For instance, when he'd assimilated the Wolven Claw, the notification said it added ten points to his speed. But when he'd checked the skill's information, which had been at Rank 3, it showed fourteen points in Speed.

That, he thought, was very interesting.

If I can somehow push this skill to the max F Grade rank of 50, then the ranks alone will add ninety-eight attribute points.

Though he still wished the skill gave him percentage modifiers, he was starting to realise how powerful it could become. On top of that, he was wondering if there might be any downsides to assimilating all these different things into his body.

It didn't take him long to start swallowing chunks of stone that he'd broken off the battlements for this very reason. Not the first time he'd swallowed stone. This time, however, he managed to succeed with assimilating the chunks, bringing up his Toughness attribute.

That was a definite boon. He'd worried he'd only be able to boost an attribute with a single material, but here he was boosting Toughness with both crucible steel *and* sandstone. It was a very, *very* good breakthrough.

Though something strange had happened. After assimilating the sandstone, he could have sworn his skin had become a little *greyer*. Perhaps he was getting paranoid. Seeing things he expected to see rather than things that were actually there. But the more he assimilated different things into his body, the less sure of that he became.

While fighting through these waves and gaining as much downtime as he could in between them, he hit a slight dead end with the materials he'd been using so far. Well, admittedly, it was more than slight. It was a *complete* dead end. After assimilating a property into his body a total of ten times—the initial time, plus nine more times—he hadn't yet managed to *keep* assimilating it.

Which meant he'd hit a limit—each property that he'd assimilated offered him only thirty-four stat points. At least until he brought the skill above Rank 4.

He brought up his stats, singling out his Strength, Speed, and Toughness to see how much progress he was making.

Strength: 569 (768)
Speed: 558 (837)
Toughness: 603 (814)

It still wasn't close enough to what he needed it to be, but at least he'd made some progress.

When his next level-up finally came, after taking out a few more waves and E Grade enemies, he couldn't help himself—he jumped into the air and pumped his fist.

He'd expected to be excited when he gained a new level. But this was more. He was *elated*. Adrenaline ran through his entire body. Suddenly, everything he'd been through during all these damned endless waves felt even more worth it.

It felt like a very long time since he'd gained his last level. When the Mastery Points he received had stalled, a small part of him had wondered if he'd ever level up again. Though he'd known it was a foolish thought, it had been a thought he couldn't help having.

That was why he unleashed an excited "whoop!" as his fist thrust high into the air on the apex of his jump.

He'd just defeated some hydra-type beast with heads that kept regenerating. The damned thing had been a wave boss, and the toughest beast he'd come up against so far. Each of the three heads had been capable of casting a different element. Fire, water, air. Whenever they opened their giant maws, one of these three elements would shoot out. It had even been able to turn the water to ice, once freezing him where he stood.

He'd had to decapitate each head *fifteen times* before the bastard thing died. Controlling the beast with Willpower Infusion hadn't been incredibly effective, either. It wasn't that the beast had been resistant to the spell—something he was eternally grateful for —it was that he could only control a single head at a time. Which begged a lot of questions.

Do each of those three heads act individually from one another?

Either way, it was enough to give him the upper hand during the fight.

His eyes skimmed the notification.

Congratulations, you have reached Level 61!
Your health has been regenerated by 70%!
Your Spirit Energy limit has increased by 200!
You have received +2 Strength, +2 Toughness,
+2 Speed, +3 Intelligence, +3 Willpower, and
+8 Spirit!
You have received +20 free stat points!
All your spells have refreshed and are no longer
on cooldown!

Although his level-up didn't bring a great deal of points to the three attributes he needed to advance the most right now, they did bring *something*. Not to mention the twenty free points he could now assign.

He distributed them, throwing all twenty straight into Strength. *Two points away from 800.*

Xavier drew in a deep breath. Not enough, no. But definite progress.

He looked down at the beast he'd just slain and tilted his head to the side. E Grades were getting easier and easier for him to kill. The sides of his lips tweaked upward in a small smirk. This mission of his. The one he was so determined to complete. The one that should be impossible. Defeating the Endless Horde, and the D Grade that headed it...

It was becoming more and more within reach.

He touched a hand to the Elemental Hydra—what the kill notification had said it was called—and deposited the massive beast into his Storage Ring. Then he went around, gathering all its decapitated heads. Whatever material this thing was made of... he could make use of it.

This was the first E Grade beast he'd encountered since the Bear King. It didn't have the Epic tag on it, though it had still been formidable. He wondered if the materials salvaged from this beast would be easier for him to assimilate than the ones from the Bear King.

Will higher-grade materials give me more attributes?

It was a thought that kept coming to him. One he couldn't shake. He also had equipment from other E Grade wave bosses he'd defeated. None of the equipment was something he or the others could wield, but that didn't mean it wouldn't come in handy... The only problem there was that none of them were able to actually *dismantle* the equipment. He couldn't chip shards of metal off the swords or spears or armour. He could dent them. He could even puncture them. But he couldn't *slice*—which meant he couldn't ingest any of the materials. And the System had prevented him from using the E Grade weapons he'd salvaged for that purpose.

Something to put on the backburner.

The wave complete, Xavier returned to the battlements. Night had fallen once more. Justin was the only one waiting for him—the others were getting some rest. He couldn't help but feel a little envious of that.

"What the hell was that beast you fought?" Justin asked. He'd been leaning over the parapet so far that he was practically hanging off it.

I suppose if he falls, he could just fly back.

"An Elemental Hydra." Xavier withdrew it from his Storage Ring, placing it straight in the middle of the battlements. The beast was so large that it was now sandwiched between the walls on either side. "Oh, and it had a lot of... extra heads." He smirked, unloading thirty-five heads, each mouth filled with lines and lines of teeth. Plenty of material for him to work with and not have to worry about wasting.

Justin stepped back and ran a hand through his hair. "That's... a lot of heads. Shame my Dismantle skill isn't ranking up anymore."

"Time?"

"Twenty until next wave. You went through that wave quite fast, but the hydra slowed you down."

Xavier grunted in agreement. He'd been hoping for more time. He tossed Soultaker over to Justin, who snatched it out of the air. He was still a little confused as to how Justin could use the weapon to dismantle beasts when he shouldn't be able to wield it, yet the same wasn't true for the E Grade weapons.

Which made him all the more worried about whether he could assimilate E Grade materials.

I'm just going to have to try.

He sat with his back against the stone parapet. Opening his mouth, he felt his teeth. He looked down at his fingernails. Then, finally, he looked at the colouring of his hand.

"What are you doing?" Justin asked, an eyebrow raised. He was kneeling down by one of the Elemental Hydra heads. The head was as large as his torso.

Xavier released a sigh. "I think Assimilate Properties is changing me." He ran his tongue over his teeth, wondering how much he should say. "It's... making my teeth longer. My fingernails... tougher and sharper. My skin—"

"Greyer." Justin nodded. "Yeah, I've noticed."

Xavier frowned. "You've... you've noticed?"

"Of course I've noticed. I'm not blind."

"You're not... worried I'm turning into a beast?"

Justin chuckled. He looked up from the hydra head. "Does it matter if you are? You can reap souls. I can grow wings. We're all changing. I don't really think we have a choice in the matter." He pursed his lips. His gaze flicked down.

"What? What did you just think?"

"You haven't felt any different, have you? Like, you're still able to keep your emotions in check?"

Xavier leant his head back until it touched the stone, thinking about the question. "I think so."

"Good. Good." Justin got back to his work. "Then I'm sure there's nothing to worry about." It looked awkward—the way he was holding Soultaker. The massive scythe-staff didn't exactly lend itself to precision work. But it didn't take him long to dislodge one of the hydra's teeth. He tossed it over.

Xavier snatched it from the air, then examined it. He tried to use Identify, but—as he'd already known—the skill wasn't strong enough.

The fang was curved. He touched the tip of his index finger to the point. *Sharp. Sharper than Soultaker.* It was also larger than any of the Wolven Fangs he'd gathered.

Too large for him to simply swallow.

"I know you haven't been able to chip armour, but can you chip this?" Xavier tossed the fang back to Justin.

"You want to assimilate it?" Justin asked, looking at the fang. He shrugged. "I can try."

It turned out Justin *couldn't* chip it. It was too tough for him. Xavier had to take over. Using his overwhelming strength and having to flow Spirit Energy into Soultaker several times to repair its edge, he finally managed to carve a small sliver off the damned thing.

A sliver small enough for him to swallow.

"Fifteen minutes now," Justin said before turning back to his work.

"Plenty of time." Xavier sat again, staring at the fang. "Here goes nothing," he muttered, tossing the E Grade material into his mouth and swallowing it with a loud *gulp.*

Chapter 34
Override Not Recommended

Xavier released a grunt of pain as the hydra fang shard slid down his throat. Far stronger than the Wolven Fang and Wolven Claw, the shard easily sliced him up, leaving blood pouring from the cuts.

He swallowed several times, knowing the wounds shouldn't take long to heal, briefly wondering if the damned Elemental Hydra had been venomous on top of everything else.

It wouldn't have been venomous. It was an elemental *beast.*

Besides, he hadn't seen any venom on the fang. Wouldn't he have seen it?

Just like with the other things he'd swallowed, Xavier could feel its path as it headed down into his stomach. Usually, this was simply a strange sensation, though one he'd been getting used to. This time, it was painful. He gripped his stomach, gritted his teeth, and tried not to make a sound. Out of the corner of his eye, he could see Justin staring at him, eyes wide with alarm, forehead creased with worry.

The pain stabbed at him. It reminded him of how bad his lungs had felt earlier that day, when he'd been buried alive. Suddenly, it became difficult to breathe.

Is it really harder, or is that only in my mind? God, I shouldn't have done this...

The shard reached the pit of his stomach, where the pain hit its peak. He could feel his body trying to destroy the foreign invader. Trying to break it down and force the impurities out of his system.

His teeth ground together so hard he felt them chip and heal, chip and heal. He didn't *want* this substance to be purged from him. He wanted to use it. Assimilate it. Just because it was painful didn't mean it wouldn't *work*.

He was about to slow the purging process—something he'd gotten a lot better at since he'd started ranking up the Assimilate Properties skill—but he found he didn't need to.

His body wasn't strong enough to purge the shard on its own. Which made him wonder what would happen if he wasn't able to assimilate it...

A few minutes went by as he willed the damned shard to assimilate.

Over that time, his breathing steadied. The pain didn't lessen, but he became accustomed to it. He didn't *like* the pain, but he could take it if he needed to. He figured that had something to do with his massive Willpower attribute.

If I can't purge or assimilate this... will the pain just never stop? He pushed that thought away. *Not helpful, brain. Not helpful at all.*

Xavier's mind was still heavily strained, split into two parts. He'd been keeping it that way for a while. It was difficult—and, at times, a little painful—but it had been the only way for him to continue gaining ranks in the Split Mind skill, which he hoped would eventually let him split his mind into more than two parts.

But right now, he needed his mind to be whole.

He snapped the two parts back together. The action was painful. He released a small hiss. Maybe he'd done that too fast. He breathed through it and focused on the shard inside of him.

Come on. Assimilate, damn it.

He'd slowly been learning a way to urge the skill on. It had worked for the other properties—especially the chunks of stone.

But it wasn't doing a damned thing on this one.

The pain in his mind went away. So did the heavy strain that had been on it since he'd first made it split in two. A sudden clarity overtook him. With his mental stats as high as they were, Xavier was used to having a clear mind. Though his mind hadn't had any rest for... well, over *six whole weeks*. So perhaps that clearness was partly an illusion.

Still, the clarity he was experiencing now was... incomparable.

My mind feels lighter.

It reminded him of runners who slap on weight vests or hikers who wear heavy packs. When they take off the weight, they feel lighter and stronger than before. His mind had been straining for the past few hours to keep its consciousness split. Now it didn't have to strain to do that at all, he could put every ounce of his concentration toward this one task with renewed mental energy.

He nudged the property into being assimilated and...

Xavier smiled through the pain. A notification appeared.

Attempting to assimilate *Unidentified Material* into muscular structure...

The pain in his stomach tripled. If Xavier hadn't been sitting down, he was sure he would have *fallen*.

He wondered why it said *Unidentified Material*. He hadn't been able to identify the items harvested from the Wolvens, yet they'd been named. Was it because the Elemental Hydra had been a whole grade above him?

Error.
The material you are assimilating is of an incompatible grade.
The impurities are too powerful to assimilate.

Attempting to purge *Unidentified Material* impurities...

Xavier's eyes widened as he stared at the text. *No, no, no! I'm strong enough!* He was sure his stats were high enough to do this—sure his body could take it, even if he wasn't the same grade. *I may be F Grade, but I'm more powerful than these E Grades!*

The pain was so intense it was making it hard for him to think.

**Error.
Unable to purge E Grade impurities in an F Grade Denizen.
Calibrating...
Calibrating...**

Xavier bit his lip. Strained his mind. The notification confused him. The first time impurities had been purged from him, the notification said it couldn't do it because he was an F Grade Denizen.

Yet he'd been able to do it since then.

Am I already doing something I shouldn't be capable of? If so, then maybe I can push this further. Maybe I can force my body to assimilate an E Grade material...

A voice of reason sounded in his mind, asking him if it was worth it. Asking him what might happen if he managed to do this. What the consequences might be.

Xavier gritted his teeth. Perhaps this was a bad decision. Perhaps he should listen to the notification and try to help his body purge the impurity. But he was so sure of himself—so confident that this would work—that he ignored that supposed voice of reason and pushed onward with his initial plan.

He fell into a deep meditative state, and pushed his mind as hard as he could, prompting the notification to appear once more.

Attempting to assimilate *Unidentified Material* into muscular structure...

It'll work this time, he assured himself. *I'll make it work.*

Error.
The material you are assimilating is of an
incompatible grade.

Xavier didn't let up. He *pushed* the process forward, willing it with everything he had. He focused on the shard inside his stomach. The pain dulled to nothing as his concentration sharpened.

Attempting to assimilate *Unidentified Material*
into muscular structure...
Error.
The impurities are too powerful to assimilate.
Error.
Purging interrupted. F Grade Denizen
attempting to override.
Override not recommended.
Purging recommended.
Do you wish to proceed with the assimilation
attempt?

Xavier's eyes widened. *Override not recommended.* Was... was it letting him do it? He bit his lip so hard he felt it bleed. The System itself was telling him this was a bad idea. That he shouldn't do this.

But Xavier never much liked being told what he could and couldn't do. His mother had tried to tell him that, back when she'd told him he couldn't be a writer. He hadn't had a chance to find out whether he would have made it or not. The System had gotten in the way when it had integrated Earth.

And now, it was almost like the System recommending him *not* to do this spurred him on. No, it wasn't *almost* like that—it was definitely like that.

Xavier hoped his stubbornness wouldn't get him into too much trouble.

Purging successfully overridden.
Assimilation in progress…
Assimilation in progress…
The material you are assimilating has various properties.
You may only draw from one.
Choose from the following:
Error.
Two of three options unavailable to F Grade Denizen.
Only one possible viable option:

   1. **Tissue Regeneration.**

Xavier frowned. The pain had flooded back, stabbing at his stomach once more. He thought Justin might have said something, but he was too focused to know what it had been. He stared at the singular option.

Tissue Regeneration.

Xavier had been hoping for something else. He had three different stats he needed to bring up to their 1,000-point thresholds, and something told him Tissue Regeneration wasn't going to get him there. Still, it interested him, and it was his only option.

Is that how the Elemental Hydra was able to grow back its heads? And if so, does that mean I'll be able to do something similar?

He had trouble imagining him being decapitated and growing back his head. Besides, if he grew his brain back, would it still even be *him*? Was that why the powerful Elemental Hydra hadn't seemed as evolved in its intelligence as the other E Grade beasts he'd encountered, because it kept growing back its head and never retained its same consciousness when it did?

Xavier shook his head. Even if he *could* grow his head back with this property, it wasn't exactly something he was willing to *test*. He wouldn't even want to test regrowing a finger.

Hopefully, I'll never find out just how effective this is.

Xavier willed the selection.

Pain flared over every inch of his body. Every one of his muscles contracted, feeling as though they were on fire.

Assimilation is complete.
Biological impurities of *Unidentified Material*
have been assimilated into muscular structure.
You have gained the trait: Tissue Regeneration!
You have gained +20 Strength!
You have gained +20 Toughness!
You have gained +20 Willpower!

Assimilate Properties has reached Rank 5!
...
Assimilate Properties has reached Rank 10!

Warning: E Grade *Unidentified Material* detected
in F Grade Denizen's muscular structure.
F Grade Denizen's muscular structure consid-
ered volatile.
Degeneration of F Grade Denizen's muscular
structure may begin within 48 hours.
Degeneration Countdown Timer: 47 hours 59
minutes 59 seconds.

Chapter 35
Battle Mind

"Xavier!" Hands shook his shoulders. He barely registered them. Barely registered his name being called. "Xavier! The wave has started!"

All Xavier could do was stare at the notification he'd just received.

F Grade Denizen's muscular structure considered volatile.

He stared at the countdown timer. It kept ticking down, and down, and down.

Degeneration Countdown Timer: 47 hours 59 minutes 41 seconds.

Degeneration...

"What the hell did I just do to myself?" Xavier muttered. He blinked. A young man, standing in front of him, suddenly came into focus. His face was frantic. His hands were still on Xavier's shoulders. "Justin?" Then the sounds of horns and war drums met his ears, and he registered what Justin had said.

The next wave had started.

Xavier stood. He touched a hand to his stomach. The agony that had taken over his body was gone. Completely. If anything, he felt stronger than he ever had—probably because of the stats he'd just gained.

Twenty points to three different attributes. And what in the Greater Universe is a trait?

And he'd gained *six* ranks in Assimilate Properties after what he'd done. Though now he realised what he'd just done might very well get him killed.

"They're heading toward the wall! Xavier! They'll come into the castle if you're not out there!"

Xavier released a sigh. He had less than two days to figure out how not to die. Because of his own stubbornness. Because he thought he knew better. Because he thought he could do *anything*, despite being told otherwise by the System itself.

All while continuing to face the Endless Horde's waves. Why, exactly, had he been so compelled to *not* listen to the System's recommendation?

Without a word to Justin, Xavier leapt back over the wall. Before he'd fallen to the ground, he'd split his mind in two parts once more.

Split Mind has reached Rank 6!

Whoa, that was fast.

Splitting his mind came far more easily this time than it had the first time. He supposed that made sense, considering he had the skill for it now. He wondered whether he could already split it into three parts, but right now wasn't exactly the best time for him to try.

He had more pressing matters to deal with.

One mind—what he decided to dub his *battle mind*—focused purely on the fight in front of him. The first thing he did was search for the E Grade boss. Xavier didn't have the best mobility on the battlefield. This wave was a mixed humanoid wave, filled with predominantly humans, elves, and demonkin. He had to kill roughly a thousand enemies before he came across the E Grade.

A damned mage.

He wasn't worried about the magic it had control of—he was worried about whether or not it would submit to his mind control.

The other part of his mind put itself toward the task of figuring out just what the hell he was going to do about this degeneration countdown.

The notification said my body will break down because of the E Grade impurity. It doesn't take a genius to think that if I advance to E Grade, the Unidentified Material will no longer be an issue, as I'll be of the same grade.

If that were true, it would mean he would have to figure out how to advance to E Grade in less than two days. He had no idea if that would be enough time to reach the 1,000-point threshold for Strength, Speed, and Toughness, but he supposed it would have to be. Assuming that even mattered anymore.

Though in came the *other* problem—perhaps the biggest problem now. He didn't actually *know* how to advance to E Grade.

One damned step at a time.

The thought didn't bring him a whole lot of comfort.

There was another possible solution. The notification didn't say he would *die* when the countdown timer reached the end—it said he would *degenerate.* And this coming just after he'd gained a trait—whatever that was—called Tissue Regeneration.

What if the trait, and my Toughness, was able to fight back the degeneration? The two simply cancelling each other out?

That wasn't exactly a *plan*, however. More like a hope. If that were true, if he failed advancing to E Grade before the countdown ended, then he would be perfectly fine. But it wasn't exactly as though there was a way for him to test out that theory.

I'm holding my own against these waves, but they're only going to keep getting stronger. My power has been inching upward, far slower than I'd like. What happens if my power goes backward?

He'd have to abandon this place. That, or get himself very dead.

I'm not going to abandon this place. I'll just have to get myself to E Grade. That's my plan anyway, isn't it?

He didn't know if two days would be enough time—he would just have to *make* it enough time.

The deadline fuelled him.

In his battle mind consciousness, he cast Willpower Infusion. Purple mist flowed out from his staff and headed straight for the E Grade mage. The mage was a demonkin. She wore blood-red robes that clung to her figure, wielded a staff with a blood-red gem, and her horns glowed... *blood-red.*

I guess I know what her favourite colour is.

The mage tried to cast several spells on Xavier, but his Soul Block spell was more than enough to keep them at bay. When the purple mist reached the woman, Xavier fully expected it not to work. Some minds were simply stronger than others, making the spell impossible.

This, however, wasn't one of those times.

The mist flowed straight into the demonkin's eyes, nostrils, ears, mouth. Xavier felt the woman's mind try to block him. Try to stop him from taking over. Felt her fear—her panic. But she wasn't strong enough to resist.

Willpower Infusion has taken a step forward on the path!
Willpower Infusion is now a Rank 20 spell.
One cannot walk backward on the path.

Xavier grinned, looking at the notification. He'd gained a fair few ranks in the past few waves. And now, *another* one.

He took control, then sicked the E Grade wave boss on her own people. The control he had over the demonkin felt stronger than any other control he'd had over the other wave bosses in the past.

This spell keeps getting stronger and stronger. I wonder what it will be like at Rank 50. Or when I'm E Grade... Maybe then I'll be able to turn an entire wave against itself. Or one wave against another...

Now *there's* an idea.

So far, in this wave, he'd been using small pulses of Soul Strike to keep his cooldowns short—sixty to a hundred infused souls per spell. Now that his control over this E Grade was so strong?

He unleashed a 1,200-infused Soul Strike on the enemies on the opposite side of the castle. The cooldown would take twenty minutes—a long-ass time when in the middle of a wave—but he reckoned the devastation would be worth it.

Thousands of enemies met their deaths at a single one of his spells.

God, he felt so... *exhilarated*! Sometimes he worried about how amazing the power he wielded felt. About that addiction he had for *more*. About how satisfying it was to harvest so many souls. But those times were becoming few and far between after all the carnage he'd caused on this floor.

With the E Grade demonkin fighting on his side, the rest of the wave was cleared before the cooldown met its end.

The E Grade wave boss went down easily enough—especially when he turned its spells on itself. For a moment, he imagined how what he was doing must look to the demonkin. He could see the fear in the woman's eyes. See the way her body shook in anticipation of her death. He didn't revel in her fear—for that, he was glad. But that didn't mean he felt pity for her.

When he returned to the parapet, Justin's mouth was agape. The teenage Airborne Duellist picked up his jaw. "You completed that wave in twenty-two minutes."

Xavier should have been proud of that—it was his best time for a long while. Instead, he just parked himself on the stone floor, back against the parapet, and told Justin about the predicament he'd gotten himself into.

Xavier had Justin rouse Adviser Kalren from his sleep. It was a strange sight—seeing the wizened old man running up the battlements' stone steps, his robes fluttering about his skinny frame. The man was some sort of a Scholar class. Yet the strangest thing about his running was that it was faster than Usain Bolt on the hundred metres.

What an odd new reality we live in.

The man wasn't short of breath when he came to stand across from Xavier. Xavier quickly informed him of what had happened.

"What blessed you with the stupidity to go against the System's recommendation?" The words tumbled out of the old man's mouth so fast that it seemed he hadn't realised he'd said them until he'd reached the end of the question. "Ah, my apologies. I did not mean to speak to you like that. After all you have done for—"

Xavier raised a hand, quieting the man. "You're right. It *was* a stupid thing to do." He didn't like admitting that much. Besides, he wondered if it even had been a bad idea—maybe that made him even more stupid.

He hated the System telling him what to do. He was grateful for all the titles he'd received. Grateful for being a True Progenitor. But that didn't mean the System was looking out for him. It was keeping him from Earth—keeping him from those who needed his help the most.

"But what's done is done. Now, I need to search for a solution," Xavier said.

The adviser slouched back against the opposite wall. He ran a hand through his beard, his head down, forehead creased in thought. He let out a sigh that made him sound like he was a thousand years old and very, very tired. "I do not see what you can do. Pushing to E Grade, as you say, is your only objective."

Xavier leant forward. "I still don't know how to *do* that. I've got my secondary core. My stats are higher than a normal Level 100 Denizen's would be. Hell, I can defeat *E Grades*. Your own legends

246

only spoke about Denizens reaching E Grade before reaching Level 100."

"As I have said before, those might very well be mere fictions. We must work with what we *know*. If levels are the only thing that will get you there—"

"I'll need to gain thirty-nine levels in less than forty-eight hours?" Xavier asked. "When the only enemies out there that are even offering me Mastery Points are the E Grades, only forty-seven of which I'll be able to face between now and then?" He shook his head. "That isn't *enough*."

"No. It is not enough." The adviser slid down to the ground. "Why did you do this to yourself? Why did you risk all you have accomplished?"

Xavier frowned. He stood, faced the Endless Horde, resting his hands on the parapet and leaning heavily on it. "Because it still isn't *enough*."

Chapter 36
Several Plans

Clouds drifted in front of the moon, further dimming the darkness of the night. Xavier held one of the Elemental Hydra's fangs between his thumb and forefinger. Moving it left and right in the torch's light. He didn't need the torchlight to see—he saw plenty well in the dark these days. But it did help him see the details.

The fang was whiter than he'd imagined it would be. He hadn't even needed to clean it. He would have thought a beast like that would have yellowed teeth, maybe some even rotted. But he supposed his own teeth grew back when he chipped them—maybe they were resistant to deterioration. Especially since this beast had Tissue Regeneration.

A small shard of this might bring my death. He hadn't even consumed an entire tooth. *But it also brought me a new trait, and a total of sixty attribute points. Not to mention the six ranks I gained, which brought me even more points.*

Justin had dismantled more materials from the Elemental Hydra. They were in a small pile by the parapet. There was still time before the next wave. The most time he'd had between waves in a while.

What happens if I consume another shard of this? Does that trait get stronger? It should certainly boost my attributes. Will that only be by two points?

He had a feeling it would be by four points each, but it was only a suspicion. He was tempted—*very* tempted—to find out. But he was also worried. There was a very good chance that consuming *more* of the E Grade material would simply speed up the countdown until his degeneration.

But what if my regeneration becomes strong enough to completely counteract whatever this "degeneration" is? Is that a risk I'm willing to take when there could be other ways out of this?

Then there were the Elemental Hydra claws. He placed the fang onto the ground, near a pile of hundreds more, and picked up one of the claws. He didn't have quite as many of those. He touched the tip with his finger. A drop of blood dripped down his skin. The wound quickly healed.

What happens if I consume this, too?

"You are not really thinking of doing this again, are you?"

Xavier looked over at where Adviser Kalren was slumped, his back against the opposite wall, a concerned look on his face.

"You want power. I understand that," the old man said. "But this is a terrible way to get it."

Xavier tilted his head to the side. "You understand it?" He frowned. He wanted to say more. *How could you understand it? You're weak.* But he bit his tongue, turning his gaze back to the claw. He sighed and placed it down next to the others. "Maybe this isn't the way," he said, thinking, *Not yet, at least.*

There was still more for him to do.

Justin was still working on the hydra, dislodging claws from its feet. It was gruesome work. He looked over at Xavier. "I think I have an idea." He stood from where he'd been kneeling, leant Soultaker against the battlements' wall, and walked over. "The trait you received—is it called Tissue Regeneration?"

"Yeah. I guess it must be something unique to the hydra. How it's able to regrow those heads—at least, to a point."

Justin nodded. "Makes sense. But there are other things that

Tissue Regeneration could do." He ran a hand over his chin, which was full of stubble—the beginning attempts at a beard. "When we build muscle, for instance—"

Xavier perked up. "The muscle tears, breaks down, before it's healed stronger."

"Exactly. For slow-twitch and fast-twitch muscle fibres. And I imagine it would work for conditioning your body against harm, right? Like, growing callouses on your skin?"

Xavier stood. "You think I should train more?"

Justin shrugged. "It's your physical stats that you're trying to get to 1,000 points, right?"

"Even if that does work for him, it will not help him advance to E Grade," Adviser Kalren cut in. "It *will* help him fight better, but otherwise..."

"What do you know about the advancement to E Grade?" Xavier asked.

The old man blinked. "Very... very little, I'm afraid. But I think you must gain enough levels—"

"No, I don't mean that. I mean, does it take a long time? Is it painful? Will I somehow be incapacitated? Unable to fight?"

Adviser Kalren raised his chin. Looked to be in thought. He bobbed his head in a nod. "Yes. I... I seem to remember something about that. I think the transformation can take several minutes."

"Several minutes," Justin muttered. "That... that doesn't sound good. What if it happens in the middle of a wave? He'll be defenceless."

Xavier was thinking the exact same thing. He could take a hit. Several hits, really. But just how many *sustained* hits could he take? And what if there were E Grade enemies involved while he was advancing?

Adviser Kalren shrugged. "He'll just have to trigger the advancement while he is between waves." He looked at Xavier. "That sounds reasonable, doesn't it?"

Xavier grunted his response. He had something else in mind.

Something that would prevent him from being able to rest between waves. He turned, rested his hands on the parapet, and looked out at the waves of the Endless Horde. Then he looked farther, at what was beyond them.

The portals the Horde came through. Portals from worlds all around the sector.

For some time now, he'd had the plan—or rather the thought—to turn the fight around. To, instead of *waiting*, take the fight straight to the next wave before it had a chance to march on him. But he hadn't known how the System would react to such a thing. It might very well let the entire Endless Horde attack him at once. Or perhaps it would simply activate the next wave right away.

He didn't know, and the only way to find out was to try. But it wasn't something he'd wanted to attempt until he advanced to E Grade.

But if the only way for me to advance to E Grade is to get to Level 100, and I have less than two days to get there, I'm going to need to get more Mastery Points than are available in the coming waves. A lot more.

"Tissue Regeneration…" Xavier muttered, contemplating what Justin had said. Strength was his weakest attribute. He still needed 135 more points until he reached 1,000 for that one, and he didn't have any skills like Running that were helping him get there.

But what if Strength Training was a skill? He'd tried to train his Strength before. He'd made some progress—gaining a few attribute points the Tower of Champions had let him start entering floors, but no skills had ever shown up. The same had been true for Running.

What if I was doing something wrong? What if there's a way to gain a Strength Training skill that I'm simply not aware of?

"How much time until the next wave?"

"Five minutes," Justin responded. "Not much time."

Xavier grunted. He turned away from the waves, sprinted for the opposite wall, and leapt straight over it. He'd spent six weeks in this place. In that time, he'd gotten fairly familiar with the outer bailey. To one side of the bailey was a line of wagons. They must have led out to the farms outside of the castle—farms that had no doubt been burned to the ground by the Endless Horde as they destroyed every inch of the kingdom before finally making their way here.

It had been a long time since Xavier had tested his Strength. He remembered, back in the tower, picking up a vending machine and pressing it over his head. He smirked. That would be child's play now.

So how in the world was he going to find something strong enough to test his Strength?

At one wall was a pile of massive boulders. A similar pile was on the battlements. These would have been used by the defending soldiers to throw down at the enemy as they tried to scale the walls, he supposed, but with Xavier there, they'd never needed to perform such a tactic.

He stepped over to the boulders and picked one up. His mind, still used to his old level of Strength back before he'd been integrated, had expected to struggle with this. But, of course, he didn't struggle. The boulder felt light. *Incredibly* light.

Soultaker is probably heavier than this thing. It's a miracle Justin can even use the weapon for dismantling.

But this is my only option right now.

He walked the boulder over to the wagon on the other side, then thought better of this strategy and pulled the wagon over to the boulders.

A moment later, he had the entire pile of boulders stacked in the wagon. *Must be reinforced to hold this much weight.* That was something he was glad for; otherwise, this foolish plan might not even be possible.

Xavier spent the next few minutes lifting the wagon off the ground to try and get some sort of pump into his muscles. At first, he performed deadlifts with the wagon. Lifting one side of it to put it on two wheels. As he did so, he frowned. It felt... somewhat difficult, but more like how difficult a push-up feels to someone who can do a hundred of them.

Not difficult enough for what I need.

Then he let go of one of the wagons' handles and used one hand instead.

That's a little bit harder...

But he was sure that he could make this harder. He did one-handed, one-legged deadlifts, smiling all the while. It still took twenty reps for it to feel hard enough, but it was good to know he was finding out what he was currently capable of.

The leverage of only lifting one side of this thing must make it a hell of a lot easier.

He lowered the wagon back to the ground and walked around it, rubbing the back of his neck, wondering what else he could do with it.

I can't bench press the thing. There isn't enough room beneath it. He tilted his head to the side. *Can I press it over my head? Would that even work?* He didn't know, but he was willing to try. The problem was that the damned wagon wasn't exactly a conventional weight. Even if he could do a lot of reps with it, it might be difficult to get the thing balanced atop his hands from where it sat, especially as he didn't want any of the boulders to fall out of it.

It took him less than thirty seconds—by crawling under the damned wagon and crouching as low as he could—to press it up over his head and then squat upward out of the crouch.

Once he picked one leg off the ground and did a one-legged squat—also known as a pistol squat—he realised he'd finally found a difficult exercise for himself.

He was on his fifth rep when the war drums sounded.

I have a plan. Several plans.

He was going to build up his Strength. His Speed. His Toughness. He was going to hit that 1,000-point threshold for each of them *within the next day*. He might not know *how*, but he would bloody well do it.

He wasn't going to sit and wait for the next waves to come, then.

He was going to finally take the fight to the enemy—it was the only way he would get to Level 100, then E Grade, in time.

Chapter 37
Too Good to Be True

Xavier had thought he'd been pushing himself as hard as he could go. He'd thought he'd been testing and stretching his limits more than perhaps anyone else ever had.

He'd been wrong.

With each new wave that came, Xavier made more and more progress.

Though he received no notifications for Tissue Regeneration, as it did not appear to be a skill, he could *feel* it at work. Xavier would have thought that Toughness, given its ability to heal, would make a trait like Tissue Regeneration unnecessary. Then again, Toughness wasn't enough to let normal beasts or humanoid Denizens *regrow their heads*, so there must have been something special about the trait.

And something else, too. His entire body was... more efficient than it had been before. There was just something stronger and more resilient about it. His cores. His Spirit Recovery. His Willpower Recovery. They were more efficient too—more than any gain in his stats could explain.

So it wasn't only his regeneration that was working better. It was everything.

He assumed it might have something to do with the fact that he had a sliver of an E Grade's fang assimilated into his body. The System had warned him against doing such a thing, and clearly his body wouldn't be able to handle it in the long term, as the countdown timer told him it was on its way to rejecting it—but before his body *did* start degenerating, it was more powerful than ever.

That was probably why he'd been able to control that E Grade demonkin mage so easily—probably why he'd defeated that wave in record time.

His Running skill, which had stalled out as he'd put his focus elsewhere, ranked up multiple times on every single wave. Something inside his muscles was *shifting*. His technique was about as perfect as it was ever going to get by this point—at least, that was certainly what it seemed like. But the efficiency of his muscles was a different story.

This was what he imagined Wolverine must feel like, with his regeneration ability. Able to stand there and lift weights and heal *while lifting weights*, becoming stronger almost with each rep.

That was how Xavier was feeling as he ran. *Maybe that's how Hugh Jackman got so buff...*

Each new rank brought him closer and closer to his goal. But even if it reached Rank 50, he knew the Running skill alone wouldn't be enough to push his Speed to 1,000. He was also getting incredibly worried about his ability to gain levels, considering he needed a *billion* Mastery Points just to get to Level 62.

A billion. It was such an absurd number. Whenever he saw it on his status screen, it made him frown and shake his head. He was hoping that when he got to E Grade, Mastery Points would be depicted differently—like how the conversion of Spirit Coins was different for each grade.

How in this world or any other am I supposed to get to Level 100 when it's going to take probably twenty waves just for me to gain a single level?

When that thought had come, Xavier had pushed it away. That was tomorrow's problem. Today was all about gaining attribute points.

So far, since Xavier had been integrated into the Greater Universe, he'd gained perhaps *two* points in Speed from his non-skill training alone. Considering how consistently he was gaining ranks in Running, he knew he would reach Rank 50 by the time the first twenty-four hours of the countdown timer were up. Doing the math, he found he needed to gain an additional seventeen points if he were going to reach the threshold.

In the first five hours, he'd gained *five*. That was how much more efficiently his body had been working.

He just hoped he would be able to keep it up.

As for Strength, being his weakest attribute, he knew he really needed to push it. And though he'd discovered a way to train, he knew that he couldn't rely on any *one* source for his attribute points. Part of him wondered if he could gain any new titles, but no titles had been forthcoming. Not since he'd defeated his first E Grade.

You'd think, after all I'd done with these waves, I would have gotten something more for it.

Fortunately, he hadn't yet assimilated *all* of the materials that Justin had gathered for him. Xavier still worried that he would soon hit a hard limit as to how many different materials he was able to assimilate. He had a feeling that he wouldn't be able to assimilate more than fifty different properties while he was still in F Grade, as each time he'd assimilated something, he'd gained a single rank. Though that theory had been somewhat blown out of the water when he'd assimilated that E Grade shard and gained six ranks in one go.

Still, even if there was a limit, right now he figured it was worth reaching it if it helped get him out of this mess.

Justin had dismantled far more than just Wolvens for Xavier. Xavier had brought him back corpses of several Winged Bears, Giant Spiders, and Flame Chimeras. Though he was fine assimilating properties from a bear beast, he did sour at the thought of the spider beast making him grow extra legs.

Fortunately, it doesn't work like that... at least, it hasn't yet.

Though if it turned me into Spider-Man, that would be pretty darn cool too.

Justin had handed Xavier several things from the beasts. From the Winged Bears he'd gotten a feather, a fang, and a claw. From the Giant Spiders he'd gotten a pincer and—ugh—an *eye*. And from the Flame Chimera, he'd gotten a lion's tooth and a snake fang.

None of these were things Xavier wanted to ingest, yet he did so for each and every one.

Assimilating all of these ingredients had taken a bit of time. He'd managed to acquire enough of each to ingest and assimilate them ten times—something he wasn't about to do for the E Grade Elemental Hydra's material.

Not that he didn't have enough. Oh, he had plenty of its fangs, and could cut plenty of slivers off them. He simply worried about what would happen if he ingested them.

I'd probably just die faster.

As he assimilated more and more of the ingredients, he felt... *changes* happening in his body. Changes that made him once more doubt the Assimilate Properties skill.

These impurities are normally purged by the body. And I'm instead making them a part of me. What... what does that mean for me? What does being "impure" mean in this Greater Universe?

He constantly ran his tongue along his teeth. *Sharper.* He looked at his skin. *Grey.* His fingernails... They looked overgrown. Sharp. More like claws than anything else. He didn't have a mirror, but after he'd assimilated the Giant Spider Eye, he wondered if that had changed him too. His vision didn't *seem* any different.

Even though these things changed him, he didn't stop. He *couldn't* stop. Consuming all of these properties? It was working— it was giving him exactly what he needed to advance. The skill he'd gained back on the battlefield with the elven and human armies was feeling incredibly overpowered now. He could tolerate its downsides.

He didn't mind looking like a beast if it made him more powerful.

In those twenty-four hours, speed was the first of his physical attributes to hit the 1,000-point threshold. A surge of energy ripped through his body and mind. Everything shifted. He was in the middle of a wave when it happened. His enemies always felt slow when he compared them to himself, unless he was facing an E Grade. Now, it was as though they were moving through molasses.

Strength, previously his weakest attribute, came next. Most of the things he consumed seemed to contribute to the Strength attribute—something he was damned glad for, as even with Tissue Regeneration, he simply hadn't been able to push his body hard enough during the breaks from the waves.

Though he had gained thirteen attribute points in Strength for his efforts, it was an absolute drop in the bucket compared with assimilating things into his body.

I'll be able to gain more by training in the future. Thirteen attribute points might not seem like a lot in comparison, but I wasn't training in optimum conditions, nor did I have the requisite time to dedicate myself to it.

There was potential there. In physical training, especially with Tissue Regeneration—but he hadn't been able to gain the Strength Training skill, if one such skill existed, from his efforts.

I'll have to try again in the future.

Having over 1,000 points in Strength made him feel more powerful than he ever had. He didn't need his scythe-staff to separate his enemies' limbs from their bodies. He found himself wielding Soultaker with one hand, slashing it left and right as he grabbed soldiers with his offhand, crushing their skulls through their helmets.

It was an insane rush. A rush that reminded him of his occasional urge to have chosen the path of the warrior. But he didn't need to go down the path of the warrior to be capable of fighting like one. He'd found that out the first time he'd killed a goblin by smashing in its skull.

This has to have some consequences I'm not aware of, Xavier thought, contemplating how many attribute points Assimilate Properties had offered him—more than his strongest titles. *This has got to be too good to be true.*

He pushed past those reservations, however, as he knew if he didn't, he would die.

When he hit his Toughness threshold, he felt as though he'd been carved from solid rock. Felt like nothing could break through his skin. For the most part, his skin still felt soft to the touch, but there was a roughness to it that hadn't been there before. He didn't know if that was because of the Toughness attribute being so high, or because of the different properties he'd assimilated into his body.

But he didn't much care. He'd bloody well done it—and with time to spare. He looked at his Assimilate Properties skill, barely believing how much it offered him.

Assimilate Properties – Rank 17
This is an epic skill that grants you the ability to assimilate foreign properties into your body, mind, and soul if the perfect conditions are met.
List of Current Assimilated Properties:
Crucible Steel (Muscular Structure) – +60 Toughness
Wolven Fang (Muscular Structure) – +60 Strength
Wolven Claw (Muscular Structure) – +60 Speed
Sandstone (Muscular Structure) – +60 Toughness
Winged Bear Fang (Muscular Structure) – +60 Strength
Winged Bear Claw (Muscular Structure) – +60 Toughness
Winged Bear Feather (Muscular Structure) – +60 Speed

Giant Spider Pincer (Muscular Structure) – +60 Strength
Giant Spider Eye (Muscular Structure) – +60 Intelligence
Chimera Fang (Muscular Structure) – +60 Speed
Chimera Tooth (Muscular Structure) – +60 Strength
Unidentified E Grade Material (Muscular Structure) – +52 Strength, Toughness, and Speed

By the time the first twenty-four hours were up, Xavier had reached Level 62 and his first goal—every one of his attributes had passed the 1,000-point threshold.

All he needed to do now was gain thirty-eight more levels and advance to E Grade in the *next* twenty-four hours.

Sounds easy enough...

Chapter 38
This Choice Has Consequences

Title Unlocked!
**All 1,000: This is a common title that everyone
receives when they have reached 1,000 stat
points in all 6 attributes.**
You have received +20 to all stats!

Title Unlocked!
**First All 1,000: You are the first person from your
world to reach 1,000 stat points in all 6 attributes.**
You have received +40 to all stats!

XAVIER GRINNED, READING THE NOTIFICATIONS OVER FOR THE
fourth time. Sixty points to *all* stats. He'd taken his stats even
further than he'd needed to. They weren't each just at 1,000, they
were *higher* than that. When he'd reached Level 62, he'd thrown
his twenty free stat points straight into Willpower, wanting to
boost his control of the enemy as best he could.

He was glad that wasn't the only boost the attribute had
received.

As Xavier stood on that parapet, having defeated the last wave in a shocking fifteen minutes, he looked out at the next, taking a deep breath.

It was time.

Playing the System's game, waiting an hour for each wave to come, would make it impossible for him to reach Level 100 in the next twenty-four hours. No, it would probably take at least two months the old-fashioned way.

The odds were against him surviving. But that just meant he needed to change the game.

"Xavier?"

Xavier blinked. He was still standing atop the parapet, staring out at the Endless Horde. He looked over his shoulder and down at Siobhan. His gaze made her take an almost imperceptible step back. He felt a hint of fear coming off her. Something primal within him stirred, glad for that.

He frowned, shrugging the feeling away. *Why would I be glad she's afraid?*

"Yes?" Xavier said.

"Are you really going to do this?" She waved out at the Horde. "What if—"

"I die?" He turned away from her. "I'll die if I don't do it." He looked at his hands. Clenched them into fists. He felt so damned *strong*. So damned *powerful*.

Degeneration Countdown Timer: 23 hours 46 minutes 27 seconds.

He sighed, looking at the countdown. He'd put it into the top-right corner of his vision as a constant reminder. To keep him grounded. To keep him pushing.

"Maybe there's a way to fix what you're going through back at the tower. Sam could have a solution."

"Even if that man knew how to help me," Xavier said, "I doubt the System would let him. And there's no other way I'd be able to gain the needed levels without the Endless Horde. Not in time. You know that."

Siobhan went quiet. All he heard was her breathing. He could tell she wanted to keep arguing, but it wasn't as though she had any better ideas. He supposed it was nice that she didn't want him to die, though.

I'm not going to die.

"I'm strong enough to take them on. I can take on more than one wave. I've done it before and became stronger for it." Xavier relaxed his hands, fists slowly opening.

"Sooner or later, those foot soldiers and beasts in the wave are going to be of E Grade," Siobhan said in a quiet voice. "You've said yourself, they're already Level 99 now."

Xavier dipped his head. She was right. But that fact didn't make him worry.

It made him *smile.*

"When that happens, I'll be ready for them."

Xavier's words came out in a low growl, one that made him pause. He looked down at himself. At his fingernails-turned-claws.

I am turning into something else.

Justin told him they'd all changed since the System came. That he shouldn't bother worrying about it. But Xavier couldn't help the hint of worry that blossomed in his chest at the sound of his own voice.

"I hope you're right, Xavier. You're Earth's only hope." Siobhan's footsteps receded along the stone.

Xavier contemplated her words. *Earth's only hope.* None of them had used those words before, but she was right. Without Earth's Progenitor, his planet wouldn't stand a chance against the invaders.

All the more reason for me to live.

The others stood on the battlements behind him. Howard, Justin, Queen Alastea, and Advisor Kalren. Their expressions varied, but he knew each of them was worried. Whatever happened, his party would survive, but something told him Kalren would refuse to step through that portal—he would die by his queen's side even though there would be nothing he could do to defend her.

Xavier wasn't sure whether to call that honourable or foolish. Perhaps it was something in between.

"Howard," Xavier called.

The cop came over to him, looking up at where he stood on the wall, an eyebrow raised.

Xavier summoned the Sector Travel Key from his Storage Ring and held it out for the man.

Howard frowned. "What's this for?"

Xavier bit his lip. "If I die out there, take the others back through to the Staging Room." He nodded at the key. "When you get back to Earth, if things are... beyond help, take the others. Take your family. Go somewhere else in the sector. Somewhere safe."

Howard looked at Xavier, then at the key. He reached up but didn't take it. Instead, he closed Xavier's fingers around it. "You aren't going to die. And we aren't going to run and hide. You can do this." He stalked back to the others, crossing his arms at his chest as he stood with them, facing Xavier's way.

Xavier smirked and deposited the Sector Travel Key back into his Storage Ring. There was still more than half an hour until the next wave began.

But that didn't matter. Xavier wasn't going to wait anymore.

"E Grade, here I come," he muttered. He looked at those gathered behind him. "I'll see you all soon."

Perhaps he should have felt fear as he leapt off that parapet and landed on the other side of the moat, summoning Soultaker to his hands and gripping its haft tight. Perhaps he should have worried about what would come next. But he didn't feel any of that. It was just him and the enemies in front of him. Him and the souls he was about to reap. The minds he was to control.

As he sprinted toward his enemies, his mouth opened wide, and a noise escaped. Not the war cry of a soldier on the front line, charging ahead. No—this was something inhuman. A bestial howl —one that sounded an awful lot like a wolf's.

Or a Wolven's.

The System's control of the Endless Horde's waves was to give those they attacked a fighting chance, so he was almost positive his plan would work.

He gazed at the front line. The next wave was mostly composed of human soldiers. The first line of which were spear wielders with large tower shields and spears longer than his own scythe-staff. Monstrous, fifteen-foot-long things.

The soldiers eyed his approach. They looked at each other. At first, they had confused frowns. Then they shifted from foot to foot. Until finally, shouts rang out all around. Shields came up, aligned neighbour to neighbour, their clang ringing out in the night. A shield wall. None of the waves within the Endless Horde had ever employed such a tactic before.

Xavier grinned. Worry and fear rippled through the lines of soldiers. The Endless Horde were the big bads of this sector. The most powerful entity within it. He wondered if something like this had ever happened to them.

He launched a 120-infused Soul Strike toward the line of enemies. It flew through their shields as though they weren't there at all. It took out an entire clump of soldiers. His Spirit attribute was still his strongest, Soul Strike his most powerful asset. He was no longer surprised by the devastation it wrought upon the enemy.

The moment it hit, there was a booming sound. It took him a while to notice what it was. To recognise it. He should have known instantly.

War drums.

But this wasn't just war drums from one wave, like he was used to. War drums were ringing out everywhere.

A notification appeared over his vision.

You have struck a blow against the Endless

**Horde before the designated time for the next
wave.
This choice has consequences.
The Endless Horde are no longer limited to
triggering their waves every hour. The Endless
Horde may start a wave every 30 minutes.
Be cautious of your next step.
One cannot walk backward on the path.**

Xavier didn't pause his run as he read the notification.

Instead, he laughed. The consequence was far more minimal than he'd anticipated. He'd expected something very, very different. Every half hour still wouldn't be enough for him, however. So far, there was only one E Grade enemy per wave, and he was only able to get enough Mastery Points to make a real difference from those wave bosses. He hesitated to even do the math—but if it took roughly twenty-four waves for him to gain a single level...

That's only two levels in the next twenty-four hours.

Xavier was fifty feet away from the front line when he sent purple mist flowing from Soultaker. Killing the soldiers wasn't worth much to him right now. His Toughness, coupled with his new Tissue Regeneration trait, was such that he didn't need to worry about them killing him—at least not easily—but what he did need to worry about was them overwhelming him and limiting his movements.

The purple mist hit the shield wall. A moment later, over a hundred soldiers were under his control.

He chuckled to himself when he gave them the first command.

Take me to your leader.

It was the best way he'd come up with for finding the wave boss.

The soldiers all turned in unison. Xavier had gotten used to controlling his enemies, so it wasn't too strange a thing to see. As he reached them, they made a hole for him, turning their shields up to block their own allies, forming an honour guard around him like the one he'd had back on the third floor.

He felt the soldiers he controlled die. Their allies didn't hesitate to strike them down, knowing they were under his control. They were well aware of Xavier's tricks by now. The waves always observed his tactics and tried to adapt to them. If he were weaker, that approach might have worked quite well. It probably would have spelled his death waves and waves ago.

Instead, it just meant they did his job for him—killing their own. He didn't need the soldiers to protect him or show him the way. Over the last twenty-four hours, he'd been practising and learning how to stretch his abilities to their current limits. Though he still wasn't able to split his mind into more than two parts, he was finding it a hell of a lot easier to slip his mind into the bodies of those he controlled. With half of his consciousness taking to this task, he'd slowly learnt how to not only feel what the Denizen he controlled felt—but he could actually read their thoughts to a small degree.

He could skim the surface of their mind. And, with the ability to command them, he could *steer* what those thoughts might be.

The moment he'd commanded the soldiers to take him to their leader, he got an image of exactly where their wave boss was and what they looked like.

Xavier leapt up over the soldiers. Though he still wished he had the type of mobility that Justin's skills offered, he'd started to learn how to get around. With his Speed and Strength as high as they were, he could leap straight over the soldiers and use their heads like stepping stones. It was almost like crowd surfing, except each time his foot came down, it gave him the chance to break one of the enemy's necks.

It took him less than a minute to find the E Grade wave boss.

And less than a minute to kill them.

Bring on the next wave.

Chapter 39
A Price Worth Paying

XAVIER QUICKLY REALISED THAT WHAT HE HAD ON HIS HANDS was a damned math problem.

At the rate he was gaining Mastery Points, he would need to kill over nine hundred E Grade enemies. It might even be more, though that was difficult to know. Though each level he gained needed more Mastery Points than the last, he usually gained more Mastery Points from each new E Grade he faced, as they tended to be of higher level than the previous wave bosses—he hoped it would balance out.

Else he would have to take out one E Grade roughly every minute and a half. And though he may have managed to do that with the *first* wave of his last day until the degeneration began, that by no means meant he could maintain this pace.

I don't even know if there are that many waves on this side of the portals.

During that minute and a half, he wouldn't be able to deal with the normal enemies of each wave, making them build and build until there were millions of the bastards all around him. Assuming he somehow even managed to do this...

God, it's impossible!

These thoughts kept raging through his mind as he fought, and he hoped what Siobhan had said might happen soon would come true—the normal soldiers in a wave becoming E Grade instead of F Grade.

So far, all these damned enemies have been Level 99 still.

War drums still sounded all around him. The Endless Horde were becoming more and more ferocious.

Xavier pushed forward, striking against the next wave before the first was anywhere near being cleared.

You have struck a blow against the Endless Horde before the designated time for the next wave.
This choice has consequences.
The Endless Horde are no longer limited to triggering their waves every 30 minutes. The Endless Horde may start a wave every 15 minutes.
Be cautious of your next step.
One cannot walk backward on the path.

The System cut the timeframe in half again.

Something told him that pattern would continue. And, like the System said, there was no coming back from this. He gritted his teeth, pushed out his purple mist to take over a nearby soldier and steal their thoughts.

Then he hunted the next E Grade wave boss.

Hours passed in this way. Xavier was becoming quite accustomed to sustained violence. He'd been fighting almost nonstop for more than six weeks. But *almost* was the important word there. During his breaks, even if he wasn't able to sleep, he was able to eat. Now, there was no time for that at all.

Fortunately, it didn't seem as though he *needed* to eat quite as much as he used to—something that didn't make a lot of sense to him, considering how much stronger he was now.

My body must be burning thousands of calories more than a normal human's would. How am I refuelling?

Perhaps it had something to do with his consumption of Celestial Energy. He already knew it fuelled his body in more ways than one, considering it fed both his cores. Maybe it fed *him*, too.

Regardless, by the time the tenth hour rolled around, Xavier felt a pit of hunger deep in his stomach and a wave of exhaustion that surged through his entire body. He'd been keeping count as the day raged on. Trying to remain aware of how many E Grade enemies he'd killed, and how much time had passed.

In ten hours, he'd killed 242 E Grade wave bosses. A feat he wouldn't have imagined was even possible even a couple of days ago. A feat that sounded absolutely impossible for an F Grade Denizen to even achieve. It should have been something that made him proud. The very fact that he was still alive was absolutely amazing, after all. To achieve something like this on top of surviving...

But it wasn't enough.

He was roughly 140 kills behind where he needed to be. He'd gained twelve levels over that time. Another feat that should have impressed him. Another feat that should have made him proud.

But the countdown timer still kept on ticking.

He'd distributed the majority of his free stat points into Willpower and Spirit. Spirit had always been—and would always be—his most powerful asset. His Soul Strike spell was perhaps the only reason he'd gotten this far in the first place. It allowed him to deal a tremendous amount of damage to the E Grade bosses he encountered. He was able to refill his soulkeeping reserve by using Heavy Telekinesis to kill beasts and soldiers on his way to the next wave boss. He didn't even have to aim the spell. The battlefield was like a mosh pit that spread for miles and miles. It was so clogged with enemies that he couldn't see the ground.

Quickly killing the wave bosses wasn't Xavier's only problem. The biggest problem he'd encountered was *locating* that wave boss in time, and moving around the battlefield fast enough to reach them. He had added points to Speed, figuring it was one of his most important attributes right now, but Speed didn't exactly give him the ability to *fly*.

Flying would certainly come in handy.

Another issue was how quickly the waves came. Of course, it was an issue he'd caused, and one he was well aware would happen.

They were down to every fourteen seconds. This only served to make the wave bosses even more difficult to find. His soul-keeping reserve could hold 1,970 souls. A part of Xavier was eager to use every single one of them in a Soul Strike, just to see how many enemies he could clear off the battlefield. To make some space to *breathe*. But that would just be a drop in the bucket.

And he'd have to wait almost thirty-three minutes for the damned spell to reach the end of its cooldown.

If I'm ever able to get past the cooldown of that spell, I'll be unstoppable on a battlefield like this.

Then again, he supposed he *was* unstoppable here. He just wasn't *fast* enough.

I wish there was someone here with me. Someone who could show me what I need to do to push forward.

A small part of Xavier wondered if he should pray. He'd been wracking his brain, trying to come up with a way to speed up his progress, but he kept hitting hard limitations. Limitations he didn't know how to surpass while in the middle of... all of this.

Xavier had never been religious. Never believed in God, or any other kind of deity. But he'd also been someone who looked to science for answers. Someone who was willing to change their mind if proof was presented to him. And though he'd seen no proof of a God that many back on Earth believed in, he did know deities existed—they'd been mentioned in the Summon spell he'd decided not to choose.

And, assuming they did exist, how would he be able to contact such beings?

His mind ran in circles. Even if he *could* contact such a being, deities in a universe that the System governed... something told him that if they were to grant him anything, they would want something in return. Whether that was devotion or some sort of pact, would he be willing to give it to them?

Then there were the presences he'd felt observing him. Two different ones, on two different occasions. The first had made him feel like nothing but a speck of dust, and it had come after he'd reached the top spot on the leaderboard. The second one hadn't been quite as intense, though there had been much power in it.

These beings... would have the answers I seek. They would know how to get me to E Grade, even without having to reach Level 100. If only I could speak to them, somehow...

It made him think about what Siobhan had recommended he do—return to the Tower of Champions and speak to Sam. But that wasn't an option. That was *far* too much of a gamble.

All these thoughts soared through one half of his mind over and over as he fought. The other half was consumed with the fight. A state of flow had overtaken him. There was nothing else in the Greater Universe but him and those he sought to kill. Nothing could stand in his way. He felt as though he was Death itself. He consumed the souls of every foe he killed. He hunted E Grade after E Grade. Saw their fear as he came for them. Saw their disbelief at what was happening.

The battlefield was his. There was nothing more powerful. Nothing more dangerous.

Wave after wave after wave began. The war drums and war cries. The horns and howls. The roars and ragged shouts. He couldn't keep up with it. More waves were beginning than E Grades he'd killed. He couldn't count how many enemies must be in the fight. Didn't know how many waves had become active. A constant stream of enemies flowed from each and every portal at the back of the enemy lines. He wondered how they could all fit.

The odds are against me. I am Death, but my scythe cuts too slow. I need to change the game again.

He leapt over the heads of his enemies. Arrows, fireballs, lightning, ice shards, boulders, air-whips and all manner of spells and weapons came for him while he soared in giant leaps. He no longer bothered using Soul Block. He knew he could take these attacks. His Toughness, his Tissue Regeneration, it made him practically invulnerable against these nuisances.

Change the game.... Change the game... Change the game...

Think, think, think.

His gaze fell on the portals once more. He imagined what must be on the other side—the Endless Horde's most powerful enemies. He bit his lip. If he stepped through a portal, what would the System do? So far, the waves and waves and waves of enemies active in the battlefield had not attacked the castle. The same truth that had been proven in the past was proven in the present—they wouldn't attack the castle until everyone defending it on the battlefield had died.

But he had to imagine it was the System that was preventing them from moving forward. That was preventing them from attacking the castle.

Xavier weighed his options. His determination to destroy the Endless Horde was still there, as insane as his task was. He still wished to protect the queen, but his desire to do so... It was not stronger than his desire to save Earth.

How could it be?

Xavier didn't know how many people were still alive back on Earth. He hoped it was in the billions and not the millions. But no matter the current population, no matter the casualties they'd endured, he needed to save them.

Siobhan's words hit him once more: *Earth's only hope.*

If stepping through one of the Endless Horde's portals to find enemies that would give him enough Mastery Points to reach Level 100—then finally advance to E Grade—meant that the waves were given permission by the System to attack the castle?

It was a price worth paying.

Chapter 40
That's Not Cowardice

HEAVY RAIN PELTED DOWN FROM THE SKY. LIGHTNING flashed and thunder boomed. The storm was violent and all-encompassing, yet still, the noise of the Endless Horde overpowered it.

Xavier whipped his head left and right, eyeing the different portals in the area. He couldn't see the portals behind the castle. Didn't know exactly how many there were. At the far back ranks of the Endless Horde, in a circle that encompassed Queen Alastea's castle, he'd counted hundreds of portals.

There must be over a thousand of them.

From each, more enemies streamed out. He didn't know who would meet him on the other side of one of those portals. He only hoped it would be what he needed.

He'd observed the portals. Seen that they were different to the portal in the castle. They were far larger—mass portals that whole armies could walk through, shoulder to shoulder—and, most importantly, they were *two-way*.

This wasn't the first time Xavier had contemplated stepping through a portal and leaving this world. He'd thought about going through the portal back in the castle. That portal, however, was *one-way,* and he'd come to the conclusion that the System would stop him and the other members of his party from accessing it.

His logic behind that was that the System didn't tolerate cowards, and running away from the Endless Horde would no doubt be considered a cowardly act.

But heading through one of the Endless Horde's own portals to try and take them down on the other side, on one of the worlds they controlled?

That's not cowardice. It's a suicide mission.

When a suicide mission was your only option, however, it started to look appealing. Not that Xavier planned on perishing on the other side.

"Just pick one," Xavier growled at himself as his gaze kept pivoting from one portal to the next. Then his eyes fell on a single portal that looked different to the rest. It was even larger than the other ones, and while the other portals glowed yellow—much like lightning—this one was blood-red, like the sky had been before the System had integrated Earth.

When he looked at it, he felt a sort of primal fear overtake him. He didn't know where that fear came from. Didn't know if it was some kind of insight, for part of him had fallen into a meditative state trying to seek insight to answer his problems, or if the fear came from somewhere else.

If an insight was warning him away from stepping through that portal, then that meant whatever lay on the other side must be incredibly dangerous.

And if it's dangerous, it will offer more Mastery Points than anything else.

Though fear blossomed in his chest at the mere sight of the blood-red portal, the temptation to enter it was stronger. Perhaps it would be a mistake—perhaps the D Grade leader of the Endless Horde was what lay on the other side, and it would crush him under its boot the moment he stepped through.

A D Grade won't bother with the likes of me. Not yet. I hope.

It was a gamble, but much in his life had become a gamble since he'd entered the Greater Universe.

What was one more?

Xavier kicked off the head of some giant humanoid Denizen that stood three times as tall as the others, making a beeline straight for the blood-red portal. Rain pattered every inch of him in a constant deluge.

Thousands of attacks streamed toward him from the enemies below, and he sensed that some of those attacks were coming from the E Grade wave bosses. He cast Soul Block, splitting it to protect him from all sides. He cast Heavy Telekinesis, pushing arrows and spears and other projectiles away.

A ripple ran through the ranks of the Endless Horde. A hush somehow quietening the millions of enemies around him enough for the sound of the storm to drown them out. The war drums and horns and roars and shouts ceased for the first time in hours.

All eyes turned toward him as he made it to the portal.

They couldn't stop him getting through.

Xavier had never stepped through a portal before, let alone *leapt* through one. Not only did he have no idea what lay on the other side, he hadn't known what it would feel like.

He imagined some sort of swirling galactic void. Stars, planets, and other celestial bodies would stream past him like he'd just stepped through a stargate.

What he encountered was nothing like that at all.

In fact, it was... *nothing*. A darkness more pure than any he'd experienced—even more pure than what the System had pulled him into when he'd been forced to choose his moral faction and when he'd chosen the path of the Champion.

But it was a darkness that seemed to have *weight*. That weight pushed down at him, as though it were trying to crush him from every side. He didn't feel pain, only pressure. One so immense that he worried it would kill him.

Xavier didn't know how long the sensation lasted. To his mind, it could have gone on for a fraction of a second or an entire eternity.

Then it was over, and Xavier came out of the portal the way he'd entered it—leaping through the air, over the heads of the Denizens that had been about to step through. He glanced down, saw shock on their faces, then clocked the area around him, taking in the architecture in an instant.

What he found took him by surprise.

The Endless Horde always felt like a primitive organisation to him. Perhaps it was the connotations a name like *horde* gave the galactic entity. Either way, he'd envisioned a world of stone and wood and castles much like the one Queen Alastea lived in.

The buildings here, on the other side of the blood-red portal, were nothing like that. In a way, they resembled that of a modern city. Skyscrapers made from what looked to be metal and glass reached higher into the sky than those in New York—so high that they pierced the clouds. He could not see the tops of many of them, obscured as they were.

But these weren't modern buildings in the way that he knew them. There was a... *presence* to them. They felt as though they were imbued with different types of energies. Some pure Celestial Energy, while others had Spirit and Willpower Energy. He was sure the others, with whom he was less familiar, held Intelligence, Strength, Speed, and Toughness Energy.

How does it help to have buildings imbued with energy like this?

What was even more eye-catching than the buildings themselves were the vehicles that flew from one to another.

The different craft varied considerably. Some were flying ships, their sails whipping in the wind—he saw several of them moored in mid-air around some of the larger buildings, and wondered how they didn't fall. Others were simple circular platforms only large enough to hold those who stood upon them. It wasn't just flying vehicles, either. Flying beasts and Denizens soared high in the sky, expertly veering around the different crafts as though they did it every day.

Are all cities in the Greater Universe as fantastical as this place?

A blaring warning sound trilled into life. Xavier had taken in all of this in the space of half a second, just long enough for the soldiers gathered near the portal to raise weapons and begin to cast spells.

Bells rang in Xavier's brain, the city's alarm somehow sounding as though it were coming from his own head.

The attacks came swiftly. Xavier, taken in by everything around him in this new environment, didn't have enough time to respond. What must have been a hundred attacks slammed into him from every side before he was able to cast Soul Block and land among the soldiers, where it was more difficult to strike him.

He hadn't even flinched as the attacks were launched at him. He'd been taking the enemies' attacks head-on for a long while now. He was confident in his ability to take a beating.

But these attacks actually damaged him, even if the damage he took from them was incredibly blunted, getting hit by that many all at once...

Your health is at 6%.

Xavier landed among the enemies, suddenly worried he'd made the biggest mistake of his life coming through that portal. He tried to scan one of the nearby enemies, but—

He wasn't able to.

How wasn't he able to? He *should* be able to identify enemies over Level 100 by now, shouldn't he? Not by virtue of his actual Identify skill—that he'd failed to rank up enough—but by virtue of the fact that he was Level 74.

But, thus far, he hadn't been able to scan a single E Grade wave boss...

The Denizens around him. They were *all* E Grade. Every single one of them.

Xavier had gotten exactly what he was looking for, and his earlier assessment may very well have been the correct one:

This was a suicide mission.

Chapter 41
Focus, You Idiot

Xavier took ten more hits after he'd landed on the stone ground. Arrows slammed into his shoulder, back, and legs. Fireballs exploded in his face and lightning bolts made his entire body shudder. His Soul Block should have been enough to stop the strikes around him, but the massive number of attacks that had come his way burned right through it, and he wasn't able to cast another until the cooldown ended.

His health regeneration was absolutely massive, which was the only reason he was still alive.

He lashed out at the enemies around him. He needed to create a circle of space. Needed to protect himself long enough to bring his health back up and get his bearings.

Soultaker separated heads from bodies left and right. He sighed internally in relief. These bastards might be E Grades, but they were *weak* E Grades—he could take them down almost as easily as the Level 99 soldiers and beasts.

Your health is at 5%.

It's gone down, not up!
Xavier's mind worked. He cast Heavy Telekinesis every

second, crushing Denizen against Denizen, but every enemy he killed was replaced a moment later. And the barrage of spells never ceased. Not many hit him—surrounded as he was, the mages and other ranged attackers were blocked—but some of the attacks were raining down from above.

A few groups of mages had taken to the circular platforms he'd seen flying between the different buildings. They had the high ground. A vantage point above where they could easily target him, no matter how many enemies were around him.

And they didn't seem to give a damn about collateral damage.

Xavier gritted his teeth. He cast Soul Strike. Pure white lightning flowed from Soultaker, branching out in different directions. A part of him wanted to throw every single damned soul he had into the spell, but he couldn't risk being without it for too long.

Hopefully a minute isn't too long.

He hadn't tested this spell on these E Grade enemies. Didn't know how many a single soul would take out. There were a half-dozen floating circular platforms around him. Each platform held at least five enemies.

Xavier infused sixty souls into the spell. Ten souls per platform. He couldn't stop to watch the white lightning branch off. Couldn't stop to watch the soul apparitions materialise.

The enemies directly around him thrust with spears and slashed with swords. Halberds and axes chopped down with ferocious speed and deadly accuracy.

Xavier's Speed was devastatingly fast. He'd maxed out his Running skill at Rank 50. Earned a few more attributes with physical training. Thrown a fair few points into Speed as he'd gained these last twelve levels—then there was the Assimilate Properties skill, and everything it had offered him.

He'd blown well past the 1,000-point threshold.

For the last ten hours, he'd been going from one target to the next, ignoring the rank-and-file enemies on the ground.

Now, he could experience the full force of his 1,445 points in Speed.

Xavier slipped away from a spear strike, moving his shoulder less than an inch to have the blade miss. He ducked a sword swipe aiming for his head. He grabbed a halberd's shaft, ripped the weapon from the soldier's hand. Sent a Heavy Telekinesis at all those striking at him from behind—they went flying backward into their comrades, their weapons never reaching him, dead before they slumped down to the ground, kept standing by the crush of enemies around them.

Breathe. Think. Act.

Purple mist pooled about him, shooting into the soldiers in the surrounding area. He tried to push it into as many enemies as possible. He'd controlled over a hundred enemies before, but they hadn't been E Grade enemies.

I can do this.

Mental blocks stopped the spell. He'd stretched it so thin that these feeble minds were able to resist him. But he didn't want to let the spell go. Didn't want to give his enemies any respite.

Your health is at 8%.

It's going back up. I just need to keep fighting.

Kill notifications kept trying to appear in front of him. He wanted nothing more than to see what level these Denizens were. To see how much Mastery Points they offered him. But there wasn't time. He couldn't spare even the fraction of a second that looking would take in either of his split minds.

Xavier *pushed* against the mental barriers of a hundred different E Grade Denizens. His Willpower was stronger than it had ever been. He could do this—he *had* to do this.

Come on, come on, come on.

Maybe jumping through that portal had been a mistake, but there was no going back now. If he leapt up into the air, he'd be hit by hundreds—maybe thousands—of strikes once more, and he simply wouldn't be able to absorb enough of them with Soul Block.

And unless he got his health back to full, he'd probably die a second or two after he leapt into the air.

I can't let that happen.

He didn't know if a System notification had appeared when he'd come here. He'd been too focused on the sight he'd seen. Too focused on the enemy attacks coming his way. He couldn't help but wonder what was happening back at the castle.

Focus, you idiot, he chided himself.

The mental blocks that the E Grades had pulled up weren't the strongest he'd broken through. Individually. Combined? He'd never come up against something this strong before. He could give up the spell. Wait for the cooldown to end and cast it again, less ambitiously. But he needed to control these bastards if he was going to free up the space around him—if he was going to turn the tide of this damned mess he'd gotten himself into.

His health ticked up another percent. Then a flash of light grabbed his attention from above. Lightning, gathering high in the sky. He clocked a ship, sailing through the air directly for him. This wasn't one of the soldiers that had been lining up, waiting to head through the portal.

This was something else.

Xavier threw his head back and released a bestial roar. Every muscle in his body tensed. His right hand, gripping Soultaker, clutched the haft like a vice. A surge of will swept through his body. Something primal.

Every single one of the mental blocks broke before his might.

A sudden calm settled over him. His mind had been in chaos since the moment he'd leapt through that blood-red portal. Since he'd seen the scope of this city. Its massive, tall buildings that pierced the clouds. The vehicles flying from one place to another. And the sheer number of E Grade enemies he had to face.

But these enemies were *weak.* Compared to him, they were nothing. They didn't possess the powerful titles he held. They hadn't pushed their bodies and minds to their limits. It didn't matter that they were a grade above him.

They were not Progenitors, let alone *True* Progenitors.

Xavier would wipe them all out and feast on their souls as their corpses rotted in the wake of his destruction.

Kill.

The mental command swept through the hundred minds he now controlled, and those warriors, mages, and archers closest to him turned on their allies.

A smirk twitched up the corners of Xavier's lips. He did not move among them. Not yet. He kept his gaze on the ship hurtling toward him. A quick glance at his Mastery Points showed he was almost at the next level. That little revelation almost shocked him out of his calm, as he felt a surge of excitement.

This would be the fastest time between levels he'd had.

My plan might actually work.

His thralls killed and died around him. More Mastery Points flowed into him.

Your health is at 15%.

He grinned.

Soul Strike still had a good forty seconds before it would reach the end of its cooldown. But if he gained a level...

Lightning flashed from the deck of the ship cutting through the air toward him. He cast Soul Block. Absorbed the spell. It came again. And again. There was more than one mage up on that deck, he was sure of it.

Xavier stood his ground. God, he was so damned tempted to leap up and take that ship out in mid-air, but that would perhaps be the most foolish action he could take right now. He figured he'd done enough foolish things in the past couple of days that he didn't need to add to the list. Despite how it might appear, he didn't *actually* have a death wish.

He waited until the ship came close enough. Soul Blocks absorbing every lightning strike that came his way. Xavier couldn't see the mages' auras—it had been a long while since he'd faced an enemy that could contain their aura—but he felt the strength in their spells.

The Denizens aboard that ship are far stronger than the ones around me.

Following the trajectory of the ship, he counted down in his head.

Three, two, one...

Heavy Telekinesis!

The sound of creaking and cracking wood was so loud that it could almost be mistaken for thunder. The ship looked as though it was slamming into a brick wall. He wasn't sure how fast the thing had been going, but it must have been damned fast. Definitely over two hundred miles per hour.

The ship flipped, nose down, ass up. He spotted the mages, wearing robes the same colour as the portal, as though they'd each been dyed in a pool of blood.

Maybe they had.

A thought like that might have made him shudder when he'd first been integrated into the Greater Universe. Now, it didn't even phase him.

The Greater Universe is a harsh, unforgiving place. And that's what I have to be to my enemies if I want to survive in it.

The mages flew straight off the deck. The spell hadn't been aimed at them, and it wasn't *actually* an invisible wall, despite how it had affected the ship, so they each went hurtling toward the ground.

Xavier counted seven of them. He hoped they would take a good amount of damage as they fell—

The mages righted themselves in mid-air. Suddenly, they were all hovering upright above him. They floated toward each other and made a circle. Their arms raised, calling to the heavens. Electricity crackled around them, then lightning struck, chaining from one mage to the other, gathering power.

Well, that's not good.

The lightning came down in the same instant a notification popped up, telling Xavier he'd reached Level 75.

Chapter 42
I Am Become Death

Congratulations, you have reached Level 75!
Your health has been regenerated by 70%!
Your Spirit Energy limit has increased by 200!
You have received +2 Strength, +2 Toughness,
+2 Speed, +3 Intelligence, +3 Willpower, and
+8 Spirit!
You have received +20 free stat points!
All your spells have refreshed and are no longer
on cooldown!

SEVERAL THINGS HAPPENED ALL AT ONCE.

Lightning struck from on high. A massive bolt that almost seemed to move in slow motion as it headed straight for Xavier's head. His spells reached the ends of their cooldown. He tossed all twenty of his free attribute points into Willpower. He cast Soul Block, infusing fifty souls into it, hoping it would be enough to absorb the spell—the one powered by seven strong E Grade mages pooling their power.

And he cast Willpower Infusion.

Lightning struck the soul apparitions. Xavier's eyes widened. The apparitions... weren't strong enough to block the strike! They

288

dissolved, the lightning tearing straight through them with devastating power.

The lightning struck him. Xavier's entire body shuddered. Pain burned through every inch of him. He felt his health, which had just inched over 90 percent after receiving that level, drop down by more than *half*.

How damned powerful was that spell!?

Xavier's body stopped shuddering and jolting. He sank down, his right knee slamming into the stone ground. Purple mist flowed up from his Willpower Infusion spell, making its way toward the seven mages.

Will it be strong enough?

The misted energy entered the mages as they floated above him in that circle of theirs. Each one of them threw their heads back. The hoods of their robes fell down, exposing their faces—all of them human. All of them strained in effort. He felt their mental resistance.

Weak.

Xavier grinned. Stood. His mind took control of the mages, turning them into his thralls.

Turn your lightning upon your allies, he said with a mental command.

There was a shift in the battlefield. When he'd come through the portal, the army on this side had looked shocked, but they'd snapped into action, no doubt thinking whoever had just leapt into their world was a raging idiot who would die in an instant.

But he was still alive, and soldiers were increasingly dying around him.

Xavier needed them to fear him. Needed them to shudder when they saw him. Needed them to falter. He was holding his own, but he still didn't know how long he'd survive over here.

He surged his aura, disrupting the balance in his core. In both his cores. A ripple swept out from him. The shock in those around him turned to fear. He could see it. Their blood running cold. The doubt overtaking each and every one of them.

Lightning rained down from the mages above. This time, it did not rain on him. The seven mages pooled their power once more. Their lightning created a chain—a violent area-of-effect spell that took down hundreds of enemies at once.

That spell definitely could have taken me out.

Xavier looked at his Mastery Points. Watched them rise. Far faster than he'd expected—far faster than he could have hoped. And that was when he realised something.

Soul Strike.

With the number of soldiers dying around him his Soulkeeping reserve was already back to full. He infused all 1,970 souls into a single spell.

Now the lightning was coming from him.

Almost two thousand soul apparitions sprang to life around him. The fear that had rippled through the surrounding soldiers turned into a surge. Xavier had heard the Endless Horde roar and shout. Had heard their battle cries.

But he'd never heard them scream in fear until now.

Death radiated out from him. Each soul apparition that materialised was another translucent, glowing soldier that fought for him. Each soul was strong enough to kill at least two or three of the enemies.

Over six thousand E Grade soldiers died after one spell.

Another roar ripped from Xavier's mouth. He couldn't believe what he'd just done—what he was capable of. These E Grades... They were so *weak*. Nothing compared to the wave bosses he'd been facing. He'd figured one soul would be able to take out one of them, as he could one-hit them with Soultaker easily, cutting off heads and bisecting bodies clean in two.

Congratulations, you have reached Level 76!
...
Congratulations, you have reached Level 77!
...
Congratulations, you have reached Level 78!

•••

Xavier stumbled back in slight shock as the level notifications sprang into view.

Three levels? He'd gained *three* levels, all at once?

That's absolutely insane!

Not only that, his health was now back at full. And Soul Strike —just as he'd realised before he'd cast it—didn't suffer from any cooldown because of the levels he'd gained.

It took a mere instant for him to reap the souls from those he'd just slain and refill his soulkeeping reserve.

And so he cast the spell again—but not before distributing his sixty free attribute points.

Spirit increased from 2,594 → 2,654!
Willpower increased from 1,591 → 1,641!

He'd split the points, putting thirty into each, and marvelled at how many that *actually* gained him with all the percentage modifiers.

Absolutely insane.

Lightning spread out from him. Hundreds and hundreds of bolts shifted into soul apparitions. Screams sounded from the soldiers as death swept through thousands more of them.

God, he'd never felt so much power!

More levels came. He felt a hunger. Deep inside of him. One he'd been holding back for so long. With all the death he caused, all the souls untethered from their bodies, that hunger threatened to take him over. It mixed in with something else. That primal, bestial will that had surged through him earlier—that had made it possible for him to take control of over a hundred E Grades around him.

The hunger is from my Soul Reaper class, but that primal, bestial energy… It's from everything I've assimilated into me.

He didn't know what the consequences of that would be, and right now… he honestly didn't care.

Part of him knew he was only as powerful as he was right now not just because of his titles but also because of the sliver of E Grade material he'd assimilated into himself—it was making his body and core work in a way that an F Grade's simply *shouldn't*.

And that was why it would kill him if he didn't advance soon.

More levels came as he wrought more destruction upon his enemies. The hunger. The primal thrill and power. Each threatened to cloud his mind. And each wanted the same thing—for him to bring more death.

Their goals were his goals. He didn't fight off the hunger or that primal ferocity. He let it all fuel him in his rampage. Those bells still rang inside his mind—the city's warning bells that had sounded when he'd first come through the portal—but those he could ignore.

Waves of lightning death rippled from him. Again and again and again. He'd built up the range of this spell until it could reach for miles—that was how he'd destroyed entire waves in an instant back outside Queen Alastea's castle.

And that was how he would devastate this world.

Congratulations, you have reached Level 87!
...
Congratulations, you have reached Level 88
...

Xavier glimpsed the countdown timer.

Degeneration Countdown Timer: 13 hours 35 minutes 18 seconds.

Xavier gave a dark grin. He'd gained more levels since he'd come through that portal than he'd gained in the last *ten hours*. He worried that soon the System would curtail his Mastery Points for a second time, considering how quickly he was levelling up. It had done it to him before, as he'd taken down wave upon wave of the Endless Horde.

He wouldn't expect anything left.

Only ten more levels. Then I should be able to advance.

Finally, advancing to E Grade was actually in sight. This floor had taken far, far longer than he'd wanted it to. He needed to get back to the tower. Needed to move *forward*.

He disturbed the points, barely looking at them as he did.

Each level didn't only bring him closer to his goal—it made him *stronger*. With every level he gained, he split his attributes to Spirit and Willpower. Spirit helped him in this moment, and he dropped more and more enemies with every Soul Strike he unleashed.

Willpower, that would help him later—when he needed to control his enemies. If not for manifesting that ability, he would have died many waves ago.

As he dropped the points from gaining Level 88, a *thrum* of power rolled through his entire body. Through his very *soul*. His core burned brighter than it ever had, his aura still unleashed. Still pulsing through his enemies and causing them nothing but fear.

He'd hit another threshold. He was gaining so many levels so fast that he hadn't even noticed it was close.

Spirit had just reached its 3,000-point threshold.

Xavier had unlocked another realm of power.

Now I am become death, the destroyer of worlds.

The words came to him unbidden as he unleashed his most devastating Soul Strike yet.

Chapter 43
An Absolute Massacre

Corpses littered the ground around Xavier. In minutes, he'd killed several hundred thousand enemies. His levels had ticked up, and up, and up with every strike. At first, he gained three levels per Soul Strike, then two, until finally each strike garnered him only one.

Only.

The very thought of a single spell "only" gaining him one level almost made him chuckle, but chuckling in this specific situation would probably make him look somewhat insane.

He was more overpowered than he'd ever imagined he could be, though he knew a scenario like this—a *slaughter* like this—was unlikely to ever happen again.

Every wave he'd defeated. Every moment of doubt. Every near-death battle he'd pushed through. Every new threshold of power, new skill, new spell... It was all, finally, becoming worth it.

A thousand times, he'd regretted and doubted his goal of destroying the Endless Horde. A thousand times, he'd pushed past those feelings and kept on moving forward.

All for this.

Somewhere along the way, as his levels kept rising, he broke through another threshold—the 2,000-point threshold for Willpower.

He felt as though he could do anything. Endure anything.

Congratulations, you have reached Level 99!

...

Xavier walked through the carnage, stepping over corpses everywhere he went. Soul Strike was different to other spells. Different to other methods of delivering death. It did not deal any physical damage whatsoever. It did not dent armour or rend flesh, nor did it burn bodies to ash.

It left his enemies pristine, the apparitions flowing through their bodies and inflicting nothing but soul damage.

The dead around him looked eerie. Untouched. As though they were sleeping. But that was merely an illusion. He drew in a deep breath, released it slowly. The hunger inside of him had not subsided. Nor had the primal ferocity. Both had melded together, taking over. He could push them back—he had more than enough Willpower to perform such a task—but he did not want his mind to be clear. Not completely.

If his mind were clear, he might see the devastation he'd caused in a different light.

I have performed an absolute massacre.

He looked at the countdown.

Degeneration Countdown Timer: 13 hours 29 minutes 18 seconds.

Good. He still had time. Far more than he'd imagined he would. And only one more level to attain. The seven mages he'd made into thralls still hovered in the sky. Were still under his control. He sent a mental command, willing them to kill each other.

But the rest of the battlefield was quiet.

No. Not a battlefield. This is a city. The army had been lining up, but beyond that are just people... going about their lives.

In the midst of the devastation he'd caused, the Denizens beyond the initial army had fled. There were still some stragglers he sent out single, one-infused bursts of Soul Strike to take them out. He almost felt guilt about killing opponents that were running away.

Though he did have to remember why he was here, that the Endless Horde had attacked Alastea's queendom, provoked generations ago by one of her ancestors. And what provocation could cause such a response? Such destruction of innocent lives? And how could they be held responsible for something none of them had even done—something done far in the past?

The Endless Horde are bullies. Tyrants. They deserve what I've given them. But maybe I should turn back. Return through the portal. There's nothing left here.

God, he was *so close* to the next level—so close to hitting E Grade. He could *feel* it. Taste it.

I can head through another portal. Do the same thing again.

Though he didn't know if that would be possible. There'd been something different about this portal. With how large it had been. How it had glowed blood-red. Maybe he wouldn't find the same level of enemies in the other ones.

But only civilians seemed to remain here. He'd already devastated the army.

Something caught his gaze, flying down at him from on high.

Airships. Sails and all. Not civilians.

Ten ships flew toward him. They were larger than the first that had come. *Far* larger. Each was a three-masted vessel that looked as though it could hold hundreds of soldiers—sailors?—aboard it.

Xavier tilted his head side-to-side, making it crack satisfyingly. He didn't know if the ship contained enough enemies for him to gain the next level, but if they were coming after him, he might as well take them down.

A System prompt shoved itself in front of his vision. It looked familiar. Through the chaos of him entering this place, he couldn't recall if anything had shown up. He'd been too busy fighting for his life, then gaining vast amounts of levels to notice.

But this notification was flashing across his vision, demanding his undivided attention. No notification had ever done such a thing before.

> **You have entered the Endless Horde's home world and angered its lord.**
> **The Lord of the Endless Horde has locked the portal to Queen Alastea's castle, barring your exit from his domain.**
> **You may no longer return to the Fifth-Floor Safe Zone.**
> **You may no longer safely exit the Staging Area.**
> **To return to the Tower of Champions, you must face the Lord of the Endless Horde and win.**
> **The Lord of the Endless Horde will arrive in 4 minutes and 43 seconds.**

Xavier stared at the notification for far too long. He read it three times, then looked over his shoulder. The blood-red portal still stood. Its glowing light bathed the corpses littering the ground in a way that almost made them look as though they were on fire.

The portal was locked to him. He *couldn't* return through it.

What does this truly change? I was always going to face the Lord of the Endless Horde.

Though this did bring his deadline to reaching E Grade down to minutes, instead of hours. And he remembered what Adviser Kalren had told him—that the transformation itself could take several minutes.

Even if I get this last level in the next few minutes, when the Lord of the Endless Horde arrives to kill me, I'll be in the middle of the transformation.

There wasn't time to think. He had barely four and a half minutes. There was only time to act.

Xavier cast several spells simultaneously. He sent a sixty-infused Soul Strike at one of the ten vessels, a Heavy Telekinesis at another, then cast Willpower Infusion on a third. Part of him wanted to devastate the entire fleet, but he couldn't know if that would be enough for him to gain his next level.

He needed to be sure he'd have something left in the tank if destroying these vessels didn't gain him enough Mastery Points for the next level.

God, he hoped advancing to E Grade would be a simple process. He'd already unlocked his secondary core. All he needed now was one more level.

At least, I bloody well hope that's all I need.

The moment the soul apparitions slammed into that first ship, its trajectory changed. Whoever was piloting it must have died instantly. It veered down, heading straight for the ground. Mastery Points and Spirit Energy flooded into him from the kills.

That's one down.

The second vessel was absolutely *crushed* by the Heavy Telekinesis spell, but those onboard were not killed. They came flying off the deck, just like the seven mages had. The Denizens didn't look nearly as powerful as those mages, however.

When he'd seen the ships on their way, he'd thought he'd be facing more powerful enemies. That some sort of elites had been summoned to take him on. But these were not elites. They were nothing.

The purple mist enveloped the third ship, enthralling the minds of those aboard it.

Ram, Xavier thought, sending a mental command to them.

The ship rammed straight into the one beside it.

With a minute still remaining on Soul Strike's cooldown, Xavier cast Heavy Telekinesis again and again.

Boom.

Crash.

Creeeeeeeeeeak.

To a weaker being, the sounds would have been deafening. Several Denizens were crushed during the onslaught. The ships slid and fell to the ground. The fall alone wasn't enough to kill the majority of the Denizens, however.

Xavier sprinted toward them. Hundreds of soldiers had leapt down onto the ground, landing in graceful crouches. These soldiers looked entirely different to the ones he'd been facing previously. Their weapons and armour were significantly more varied.

Maybe these aren't soldiers. But they came after me.

Before Soul Strike finished its cooldown, every Denizen from all ten ships met their demise.

He glanced at his Mastery Points.

Not enough. I need more.

Xavier gazed up and smiled.

More ships were heading his way. Clearly, they hadn't seen what he was capable of. He'd spread fear into every soldier on the ground. Seen them flee after he'd devastated the army. Yet more enemies were coming toward him?

That made him wonder about what might have happened to the soldiers that had fled. Made him remember the words of that sergeant from the third floor: *The System doesn't stand cowards.*

He realised what must be happening. All the Denizens in the area... They must have gotten a System notification, maybe a new quest, tasking them to kill him.

Xavier could only imagine what kind of reward the System must have offered for something like that.

Certainly, these Denizens thought it was enough to risk their lives. A part of him pitied them. Felt bad for them. But that was a very small part. The System may have prompted them to do this, but it was their own decision to come after him.

At least, he hoped it was.

Too much thinking.

He blocked out his thoughts and leapt straight into the air, heading for one of the newer vessels. His Soul Strike spell was still cooling down. Heavy Telekinesis would take out the ships, but he'd need to get up close and personal if he wanted to take out those aboard.

Attacks streamed toward him. Arrows, spells, even massive ballistae bolts. His Soul Block apparitions were more than enough to absorb the impact, though he wished he had better mobility while in the air, enough to dodge these kinds of attacks.

His leap had him landing on one of the decks to shocked faces. Fear seized those in front of him, but it didn't stop them from acting.

Xavier tore through every Denizen aboard, then leapt straight to the next ship.

He'd taken down sixteen more ships in two minutes and fifty seconds by the time the notification finally came.

Congratulations, you have reached Level 100!
Your health has been regenerated by 70%!
Your Spirit Energy limit has increased by 200!
You have received +2 Strength, +2 Toughness, +2 Speed, +3 Intelligence, +3 Willpower, and +8 Spirit!
You have received +20 free stat points!
All your spells have refreshed and are no longer on cooldown!

By reaching Level 100, you are now able to activate the advancement from F Grade to E Grade and upgrade your class. This can only happen while you are outside of combat.
You will not receive any further Mastery Points until you have advanced to E Grade.
However, you can still upgrade spells, skills, and gain attributes while in this state.

Chapter 44
Little Anomaly's Death

Title Unlocked!
Level 100: This is a common title that everyone receives when they reach Level 100.
You have received +20 to all stats!

Title Unlocked!
First to Level 100: You are the first person from your world to reach Level 100.
You have received +100 to all stats!

THAT'S INSANE, XAVIER THOUGHT. ALL JUST FOR GAINING Level 100?

He shook the thought away, focusing on the problem at hand. He had barely two minutes until the Lord of the Endless Horde arrived, and he needed to advance to E Grade—a process that could take several minutes—before that happened.

And apparently, he wasn't able to initiate the transformation while in combat.

Not only that, I'll have another class to choose. Will I even have any time to go over the options?

Hell—assuming he even survived the transformation—he probably wouldn't be able to choose his upgraded class while in combat with the Lord of the Endless Horde.

Of course I won't be...

If only he had just a little more time.

Xavier snapped into action. As far as he was concerned, he didn't have a choice. There was only one viable option in front of him.

He had to run.

He'd been aboard one of the flying ships as all these thoughts swirled through his mind. He was beginning to notice some of the other vessels that had been heading his way were abruptly turning around, making a run for it after they'd seen the sheer devastation.

At least some of these people have some sense.

Something inside of him flared at the sight of them running. A primal sensation took over, making him want to run after them. Hunt them. Kill them. Like a predator seeing prey flee. He clamped that feeling down and leapt off the ship's deck. As he fell, he balanced the energy in his cores, preventing his aura from shooting out.

He needed to get out of combat, find somewhere safe to advance, and hope it wouldn't take too long. If his aura could be felt, it would be like a beacon leading the Lord straight to him.

Where will the Lord of the Endless Horde appear? Right in front of wherever I am?

He sprinted down the wide street, tall buildings rising up on either side of him. A quick glance over his shoulder showed none of the enemy ships were in pursuit. He could no doubt take them all out with a single Soul Strike, but no way was he going to waste any souls right now, or even put the spell into cooldown.

They aren't chasing me. They're no longer relevant.

The System must consider him outside of combat by now, but he wasn't exactly safe in the middle of the street. He ducked into an alley, figuring it was the best place for him to hide. Part of him wished he'd snagged some of the Denizens from those ships as thralls. Had them to protect him while he would no doubt be defenceless, but there were two glaring issues with that plan.

First, he doubted he would be able to hold control of them during the transformation. And second, even if he *did* manage to remain in control, they wouldn't stand a chance against the D Grade monster he was about to face.

Xavier wasn't much for prayer. Well, he wasn't *anything* for prayer. The thought of asking a deity for help had entered his mind before, when the goal of reaching Level 100 in time had seemed out of reach. But he'd done it. On his own. He hadn't needed any damned help.

But that was when he could stand on his own two feet and fight. What was going to happen when he couldn't fight? When he was stuck in this transformation? Would it make him convulse and fall to the ground? When the Lord of the Endless Horde found him, would the man simply *kill* him in an instant?

He's not going to just wait for me.

The Lord of the Endless Horde will arrive in 1 minutes and 33 seconds.

Xavier swallowed his pride. He put his back to the alley wall, sank down into a crouch, clutching Soultaker's haft in a vice grip, and shut his eyes. Before he activated the transformation, he whispered a swift prayer.

"If anyone is out there, anyone listening, please help me get through this. If you do, I'll owe you—" Xavier paused. He'd been about to say, *I'll owe you my life.* It seemed like what one would say in his current position. But he didn't want to agree to such terms. He didn't want to shackle his freedom to another's will.

Hell, he didn't even want to ask for help—he was simply feeling desperate.

So he left it at that. *I'll owe you.* It seemed like more than enough, and all he was willing to offer.

"All right. Let's get this started then," he muttered. A thrill of excitement ran through him as he activated the transformation.

Are you sure you wish to activate your advancement from F Grade to E Grade? If you have not prepared your body, mind, and cores appropriately, your attributes, spells, and skills might be damaged, or the transformation may cause your death.

One cannot walk backward on the path.

Xavier stared at the notification for five whole seconds after he'd read it. This... this could cause his *death*? No one had told him that. If it were something Adviser Kalren knew, the man had kept it to himself.

He bit his lip. It wasn't as though he had another choice. And how much more prepared could he be?

Yes, he willed. *I'm sure.*

A bright light enveloped Xavier. His entire body convulsed. He lost awareness of everything around him.

Empress Larona floated in the black, amongst the stars. She could See so much from here. A deep frown was set upon her face. She was worried. The future she envisioned—the future she was aiming for—felt as though the very threads of fate did not wish it to come to pass.

Something invaded her awareness.

A plea for help?

She recognised where it was coming from.

The young one.

A smile twisted the sides of her lips. Somehow, this man had tugged on the connection that had been made between them when she'd observed him, sending his prayer through it across the stars.

Not just across the stars, either—he is on a tower floor.

This intrigued her greatly, but she could not respond to his plea. She was the most powerful Denizen in her entire sector, but that did not mean she had the ability to influence what happened on a tower floor. All she could do was observe it. Though even that was a great feat for someone of her grade.

Yet this brought her great pleasure, for she could see what he had done—what danger he had gotten himself into.

He has taken the hard path.

The hard path was the only one that would lead him toward The End. The line that she'd followed the first time she'd observed him... it wasn't so faint as it had once been.

Even if I could help you, Xavier Collins, I dare not influence your next step on the path.

A monster of a man strolled across his rooftop garden, gathering magical herbs and throwing them into a cauldron at the centre of the courtyard. He could have instructed literally anyone to do this task for him, but he enjoyed small labours such as this.

In the eons that he had lived, he had learnt much. Mastered much. Often, there was little else to do when the years drifted by like dust in the wind. The passing of time was inevitable, and he had long discovered that he could not lose himself to mindless pleasures—they did not bring fulfilment, only fleeting moments of joy.

Fleeting moments of joy were nothing when you lived for an eternity.

The man cocked his head to the side, as though he'd heard something. He grunted, instantly realising what it was.

He chuckled. A plea for help, from the Child from Earth.

Perhaps you are not what I thought you would be...

He sighed.

His eyes widened as he slipped into the Tower of Champions and onto one of its floors, observing what the young one was doing. Time seemed to stop as he did so—the flow of time was different where the baby True Progenitor was, and his mind compensated for that.

How...?

The young one had reached Level 100.

Not possible.

Even stranger was the fact that he was only on the fifth floor of the Tower of Champions. The monster of a man remembered that floor. His memory stretched far back, and though there were gaps, it was almost perfect.

The Endless Horde. He's trying to take it out.

This... this was interesting. Perhaps the most interesting thing that had happened in the last few billions of years. He tilted his head to the side. Though it was a shame that the young one's life was about to come to an end.

I could not help you, even if I wished.

He sighed once more.

I suppose there is no reason to send Adranial to this sector at the edges of the Greater Universe after all.

He sat on a bench in his garden, the herbs and cauldron all but forgotten—he'd been making an alchemical potion for his favourite descendant before she returned from her own Tower of Champions and he sent her on this journey.

It was time to observe this little anomaly's death.

Chapter 45
Advancement Completion Imminent

XAVIER FLOATED IN DARKNESS. OR STOOD IN IT. HONESTLY, HE wasn't really sure. This feeling was a familiar one, however. It reminded him of the room he'd been taken to when the System had begun integrating Earth. Black. Formless. Unending.

Initiating advancement of Denizen XAVIER COLLINS from F Grade to E Grade.
Checking attributes...
Denizen's attributes deemed as: Exceptional

Xavier blinked, staring at the notification. This was familiar. Very familiar. Reminiscent of when the System had judged his physical, intellectual, and spirit skills.

Except "exceptional" hadn't been an option at that time—not as far as he'd known.

He blinked, wondering about his attributes. Time seemed frozen in this place, and he got the feeling that nothing *he* did would speed this process, which meant he could finally stop and *breathe.*

Xavier had been in a mad dash to reach E Grade since finding out it would be possible on this floor. He'd no doubt pushed himself farther than any Champion on this floor ever had. But it also meant that there were a lot of floor titles other Progenitors—especially *True* Progenitors—would likely have gotten before reaching E Grade that he hadn't.

Though my attributes are incredibly high for someone at my level, I probably haven't broken any records. I doubt I would be the strongest Denizen in the Greater Universe to be advancing to E Grade, for instance. Though having an epic class and a lot of the titles I do possess mean I must be in the top tier.

He felt a small note of disappointment at that—at not being *the best*. He could have taken a different path. But it was too late now.

On the other hand—assuming he survived what came next—he would still have the opportunity to gain all of the titles from the next floors. And, being E Grade, there was every chance he would rank as number one for each floor, breaking the previous records easily.

I can't imagine there are other Denizens out there that have reached E Grade by this point in the Tower of Champions. Maybe that will garner me a title as well.

Becoming as strong as he could as fast as he could was his goal —it was what would make him the best asset to his planet. The best defender of it.

He looked at the other notifications that had appeared.

Checking spells...
Denizen's spells deemed as: High
Checking skills...
Denizen's skills deemed as: High

Xavier tilted his head to the side. He'd been hoping for a better outcome than that, now that he knew that exceptional was an option. All of his spells were Rank 50, and all but two of his skills were Rank 50 as well. Perhaps there wasn't something higher than "High" for these two properties.

Checking Spirit Core…
Denizen's Spirit Core deemed as: Exceptional
Checking Willpower Core…
Denizen's Willpower Core deemed as:
Exceptional

Xavier smiled. When the notification had told him that not being prepared could damage his spells and skill, or even get him killed, he'd been momentarily worried. Logically, he'd known he was prepared enough, but *seeing* that was the case took a weight off his shoulders.

Advancement to E Grade initiated.
Advancement cannot be interrupted.
Prepare yourself.

Prepare myself? I thought I was pre—
Pain slammed into him. It felt like his very being was split in half on a molecular level. How he knew that was what it felt like was beyond him—but it was. The pain split him in a trillion places, all over his body, inside and out, made him convulse and shudder and writhe.

The pain was so intense that he wasn't even able to scream.

Crellstello, Lord of the Endless Horde, floated down to the surface of his home world, humming a low tune. A funeral dirge, for the Champion he was to kill. The Lord had been exploring the hidden nooks and crannies of his home world's third moon. Exploration was something he greatly enjoyed—his discoveries were the reason he'd managed to become so powerful in the first place—and he'd been meaning to map out the moon for years.

As far as he knew, there wasn't anything of significance on the moon, hence why it had been neglected for so long. Better to go for treasure and resources he knew existed. But he already knew what the entire sector had to offer, and he had to do something with his spare time.

He'd of course been aware of what was happening with the siege upon the Queendom of Arala's final stronghold. Though he had not been the one to order the siege—such minutiae as the scheduling of when to attack other planets was not something that needed occupy his time—he had plenty of lieutenants to keep an eye on things.

Or so he'd thought.

But the handling of this siege had been an absolute disaster. Much of that was attributed to what the System allowed his Horde to do. In this sector, the System had certain restrictions in place when it came to invading weaker domains. Crellstello knew there were other places in the Greater Universe where such rules were different, but he also knew that if he were to step away from his sector, he would no longer be considered the *most powerful*.

There would be others to contend with. Denizens of equal and far higher ranks. Right now, he was a big fish in a small pond. He didn't want to change that.

Perhaps in a few hundred years, or even a thousand, things would change. But the advancement to C Grade had eluded him, and he'd long ago told himself he wouldn't step away from his sector until two things were achieved: Total domination of every planet in the galaxy, and his advancement to C Grade.

Now some Champion of the Void was burning through the lower ranks of his Horde. The System should have compensated for that. Clearly, the waves it had allowed weren't *enough*.

This damned Champion should have been crushed long ago.

Somehow, the Champion was gaining more and more strength from each wave that came. Now, however, the Champion had pushed too far—come to *his* home world. It was not that the Lord cared for those the Champion had killed. His soldiers and beasts were disposable. They always had been. He saw them closer to slaves than citizens, and one does not mourn the death of slaves.

What he cared about was the setback this Champion had caused to his plans and the fact that his actions made the Horde look weak.

That was not something he could tolerate, and finally, the System was allowing him to remedy the situation.

You've attacked my world now, Champion. All restrictions have been lifted.

Truly, it had been the most foolish of choices.

The Lord of the Endless Horde easily pinpointed the man's location in his city and landed at the mouth of an alleyway. He chuckled at the sight before him. The Champion wore dark robes and clutched a weak weapon that was beneath his power. And he was shuddering.

"This is where I find the great Champion of the Void that has been giving my Horde so much trouble? Cowering in fear at the back of an alleyway?" The System must have made the Champion aware of the Lord's imminent arrival. He released a deep chuckle, then made a *tsk, tsk,* sound with his mouth. "You made a dire mistake, coming to my home world. You should have retreated through the void, back to whatever backwater universe you came from."

As the Lord of the Horde neared the shuddering man, he paused and tilted his head to the side. There was a power enveloping the man. Energy hovering around him. It wasn't the man's aura. It was something else.

System Energy.

This got the Lord's full attention. "You aren't cowering," he muttered. "You're advancing." The transformation looked as though it still had a few minutes until it would be complete. The Lord rested a hand on the hilt of his sword. "One cut, and you would be done for."

He didn't feel any resistance to the course of action. The System would allow him to do this.

The Lord sat down on the cold stone of the alleyway, crossing his legs beneath him. He rested his hands on his knees and closed his eyes, taking a deep breath.

It was true; he had done what people might consider terrible things in his life, and he did not much care for the lives of others—unless they could advance his own cause. But he lived by a code of honour, one his mother had taught him many years ago.

"You do not fight someone who is unarmed, little Crell," his mother had said, placing a hand on his chin and pulling his eyes up to meet hers. "Do not dishonour your family."

I won't dishonour you, mother.

He'd made sure to always adhere to her code of honour. That was why, when he'd burst into her throne room during his coup, he had not attacked her unawares—he'd waited until she'd summoned her weapon.

Crushing this Champion of the Void would be child's play, and far more enjoyable when the man was conscious. Though it did surprise him that the man was advancing to E Grade. The System would not have thrown such low-level waves at this Champion if he'd been this strong when he'd first arrived.

He has tempered himself on my Horde, in a way that no one else ever has, but he shall regret it.

Xavier's pain felt as though it would never cease. It was as unending as the Horde he faced—as unending as the Greater Universe itself. His body split a trillion ways, and with it, his mind. Perhaps even his soul.

His consciousness was not a tangible thing. He could not take hold of what was happening. His awareness was more than fractured—it was glass shattered by a meteorite the size of Earth's moon. Whenever it tried to reform, to get a handle on what was happening, that meteorite would strike once more, shattering everything he was.

The System was breaking him down. Down into nothing.

Not nothing. Almost nothing.

Time was irrelevant. This was all he knew.

Until things changed.

Bit by bit, the core components that comprised the being that was Xavier Collins stitched themselves back together. The System was rebuilding him. He could feel its presence around him, and he realised that he recognised it. He had felt this before. When he'd first been fully integrated and given his class—that was when he'd felt it the most.

He'd just never noticed it before. Now, with the presence of the System around him so strong, it was clear.

There's an energy around me... It's around me every time I earn a title. I just never knew.

A word for the energy came to him unbidden. An insight provided to him from the Greater Universe itself, even though he wasn't meditating right now—even though there was no way that he *could* meditate right now.

System Energy.

The pain had not gone away. If anything, the pain was worse now that his mind was slowly becoming whole once more. He could fully perceive it. But Xavier had the strength of will to look past that pain. Had the strength of will to see through it and to the other side.

He was changing.

Error.
Multiple impurities detected in XAVIER COLLINS.
Assimilated impurities unable to be purged.
Impurities may affect the efficacy of your advancement.
Advancement completion imminent.

The pain doubled.

Chapter 46
Advancement Complete

XAVIER OPENED HIS EYES IN A FLASH.

He was lying on the cold, hard stone of the alleyway he'd run to. He felt no pain anymore. It looked as though his body hadn't been attacked while he'd been unconscious.

His body, mind, and soul was whole again.

The impurities the System had detected—everything that he'd assimilated into his body to gain more power, more attributes. The things that had been changing him... How had it all affected his advancement?

There isn't time to think about that. The Lord of the Endless Horde will be here soon.

He tried to open the timer that would tell him when the Lord of the Endless Horde would arrive, but he wasn't able to—because the Lord of the Endless Horde was already here.

"You have caused me an awful lot of trouble, Xavier Collins." The voice was deep. Powerful. And... bored?

Xavier forced himself to his feet in less than a second. Soul-taker was still gripped tightly in his hand. The staff-scythe felt... weak in his grasp. The weapon hadn't been fit for him for a long time.

Notifications were launching into his field of view, trying to gain his attention. He wished to look at them—wanted to know what the transformation had caused.

I still have to upgrade my class.

There might be other things he needed to do. Had his skills or spells changed? Had he gained more attributes? He felt... different. More aware. Of the energies around him. The Celestial Energy, for instance, stood out like it never had before, starkly contrasted against the background of the tall buildings that bracketed the alleyway.

And his body was definitely more powerful. His magic. His core. His soul. God, he wanted to know what had changed!

But the man who stood at the mouth of the alleyway took up all of Xavier's attention. Xavier wasn't sure who he'd imagined when he'd thought of the Lord of the Endless Horde. Perhaps a man in dark black full-plate armour. Or some demon lord with horns sharper than any sword. Maybe an ancient elf whose soul had grown dark as time ravaged their will.

What he saw was nothing like that.

The Lord of the Endless Horde wore something akin to martial arts robes. The robes were white and thick, almost like he was walking out of a Karate dojo or Taekwondo dojang. He had dark hair, tied into some sort of warrior's braid that hung down his back absurdly long. At his waist, a jade scabbard held what looked to be a rather slender sword. He didn't have a shield.

Why is he just standing there?

The man must have arrived while he was in the middle of his transformation, yet he hadn't attacked. He was just looking at Xavier with clear contempt, like an arrogant nobleman glancing at a beggar in the street.

Xavier felt no power radiating from the man, but he didn't need to feel the power to know it was there.

His mind worked at a mile a minute. Every split second counted. Xavier had thought the man would attack him the instant he arrived. Honestly, he'd not expected to wake up after the transformation—he'd thought this truly had been a suicide mission.

But he was still alive, and the degeneration countdown that had plagued him since he'd integrated the E Grade material into himself had finally disappeared.

Could I buy some more time? Enough to choose my class?

The Lord of the Endless Horde rested a hand on the pommel of his slender sword. The pommel was a large emerald, the green of it matching the jade of his scabbard. It did not glow.

Xavier shifted where he stood, readying himself.

I should move. Now.

He already knew the chances of him defeating a D Grade Denizen were incredibly low. If he allowed that D Grade to make the first move? They would be zero.

But maybe if I get him talking...

"Why did you not kill me while I lay defenceless on the ground?" Xavier asked. He split his consciousness and checked his soulkeeping threshold, found it to be full—the number of souls he kept hadn't changed.

The Lord of the Endless Horde raised his chin. "My mother raised me never to attack an unarmed, defenceless enemy." He made a *tsk* noise with his tongue. "Of course you are still defenceless. There isn't much I can do about that." He tilted his head to the side and took a step forward. "You are a curiosity, Xavier Collins."

There he goes, using my name again. He must have a very advanced Identify skill.

Xavier didn't even bother trying to scan the man, or using his own Identify skill. He knew there was no chance of it working. "Strange sense of honour you have, sending your army to attack a Queendom that has done you no harm."

Keep him talking. For as long as possible.

As swiftly as he could, Xavier read through the different notifications that vied for his attention, knowing this fight could begin at any moment.

Congratulations, XAVIER COLLINS. By

advancing to E Grade, you have taken the next step of your journey on the path.
You have received +100 to all stats!
Your body, mind, and soul have been transformed and will now work more efficiently.
Your skin has been hardened, your strength improved. Your mind has been enhanced, your thoughts cleared. Your soul has been tempered, your spirit emboldened.
Your cores have become more robust. Your awareness of them increased.
The transformation to E Grade has changed you at the very foundation of your being. Each step forward on the path of advancement not only increases your power and lifespan but also increases your potential within the Greater Universe.
One cannot walk backward on the path.

Title Unlocked!
E Grade: This is a common title that everyone receives when they advance to E Grade.
You have received +50 to all stats!

Title unlocked!
E Grade Progenitor: You are the first person from your world to advance to E Grade.
You have received +100 to all stats!

Title unlocked!
E Grade Speedrun (Unmatched): You have reached E Grade faster than anyone in the Greater Universe, displaying a potential that has never been seen before.
This is an unmatched title.

The System is watching.
You have received +25% to all stats.

Congratulations, XAVIER COLLINS, a class
upgrade is now available to you.
You have 24 hours to make your choice. You
will not gain any Mastery Points until you have
upgraded your class.
Would you like to see your options?

Xavier could barely contain the excitement he felt at all the power he'd just received. He'd just gained far more power than he'd imagined he would. God, no wonder he felt so different—he'd broken through several more thresholds.

And the way the System had broken him down and put him back together... It affected him in more ways than simple attributes boosts. Ways he couldn't begin to understand.

Then there was the final title he'd received. E Grade Speedrun (Unmatched). Had he truly reached E Grade faster than any of the trillions and trillions of people that had come before him? How could that even be possible? Other Denizens would have advantages he didn't have access to—powerful ancestors with close to limitless resources. Wouldn't they powerlevel their kin—and get them to this stage—if they knew such a title was possible?

He had gotten there in under two months. Was that truly such an accomplishment?

The second-last line in the title was what hit him the hardest.

The System is watching.

It sent a shudder up his spine.

Xavier had read all of this in almost an instant, his thoughts moving more swiftly than ever, contained in the second part of his split consciousness.

Split Mind... Usually, using that skill hurts me, requiring a certain amount of strain. This time, I was able to activate it without any trouble whatsoever.

Was that because of his attributes, or because he was E Grade now?

The Lord of the Endless Horde took another step forward. "You speak of things you do not understand, Champion of the Void. Honour is... individual. We each have to choose what it means to us. To live by a code." He raised a hand, pointed at Xavier. "You have made my horde look weak. That, I simply cannot abide." He looked at the sky, breathed deeply through his nose. "Fortunately for me, you are a fool. A curiosity, yes, but a foolish one. You are very ambitious, attacking my home world. Usually, one such as I would not be allowed to attack one as weak as you. Not in this sector. Not unprovoked."

Xavier contemplated the last notification. He had a day to choose his next class, and he wouldn't receive any Mastery Points if he killed this man before doing that.

What a waste.

He looked at his status information.

XAVIER COLLINS
Age: 21
Race: Human (?)
Grade: E
Moral Faction: World Defender (Planet Earth)
Class: Soul Reaper (Epic) – Class Upgrade Available
Level 100
Strength: 1,379 (2,206)
Speed: 1,272 (2,480)
Toughness: 1,297 (2,075)
Intelligence: 1,263 (2,728)
Willpower: 1,623 (3,181)
Spirit: 2,083 (4,687)

Mastery Points (E Grade) until next level:
0/100
Available Spirit Energy (E Grade):
46,970/46,970
Available Willpower Energy (E Grade):
10,000/10,000
Available Skill Points: 0
Free stat points remaining: 20
Titles:
Bloodied Hands, Born on a Battlefield, Settlement Defender, Quester, First Defender of Planet Earth, Survivor, All 100, First All 100, 1,000 Stats, First to 1,000 Stats, Greater Butcher, Fourth-Floor Climber, Solo Tower Climber 4, 1st Fourth-Floor Climber, Fourth Floor Ranked 1 – RECORD HOLDER (Completion Time – 4 sec), Ahead of the Pack, Goliath Killer, All 1,000, First All 1,000, Level 100, First to Level 100, E Grade, E Grade Progenitor, E Grade Speedrun (Unmatched)
Spells List:
Spiritual Trifecta – Rank 50
Heavy Telekinesis – Rank 50
Spirit Break (All) – Rank 50
Spirit Infusion – Rank 50
Soul Harvest – Rank 50
Soul Strike (Ranged) – Rank 50
Soul Block – Rank 50
Soul Harden – Rank 50
Willpower Infusion – Rank 50
Skills List:
Physical Resistance – Rank 50
Magical Potency – Rank 50
Magical Resistance – Rank 50
Physical Damage – Rank 50

Assimilate Properties – Rank 17
Scythe-Staff Mastery – Rank 50
Meditation – Rank 50
Aura Control – Rank 50
Core Strength – Rank 50
Cultivate Energy – Rank 50
Identify – Rank 23
Split Mind – Rank 13
Minor Spirit Coins: 394,249
Lesser Spirit Coins: 8

Xavier noticed several differences. The first difference was the question mark by his race. That... that was definitely new. Had the items he'd assimilated somehow changed his race? It did say the impurities might affect his transformation.

I wonder if that will have any negative effects.

His Mastery Points, Spirit Energy, Willpower Energy, and spirit coins had all been altered. He'd been slightly baffled when he'd seen only "100" Mastery Points needed for him to gain his next level, until he'd noticed the "E Grade" descriptor.

The numbers for his Spirit Energy and Willpower Energy were still quite high, but they'd definitely been altered as well.

And God, his attributes! They were absolutely insane. He just hoped they were insane *enough*.

The Lord of the Endless Horde had taken a third step forward. His fingers wrapped around the hilt of his slender sword. Xavier knew there was no more stalling anymore. No chance of him upgrading his class before this showdown began.

Time to fight a D Grade Denizen.

Chapter 47
At Least I Made the Bastard Flinch

XAVIER BURST INTO ACTION BEFORE THE LORD OF THE Endless Horde could make the first move. His soulkeeping reserve was full with almost two thousand souls, but there was no one around him that he could easily kill—the alleyway was deserted.

Part of him wanted to drop a fully infused Soul Strike at his D Grade enemy, but if that wasn't enough, he wouldn't be able to use Soul Block.

Several things happened all at once.

Xavier sprinted to the left, straight toward the wall of the tall skyscraper—the alleyway he'd run into had been a dead end, not providing much space to move. He had no idea what the Lord of the Endless Horde was capable of, but as the man wielded a sword, the last thing he wanted to do was face him in a close-up, melee fight.

As he moved, he cast Spiritual Trifecta on himself and Spirit Infusion into Soultaker. His Spirit attribute was currently at 4,687 points, and the power that rolled over him felt absolutely *insane*.

Not only that, his body moved so much faster that he wondered if his friends back at the castle would even be able to perceive his movements. Still, he knew it likely wasn't fast enough. He needed better mobility—a way to get out of this alley.

Heavy Telekinesis! Spirit Break! Willpower Infusion! Soul Strike!

Each spell was cast with incredible speed and precision. His enemy hadn't moved from where he stood. The man's gaze simply tracked Xavier's movements, a single eyebrow raised, the corner of his mouth twitching upward in amusement.

Then the first spell hit the man.

The Lord of the Endless Horde was pushed back two feet. His eyes widened. The amused smirk fell away. The raised eyebrow dropped. A look of wild confusion replaced it.

Yes! Xavier shouted in his mind. He'd half-expected the spell to do absolutely nothing. He may have been able to mow down E Grade enemies while he was F Grade, but he'd been a *strong* F Grade.

He had no idea where he stood now. He just had to hope that this sector was as weak as it seemed. That it lacked the advantages of others.

None of the enemies I faced were unique.

If they'd possessed titles, they'd been incredibly basic. And no one in this sector was old enough to be a Progenitor, for the System had been here long before any of them had been born, and the strongest Denizens in the sector ended up leaving to find power elsewhere.

Yet the Lord of the Endless Horde had remained.

He likes being the strongest here. I suppose I can't blame him. Or maybe he feels he's too weak to survive outside this sector.

Spirit Break hit next. Xavier wasn't sure what to expect from that. He certainly didn't think it would break his enemy's body, mind, and magic.

Fwoooom.

The spell slammed into a barrier, one that had sprang up the instant after Heavy Telekinesis had hit. It made the Lord of the Endless Horde glow golden.

Xavier, still running off to the side, watched the man as closely as he could, and saw the slightest hint of pain alight on his face.

The barrier clearly offered some sort of magical defence. But the defence wasn't completely impenetrable.

At least I made the bastard flinch.

Though Xavier could admit that wasn't very promising.

The purple mist from Willpower Infusion was the spell Xavier was least confident in, especially now that damned golden barrier had been raised. Xavier held his breath as the mist reached his enemy.

It seeped *through* the barrier.

The magical defence is useless against mental attacks!

If Xavier could get a hold of his enemy's mind, all would—

A mental block stronger than anything he'd ever encountered snapped up. For a split second, Xavier had *almost* been able to feel his enemy's mind. Now, it was as though a wall of reinforced steel a mile long had materialised.

Xavier pushed against it, as hard as he could. He was able to pull upon more mental strength than ever before now that he'd advanced.

It wasn't enough. He saw no possible way he could break through the man's mental defences, not while they were this strong.

Finally, Xavier's final and most powerful spell hit—Soul Strike.

Xavier had infused one hundred souls into the spell, trying to be conservative to test the man's defences. The apparitions sprang into life. A hundred of the man's dead soldiers materialised at the end of pure white bolts of lightning, surging toward their former master.

The Lord of the Endless Horde gazed at the apparitions. He still had not drawn his sword. He tilted his head to the side as they came for him, clearly seeing them for what they were.

His lips twitched upward as the apparitions slammed into his golden barrier. The golden barrier flickered—briefly—but didn't falter. It solidified a moment later. The attacks hadn't harmed the man in the slightest.

When the four spells had all been cast, Xavier reached the left wall. All this had happened in one small moment. He'd not had anywhere to go when he began his run—he'd simply wanted to be on the move. Though his enemy wielded a sword, there was a chance the man had ranged spells. It'd be better for him to remain in motion, able to dodge the attacks if they came.

The Lord of the Endless Horde chuckled, shaking his head slightly. Finally, he pulled his slender sword free of its jade scabbard with a slight scrape, his gaze on Xavier. "Is that truly all you have to offer?" He cracked his neck. "I'll admit, that first spell took me by surprise." He looked at the stone ground. "I hadn't expected to be moved backward by someone as weak as you."

He took a step forward.

"But those other things you had to offer?" He made a *tsk, tsk* noise with his tongue. "Very disappointing. That final attack of yours, oh, it looked flashy, but if that is the limits of your power? Well... I'm surprised you managed to get this far in the first place."

Xavier had stopped running. Apparently, he hadn't needed to. This D Grade bastard seemed happy enough to toy with him—to treat him as though he wasn't a threat. Xavier had expected the man to come at him right away, yet he'd just stood there, taking every spell he had to throw.

Now he was running his mouth, monologuing like some lame movie villain.

Not the first time I've found myself in this situation...

The question was, how in the hell could he use this to his advantage? Though the Lord of the Endless Horde was running his mouth, the D Grade bastard had a point. As strong as Xavier had become—as much as he'd been able to accomplish—he was still nothing compared with this man.

How could he possibly change that?

There wasn't enough time for him to upgrade to his next class. The process would take too long. His test of Soul Strike, using only one hundred souls, had been somewhat effective—it had made that golden barrier flicker. Maybe if he used enough souls, it would break the damned thing completely.

But now he had to wait over a minute for the spell to reach the end of its cooldown. Something protested within his mind at that thought. His assertion had a feeling of *wrongness* about it.

Standing there, watching the Lord of the Endless Horde smirk at him, Xavier looked at the cooldown for Soul Strike.

Soul Strike has a varied cooldown, dependent on how many souls are infused into the spell. It cannot be used for another 45 seconds.

What? Xavier thought, thinking his eyes must be deceiving him. It had been a few seconds since he'd cast the spell, but the cooldown remaining was *half* of what it should have been.

What else has changed?

This was a definite boon, though forty-five seconds was still a very long time. Especially in a fight like this, where every split second no doubt counted.

I wish I had another way to refresh my spells besides levelling up.

That would certainly solve a lot of his problems.

I just have to keep him talking.

"If I am so below you, why do you demean yourself by fighting me?" Xavier asked, his grip on Soultaker still strong, tight. He let out a silent breath and relaxed. His high Willpower made keeping his emotions in check very easy, as long as he was aware of them.

The Lord of the Endless Horde didn't look at Xavier. His eyes were on his sword. He held it up, let the light catch the side of the blade. He still looked mostly bored. "If I did not allow myself to fight those below me, I would never have anyone to fight."

Xavier raised his chin. He saw a way to infuriate the man. To goad him. But that didn't seem like a wise approach. There was still forty seconds on his Soul Strike.

How long will I last when he attacks me? How foolish was I to think I could go up against a D Grade?

Xavier steeled himself, realising something—he *was* being a fool. But not because he'd gotten himself into this mess. He was being a fool because he'd lost his confidence at the time when it should have been at its highest.

He forced himself to think of all that he'd just accomplished. Of everything that he'd just done in the last day and a half, let alone the last few weeks since the integration. He had achieved feats that literally no one in the Greater Universe had ever achieved. He'd somehow attracted the attention of powerful Denizens without having even finished the first ten floors of the Tower of Champions. Powerful Denizens that observed him in ways that shouldn't be possible because they saw his potential.

He had an *unmatched* title for becoming the fastest Denizen to ever reach E Grade.

And he was standing there, trying to make his opponent talk because he was afraid to face the man before his cooldown ended? Was that truly how he wished to face his enemies?

So goad him, then. Change the damned game.

Xavier smiled. As he did so, he felt his teeth—slightly pointed— dig into his lower lip, and he knew what he needed to do to get more powerful. "That's why you've remained here, in this sector." He paced across the alleyway. He let go of Soultaker, placing the now-free hand on his mouth and shaking his head, as though embarrassed for the man.

He slipped something into his mouth, swallowed imperceptibly.

"You're afraid of facing someone on your level. Afraid of a true challenge." Xavier made a *tsk, tsk,* sound identical to the one the Lord of the Endless Horde had made. "How long have you been like this, stagnating in your power? No wonder the System holds your Horde back so much. No wonder it places so many restrictions on this sector." He stopped pacing, looking up. "It doesn't tolerate cowards."

Chapter 48
Death by a Thousand Cuts

SEVERAL NOTIFICATIONS POPPED UP IN XAVIER'S VISION AT once, all while he stood across from the Lord of the Endless Horde, speaking taunts at the most powerful Denizen he'd ever faced.

> *Unidentified Material* **categorised as** *Elemental Hydra Fang!*
> **Biological impurities of** *Elemental Hydra Fang* **have been further assimilated into muscular structure.**
> **Tissue Regeneration trait strengthened!**
> **You have gained +4 Strength!**
> **You have gained +4 Toughness!**
> **You have gained +4 Willpower!**

Eight times, the notification appeared. He marvelled at the speed at which he used his Assimilate Properties skill, holding back a smile as the skill ranked up three times, adding to every attribute he'd gained with the skill.

He also couldn't help but notice that E Grade properties gave him four attribute points each time he assimilated them, rather than the two that F Grade did. It wasn't a huge boost, but every little bit made a difference.

The skill worked with an efficiency he hadn't imagined possible. He'd swallowed several shards of Elemental Hydra Fang at once, hoping he could assimilate them one after the other before his body forced them to be purged.

And it wasn't the only shards he swallowed.

Attempting to assimilate *Elemental Hydra Claw* into muscular structure...

The material you are assimilating has various properties.
You may only draw from one.
Choose from the following:

    1. **Passive Elemental Damage (Fire)**
    2. **Passive Elemental Damage (Air)**
    3. **Passive Elemental Damage (Water)**

Though surprised by the options before him, Xavier chose swiftly, doubting he would have time to assimilate anything else. There was an addictive quality to the skill.

God, he wished he could assimilate the Bear King's material.

Assimilation is complete.
Biological impurities of *Elemental Hydra Claw* have been assimilated into muscular structure.
You have gained the trait: Passive Elemental Damage (Fire)!
You have gained +20 Intelligence!
You have gained +20 Willpower!
You have gained +20 Speed!

Assimilate Properties has reached Rank 21!

...

Assimilate Properties has reached Rank 25!

Passive Elemental Damage, Xavier thought, revelling in the new trait he'd just gained. When he'd given up the Cast Element spell, he hadn't expected to be able to cause elemental damage again.

I'm a whole different beast now.

The Lord of the Endless Horde's expression shifted from one of boredom to one of mute curiosity. Though there was a hint of something in the man's eyes. Something dark and angry. "You dare call me a coward? I was going to make your death a swift one, lest you waste more of my time." He raised his chin, eyes boring into Xavier. "Now... I think I'll make your death last." Suddenly, a power radiated from the man.

His core.

The energy flowed outward, like a dam breaking. The wave forced Xavier to take a step backward. The pressure was like nothing he'd ever experienced. Sam, the barkeep, had said that a powerful Denizen could harm others with nothing but their aura alone.

His aura might be powerful enough to kill my entire party.

Something made Xavier want to fall to his knees. To bend at the waist and neck and beg this man forgiveness.

But he would never stoop so low as that. Not in a million years.

He gritted his teeth and fought the pressure of the man's aura.

The Lord of the Endless Horde clearly hadn't expected this. Perhaps he'd thought he could cow Xavier with this alone. If so, he was a damned fool.

Xavier cast Heavy Telekinesis on the man. He didn't expect anything to happen. The first time he'd cast the spell, the golden barrier around his enemy hadn't been active. But he needed to put pressure on it. If he'd learnt anything about defensive barriers from Howard, it was that they had two limitations—how much damage they could take, how long they could last.

This man didn't look like a tank class.

The spell isn't going to last long. Not if I can help it. And once I break through... I'll break him.

Xavier turned thought into action. He fell into his battle mind, into a new level of focus. The spell hit. The golden barrier flickered —ever so slightly. Though not as much as it had flickered when he'd struck it with Soul Strike.

Still, it's vulnerable.

And it didn't protect from mental attacks. That was something he'd already learnt.

Xavier took a gamble. A small one, at first. He sank one hundred souls into Spirit Break. This was a property of the spell he'd gained when he'd taken up the Soul Reaper class—one he didn't take advantage of near enough.

The Lord of the Endless Horde flung himself forward. And god damn could the man *move*. Xavier grinned. Raised Soultaker. He wasn't going to run from a confrontation.

Spirit Break slammed *through* the man's barrier. The D Grade bastard's right eye twitched, betraying the pain he felt when the spell hit him. Physical. Mental. Magical. Those were the three aspects of Spirit Break. The mental pain was what the Lord must have felt the most, as the barrier no doubt blocked the physical and magical damage very effectively.

Heavy Telekinesis and Spirit Break both had low cooldowns— less than a second—but the cooldowns weren't faster than the Lord.

His sword came down for Xavier's head with devastating speed. Xavier brought up Soultaker. The scythe-staff glowed silver from his Spirit Infusion spell. That spell infusing it was the only reason he felt confident trying to block with it at all.

The Lord's sword hit Soultaker's haft. Hard. The impact pushed Xavier down into the stone ground, cracking it and cratering it a foot deep.

It wasn't only the stone that cracked. Xavier felt something break in his scythe-staff, picking the sound out through the noise of the stone breaking beneath him.

Perhaps he'd been wrong about Soultaker surviving.

There were still twenty-three seconds until Soul Strike was ready to be used again. He hadn't even gotten the man to talk for a full minute.

Xavier leapt backward, out of the small crater that had been created, dodging a slash aimed for his midsection by less than a hairsbreadth.

A notification had appeared the moment the sword had impacted his staff.

Staff-Scythe Mastery has reached Rank 51!

Xavier's eyes widened. He'd blocked the man's attack once, and he'd gained a rank? That didn't seem like it should be possible.

The System sees this man as completely out of my league...

It was compensating for him. It didn't reduce the challenge of the fight; rather, it was upping the reward for even the smallest of Xavier's successes.

I can use this.

The Lord of the Endless Horde was faster than Xavier—that was clear. He had him on the back foot. Each of the man's strikes pushed Xavier backward another step. The man hadn't even used any spell yet—nothing but the golden barrier that surrounded him.

He's still going easy on me.

Xavier wasn't sure why he was frustrated by that fact.

He blocked another strike, one coming from the left. It sent him flying straight into the alley's right wall, cracking the stone of the tall building. He felt Soultaker break just a little more this time and wondered how in hell the thing was even still together.

Scythe-Staff Mastery gained another rank. Though he was beginning to wonder if that would matter much, soon.

It's going to be tough to utilise the skill if Soultaker breaks.

All the while, he kept cycling through the same few spells.

Heavy Telekinesis was definitely doing something to the golden barrier. Xavier's perception had become incredibly fast, especially after he'd advanced to E Grade. To a weaker Denizen's eyes, they wouldn't have been able to discern the increased duration of the golden barrier's flickering.

To Xavier, the shift was as clear as day.

It spurred him on.

He cast Spirit Break three more times. He worried about the number of souls he was using. He needed to get out of this alley. Needed to find more soldiers. Something to help him refill the reserves. One-on-one fights were not his forte.

He packed two hundred souls into each casting of Spirit Break.

Just as the golden barrier flickered longer, so did the man flinch more each time.

It's working. I'm breaking him down!

He was just doing it too slowly.

Willpower infusion!

Xavier cast the spell with unrestrained vigour. He'd been holding off. Wanting to break down the man's mind with Spirit Break as much as he could before trying the spell again.

The mist flowed from Soultaker's blade. It made it to the Lord of the Endless Horde in a mere instant, as the man was in close, slashing his sword at Xavier with violent precision. The mist flowed through the golden barrier just as it had the first time.

The wall came up once more. Xavier could feel it easily with his mind. Could feel how powerful it was. A grin slipped onto his face.

It wasn't just the wall's strength he felt—he also felt its vulnerability. Just like there was a crack in Soultaker's haft, there was a crack in the enemy's mind.

He's not taking his defence seriously.

The Lord of the Endless Horde was still toying with Xavier. Slashing at him with testing strikes. He was fast, but he surely wasn't using all the power at his disposal. That posed multiple problems for Xavier. One of which was the fact that if he forced

Willpower Infusion through that gap and took control of his enemy, it wouldn't be a *strong* control. The crack in the man's mind wasn't large enough.

And the moment that control fell away... the crack would be filled.

"I tire of this!" The Lord of the Endless Horde swung his sword down again. An overhead strike, like the first he'd performed. Except faster.

Xavier didn't have time to get out of the way. He raised Soultaker, holding it in a solid two-handed grip, horizontally above him.

Crack.

The scythe-staff broke down the middle. The Lord of the Endless Horde's slender blade kept moving.

No!

Soultaker broken, the blade came straight down at Xavier's forehead. He tried to throw himself out of the way, but he wasn't fast enough—couldn't be fast enough.

The Lord's slender sword bit deep into his shoulder.

Pain flared. A hiss released from Xavier's gritted teeth.

A smile blossomed on the Lord of the Endless Horde's face.

"I told you your death would be slow." The man yanked the sword out of Xavier's shoulder.

Xavier stumbled back, his breath coming fast and shallow.

"Have you ever heard of death by a thousand cuts?" A slimy smile slid onto the Lord's face. "Well, something tells me you won't last that many." He tilted his head to the side. "But let's start the tally at one."

Your health is at 70%.

Xavier hadn't known what to expect. Part of him thought he would have died instantly the moment that man's sword hit him. He was glad he'd been wrong—though maybe death would have come if the blade had dug into his forehead instead of his shoulder.

Physical Resistance has reached Rank 51!
...
Physical Resistance has reached Rank 55!

Holy crap!

Xavier had been right. The System *was* compensating for him. The percentage boost from those rank-ups had gotten him over thirty points in Toughness.

Your health is at 73%.

Xavier grinned over at his enemy. He didn't know how much health he had now. The well of energy that was his life force was so much deeper than before. But so was his level of health regeneration. His Toughness might not be his highest attribute, but it was now at 2,241 points.

The Lord of the Endless Horde was toying with him. Wanting to make his death a slow, agonising one.

Looks like I can use that to my advantage.

His grin fell away as he glanced down at his scythe-staff. Soultaker was now in two parts, one held in each hand.

I guess I'll have to learn how to fight like this now.

Chapter 49
Always Mind Your Surroundings

THE NEXT FEW MINUTES WERE A WHIRLWIND OF PAIN.

The Lord of the Endless Horde's smile grew more and more sinister as the fight went on. Xavier continued to cast spells at the golden barrier, hoping that his Magical Damage skill would rank up, but nothing at all was coming from it. The barrier flickered more and more, but Xavier quickly realised the damage he was inflicting upon it wasn't *enough*.

And because he wasn't damaging the Lord himself, it didn't help him receive any ranks in the skill.

He would need soul damage to truly hurt the man. When Soul Strike had reached the end of its cooldown, he'd once again considered infusing all of his souls into the attack. It might very well be his only option—but he wasn't ready to do that.

He had other plans for this fight.

Physical Resistance has reached Rank 60!
...
Physical Resistance has reached Rank 65!

Your health is at 43%.

Xavier pushed through the pain. It was nothing compared to what he'd experienced during his advancement. Each time he took a hit, it took less of his health from him. But even if Physical Resistance gained a hundred ranks, he knew it wouldn't be enough to keep him alive from a true onslaught of attacks from this man.

As the fight progressed, Xavier always on the backfoot, he practised his ability to evade the Lord of the Endless Horde's strikes—in hopes his health would have enough time to regenerate.

You have learnt the skill Evasion!
Evasion – Rank 1
Evasion is half speed, half anticipating your
enemy. You are practised in the art of not
getting hit, and now you have the skill to
prove it.
+5% perception of enemy's attacks.
+5% Speed.

The notification had taken him by surprise. The skill rank-ups he'd expected, but learning *another* skill while in the middle of battle?

Xavier hid the smile from his face. He hadn't earned it yet. Besides, he needed the Lord of the Endless Horde to see him suffer.

I will tear every ounce of possible advantage out of this fight as I can!

The difference was instantaneous. The skill ranked up quickly. Every single time he dodged one of the man's lightning-fast sword strikes—which had become easier than ever as instincts he'd never had became ingrained in his mind—another notification popped up. He felt his Speed notch up and up.

And it wasn't just his Speed.

Just as the skill had said, his perception of the Lord of the Endless Horde's attacks improved tremendously. He'd already been getting a feel for how the man fought, the skill simply helped him advance that.

Xavier didn't only focus on evading the man's attacks, but he also used the two halves of his broken staff-scythe. He no longer blocked the man's strikes head on. Instead, he angled them away, ensuring Soultaker's hafts never touched the man's blade. Even turning away, the man's strikes put an immeasurable toll on his body.

But he knew the Lord of the Endless Horde would tire of this soon enough. At any moment, he could turn. Show Xavier his full power.

I need to be ready.

"Are you hurting yet, *boy*?" The Lord broke through Xavier's guard and dug his sword straight into his side. His mouth was close enough that Xavier could feel his breath on his own face.

Xavier held the Lord's gaze. The pain bit into him—another rank of Physical Resistance gained—but he only let a flicker of that pain onto his face.

There was a look of confusion in the man's eyes. "Why aren't you begging for death? You should be begging for death!" He pulled the sword out and kicked Xavier in the chest.

Anger overtook the Lord of the Endless Horde then. Anger that had been simmering slowly behind the man's eyes. His aura, which had already been unleashed, putting constant pressure onto Xavier's shoulders, flared even more powerfully than before.

The kick sent Xavier flying. The pain in his side was intense. He felt his health tick under ten percent. A weakness overtook him. A futility.

He tried to reorient himself in the air. To land feet first against the wall behind him. But as pained as he was, he wasn't able to. He slammed into the rock. This building, unlike the last he'd slammed into, wasn't made from stone. It was made from metal— one of the grand skyscrapers he'd gazed at when he'd first entered this place.

The force of his impact dented the metal wall. He heard a

massive metallic creak, as though the very foundation of the tall building had been compromised.

Perhaps it has been.

Xavier slid down the wall. He had the presence of mind to land on his feet in a crouch. He stood, wincing at the pain in his side. The wound was healing, but his health was incredibly low. Even with all the new ranks in Physical Resistance, he wouldn't be able to take another hit from the Lord of the Endless Horde.

I'd die in an instant.

But the sound of that metallic creak had given him an idea. He'd been so focused on his enemy that he hadn't been paying attention to his surroundings. Words from one of his favourite movies played in his mind.

Always mind your surroundings.

He didn't know how strong these buildings were, but he now knew they were vulnerable.

The Lord of the Endless Horde's steps were featherlight and silent. His laughter, on the other hand, echoed off the alley walls. "You're turning out to be quite the disappointment, Xavier Collins. Did you really think coming to my home world was a *good* idea?"

Xaiver didn't respond. He tried to look weak, vulnerable. Wasn't hard, considering how damned low his health was. The two halves of Soultaker were still gripped tightly in his hands. The black blade was deadly sharp, even if it was nowhere near as powerful as the weapon his opponent wielded.

Xavier threw a glance upward and hid a smirk. He'd definitely been blind to his surroundings. He'd assumed that everyone in the area had simply run away from the fight—then he remembered the flying ships that had come for him. The quest they must have received to kill him.

He imagined no citizen of this world or any other within the sector would be foolish enough to come between the Lord of the Endless Horde and whoever he intended to kill.

But that didn't mean they wouldn't wish to observe the fight.

I've been thinking too small.

He slashed behind him, at the wall he'd just been flung into and dented, hoping he wasn't a fool. Hoping he was right. The alleyway had three walls, each a building. The one that marked the dead end was so close to the others that they were almost touching. One could only fit a hand through the gap.

But they *weren't* touching. Which meant it could fall, straight down in the alley, if the right amount of pressure were applied...

"What are you doing?" the Lord asked, a hint of amusement in his voice.

Xavier's blade cut straight through the metal. He didn't know a damned thing about construction, but he'd played a fair amount of Jenga in his time. He knew that if you took a chunk from the bottom of something tall...

To his great pleasure, the strikes he inflicted didn't only cut, they *burned*. It was the first time he'd seen his new trait in action—though, as the building was metal, he doubted the fire damage would be of much help.

Most of Xavier's physical spells didn't cause much damage, but the first spell he'd ever chosen would be perfect for this.

Heavy Telekinesis!

Xavier's Intelligence was his third-highest attribute. Close to breaking three thousand points. Since advancing to E Grade, he'd only ever used his Heavy Telekinesis spell on the Lord of the Endless Horde.

And so he hadn't realised just how powerful it had become.

Boom!

Creeeeeeeeeeeeeeeak!

He'd slammed the spell straight into the dent his body hitting into the building had created. Straight where he'd put the cuts.

I've done it, Xavier thought. *The building's going to fall.*

All he needed to do was get the hell out of the way—and hit the Lord of the Endless Horde with a distraction that would stop *him* from getting out of the way.

While he'd been taking the bastard's strikes, ranking up his Physical Resistance skill and his new Evasion skill to boot, Xavier hadn't simply been moving onto his back foot. He'd been throwing Spirit Breaks at his enemy, weakening his mind as much as he could manage.

His soulkeeping reserve had fallen to just above a thousand.

This might be my only chance.

The Lord of the Endless Horde, still seeing Xavier as no threat at all, was idly staring at the skyscraper as it continued to creak and veer downward toward them. Any moment now, it was sure to fall.

"That's your plan?" The man shook his head, a look of utter disappoint on his face. "You've seen how fast I am. You truly believe that thing's going to fall on me? Or are you trying to anger me by damaging my city, as though I would care?"

That's right, you bastard. Keep talking.

Xavier took a step toward the man. He raised the two halves of Soultaker. This only made the Lord of the Endless Horde laugh all the more.

"I admire your... level of foolishness. Something tells me you do not understand the difference between us. That you do not understand the sheer gulf that separates the power of our grades. There is nothing that you can do to defeat me, child. Even if you had my entire Horde by your side."

"We'll see about that."

In quick succession, Xavier cast four spells.

Heavy Telekinesis came first, flickering that damned golden barrier. Spirit Break came next. With five hundred souls infused into the attack—more than he'd ever used with it—the reaction it caused on the Lord was far more than a simple flinch.

He took a whole step back, a look of pained shock afire on his face.

Something told Xavier the man wasn't used to feeling pain, and hadn't been for a long, long time.

Soul Strike came next. As with Spirit Break, Xavier infused it with five hundred souls. His soulkeeping reserve was down to twenty-three. And though it would cause no mental damage,

Todd Herzman

Xavier hoped the soul damage would be enough of a shock to make the man's focus crumble.

Finally, he cast Willpower Infusion.

Willpower Energy flowed through Xavier and out both halves of the scythe-staff until a thick purple mist filled the alleyway. It sped straight for the man in front of him.

Creeeeeak.

The skyscraper was falling. Ever faster. It blocked out the sun as it veered toward them.

Not much longer now.

The Lord of the Endless Horde, in his abundant arrogance, had simply stood there and taken the spells, for he had taken Xavier's spells before and no harm had come to him.

What harm could an E Grade possibly cause to a D Grade, after all?

He'd resisted Willpower Infusion several times, and again, no harm had come to him.

But this time, things were different.

There was a crack in the wall that was the Lord of the Endless Horde's mental block. A crack that Xavier was about to take full advantage of.

The apparitions from Xavier's 500-infused Soul Strike and the mist both reached the D Grade Denizen in the same instant.

Chapter 50
The Time for Games Is Over

On the Lord of the Endless Horde's home world, Xavier leapt.

Behind him, a building was falling. In front of him, a powerful D Grade Denizen stood. The man's mind was captured. In control. The crack in his mental defences, after being hit by a 500-infused Spirit Break, had become large enough for Xavier's control to slip in.

Willpower Infusion has reached Rank 51!
...
Willpower Infusion has reached Rank 60!
...
Willpower Infusion has reached Rank 65!

Holy crap, Xavier thought. The rank-ups wouldn't help him now that the spell had already been cast, but the next time he used it, it would be much stronger. *The fact I managed to control his mind at all is a miracle.*

Though he had no idea how long that would last, as every split second, the Lord of the Endless Horde fought Xavier's control like a cornered rabid dog.

Xavier, his mind still split, had put one of his consciousnesses toward the singular goal of simply holding the D Grade Denizen where he was. He didn't know if dropping a building on the man would be enough to kill him, but he hoped to all hell it would be enough to at least *harm* him.

Your health is at 13%.

Though it didn't look like it, Xavier's health was rising quite fast. He just needed it to rise *faster*. God, he wished he had time to pick his new class. He didn't know what it would bring—what new spells he might have access to—but it could offer him an advantage he currently lacked.

But the last thing he needed was to be unconscious if—most likely *when*—the Lord of the Endless Horde dug his way out from beneath that falling building.

As he leapt, shooting high into the air off powerful legs, Xavier flew straight toward one of the ships he'd seen hovering above the alley. The building fell straight past him. Was a handspan from clipping him in the legs.

He'd gotten away just in time.

Xavier couldn't look back. Not yet. The control he had over the Lord of the Endless Horde was slipping fast. He'd given the man one command—*be still*—and that command was being fought. He was moving. Very slow, like a tired turtle, but he was moving nonetheless.

The ship he'd leapt toward was turning about with great speed. Fortunately for Xavier, it wasn't nimble enough to avoid him.

Xavier latched onto the side and pulled himself up onto it. The force of him hitting the ship had made it sway violently downward, which made him wonder just how much he weighed now. Had his body become denser after his advancement? Or was it his Strength attribute that made him so heavy?

Not important right now.

The Denizens aboard the ship he'd just clung to came running for him. He couldn't feel their auras, which meant they were likely E Grade, or near to it. Either way, they were no threat to him.

As Xavier raised his weapon—or *weapons*—he felt the mental connection between himself and the Lord of the Endless Horde *snap*. His control over the man was gone.

At the same time, a massive *boom* sounded behind him as the skyscraper crashed to the ground. As tall as the damned thing was —piercing the sky as it had been—Xavier hadn't given a thought to whether there had been people inside of it, or people below it, for that matter.

What he was glad for was that it had fallen across a wide road. The alleyway he'd run into had been at the end of a T intersection. The way had been clear. He'd been lucky, he knew, for any other place he could have been, the building would have slammed into another long before it reached the ground.

He hadn't sensed any auras inside the building. Then again, not everyone had an aura, and there was a chance the building could have been shielded somehow, containing people's auras within its walls.

Xavier crushed one Denzin's skull with the bladeless half of Soultaker and decapitated another with the other. Kill notifications began to pop up into his vision, but it wasn't only two he'd just defeated.

It was several *hundred*.

He felt their souls freed from their body. The building that had fallen...

Soul Harvest!

Hundreds of souls made their way into him, all at once. The kill notifications were for Denizens of assorted levels—from as low as Level 1 to as high as Level 140.

He skimmed them, some slim hope within him that he might have killed the Lord of the Endless Horde with that building. But he knew if that had happened, he would have gotten other notifications—the completion of the fifth floor, for one.

The remaining Denizens aboard the ship swiftly turned

around, running away from him instead of toward him. Some even dove overboard to get out of his reach. He let them go, instead leaping to the next ship.

Soul Strike has a varied cooldown, dependent on how many souls are infused into the spell. It cannot be used for another 4 minutes and 3 seconds.

Not bad, Xavier thought. It was definitely a long time, but before his advancement to E Grade, the cooldown for using five hundred souls in Soul Strike would have been twice as long.

There had been several ships above the fight with the Lord of the Endless Horde—he'd counted six at his first glance, and he'd been right. They were all fleeing now, at the sight of the building falling, at the sight of him leaping out of that alley. But they weren't far enough away.

Willpower Infusion's cooldown ended. God, he was never more glad than now that it had a short cooldown.

There were dozens of people on these ships. He'd leapt to the next one to get into the centre of them. The moment he landed, he cast Willpower Infusion. This time, he didn't just have a single target.

The mist shot from him and went to everyone aboard not just this ship, but every one of the half dozen flying ships in the area. Mental blocks sprang up. Hundreds of them. But even with his focus split as it was between so many targets, not a single mind among them was strong enough to resist his influence.

He commanded those aboard each of the ships to turn them back around. To face the alley once more. His soulkeeping reserve had been replenished when that building fell, though it was only a little over eight hundred. Halfway to being full.

Standing at the prow of the centre ship, Xavier stared down at where the building had fallen.

It *had* to have fallen atop the D Grade bastard, hadn't it? And though it clearly hadn't killed him, perhaps it might have—

The part of the building that had fallen upon the alleyway exploded, breaking in half. A figure shot out of it. A figure in white martial arts robes, wielding a slender sword. The man leapt through the air…

No, he didn't leap. He *flew*. Straight at Xavier.

Xavier steeled himself. He commanded every one of his thralls to attack. With spells. With the ships they captained. With anything and everything.

Fireballs, lightning bolts, shards of ice—they all sailed toward the D Grade bastard as he shot through the air.

Xavier cast Heavy Telekinesis. His casting was faster than all of the thralls, and the first spell to hit. He'd expected the man's golden barrier to stop the attack, but it did nothing.

The man wasn't thrown back, but he was halted in mid-air.

With all his power, Xavier tried to hold the man there. It wasn't a simple *push*. He was trying to crush the man with his Heavy Telekinesis. Practically frozen in the air as he was, he got a good view of the man.

He didn't appear wounded. There was no blood marring his white robes. No marks on him at all—not even soot or dust or anything from the building's collapse.

How is that possible? How powerful is this man?

The spells hit then. Dozens of them, from every Denizen with ranged abilities. Arrows and crossbow bolts hit the Lord of the Endless Horde as well. A wave of fear exploded outward from all of the thralls he controlled. Fear at having attacked their Lord. The attacks did nothing. There was no golden barrier, and still, they caused the man no visible damage.

Ships sailed through the air toward the Lord, to ram into him, but Xavier knew that would do nothing too. If a building crashing into him hadn't hurt the man, what could ships do?

Xavier cut the lines of energy that held his control over his thralls. Before he did, he pushed a final command into their minds for them to *hold their ground*. He didn't know if it would work. He didn't much care, either.

The Lord of the Endless Horde was only held by the Heavy Telekinesis spell for a mere second and a half. He broke free. Anger was written all over his face. Burned in his eyes. He didn't fly at Xavier. Not right away.

Instead, he raised his sword. Pointed it at one of the ships sailing toward him. No words were spoken. He cast a spell. His sword glimmered in a golden light—much like the barrier he'd used on himself. He slashed.

A blade of golden energy materialised in the air, an extension of the D Grade Denizen's sword. It cut through one ship.

Slash.

Another.

Slash. Slash. Slash.

Every ship but the one Xavier stood upon was sliced completely in two. Then the sword was pointed at him.

"The time for games is over."

The Lord of the Endless Horde slashed his sword.

Xavier's mind reeled. He saw the slash coming. The attack falling. The man's emotions. His anger. It boiled to the surface. The Lord of the Endless Horde's mind had been controlled, and he must have felt nothing but horror that someone as weak as Xavier had managed such a thing.

Your health is at 21%.

The golden blade of energy materialised in the air. A normal cut from the D Grade Denizen's blade would be enough to kill Xavier right now.

A blow like this? It would obliterate him.

He saw it coming. Knew its exact trajectory. And he knew he was fast enough to get out of its way.

But Xavier didn't move, because he also knew exactly what he needed to do to have a chance at killing this man. This man, whose aura was raging as much as his face was, the power radiating outward, crushing the less powerful Denizens in the area. The pressure Xavier felt from the man's power was nothing compared with the surviving thralls still under his control.

The power he's let loose... the chaotic, uncontrolled nature of it... That will be his demise.

Xavier just hoped he would survive killing his enemy.

Chapter 51
Burn, You Bastard, Burn!

AT THE PROW OF THE LAST REMAINING FLYING SHIP ABOVE the floating Lord of the Endless Horde, Xavier steeled himself and stood his ground. A strong wind blew in, flapping the sleeves of his robes and pulling the dark hood back to rest on his upper back.

Xavier had a plan. But if he was strong—if the plan failed—he would die in the next second.

He didn't know if what he was about to attempt would work. He'd never tried something like it before. And the only reason he thought it was even possible was because of a confluence of events.

Candleflames don't produce smoke.

The fire that was the Lord of the Endless Horde's core was out of control. He'd let it loose—let it run wild to put pressure on Xavier. To the point where he was sure there must be weaker Denizens out there in the city, falling unconscious, even dead because of its power.

The Lord of the Endless Horde had underestimated Xavier just enough to be angered by his actions. He'd let his guard down, and Xavier had been able to take control of his mind. Even if only for a brief moment.

His emotions are out of control. He killed his own people

because I put them under my thrall—if he were thinking straight, would he do such a thing?

Xavier gritted his teeth. A blade of golden energy hurtled toward him. It was too late to get out of the way.

Now!

He cast Soul Block, Spirit Break, and Willpower Infusion almost at the same time. With the death of so many caused by the falling skyscraper—and those deaths attributed to Xavier's actions —he'd been able to reap over eight hundred souls.

Xavier didn't know how strong this golden energy blade was. He had to trust that his defences would be enough. The spell was clearly a magical one, and though it was his Toughness attribute that gave him more health, it was his Willpower attribute that gave him resistance to magic. And his Willpower attribute was well at 3,248.

He infused two hundred souls into Soul Block, hoping it, along with his resistance to magic, would be enough to withstand the attack. The apparitions sprang up in an instant. He then threw the rest of the souls into Spirit Break. Over five hundred—the most he'd ever infused into the spell. God, he wished he'd been able to use more. Wished he'd been able to use over a thousand.

For this to work, what he assumed was true *had* to be true—that after the first time he'd broken into the man's mind, he'd weakened it. That the man hadn't been able to shore up his mental defences —if he had, his emotions wouldn't be so volatile, would they?

Spirit Break hit. The golden barrier that had surrounded the Lord of the Endless Horde for almost the entire battle was gone. It had disappeared after the building had fallen atop him. Which meant this Spirit Break was stronger in more ways than one.

In the same instant that Spirit Break struck, so did the Lord of the Endless Horde's golden blade of energy. It tore through the apparitions like they were as weak as spiderwebs. But the glowing light in the attack dimmed with each soul that it passed through until it reached him.

The blunted attack slammed across Xavier's torso. His robes

were already a tattered ruin of slashes and blood—he hadn't had a moment to infuse Spirit Energy into them for repairs. Now, a new slash joined them.

Your health is at 3%.

The attack brought him to his knees. But he was alive. Alive long enough to fulfil the next step of his plan.

A hiss released from the Lord of the Endless Horde's lips. Pain slipped onto his face. Far more than a flinch. Without his golden barrier, the spell didn't just break him mentally—it hit with a trifecta of pain. Physical, magical, and mental. It did not snap his limbs backward like it would on a lesser enemy, but it didn't need to.

Purple mist seeped through the man's nose, eyes, ears. The misted Willpower Energy was thicker, more concentrated, than any he'd ever been able to summon. The Willpower Infusion spell had ranked up several times the last time he'd been able to use it on this bastard.

He just hoped it had ranked up enough.

Once again, Xavier felt the man's mental block spring up. Once again, he felt the cracks. There were more than last time. Far more. And they were larger. Usually, when Xavier tried to take over a mind, he would put one half of his consciousness toward the task.

He couldn't do that this time. Not if he wanted this to work.

Xavier put his entire mind, all of his focus, every single part of it, toward this. He pushed through the cracks and took control. The line between himself and the Lord of the Endless Horde was like a steel cord. He felt the man's emotions. Felt the surface of his thoughts.

And he felt the man's tumultuous core. The raging fire of power he had within him.

When Xavier had first learnt about the concept of controlling his aura from Sam, the barkeep back at the Tower of Champions and guardian of his cohort, he'd almost burned through his core in his attempt. He would have, if not for Sam.

And once he burned through all the Spirit Energy in his main core, he would have burned through his health until there was nothing left.

Xavier, however, didn't only feel *one* core—he felt *three*.

Of course the man would have three active cores. He was *D* Grade.

This might be harder than I thought.

But that didn't matter. This was his plan. He was down to 3 percent health. If he didn't do this...

I will do this!

Xavier set things in motion. He threw his consciousness. His *whole* consciousness straight into the Lord of the Endless Horde's mind, just as he'd done to that one Denizen during the waves back outside Queen Alastea's castle.

Suddenly, his control over the man strengthened even more. More than he would have thought possible. In that moment, Xavier *was* the Lord of the Endless Horde.

Burn!

The command was yelled with all the power of his mind.

Burn through your cores!

He didn't just set one to burning—he set them *all* to burning. Xavier identified the three cores. A Spirit Core. A Strength Core. And an Intelligence Core—the Intelligence Core was the weakest of the three.

He could feel it. Feel the pressure, blazing outward. When he'd done this to himself, his aura had flared brighter than ever.

The Lord of the Endless Horde's aura, flaring as it was, might very well crush everyone in the city.

Everyone but me. I'm strong enough to resist.

He could feel the energy of the man's core. It was a blazing inferno. An inferno the size of a city—of *ten* cities.

Burn, you bastard, burn!

He pushed the process ever forward. If it were his own cores, at the rate these were burning... he would have been dead in seconds.

As the cores burned, the Lord of the Endless Horde fought for control of his own mind. Seconds passed. One. Five. Ten. With every second, Xavier felt his control slipping away.

And with each second, the Lord of the Endless Horde grew ever weaker.

How? How is he doing this?!

The Lord of the Endless Horde was trapped within his own mind, his cores burning through all of their energy. Soon, they would burn through his very life force.

This was the second time that meddlesome child had taken control of him. But this time, his control was far more intense.

Crellstello was stronger than this foolish Xavier Collins. He was stronger than *anyone!* No one—no one who stepped foot in his sector—could ever face him! Could ever even put up a challenge!

No. They couldn't defeat him even if all the worlds in the sector gathered together under the same banner and declared war on him. He would crush them like the bugs they were.

And Crellstello had known that coming into the fight with Xavier. He'd known he needn't worry, and so he *hadn't* worried. Even when the boy's first spell had knocked him back two feet, it hadn't *hurt* him.

This child *couldn't* hurt him.

He'd only just advanced to E Grade.

The Lord of the Endless Horde tried to take control of his own mind once more. The last time, it had taken a mere moment for him to take control again—a moment that had seen a building fall on top of him. But that had barely hurt.

Why... why didn't I just crush the child at the start? How did he even survive my True Blade spell?

His mother's words entered his mind. Words he'd despised for centuries. Words that had been the reason he had finally killed the woman.

You are weak, Crellstello. You will always be weak.

But he proved her wrong! He'd been strong enough to kill her! Strong enough to take over this entire sector!

The fires of his cores burned. He could feel them, snuffed out, one by one. His Intelligence Core was the first to lose everything.

You are weak, Crellstello.

His Strength Core went next.

You will always be weak.

Then his Spirit Core. The main core of every Denizen. His Spirit Energy had not been low for centuries. Not since he himself was E Grade.

Crellstello, the Lord of the Endless Horde, could feel how close he was to taking back control of his body. But he knew all the energy in all of his cores... would be gone by the time he did.

I'm not weak! he yelled within his mind. *I am strong!*

Though he thought it with all the determination he had, he no longer believed it. Maybe he never had. That was why he was still here, lording over those weaker than him, instead of trying to become stronger. Instead of facing new challenges.

I toyed with this man when I should have crushed him. So sure I was in my own power.

His mother had always told him his weakness, his arrogance, would be his downfall.

When the Lord of the Endless Horde finally took control of his mind once more, all three of his cores were burned out of their energy.

But his cores, they were *still* burning. Burning through his health!

He woke on the ground, in the rubble of the fallen building. His Flight spell had been interrupted when that bastard had taken control of his mind. Pain stabbed at each of his cores. It wracked his entire body.

Not since he was F Grade had he so little control of his energies.

The Lord of the Endless Horde opened his eyes to see a man standing over him. A man in dark robes with glowing silver eyes. A man that shouldn't have been able to take control of him—shouldn't have been able to *defeat* him.

Yet here, Crellstello lay at that man's mercy.

His body, his mind, his spirit—it was weak. He struggled to reverse the burning of his health. Doing such a thing should have been child's play, but something within his very soul had broken, and all he could hear, over and over, was his mother telling him how *weak* he was.

"Please..." the Lord of the Endless Horde begged the man standing above him. "Help me."

Xavier Collins raised the bladed half of his broken scythe-staff and uttered a single word, "No."

The blade came down.

Chapter 52
The System Is Watching

Xavier went for the man's neck.

The Lord of the Endless Horde lay upon a ground of rubble. It wasn't just the metal and glass of these strange skyscrapers—stone and wood and dust and splinters had poured out of the innards when the building had fallen.

The D Grade Denizen had been weakened. Once, he had been the most powerful being in the entire sector. Now, all three of his cores had burned right through, and his health had come next.

Still, Xavier hadn't known if he would be strong enough to kill the bastard—didn't know if the Lord would be able to come back from what he'd done to him. A feat he hadn't thought possible.

I dropped a building on top of him.

Thunk went his broken scythe-staff as the blade dug into the Lord of the Endless Horde's skin.

Physical Damage has reached Rank 51!
...
Physical Damage has reached Rank 55!

I took control of his mind.

Thunk!

...

Physical Damage has reached Rank 58!

I made him burn his own body.
Thunk!

...

Physical Damage has reached Rank 62!

I made him fall from the sky.
Thunk!

...

Physical Damage has reached Rank 65!

I made him beg for my help!
Thunk!

Twenty swings it took. Twenty swings to kill and behead the most powerful being in the sector. A man who'd killed only for power. Only for dominance. Who invaded worlds on a whim.

Each strike had brought more ranks, the System still compensating in his favour even now. And thus, each strike had more Strength behind it—had more damage behind it.

When the last strike fell and the kill notification finally came, Physical Damage had reached Rank 70.

You have defeated a Level 201 Human Master of the Golden Sword!

No Mastery Points were shown for the kill.

Xavier's energy left him. It drained from every one of his muscles, and he collapsed to the ground. A sharp pain stabbed at his head. His entire body ached.

Your health is at 5%.

Xavier smiled, despite his weariness, despite his pain.
He was alive.
The notifications flooded into his vision. The first was one he'd
been aching to see for so long.

**Congratulations! You have cleared the Fifth
Floor of the Tower of Champions.
Party Member Contribution:
Xavier: 100% of XXXX waves.
Howard: 0% of XXXX waves.
Justin: 0% of XXXX waves.
Siobhan: 0% of XXXX waves.
Error – Endless Horde Defeated.
No shared attributions apply on this floor.**

**Title Unlocked!
Fifth-Floor Climber: This title has been
upgraded. You have cleared the Fifth Floor of
the Tower of Champions and shall be
rewarded.
You have received +10 to all stats!
Note: The title "Fourth-Floor Climber" has
been stricken from your soul.**

**Title Unlocked!
Solo Tower Climber 5: This title has been
upgraded. You have cleared a floor of the
Tower of Champions by yourself. You are
either very brave or very stupid for attempting
such a feat. Know that whether this feat was
achieved through sheer skill or unbridled luck,
you shall be rewarded.
You have received +40 to all stats!**

Note: The title "Solo Tower Climber 4" has been stricken from your soul.

Title Unlocked!
1st Fifth-Floor Climber: Out of Champions from five competing worlds, your party is the *first* to clear the Fifth Floor of the Tower of Champions within your instance.
You have received +25 to all stats!
Note: As you have a similar title, "1st Fourth-Floor Climber" has been combined with this title and shares its stats.

Title Unlocked!
Fifth Floor Ranked 1 – RECORD HOLDER (XXXX Waves – Error – Endless Horde Defeated): Out of all the Champions from all the worlds in the Greater Universe who have completed the Fifth Floor of the Tower of Champions in every possible instance, you have defeated the highest number of waves. This title is a Temporary Title. If your record is edged out of first place, your title will be turned into a normal top 100 title.
If your record is edged out of the top 100, your title will be lost.
You have received +60 to all stats!
Note: As you have similar titles, each has been combined with this title and shares their stats. You may still view the previous titles and your standing on the leaderboards, if you will it.

Title unlocked!
Destroyer of Hordes (Unmatched): You have exceeded the expectations of the System,

completing a floor of the Tower of Champions in a way that was never envisioned.
This is an unmatched title.
The System is watching.
You have received +30% to all stats.
You have received a Unique Spell: Core Burn
You have received a System Boon: Usurper

Title Unlocked!
Ahead of the Pack 2: You are well ahead of those from your world. You have become the first fully integrated person from your world to defeat a D Grade Denizen.
You have received +100 to all stats!
Note: As you have a similar title, "Ahead of the Pack" has been combined with this title and shares its stats.

Title Unlocked!
Goliath Killer 2: You have defeated a Denizen of a grade one above your own for the second time, at a different grade. This is a feat few in the Greater Universe ever manage and is often an indication of greatness.
You have received +120 to all stats!
Note: As you have a similar title, "Goliath Killer" has been combined with this title and shares its stats.

In 1 minute, you and your party will be returned to the Staging Room.

Xavier couldn't help but gawk at all of the notifications as he read them.

Power pulsed in him as one attribute after another broke through *another* threshold of power.

Intelligence, over 3,000.

Throom.

Speed, over 3,000.

Throom.

Strength, over 3,000.

Throom.

Toughness, over 3,000.

Throom.

Willpower rose over 4,000 points.

Then finally Spirit. His strongest attribute of all. It rose higher than he'd ever expected it to.

Over 5,000 *points.*

Throooooom.

He was practically radiating power. He hadn't gained a single level from the man's death—he wouldn't gain any Mastery Points until he chose his next class. But god, was he *strong.*

He felt... Unmatched.

His combined stats must be massive, though he hadn't received any titles for his stats since he'd reached 1,000 in all of them—nothing for two thousand or three thousand. And nothing for his combined stats since 1,000.

Maybe the System only does that at the beginning?

But there wasn't time to think about that. He'd read through the titles incredibly fast, but he still had less than a minute until the System booted him from this floor, sending him back to the Staging Area.

A part of him had wondered if he would somehow be able to bring Queen Alastea and her adviser back with them, but such a thing never seemed possible. And now, he wouldn't even be able to see her again.

At least she'll be free, now. The Endless Horde will no longer come after her, or her people.

Now that their D Grade leader had been defeated, he was sure remnants of the Endless Horde would return through the portals.

Xavier knelt down by the Lord of the Endless Horde. He looked at the man's robes. At his slender sword and jade scabbard. The man wore other things, too, things Xavier hadn't noticed at first. A golden bracelet on his left hand, an anklet on his right ankle, and six rings on his fingers.

Are they all Storage Rings, I wonder?

He grinned and looted it all. The jewellery. The sword, scabbard. The martial arts robes. The Lord of the Endless Horde lay in the rubble in nothing but his underclothes, his head separated from his body. A once-powerful man, fallen from his heights.

Xavier stood, closed his eyes, and basked in the sunlight falling upon him through the tall buildings.

It was finally time for him to return to the Tower of Champions. There were many things he needed to discover. One of those titles had granted him something called a Unique Spell named Core Burn, another a System Boon—whatever that was—called Usurper.

All of the titles he'd received were... amazing. But the unmatched titles did make him narrow his eyes and wonder, yet again, what it meant by "The System is watching."

Not for the first time, Xavier felt a presence watching him. Or, was it two presences? Powerful presences that he'd felt before. He picked them out easily—the most powerful one, the one that made him feel like a speck of dust... It had observed him at the end of the last floor.

Here it was again.

Not the System.

The other was weaker, but by no means weak.

Again, neither of these presences was the System watching him. He was sure of it. But those titles proved he *was* being watched by it.

The most powerful entity in the Greater Universe has its eye on me. I suppose I'll have to make my life a story worth watching.

Xavier smiled as he felt the pull of the System taking him away from this place. When he'd entered this floor, he hadn't known how long he would spend on it. Hadn't known how powerful he would grow. Hadn't known he would—even *could*—achieve the impossible.

Yet he'd done it.

Soon, he would burn through the next five floors and finally return to Earth.

And nothing would be able to stop him from keeping it safe.

Chapter 53
Usurper

Someone slammed into Xavier the moment he appeared in the Staging Room.

Siobhan wrapped him in a tight, but brief, embrace. "You're alive!" She stepped back, cleared her throat. "We... we thought you might die out there."

"We saw you leap through that portal," Howard said. "What on Earth were you thinking?"

Xavier rubbed the back of his head. "Well, I wasn't *on* Earth at the time." He smirked, but his weak joke only got a groan from Justin and a raised eyebrow from Howard.

His party were gathered in front of him. They each looked a little bit shocked. Clearly surprised that he was alive at all.

"What happened?" Howard asked. "Did you face the Lord of the Endless Horde?" He stepped forward, brow creased. "The contribution notification for the floor... said you *defeated* the Horde?"

Xavier raised his chin. He smiled. Couldn't help it. He was back! Finally, they'd finished the floor, made it back to the tower! Their loot boxes sat in the middle of the Staging Room, as they always did, waiting for them to open them.

And he had a class upgrade to choose.

Not only that, but he also had a new spell that he'd gotten from one of his titles, as well as a System Boon, to discover the details of.

As thrilled as he was to do all of that, he told the others what had happened first. He led them to the loot boxes and took a seat on his own. He wasn't worried about the time they might take between floors. He was well and truly in the lead. He'd likely have to take off an entire week if someone were to ever catch up.

And the six or so weeks he'd taken on that floor? Well, here, technically, only an *hour* had passed. Two, if he counted his first time on the floor.

I wonder what Sam will think when I return to the tavern, already E Grade. That's assuming I should even tell him.

"You really defeated him? A D Grade Denizen?" Siobhan shook her head, a look of awe on her face. "That's amazing!"

Siobhan wasn't the only one shaking their head. Howard and Justin were too.

"You... took control of him?" Howard asked in slight disbelief. "Made him burn his core from the inside?" He blinked. "That's, well... that's damned overpowered." He ran a hand through his beard. "Could you do that to... to anyone?"

Xavier thought about that for a moment. "I'm not sure. Honestly? I think it was only possible because the man's core was so volatile. He'd let his guard down. Got emotional. And his barrier wasn't a mental one. He had a strong mental defence, but it was clear he didn't have any spells to reinforce that." Not that Xavier had any mental resistance spells.

Maybe I should look into better mental defences myself.

It was definitely terrifying—what he'd been able to do to others with Willpower Infusion, and he was sure he wouldn't be the only one to have a spell like that.

The Lord of the Endless Horde might have been D Grade, but he was only Level 201. A weak, low-level D Grade at best. He may have ruled a sector, but it was a weak sector, one he was clearly afraid of leaving.

He'd mentioned these things to the others. Not because he was trying to diminish his accomplishments, but rather because he was trying to put them into perspective. He *was* powerful—and he'd only grown *more* powerful after he'd defeated the Lord of the Endless Horde, after the titles he'd gained—especially the unmatched title, which gave him a massive 30 percent boost to all stats.

But he was by no means unstoppable.

Not yet.

The Lord of the Endless Horde had been an arrogant fool, and it had been the man's downfall. The last thing Xavier needed was to become arrogant himself just because he'd defeated a weak D Grade.

Still, he could bask in the joy of his accomplishment for a little while.

Two unmatched titles. Those words about the System watching... I definitely did something to be proud of.

"I don't know why you three are so surprised I won." Xavier smirked. "Weren't you the ones who gave me the idea in the first place?"

Siobhan glanced at the others, lips pursed. "True, we did give you the idea, but, well..."

"We didn't think you'd actually be able to do it," Howard said, rather bluntly, with a shrug.

Xavier leant back. "What? You didn't think...?" He laughed. "You set me onto this path, and you didn't think it would *work*?"

"We knew you could get farther than you thought," Justin said. He bit his lip. "My Olympic fencing coach used to always talk about how confidence, being sure of oneself, was what *made* the seemingly impossible possible. All athletes have to think they can achieve something others can't. What would be the point of competing if we didn't think we could win?"

"You went farther than any of us expected you to, Xavier," Siobhan said. "You're amazing. Truly."

Xavier wasn't sure how to feel about what they'd done, but he took it in stride. He was glad for their initial encouragement, though his confidence had wavered several times—and the confidence of his party had definitely wavered too.

Hope, he realised. *They were trying to instil hope.* He would remember that, for when they returned to Earth. He assumed there were a lot of people back there who would be in need of hope.

Xavier clapped his hands together. "Well, uh, I suppose I should thank the three of you. I'm not sure I would have gotten as far as I did if you hadn't put that idea in my head in the first place. There were so many times when I wanted to give up. If my plan had only been to get the best record for the floor, I might have returned here soon after wave 1,000, when things were getting... very difficult."

That was when he'd developed Willpower Infusion in the first place. He would have come back strong, even without that spell, even without advancing to E Grade... but doing what he had? That was so, *so* much better.

Xavier was eager to look at his new class selections, and so he broke off from his party. The others opened their loot boxes, but he figured he shouldn't do that until he had his next class. He knew the amount of Mastery Points he would gain from the loot box wouldn't be much, but he'd waste them if he hadn't chosen his class before opening it.

He stepped over to the opposite side of the Staging Room, near the heavy balls that could be hefted up to increase one's Strength, and sat cross-legged on the ground facing away from the others.

First, he looked at the new spell he'd received.

Core Burn – Rank 1
Core Burn is a unique spell only available to those who have tapped into the ability to influence another's core. It cannot by learnt from any book, scroll, or class upgrade.
This spell makes an enemy burn through the energy within their main core and can cause a chain reaction,

*burning through the energy of the enemy's other cores if
they have been revealed.*
*This spell is most effective against those with weak
mental and spiritual defence.*
This spell has only one path.
*As this is a unique spell, handed out by the System
because of your accomplishment, it is bonded to your
soul and cannot be unlearnt.*
One cannot walk backward on the path.

Xavier smiled. When he'd seen the name of the spell, he'd
expected it to be something like this. *That's exactly what I did to
the Lord of the Endless Horde.* He was a little surprised to find that
the spell was only Rank 1. A part of him had hoped that when he
learnt a spell as an E Grade Denizen, it might start at Rank 50.

But he supposed that was too much to ask for.

Still, he was eager to test out his new spell. He looked over at
the door to the next tower floor, tilting his head to the side,
wondering what the sixth floor might be like.

*Surely it will be nothing like the fifth floor, with near-endless
waves attacking me over and over...*

He knew there could be a huge benefit to another floor like
that, but he was tired of the same old thing. Besides, he wanted to
get back to Earth as soon as possible.

*I could probably clear the rest of the floors today... though I
suppose I haven't slept in a very, very long time.*

He blinked, realising... he wasn't exhausted. His robes weren't
damaged, either, so he didn't need to infuse Spirit Energy into
them to repair them.

*Maybe advancing took away my need for rest, and the System
healed me when it returned me here.*

He looked at the next thing the System had granted him.

System Boon – Usurper

System Boons are one of the rarest gifts granted by the System in the Greater Universe. Usurper is a one-use-only System Boon. This boon gives a Denizen the ability to challenge the ruling Denizen in any region they are currently in. Once activated, it will teleport the user to their desired enemy. The System will then preside over a death duel between the user and the ruling Denizen. Each Denizen will have one day to prepare for this duel, and neither can be harmed or harm others during that time.

Xavier's eyes widened as he read through the boon. Not only had he not known System Boons existed, he'd had no idea what the System Boon would be able to do for him.

This is a powerful gift, but one I must use very, very carefully.

He supposed it made sense to receive something like this after what he'd just done—defeating the ruling Denizen of an entire sector. But it wasn't just a challenge, it was a *death duel*. He would have to be sure he could defeat whoever it was he faced if he were to ever use this.

The fact that both Denizens would have a day to prepare, but wouldn't be able to harm others or be harmed during that time was rather interesting.

If I can't harm others, it will be difficult to gain Mastery Points during that time.

It also only specified that *he* would be teleported, meaning he would be taken into the depths of enemy territory for this death duel.

What would protect him *after* the duel?

I guess that's something I'll have to figure out if I ever have reason to use this.

Considering all he'd been through so far, he imagined he would *definitely* have reason to use a boon like this.

Finally, it was time to look at what classes he had available to upgrade to.

Chapter 54

Insidious

XAVIER SHIFTED WHERE HE SAT, FIDGETY AND GIDDY WITH excitement. After all the carnage he'd inflicted upon his enemies, perhaps his mood should have been a bit more sombre.

I did what I did because I needed to, he thought. *And I saved Queen Alastea from a fate she didn't deserve, even if I didn't get to see her in the end.*

And he accomplished something no one else ever had. He was proud of what he'd done, and excited for what it could mean. He could only imagine how powerful his next class choice might be when every one of his attributes was over the 3,000-point threshold, with one above 4,000, and another above 5,000.

Not to mention having the title for achieving E Grade faster than any other Denizen in the Greater Universe. Surely that must count for something.

He drew in a deep breath and forced himself to lower his expectations. He didn't want to imagine his class upgrade being something far more than it truly was and be disappointed.

He brought up the selection list. There were five different classes to choose from.

Reaper of the Mind – Epic Class

Puppet Master – Epic Class
Insidious Reaper – Epic Class
Soul Reaper – Legendary Class
Otherworldly Reaper – Legendary Class

Xavier tilted his head to the side as he read the different class names. Every single one of them was intriguing to him. For one, it was interesting to find that none of the classes were below epic.

I guess it wouldn't be considered an upgrade if the classes weren't at least epic or above.

The second thing he found interesting was that Soul Reaper—his current class—was still available, only this time it was classified as legendary. And though each of the names was interesting, it was the two legendary classes that his gaze fell down toward.

He wanted to read their descriptions first, but assumed that might be foolish. Though he wasn't likely to choose the epic classes, he should discover what they actually did before discarding them.

Reaper of the Mind Class (Epic):
A Reaper of the Mind is a mage that focuses on magic of the mind and spirit. They are primarily long-range fighters and have the ability to imbue Spirit Energy into their equipment to strengthen its qualities—though this lasts for a limited time.
Reapers of the Mind, as part of the Reaper line of classes, have the special ability to harvest the souls of those they slay and can call upon those souls in moments of need.
Reapers of the Mind can also harvest an opponent's mind, gain knowledge, and consume some of their memories after death. This can give the user the ability to learn spells and skills from slain opponents.

Attributes per level: +15 Willpower, +15 Intelligence, +15 Spirit, and +15 free stat points.

Xavier's eyes widened slightly at what the Reaper of the Mind class would allow him to do. He could definitely see the advantage in being able to harvest not only memories, but spells and skills, from those he defeated.

I wonder what I could have learnt from the Lord of the Endless Horde.

For a moment, he imagined himself using such an ability. Wondered how many different spells he could learn. And skills, too, he had come to find were incredibly valuable.

They help attributes far more than I ever imagined they would.

But he had to say he didn't like the fact that it was a long-range only class. Though much of what Xavier could do was long-range, and he was still technically a mage, he liked the versatility of being able to fight up close.

He also already had the ability to imbue Spirit Energy, *and* Willpower Energy, so that wouldn't be an added benefit.

Xavier noted the fact that the class offered twenty more attribute points than his current Soul Reaper class, despite them both being epic classes. That must have been because it was an E Grade class, not an F Grade class. Though he didn't like that it offered none of the physical stats on a level-up.

He looked at the next available class on the list.

Puppet Master (Epic):
A Puppet Master is a mage that focuses on magic of the mind and spirit. They are primarily long-range fighters and have the ability to imbue Spirit Energy and Willpower Energy.
Puppet Masters have the special ability to take over the mind of an opponent, or multiple opponents, with several spells in this area,

including the option of mind-controlling opponents in a permanent manner.
Puppet Masters often control small groups or large armies of Denizens and beasts to do their bidding.
Attributes per level: +20 Intelligence, +20 Willpower, +14 Spirit, +6 free stat points.

Xavier grimaced as he read the Puppet Master's class description, shaking his head in slight disgust. Though he could see how it might be a very powerful class in its own right, it mentioned nothing of harvesting souls.

It's clearly not in the Reaper line of classes, which means I could lose all my soul reaping spells...

Not only that—while it offered the same sixty attribute points each level-up, it was far more restricted, only offering a meagre *six* free stat points, with the rest going into only mental attributes.

It would certainly be interesting to have a permanent army... but considering all Xavier had done, he felt like he was already an army of one.

This class would not serve me well.

He moved straight onto the next.

Insidious Reaper Class (Epic):
An Insidious Reaper is a mage that focuses on magic of the mind and spirit. They are primarily long-range fighters and have the ability to imbue Spirit Energy and Willpower Energy.
Insidious Reapers, as part of the Reaper line of classes, have the special ability to harvest the souls of those they slay and can call upon those souls in moments of need.
Insidious Reapers have the special ability to set triggers in the minds of opponents, effectively

creating sleeper agents. These sleeper agents can perform specific tasks for the user even if they are a planet away when a trigger is encountered, and they will have no memory of the task they perform.
Attributes per level: +15 Willpower, +15 Intelligence, +15 Spirit, and +15 free stat points.

Xavier smiled. Though Insidious Reaper didn't feel like his style of class, he could imagine how important it could be for someone who wished to perform political assassinations, or other types of espionage.

He could also see how those triggers could be used in a combat situation, wondering how powerful they might be... but he didn't see how the class offered him much more than he already had. Perhaps it could be used to help him get information on an enemy, or even cripple them from the inside, but Xavier wasn't quite that subtle.

Besides, he would rather have a class that excelled primarily in combat. That would be the only way he could truly take out enemy leadership. He doubted he would be able to put triggers in the minds of those that were much more powerful than himself.

No, Insidious Reaper wasn't the class for him, but it certainly showed him something of what could be possible within the Greater Universe. More than just being able to grow wings or control the minds of those in front of him.

Are the possibilities in the Greater Universe limitless?
Perhaps one day he would find out.
He looked at the first of the legendary classes.

Soul Reaper Class (Legendary):
A Soul Reaper is a versatile mage that focuses on magic of the spirit. They can be a long-range fighter, a close-range fighter, or a mix of both, and they wield a scythe-staff in battle—a

**hybrid, melee / magical weapon. They can wear
any armour they wish and have the ability to
imbue Spirit Energy into their equipment to
strengthen its qualities—though this lasts for a
limited time.**

**Soul Reapers also have the special ability to
harvest the souls of those they slay and can call
upon those souls in moments of need. This
differs from necromantic spells, as the Soul
Reaper class lacks the ability to communicate
with the souls they reap and lacks the ability to
reanimate the dead.**

**Attributes per level: +10 Strength, +10 Tough-
ness, +10 Speed, +15 Intelligence, +15
Willpower, +20 Spirit, +20 free stat points.**

Xavier tilted his head to the side. From the description, he
didn't notice any significant difference to what the original Soul
Reaper's class description had been.

*It's a straight-up upgrade; the only thing seeming to change here
is the number of attributes I'd get.*

The attributes were certainly nothing to sniff at. Currently, he
received forty attribute points per level. With the E Grade epic
classes, he would get sixty.

With this E Grade Legendary class? He would get a *hundred*.

That would be a massive improvement.

But Xavier couldn't help but think that it was *missing* something. Reaping souls was a massive part of what he did. It was the
reason he'd been able to take on the Endless Horde in the first
place. But it wasn't the extent of what he was capable of.

*I wouldn't have been able to defeat the Lord of the Endless
Horde, or even all those waves of the Endless Horde itself, without
the use of Willpower Infusion.*

It had become a large part of who he was as a fighter, and he
was hoping it would have better influenced his next class choice to

give him some more diversity in his spell options—though choosing something like Reaper of the Mind or Insidious Reaper simply didn't seem like an option.

Those classes would limit me far too much, and they don't offer as many attribute points.

Xavier was well aware of the importance of attribute points. He knew how much a seemingly small difference per level made in the grand scheme.

Besides, out of all different class names in the list in front of him, it was the final class that drew his eye more than any other. He'd seen a name similar to it before. In a way, he'd been reaching toward it ever since he'd seen it.

Xavier looked at the description for Otherworldly Reaper.

Chapter 55
Otherworldly Reaper

XAVIER SAT, CROSS-LEGGED, IN THE STAGING ROOM OF THE Tower of Champions. The stone floor was cold beneath him. The others were chatting quietly at the other side of the room about what they'd received from their loot boxes. He tuned them out.

The first time Xavier had opened up the System Shop, he'd seen a weapon that intrigued him. It was incredibly expensive, requiring the use of Grand Spirit Coins. One *billion* Grand Spirit Coins. Considering the rate of exchange between the different coins... it was a sum he could never imagine being able to afford.

Yet he couldn't help but covet the weapon.

Stave of the Otherworldly Void Reaper.

There was something about it that attracted him. He hadn't looked at its details. He didn't think he would be *able* to look at its details. Still, he was certain that the weapon wasn't a normal staff, but a scythe-staff—it must have been, considering it was for a Denizen who held a class in the Reaper line.

Otherworldly Void Reaper...

That name had most definitely intrigued him.

And now, the class he was looking at was called the Otherworldly Reaper. He had to imagine that there must be some sort of connection.

He brought up the description.

Otherworldly Reaper Class (Legendary):
An Otherworldly Reaper is an ultra-rare class
of versatile mage that focuses on magic of the
spirit, mind, and will. They can be a long-
range fighter, a close-range fighter, or a mix of
both, and they wield a scythe-staff in battle—a
hybrid, melee/magical weapon. They can wear
any armour they wish and have the ability to
imbue Spirit Energy into their equipment to
strengthen its qualities—though this lasts for a
limited time.
Otherworldly Reapers have the ability to
harvest the souls of those they slay and can call
upon those souls in moments of need. They
also have the ability to call upon spirits from
the Otherworld.
The Otherworld is a land between universes. A
land where the impossible dies. Little is known
about this place by most Denizens of the
Greater Universe.
Attributes per level: +10 Strength, +10 Tough-
ness, +10 Speed, +15 Intelligence, +15
Willpower, +20 Spirit, +40 free stat points.

Xavier stared at the description for a long while, not really understanding what the class was offering. This class sounded most similar to the normal Soul Reaper class, but this reference to the Otherworld, and calling spirits from it?

It sounds more like a summoning spell than a reaping spell. What exactly would these spirits do? What are they capable of?

And what is the Otherworld?

A land between universes... was that referring to the multiverse? Soon after entering the fifth floor for the second time, he'd discovered that it was in a different universe. Discovered that every time a Tower of Champions' floor was entered, it created *another* universe, branching off from that one action.

Every time a Denizen farmed a single floor, they created another universe, which made it sound as though Denizens had incredible power—but it was the System that was sending them there. The System that was allowing them to travel to a different universe.

But what exactly would be *between* universes? How could there even be a place in between?

Xavier bit his lip, then noticed something about the attributes. His forehead crinkled, deep ruts cutting into his brow. This class, like the last one he'd looked at, was classified as legendary, and yet it offered twenty more attribute points.

I thought classes of the same type all offered the same number of attribute points, just distributed differently?

He wasn't annoyed to be proven wrong. Gaining 120 attribute points per level would definitely be better than gaining 100, but how could he choose this class when he didn't really know what it would offer?

It was a gamble, that this connection to the Otherworld would actually help him.

I doubt I'll lose any spells from choosing this class. I'll still be able to do everything a Soul Reaper can do, right?

Though that did make him wonder if the Legendary Soul Reaper class in E Grade would have more spells to offer than the Epic Soul Reaper class in F Grade had.

Still... he was intrigued. It kept coming back to the Stave of the Otherworldly Void Reaper. It was the most expensive item for his class that he'd seen in the store, which made it seem like it must be the most powerful.

Little is known about this place by most Denizens of the Greater Universe.

If little was known about this Otherworld, it would be difficult for him to find information about it. Difficult for him to learn from others about it. But it would also mean he would be able to take hold of valuable information himself. Information that others didn't have could always be used to one's own advantage.

That's why Champions from integrated worlds tend to fare better than those from newly integrated worlds. Except for Progenitors, of course.

Xavier could have talked with the others about his decision. Hell, he could go down to the tavern and speak with Sam. But he'd always made these decisions on his own, and they'd paid off so far.

If nothing else, this would gain him more attribute points.

Besides, this was always going to be his choice. The unknown was so much more enticing than the known.

Xavier willed the class selection.

Are you sure you wish to choose OTHER-WORLDY REAPER (LEGENDARY) as your class?
Becoming an OTHERWORLDY REAPER (LEGENDARY) may result in the loss of spells and skills that are incompatible with the class. This is a choice that cannot be unmade.
One cannot walk backward on the path.

The warning that he might lose spells or skills made him pause for a moment. His mind instantly went to Willpower Infusion—except he *couldn't* lose that spell. In the description, it had said that it was bonded to his secondary core and couldn't be forgotten.

He hadn't lost Heavy Telekinesis when he'd chosen Soul Reaper, so he doubted he would lose it this time. He couldn't lose his Core Burn spell, either. It was bonded to his soul.

Yes, he willed in response to the notification. *I'm sure.*

Class selection complete.
Evaluating Class Upgrade of Denizen XAVIER

**COLLINS from SOUL REAPER (EPIC) to
OTHERWORLDY REAPER (LEGENDARY).**
Checking compatibility of spells:
Heavy Telekinesis...
Compatible!
Spiritual Trifecta...
Compatible!
Spirit Break (All)...
Compatible!
Spirit Infusion...
Compatible!
Soul Harvest...
Compatible!
Soul Strike (Ranged)...
Compatible!
Soul Block...
Compatible!
Soul Harden...
Compatible!
Willpower Infusion...
Compatible!
Core Burn...
Compatible!
Checking compatibility of skills:
Physical Resistance...
Compatible!
Magical Potency...
Compatible!
Magical Resistance...
Compatible!
Physical Damage...
Compatible!
Assimilate Properties...
Compatible!
Scythe-Staff Mastery...

Compatible!
Meditation...
Compatible!
Aura Control...
Compatible!
Identify...
Compatible!
Cultivate Energy...
Compatible!
Core Strength...
Compatible!
Running...
Compatible!
Split Mind...
Compatible!
Evasion...
Compatible!
Class Upgrade Evaluation Complete.
Commencing Class Upgrade!

Xavier steeled himself for the pain he knew was coming. It hit him in a wave. The last time he'd felt it, it had been so unbearable that he'd fallen unconscious.

This time, he bore it well. He remained sitting where he was. It made him shudder. Made him throw his head back. But he didn't so much as release a single hiss. He clenched his jaw shut, clenched his eyes shut, and kept his pain silent.

It didn't make him fall.

When it was over, he opened his eyes once more. He took a measured breath, felt it in his belly, and let it out slow. The pain had disappeared as quickly as it came. He didn't know how long it had lasted. Several minutes, at least. Proving that he wouldn't have been able to upgrade his class while he'd been fighting against the Lord of the Endless Horde.

I already knew as much. But at least I took the upgrade better than last time.

There were several notifications waiting for him.

Congratulations, XAVIER COLLINS! You have upgraded your class from SOUL REAPER (EPIC) to OTHERWORLDY REAPER (LEGENDARY).

You have 0 Spell Upgrades and 0 Skill Transfers pending.

You have gained the spell Summon Otherworldly Spirit.

You have gained the spell Otherworldly Communion.

You have gained the spell Soul Shatter.

You have gained the spell Soul Puppet.

These spells are locked to your class and cannot be forgotten unless you change to an incompatible class.

Xavier smiled. God, it felt good to learn so many new spells all at once! It wasn't as many spells as he'd learnt when he'd originally chosen the Soul Reaper class, but he still had those spells, so it was a great boon.

For a moment, he wondered if everyone choosing the same class would receive the exact same spells or if the individual path they were on would somehow influence that.

Xavier leant forward and rubbed his hands together. Ever since he'd returned to the Staging Room, it felt as though a massive weight had been lifted off his shoulders. The burden that had been fighting the Endless Horde, protecting Queen Alastea, was now gone.

The burden of protecting Earth was still there, but he knew for sure he would be capable of that now.

Maybe these next few floors will actually be fun.

He grinned, excited to see what his new spells had to offer him.

Chapter 56
Soul Puppet

Xavier found he was equally curious about each of his new spells. He looked at the first of those he'd just received after choosing his new Legendary Otherworldly Reaper Class.

> **Summon Otherworldly Spirit – Rank 1**
> *Summon Otherworldly Spirit is a legendary spell*
> *specific to the Otherworldly line of classes.*
> *Summon Otherworldly Spirit is a spell that gives the*
> *Denizen the ability to call forth a spirit from the*
> *Otherworld.*
> *One cannot walk backward on the path.*

Xavier blinked. *That's it?* The description barely told him anything. It didn't at all hint as to what the spell was *capable* of. Whether it was offensive or defensive in nature. Whether there were different paths to take it in, specialising or generalising...

It doesn't tell me any more than the name of the spell does.

He shifted where he sat, feeling a little disappointed. Then again, it could be a lot of fun experimenting with the spell when he got the chance. That sparked a bit of excitement within him. The spell was still unknown to him. Right now, he could imagine it capable of almost anything. Mysteries, and the solving of them, had always been appealing to Xavier.

He looked at the second spell.

Otherworldly Communion – Rank 1
Otherworldly Communion is a legendary spell specific to the Otherworldly line of classes.
Otherworldly Communion is a spell that gives the Denizen the ability to commune with the Otherworld and gain insight.
One cannot walk backward on the path.

Xavier shook his head and sighed. From the spell name alone, he would have guessed that was what it did. And though he'd just admitted that he liked mysteries, it would have been nice to have a bit more to go on.

I guess I'll get to find out.

It set his mind to wondering. When he meditated, he gained insights—bits of knowledge that he assumed were given to him by the System, or the Greater Universe itself. This Otherworld, a place between universes... Could it be somewhere that was beyond the Greater Universe?

How could anything be beyond the Greater Universe? Xavier thought. Then again, until not long ago, *Earth* had been beyond the Greater Universe. Beyond the System, even with its unimaginable power.

The System hadn't taken over everything yet.

This is all speculation, he chided himself. There would be time to experiment with the spell soon. He tried not to feel under-whelmed by the descriptions. This had been the strongest class choice for him, and there was no room, nor need, for regret.

Besides, the final two spells sounded particularly promising.

Soul Shatter – Rank 1

> *Soul Shatter is a legendary spell specific to the Reaper*
> *line of classes. This spell has several paths.*
> *Soul Shatter is an offensive spell that harnesses an*
> *enemy's soul while it's still in their living body. Soul*
> *Shatter causes a burst of soul damage by detonating a*
> *portion of, or all of, an enemy's soul.*
> *This spell has three paths: single-target damage, area-*
> *of-effect damage, or generalising between the two.*
> *The power of the spell depends on both the strength of*
> *the soul it is used upon and the strength of the user*
> *casting it. Shattered souls cannot be harvested.*
> *Generalising with Soul Shatter weakens the strength of*
> *each attack by a third.*
> *One cannot walk backward on the path.*

Xavier grinned. *That's more like it.* Though he didn't like the fact that he wouldn't be able to harvest a shattered soul, it was nice to acquire a purely offensive spell. The spell reminded him of a spell necromancers in video games often received, Corpse Explosion, which made him realise that in the new reality he found himself in, spells like that no doubt existed.

He looked down at himself, put a hand to his stomach, where the empty, hungry pit had resided ever since he'd chosen the Soul Reaper class. That part of him that had urged him to harvest the souls of the other Champions down in the tavern. Though he'd been able to control it much better after that.

He would have assumed that this new spell, Soul Shatter, would have upset that empty pit within him. That it would have been seen as a waste. But the pit was quiet. More in control than it had ever been.

Xavier barely felt it at all.

That stands to reason. My Willpower attribute is over 4,000 points.

He was glad to know that wouldn't be giving him any issues, at least in the near future.

Soul Puppet – Rank 1
Soul Puppet is a legendary spell specific to the Reaper line of classes.
Soul Puppet is a control spell that requires at least one harvested soul to cast. Soul Puppet places a harvested soul inside of a recently deceased Denizen or beast, allowing the user to give the corpse limited instructions.
Though this spell has the ability to reanimate the dead, it is not a necromantic spell, as it relies on a soul controlling the corpse. Each moment the soul resides within the corpse it degrades. When the soul dies, control is lost.
Soul Puppet only has one path.
One cannot walk backward on the path.

Xavier's eyebrows rose. Despite the spell saying it wasn't a necromantic spell, it certainly *sounded* like a necromantic spell to him. He remembered feeling an aversion to necromantic magic when he'd first discovered it was real within the Greater Universe. He didn't like the idea of having corpses walking with him.

Since his ordeal with the Endless Horde, Xavier had become... far too familiar being in close proximity to the dead. He already had a spell that gave him the ability to control others, but this seemed like it could work differently, allowing him to control even more enemies.

He imagined a scenario where it could come in handy, and it wasn't difficult to think of one. If he were, perhaps, facing a wave of low-level enemies with a single boss in their midst... he could control the low-level enemies with Willpower Infusion, harvest their souls when they died attacking the boss, then place a soul inside of them, making them get right back up and keep attacking.

It certainly suited Xavier thinking of himself as Death...

Xavier stood and stretched. He hadn't known what spells to expect when he chose the Otherworldly Reaper class, but he found he was quite intrigued with the selection. He now had fourteen spells to choose from within battle—which also meant he had a lot of spells to rank up, especially since these new spells were only Rank 1.

As he stretched, he thought of even more uses for Soul Puppet. Soon, he would be returning to Earth. His priorities would shift. For the longest time, he'd barely needed to worry about protecting others. Yes, he had been protecting the castle on the fifth floor, the queen, her adviser, and his party, but the Horde refused to attack the castle until they killed him, so he hadn't needed to do much beyond stay alive and slaughter the enemy.

Something told him the invaders on Earth would not do the same thing.

There'll be many, many lives at stake. Perhaps I'll be able to use Soul Puppet to control corpses and make them into corpse-shields to protect those in danger. That's the reason I've been accumulating so much power, isn't it? So I can protect others?

Thinking about returning to Earth made him wonder how his mother would react when she saw him. When she found out what he'd become. The woman had never really approved of his life in the past, and that was when he wanted to become a writer.

Now, he harvested souls, controlled other people's minds, could summon spirits from the Otherworld. Shatter souls, make corpses walk and listen to his demands...

She's going to be in for a shock. That's for damned sure.

Xavier chuckled to himself, imagining her shocked reaction. He stopped chuckling when the thought occurred to him that she might have died in the first few days post-integration. He didn't know what was happening back on Earth.

I'm getting back there. Soon.

He headed over to the others and told them about the spell and book the System had given him, as well as his class choice and the spells he'd gotten from it—not to mention the number of attribute points he would receive per level.

"A Legendary class? That's insane!" Justin said. "I wonder if we'll get to choose a Legendary class..." He drifted off, his eyes getting all starry.

"I'm still curious about this System Boon, Usurper." Siobhan crossed her arms. "I wonder why the System gave it to you." She cocked her head to the side. "It's as though it wants you to challenge those in charge."

Howard scratched his beard. "I think it's just responding to his actions. The way he took out the Lord of the Endless Horde. The choices of his class. The System is responsive. It always has been."

Siobhan nodded several times. She paced, tapped a finger to her lip. "You're right. And this new development, that the System is watching you... I wonder if we can somehow use that to our advantage."

Xavier tilted his head to the side, intrigued by her words. "Use it to our advantage? How would we go about that?"

The woman shrugged, tucked a strand of her red hair behind her ear. "Honestly? I'm not sure."

"Still, we should keep it in mind." Xavier clapped his hands together. "But there are other matters to attend to." He looked at his loot box. Honestly, he wasn't excited for whatever was inside. Though maybe he should be. The last time he'd opened up a loot box, he'd found a Sector Travel Key inside.

Would there be a chance of finding another one? Or some other interesting, valuable item?

I felt their presence. The two powerful Denizens who are watching me. It's not only the System that has its eyes on me.

Didn't he deserve to get a higher reward, considering what he'd done? Or was he simply asking for too much?

I already have so much wealth at hand.

He hadn't even begun to think about that. Before he stepped onto the next floor, he would need to outfit himself again. It wasn't simply that he'd outgrown his gear—though he most certainly had, considering he'd gotten Soultaker all the way back when he was Level 10—the poor staff had broken in half during his last fight.

And it wasn't only him that needed to be outfitted. The others would need better gear. They would be heading back to Earth soon, and as powerful as Xavier was, he knew he couldn't defend the entire planet on his own. If only because he couldn't be everywhere at once.

I need a more effective way to travel. He looked at Siobhan. *I need someone who can protect others.* He looked at Howard. *And I need someone who can fight well enough when I'm not around.* He looked to Justin.

Each of them had a role that would serve him well in his party, and back on Earth. But those roles had been sorely neglected ever since he'd entered the fifth floor. All they'd each gotten to do was read and research in that tower library and practice the skills they already had available to them.

Technically, Xavier was sure he could get back to Earth quickly. He doubted the next five floors would take him very long to complete, even if he was going for the best record on each of them. He was far beyond what the Tower of Champions would expect of a Denizen at this point in the floors. But he couldn't simply sprint through them if he wanted the others to be valuable to him when they returned.

He needed to powerlevel them up first.

Xavier stepped over to the loot box, ready to open it.

Chapter 57
Portal Stones

Xavier threw open the lid on the loot box.

You have gained +2 Skill Points.
You have gained 1 Mastery Point (E Grade).
You have gained 100,000 Lesser Spirit Coins.
You have received 2 Portal Stones.

Xavier tried to hold back his sigh. Two skill points wasn't bad. He'd long ago found out how helpful his skills could be, so that actually gladdened him.

The single Mastery Point had momentarily shocked him, until he remembered he was E Grade now and Mastery Points worked differently to how they did when he was F Grade. He bit his lip. He supposed being 1 percent on his way toward Level 101 wasn't a total loss... even if it felt that way.

Something tells me I'm not going to be able to gain any levels from the enemies I face on the next few floors, considering how much the System has restricted me in the past...

Previously, he'd thought the first ten floors of the Tower of Champions might be there to help get a Champion to E Grade, or close to it. Now, he knew that was incredibly unlikely, since he'd discovered just how much was needed to get there.

I've certainly messed up the normal bell curve.

Maybe the first fifty floors would be enough to get someone to E Grade, or maybe they would need one hundred... He supposed he would find out by looking at the other members of his cohort, assuming they ever got that far.

That gave him an idea. One he would work on soon.

He chuckled at the sight of 100,000 Lesser Spirit Coins. That would barely make a dent. Xavier looked at what he had—it had added 10,000 Minor Spirit Coins into his Storage Ring. He noted the fact that it automatically turned them into Minor Spirit Coins now that he was E Grade.

I wonder how many coins the Lord of the Endless Horde's possessions I looted will get me.

There would be time for that soon, too. Honestly, he found himself excited for all that needed to be done. Especially since there was a lot more variation in what he needed to do now than there had been for the last six or so weeks.

The last item—or rather, items—intrigued him. He asked the others if they'd received Portal Stones. They each shook their heads.

Siobhan stepped forward. "What's *is* a Portal Stone? They sound like valuable items."

Xavier had one Portal Stone resting in each of his hands. They were gemstones, red ones that almost looked like rubies. Each was roughly the size of a baseball. Those would be some expensive rubies. They were also exactly the same size, cut identically.

"They do sound valuable," Xavier muttered. He used his Identify skill on one of them.

{Portal Stone – Restriction: Sector}
A Portal Stone has the ability to connect one place to another, creating a two-way portal between two points. The power of this Portal Stone is restricted to a single

sector and does not allow the user to travel between sectors.
A Portal Stone is useless if it is not paired.

Identify has reached Rank 24!

"Huh," Xavier said. "That's pretty amazing."

"Well, what does it do?" Siobhan asked.

"I mean, I assume it makes a portal." Justin grinned.

Siobhan rolled her eyes. "Yes, that's obvious enough."

Howard released a deep chuckle as he crossed his arms.

Xavier explained what the stones did. He tossed one up in the air and caught it, then idly started juggling them both one-handed. With his Speed, keeping them up in the air was almost as easy as holding them in his hand. He barely needed to think about it.

"Connect two points..." Siobhan trailed off, tapping her finger to her mouth again. "That *is* amazing! Of course, you wouldn't be able to take the Portal Stone *through* the portal. Perhaps you could keep one at a home base, then travel with the other. You could make a swift retreat with it, but—"

"But you wouldn't be able to retrieve it, only travel back through," Xavier cut in.

Siobhan nodded. "And what happens to the stone while you're gone? When you close the portal, your enemy could pick it up, throw it in a dungeon..."

"Sounds like there's a lot of possibilities," Howard said. "And it's limited to a sector?"

Xavier nodded.

"Well, considering you have a Sector Travel Key that could take you anywhere within the sector, it sounds as though you could connect two places within the sector fairly easily. You wouldn't have to spend an entire year somewhere if you didn't want to."

Xavier smiled. "That was my first thought as well. Though I'd want to be sure of the places I connected." He couldn't help but recall Sam's warning about Denizens luring him places with sinister motives. "I wonder how rare these things are." He looked at the others. "Neither of you came across word of things like these in any of the books you read back at the castle?"

Siobhan shook her head. "Unfortunately, no, we didn't. Those books were useful, sometimes... but mostly they were on the history of the sector that we were in. There were many legends, even fictions. And some, ah, romances." Siobhan blushed, then cleared her throat and shrugged. "None of the people who wrote those books were as powerful as you. There was talk of making portals, but the classes needed to do that were all support classes, and it didn't say there were items that could do it."

Xavier nodded. He'd thought that library would be a loophole for them finding information that the System had hidden from them. But perhaps the System had factored that in when it had made that place a tower floor. There hadn't been access to the System Shop there. No one was above F Grade. And the books, while useful, didn't give them a strict path to E Grade at all. It was only by the grace of Adviser Kalren, who stayed behind instead of going through the portal during the exodus, that Xavier learnt how to discover his secondary core.

The System does a good job of hiding information it doesn't think we're ready for.

He stared at the Portal Stones for a moment, wondering how they'd come to be in his possession. Just like the Sector Travel Key, a part of him didn't know if these came from the System or not.

An entity powerful enough to change what the System rewarded me with in one of its loot boxes... that would be quite the power indeed.

If it were true, it seemed as though he had a benefactor out there, somewhere. Someone who was trying to curry his favour. Someone who was dramatically more powerful than him yet had their eye on him still.

Haven't even left the tower and I'm already making a name for myself. I wonder what things will be like when I step into the wider sector, or even out into other sectors.

Xavier deposited the two Portal Stones into his Storage Ring. He definitely wanted to experiment with them, but there would be time for that later.

He'd placed the Lord of the Endless Horde's equipment into his Storage Ring. The man had had six rings on his fingers. He hadn't been able to put the rings into his own Storage Ring, which meant each of them must possess spatial storage of their own.

His entire party huddled around the System Shop's terminal, placing their hand on the glowing crystal atop the pedestal. There had been plenty of things to loot during his time facing the Endless Horde, but there hadn't been enough room to keep it all. All the others' Storage Rings were completely full by this point as well. He let them sell off any items they wished, even if he'd been the one to kill the enemies. They needed money of their own, after all, and this would be the fastest way for them to get it. They'd been giving him their Lesser Spirit Coins from their loot boxes ever since the end of the first floor.

Now, he didn't need them anymore.

First, Xavier sold off everything except for a few choice items that he kept for himself. He had various weapons, armour, and other equipment that he'd looted off E Grade wave bosses whenever he'd had the time to do so—which hadn't been as often as he'd liked.

By the time he'd sold all of that off, he'd gained over 600,000 Minor Spirit Coins, more than doubling what he already had and putting the figure over a million. If there were still Lesser Spirit Coins, he'd have ten times that number.

God, that's a lot. Or it certainly seems like it.

He looked at the slender sword he'd taken from the Lord of the Endless Horde. At the beautiful jade scabbard. For a moment, he thought of keeping the weapon for Justin. But this was a D Grade item, one he wasn't even able to Identify. It would take far too long for Justin to be able to wield it. They needed the money more.

I'll outfit him with weapons whenever he needs them. I'm sure I'll be wealthy enough to.

Part of him knew that selling items straight to the System was no doubt losing him a great deal of money were he to simply sell them straight to interested buyers, or auction them off somehow, but as he had no way to do that... it seemed like the right choice.

The more money we have, the more security and power we can buy ourselves now, which will get us even more later.

It seemed like sound logic to him. Or perhaps he was simply impatient. Either way, he sold the sword, the scabbard, the robes, the golden bracelet, and the golden anklet straight to the System.

Xavier's eyes widened in shock as he received his payment.

The System paid him 15,800,900 Minor Spirit Coins.

I have over 16 million Minor Spirit Coins... That... that's insane.

Growing up, Xavier had wild dreams of becoming rich. He supposed most people did. When he decided to become a writer, he knew those dreams would likely never come true. But a part of him also knew that if he got lucky, if he did well enough, maybe they would. Maybe he'd be able to buy a mansion, get any car he wanted, travel on a whim...

The world, the universe, was a different place to when he'd had those dreams, but he couldn't help but wonder what all of these coins would buy him. He had a responsibility to protect Earth, and something told him being as powerful as he was this soon after his world's integration was going to attract attention he didn't want. Threats he couldn't even contemplate in that moment.

But his power, his money, his long lifespan... perhaps there would be more to his life than simply fighting. Perhaps he would be able to fulfil those frivolous dreams he'd had. Assuming he even wanted them anymore.

When I return to Earth, I will be the most powerful person there...

Xavier stood there, day-dreaming about owning a massive castle. About having the freedom to do... whatever he wished.

He shook his head. Maybe that would happen, but there was a lot to get done before then.

The six Storage Rings he'd taken from the Lord of the Endless Horde were on his fingers. They felt a little awkward, clinking against each other. He didn't plan to keep so many. Maybe one on each hand, taking the largest of the two of them.

Xavier looked inside the first of the Storage Rings, wanting to inspect its contents, but something was blocking him. It was familiar—much like the mental block the Lord of the Endless Horde had put up before Xavier had taken control of the man with Willpower Infusion.

Except this block wasn't cracked.

Lines creased Xavier's forehead as he pushed against the block, pouring all his focus into this task.

Crack.

Xavier widened his eyes, staring at the ring.

{Storage Ring} of unknown grade has been destroyed, along with all of its contents.

"Oh crap," Xavier said, then swore under his breath.

Chapter 58
Charon

ONE OF THE LORD OF THE ENDLESS HORDE'S STORAGE RINGS had broken, and all of its contents had been destroyed. Xavier ran a hand through his hair. He couldn't begin to imagine how much wealth must have been stored in that one little ring. How many items. How many spirit coins.

And now it was all simply... gone.

"What happened?" Howard asked. The man had a raised eyebrow. Must have heard Xavier swear.

"I took six Storage Rings from the Lord of the Endless Horde."

"Whoa," Justin said. "That's awesome. What's inside them?"

"I don't know." Xavier took the broken ring off his finger. "When I tried to look in this one, it blocked me. I tried to push past it, and... the ring and everything within were destroyed."

"The Lord must have put some sort of safeguard into it," Siobhan muttered. "He mustn't have wanted anyone to get their hands on his wealth. I didn't even know such a thing was possible."

"Anything's possible," Xavier whispered. He shut his eyes for a moment and sighed. "I suppose it's not a big loss, in the grand scheme." He looked at the other five rings. "I guess... I won't be able to open these."

"Not yet," Siobhan said. "But you might be able to open them

401

in the future. Surely you're not the only one who's ever tried to get to the contents of another Denizen's Storage Ring."

Xavier nodded. He hadn't gotten that far, but she was right. "I guess I'll have to hold onto them. Keep them safe." He raised a hand. "But I can't put them in my ring, and I'd rather not wear them like this."

Siobhan put her hand on the System Shop's crystal. A moment later, she held a looped chain in her hand, one with a small clasp. She opened the clasp. "You could wear them beneath your robes, like a necklace."

Xavier looked at the rings again, contemplating all the wealth within them. It felt a little like giving up, not trying to open them now. But who knew what opportunities would arise in the future? Besides, he had plenty of spirit coins after selling off that D Grade equipment.

He slid the rings off his fingers and onto the chain she offered him, then put it on around his neck, tucking it under his robes where it couldn't be seen. He felt the weight of them. It was oddly comforting.

What treasures lie within...

Xavier shook his head. It was time to stop daydreaming. He needed to buy some new robes, and most of all, he needed a new scythe-staff. Which made him wonder whether the System would buy back his broken one. Surely there would be a crafter or black-smith of some sort out there who could repair it.

He opened the System Shop and looked at what was available to him. Last time he'd done this, he'd filtered the items so it showed him the most expensive ones he could afford, restricting it to scythe-staffs he was able to equip.

The last weapon he had bought had cost 240,000 Lesser Spirit Coins. He couldn't help but wonder how much the next weapon might cost. Considering his considerable wealth, it would be foolish to spend it all on a single weapon. He imagined it might be a little while until he was able to gather a similar amount of wealth again.

It's not every day I kill a D Grade Denizen... at least, not yet.

He restricted his purchasing power for his scythe-staff to 2,500,000 Minor Spirit Coins. He had to imagine that would be more than enough to outfit him with a powerful weapon for his level and grade. He could have allowed himself to spend more—a lot more—but something told him that money would come in handy.

Especially since it wasn't only his party that he wanted to outfit with weapons.

One step at a time.

Xavier restricted himself to looking at the top three most expensive items within his chosen criteria.

As he had in the past, he intended to look at the last item first, working his way up from the cheapest to the most expensive. He figured it would give him an idea of how powerful the weapons in this price range were and how they might vary.

Though before he did that, he looked at the description for his own scythe-staff.

Soultaker

Warning: This scythe-staff has been broken and must be repaired. The benefits to the wielder will disappear within 24 hours of its breaking.

This scythe-staff requires 150 Intelligence, 150 Spirit, 100 Willpower, and 100 Strength to wield.

+30 Intelligence

+35 Spirit

+15 Speed

+20 Strength

+30% Spirit Energy recovery

+35% magical damage dealt

+35% physical damage dealt

Xavier frowned when he read the warning at the top of the

scythe-staff's description. He hadn't realised the weapon was still offering him any attributes at all. *Even when I'm not wielding it, I benefit from its stats even when it's in my Storage Ring—I know that; I've tested it in the past.*

But he didn't realise that would have a lasting effect *after* it broke.

It hasn't even been twenty hours yet...

He looked at the cheapest of the three scythe-staffs in the System Store.

Wisdomous Scythe of the Umbral

This scythe-staff requires 1,000 Intelligence, 1,000 Spirit, 1,000 Willpower, and 1,000 Strength to wield.

+300 Intelligence
+350 Spirit
+200 Willpower
+100 Speed
+100 Strength
+100% Spirit Energy recovery
+100% magical damage dealt
+100% physical damage dealt

Imbued ability: When this scythe-staff is in the hand of its wielder, it bestows upon them the **Soul Target** ability. Soul Target allows the wielder to tag an enemy and know their whereabouts until that enemy is untagged, or they have tagged another.

Distance restriction: Sector-wide

This item costs 2,000,000 Minor Spirit Coins

Xavier's mouth fell open a little as he read the first scythe-staff's description. The number of attributes it offered felt... rather incredible, at least compared to what he was used to. They offered more than his most powerful titles, except for the titles that offered percentage-modified boosts.

The imbued ability drew his attention even more than the attributes did. He didn't know abilities could be imbued into weapons or other equipment. That knowledge would definitely come in handy, and it made him wonder what other equipment he should try and arm himself with.

I wonder if there's equipment with defensive enchantments that I could buy. Something that could spring up a shield if I'm in danger. If there are, why didn't the Lord of the Endless Horde have such things?

The reason came to him instantly: arrogance. The man never expected he would need one. Not while he was the most powerful Denizen in his entire sector.

I must make sure that I never think I'm too powerful to be beaten. That I never think myself so high above others that it's no longer possible for me to fall.

The imbued ability, Soul Target, was very intriguing. He could certainly see how it could come in handy, but he also didn't feel as though it would be beneficial to him on a regular basis. If the weapon he wielded had an imbued ability, he wanted it to be something that he could use regularly during encounters.

He moved onto the next weapon.

Spirit Scythe of Darkest Night

This scythe-staff requires 500 Intelligence, 1,500 Spirit, 500 Willpower, and 500 Strength to wield.

+200 Intelligence
+500 Spirit
+100 Willpower
+100 Speed
+100 Strength
+110% Spirit Energy recovery
+100% magical damage dealt
+100% physical damage dealt
Imbued ability: When this scythe-staff is in the hand of its wielder, it bestows upon them the **Restorative Spirit**

ability. For half of the wielders Spirit Energy reserve, it can restore a single spell from cooldown.

Time restriction: This ability can only be used once every 12 hours.

This item costs 2,250,000 Minor Spirit Coins

Xavier frowned. This scythe-staff was intriguing, even if the name reminded him of something out of Green Lantern. It didn't require as many attribute points in most attributes as the last one yet required more in Spirit. Though none of these requirements were anywhere near what he had.

For the most part, it offered *less* attributes, and yet it added 500 Spirit. That kind of advantage would make a huge difference.

And the imbued ability was indeed intriguing. In fact, he'd only recently been thinking it would be able to restore his spells from cooldown. Though this would only allow him to use it on a single spell, it was only Soul Strike that he would need it for.

I have so much Spirit Energy. I can't imagine when losing half of my Spirit Energy would do me any real damage...

It could only be used once every twelve hours. Quite a long time to wait, but if he were to use every single soul in his reserve, harvest the souls of those that strike killed, then re-cast Soul Strike in almost an instant?

That could very well save his life.

He tilted his head up. Part of him wanted to buy the scythe-staff based on that ability alone and not even look at the next option, but he knew that would be foolish.

So he moved on.

Charon's Scythe

This scythe-staff requires 2,000 Intelligence, 2,000 Spirit, 2,000 Willpower, and 2,000 Strength to wield.

+300 Intelligence

+500 Spirit

+300 Willpower

+200 Speed

+200 Strength

+120% Spirit Energy recovery

+110% magical damage dealt

+110% physical damage dealt

Imbued ability: When this scythe-staff is in the hand of its wielder, it bestows upon them the ability to **Soul Step**.

Soul Step allows the user to latch onto the soul of any newly deceased Denizen or beast and move through the Otherworld to transport to the location of the soul instantaneously.

Time restriction: This ability can only be used once per minute.

Distance restriction: This ability is restricted based upon how far away a user can sense souls.

This item costs 2,500,000 Minor Spirit Coins

Holy crap!

Xavier grinned, reading the description. This scythe-staff required considerably more attribute points than the past two scythe-staffs, but the number of attributes it offered was far superior.

And it still offers 500 points in Spirit!

This made him bite his lip and wonder if he should look at weapons that were more expensive than this one. He could afford it, after all, couldn't he? But again, he knew it might be a long while before he saw this kind of money a second time, which meant he needed to spend it wisely.

Right now, he didn't need to buy the most powerful weapon that he could find. Though he'd told himself not to be arrogant, he didn't think he *was* being arrogant when he looked at the challenges he would soon face.

Those challenges didn't require a weapon that cost over 15 million Minor Spirit Coins.

The imbued ability interested him as well. It dealt with the Otherworld—something specific to his new class—and it would allow him to teleport. He'd been wishing for a better way to move around the battlefield for a long while now. Of course, this required that someone be recently *dead* for him to travel toward them, and it could only be used once per minute, but it still seemed plenty powerful to him.

It would also more than double his damage, both physical and magical. That added 10 percent over the other scythe-staffs would make a very big difference.

Though the temptation to look at more expensive weapons hadn't left him, Xavier knew he should stick with his decision.

He couldn't help but linger on the scythe-staff's name for a moment. It begged many questions. Charon. He knew that name. The ferryman who transported the dead to the underworld. A Greek myth, yet here the name was, as though this scythe-staff belonged to him—or was named after him.

Was Charon real? Is he still? If he is, how do we know of him, just like we know of elves, demons, and other races I've encountered that humans have been dreaming about for years?

He shook his head. Maybe one day he'd learn the answer to that, but right now it wasn't important.

Xavier purchased Charon's Scythe.

Chapter 59
Anointed Robes

Xavier stood in the Staging Room, a hand on the glowing crystal atop the pedestal that was the System Shop's terminal. Charon's Scythe appeared in his hand in an instant.

"Whoa."

The change was miraculous. The second the scythe staff was within his hand, two of his attributes reached new thresholds of power. His Willpower and Spirit. They were already his two most powerful attributes, powering his two most powerful spells... To have them reach a new height of power just from his selection of weapon? That felt kind of insane to him.

He let out a breath and savoured the moment. God, it always felt so thrilling whenever his power grew. He knew that weapons and equipment were how many Denizens improved their strength. It was how the Denizens from long-integrated worlds were able to keep their leads in the Tower of Champions. Wealth. Money. And power. It was how the old ones remained in charge.

If this weapon, which wasn't even the most expensive he could afford, offered him this much power... How much power would he be able to buy with the rest of his money?

He put those thoughts out of his mind and examined the new weapon he'd just received.

The weapon wasn't what he'd expected. The haft's wood was different to the smoothness of Soultaker's. It wasn't perfectly straight like Soultaker's had been. There was an unevenness to it, like the haft had been made from a fallen branch rather than wood honed for the purpose.

Like it was more... natural.

Except it was anything *but* natural. It weighed more than Soultaker had. A lot more. The weight was the first thing he'd felt when he'd summoned it. It certainly didn't weigh too much for him. It required 2,000 Strength, while he had over 2,500.

The heft to it was comforting. He remembered a time when Soultaker had felt heavy, now it was like picking up a feather.

Hitting someone with any part of this is liable to send them flying...

The blade was unique, too. It wasn't the solid black of Soultaker. It was silver—the same silver that his eyes glowed. Though he was sure the actual metal wasn't silver.

The blade was also longer. While Soultaker's blade had been as long as his forearm, this was as long as his *arm*. It almost looked absurd. There was another difference with the blade, too. Whereas Soultaker's blade looked like a more traditional scythe, with the blade almost at a ninety-degree angle to the haft, this was more reminiscent of a polearm. The blade was slightly curved, but it followed the line of the haft, making it look more like a war scythe than an agricultural scythe.

Xavier could instantly see the advantage to this.

He stepped into an open area of the Staging Room and held the weapon before him, admiring it for a moment. Then, he tested its swing. Tested its thrust. Its heft.

It took a moment for the weapon to feel right. He'd been wielding Soultaker for so long that picking up anything different was always going to be a transition.

But once he got used to the feel of the weapon, he knew it was far superior to anything he'd held before. The haft wasn't as long as Soultaker's had been—it was only about seven feet, where the last one had been nine feet—but the blade itself made up for that length.

He moved like the wind. His Speed, his Strength, made him whirl around the Staging Room like a dervish. He performed strikes, flips, swings, and sweeps that would bring a pre-integration martial artist to tears.

When he finished, he found that the others were staring at him.

Justin's mouth was agape. "You... you move so *fast!*" He shook his head in disbelief. "I couldn't even make out your attacks. It's like you have superspeed!"

Xavier smirked. "What, seeing me practice doesn't make you want to spar me?"

Justin put his hands up defensively. "No. No no no. Definitely not. Sparring you would be suicide."

"Suicide? You think I would kill you?"

"Well, no... But it would certainly kill my confidence."

Xavier chuckled. He couldn't help himself. "Don't worry about that. After I buy some more equipment and the three of you get outfitted, we're going to be doing a bit of power-levelling." He rubbed his hands together evilly. "It's about time the three of you got strong."

Howard raised an eyebrow, but a hint of a smirk played on his lips. Siobhan raised her chin and smiled. Justin put a hand on the hilt of his sword and grinned.

"Finally!" Siobhan said. "Don't get me wrong, it's not that I don't like being cooped up in the library and reading books for days on end; in fact, it's one of my favourite things to do... But when it's the *only* thing, it does grow a bit tiresome."

"Tiresome. That's definitely putting it mildly." Justin drew his sword. He did a few practice thrusts at the air. "It's been far too long since I fought something!"

Howard crossed his arms over his chest. "I'm inclined to agree. Though I do wonder—how long do you plan on remaining here? You should be able to clear the last few floors rather quickly, without losing out on any titles. What's your priority? Returning to Earth is certainly mine."

Xavier tossed Charon's Scythe to his left as he stepped forward. He placed a hand on Howard's shoulder and gave it a gentle squeeze. "I know you want to get back to your children. To your wife." He looked to the others. "We each have loved ones to return to. People we want to protect. But we don't know how long we'll have back there. I, for one, want to be prepared."

Siobhan nodded. "I'm nowhere near as strong as I thought I would be when it came time to return."

Justin sheathed his sword. "I still have a long way to go too."

Howard grunted. "How much do you think you can do for us in two days?"

Xavier stepped back, looked at his new weapon. "Two days? I think we can do quite a lot."

Xavier didn't spend a great deal of time selecting his equipment. Perhaps he should have, but he felt as though there were more important things to do.

He provided each of the others with 500,000 Minor Spirit Coins. A substantial sum, especially when converted into Lesser Spirit Coins.

Justin bought a new sword and some new armour. Now, he wore ringmail, what looked to be leather gloves—but from what beast that leather came from, Xavier didn't know—and a long, slim sword. The sword reminded Xavier of the Lord of the Endless Horde's sword, except the scabbard was nowhere near as fancy.

Howard went a different route. His armour was full plate. And he had discarded his sword for a double-bearded axe. The blades on the thing were huge, and Xavier knew a normal human wouldn't be able to wield such a thing. Too much metal. Too much weight. He also had a helm, gauntlets and greaves.

He looked like the picture of a traditional knight.

His new tower shield was absurdly large—as tall as himself. He could place it in front of him and not a single part of him was exposed to a frontal attack.

Siobhan acquired new robes. Purple ones that were cinched in at the waist and went well with her red hair. Her new staff looked much the same as her old one, except for the crystal at its top. Like her robes, it was purple. And also massive. It looked like it could brain a goblin quite effectively, though he knew the Divine Beacon would never use it for such things.

Xavier had outfitted himself with a new set of robes.

The robes looked remarkably similar to his old ones, but the attributes they endowed him with were far superior. And, just like with Charon's Scythe, they came with an imbued ability. One he knew would come in handy.

Anointed Robes of Umbral
These robes require 1,000 Intelligence, 1,000 Spirit, and 1,000 Willpower to wear.
+200 Intelligence
+200 Spirit
+200 Willpower
+60% Spirit Energy recovery
+60% magical damage resistance
Imbued ability: When these robes are worn, they bestow upon the wearer the ability to **Otherworld Phase**.
Otherworld Phase allows the user to phase into the Otherworld for a period of 2 seconds, effectively making them incorporeal.
Time Restriction: This ability can only be used once every 10 minutes.
These robes have a self-repair feature fuelled by Spirit Energy.

The Anointed Robes of Umbral had cost him 2,000,000 Minor Spirit Coins, and they'd been worth every one of them for the attribute boost alone. The robes shot his Willpower and Spirit attributes through yet *another* threshold. God, they made him feel *powerful*. His percentage modifiers... were absolutely *insane*, offering him more power than he'd ever imagined.

And I'm still merely a child in the Greater Universe.

The imbued ability intrigued him. Otherworld Phase. Xavier didn't know when such a defence would be needed—certainly not in the next five floors of the Tower of Champions—but he didn't want to grow so overconfident that he neglected his defensive capabilities. Having the ability to shift out of phase into the Otherworld when being attacked could likely save his life in the future.

It intrigued him that both his new scythe-staff and his new set of robes had skills related to the Otherworld. He knew that knowledge of this place was rare among Denizens. Yet both of his main pieces of equipment referenced it?

Perhaps it was because the System Shop contained items from all over the Greater Universe, and he'd filtered his search preferences to weapons and equipment that were suitable to him.

Xavier looked at the last piece of equipment he'd bought.

Dark Steel Bracer

This bracer requires 1,000 Toughness to wear.

+100 Toughness

+20% health recovery

+20% physical damage resistance

Imbued ability: When this bracer is worn, it bestows upon the wearer the ability to **Buffer**. **Buffer** allows the user to push all enemies in close proximity twenty feet away from them for ten seconds.

Time Restriction: This ability can only be used once every 24 hours.

These robes have a self-repair feature fuelled by Spirit Energy.

He hadn't bought the Dark Steel Bracer for the stats. Though, he would never say no to more stats—especially since Toughness was his weakest one. He had bought it for its imbued abilities. The ability was nowhere near as powerful as the abilities his new scythe-staff and robes gave him, but he was sure it would come in handy.

Buffer, at first glance, didn't seem all that helpful to him. He had his Heavy Telekinesis. Couldn't that push his enemies away?

In theory…

But he had to take into account the situations he might find himself in when back on Earth. Though his accuracy with Heavy Telekinesis had improved dramatically, he would not be able to distinguish between friend or foe with a violent push to create space for himself. If he were protecting an ally, the Buffer ability would only target his enemies.

Besides, if he were to be honest, there simply weren't a great many imbued abilities for him to choose from with this kind of equipment. Maybe it was the price ranges he was looking in, but all of the other imbued abilities seemed inadequate, giving temporary boosts to his Toughness, or creating limited floating shields or Bulwark-type barriers.

None of those options seemed suitable to him. The defences simply wouldn't be enough. If anything were to put him in real danger, the flimsy imbued abilities that he had seen would do nothing against a threat that could get past his relatively high level of Toughness. That wasn't his arrogance speaking—as far as he knew—it was simply practicality.

Happy with his equipment choices for the moment, Xavier walked up to the door. The door that would take him to the next floor.

Finally, it was time to keep moving forward.

He wondered what the sixth floor of the Tower of Champions would have in store for them.

Chapter 60
Bearded Menace

Howard gripped the haft of his double-bearded axe. The weight of it felt perfect in his hand. When he'd purchased it, he'd gone right ahead and gotten the Axe Mastery skill, using one of the two skill points he'd received from the loot box after the fifth floor.

Previously, he'd been training with a sword, but the sword had never felt right to him. Never felt natural. Not like he knew it must feel for Justin. Perhaps it was simply seeing that boy wield his own sword with such skill and ease compared to him, or maybe he was just built differently. He didn't know.

In those weeks he'd spent cooped up in the tower library of Queen Alastea's castle, he'd become enamoured with the legend of one of the Denizens he'd read about.

Sir Gambion. The stories called him the Walking Fortress. The legendary Denizens the stories spoke of were always those that ended up leaving the sector Queen Alastea resided within—no one truly powerful ever stuck around that place.

While stuck in that library, Howard kept stumbling upon more and more stories about the Walking Fortress. A tank so powerful that nothing could ever harm him. The man, of course, had wielded an axe.

That was where Howard's fascination with them had been born. At first, it had felt a little childish. Like he was reading fairy-tales and wanting to live them out. At his age, he was far too old for such things. But when they'd finally returned to the Staging Room and he'd stepped up to the System Shop's terminal, he just couldn't help himself.

His axe, Bearded Menace—not a name Howard chose, though one he was growing fond of—cleaved through the neck of a leaping goblin, then another on the backswing as he wrenched the blade out of the first one's neck.

Howard didn't know how to feel about the fact that he enjoyed combat so much, or that the feeling of gaining Mastery Points never failed to thrill him. There were some cops that got off on confrontation. On using their badge to get away with beating the crap out of someone.

Howard had never been one of those. Violence was a last resort —one only used when every other option had been exhausted or when there simply was no other option to begin with.

Yet he felt as though now, violence was always the first option. The world was a different place. The threats around him were different. Therefore, the methods needed to deal with them were different too.

I'm still a protector at heart, he thought, not sure who he was trying to convince. *That's why I ended up with the tank class. That's why I have to do what I'm doing.*

The faces of his wife and children were burned into his mind. God, he worried about them every day. He hoped his wife was with them. He knew children under the age of sixteen were taken to Safe Zones. Though who knew if those Safe Zones were actu-ally *safe*. Stephanie was fifteen now. She'd be sixteen soon enough.

He wanted to be there for her before she was integrated.

At first, he'd known the advice he would give her—*don't choose Champion. Whatever you do.* He would have told her that for so many reasons. Howard and the other members of his party hadn't talked about what they'd had to do to get where they were. Hadn't talked about the innocent people they'd needed to kill just to get past the first test to "prove" they were worthy of coming to the Tower of Champions.

And what an awful test that is. One that forces us to kill another, someone who doesn't deserve to die, simply to save our own skin.

But he'd thought long and hard about that test since. The System wanted conflict. He knew that. He'd read about that, in the library. There were many theories. One of the moral paths people could choose was the path of chaos. If the System was in any way *good*, it certainly wouldn't push that path on people.

It wouldn't push us to fight, either.

The test, however, wasn't *evil*, not if one were thinking like the System must—assuming the System had thoughts, he still knew very little about it and how it worked. The System wanted to find people who did what was necessary to protect their world. Sometimes, the darkest of acts were what was required to keep the peace. It was a reality Howard hated to admit. But that was how many leaders throughout history had managed to stay in power, and staying in power meant stability for their country or kingdom, and stability meant safety.

Safety was what he wanted for his children. Safety was what he *needed* for them. He wasn't foolish enough to think that he alone could keep them safe for all eternity. No, this new world would throw so many threats at them.

Maybe choosing Champion is what they'll need to do to survive. And if that's the case, then I need to prepare them for that.

The very idea was still abhorrent to him, even if the seed of it was slowly growing, sprouting to the surface of his mind.

How could he encourage, train, *ask* his daughter, his son, to kill?

Because this is a new world.

The corpses of a hundred goblins surrounded Howard. He wasn't even breathing heavily. "Clear!" he called out to the others. Xavier was outside, in the courtyard of the keep. The sixth floor, it turned out, was a reversal on the fifth floor. Instead of protecting a fortress—Queen Alastea's castle—they were taking down a stronghold.

When they'd arrived, they'd found themselves at the head of an army of a hundred soldiers. The numbers felt so miniscule after seeing the ranks of the Endless Horde charge the queen's castle every hour for so many weeks. A prince had approached them. *More royalty.*

The man had hailed them, called them Champions, and told them they'd been summoned to lead his army into battle.

"No," Xavier had said, his hands folded behind his back. He hadn't even bothered summoning his new weapon—Charon's Scythe, a fierce-looking thing. Nothing could harm him in a place like this. He'd looked up at the keep in the distance. "You want us to take that keep?"

The prince had nodded, looking a little uncertain, not to mention a bit offended at being spoken to in such a way, but he had a wariness about him when he looked at Xavier, as though he sensed the strength the man had despite the fact that he was hiding his aura.

"We will take the stronghold alone."

"Wait!" the prince had called out as Xavier marched toward the keep. "My father. He's at the top of the keep." The man had glanced up at the sun. "The Goblin Lord said he would be executed at sunset. They're... performing some sort of ritual. I'm certain you are brave and powerful, but please don't risk my father's life by going alone. Arrogance will not be enough to save him."

Xavier had paused then, staring at the man, the gears turning in his mind. "I will ensure your father's safety."

The prince hadn't looked convinced, but he also hadn't argued.

Xavier wasn't a man one wanted to argue with.

It was still strange—seeing how much that man had changed. He was still so young. Early twenties. Perhaps that was part of it. It wasn't exactly as though he were a blank slate, but his philosophy of life had not yet had a chance to become set in stone. And here he was, falling into being a Progenitor. No strong ties to hold him back from becoming what he needed to be.

The sixth floor's goblin keep—that was what they were calling the stronghold they lay siege against—had at least twenty different floors. Howard had just cleared the fifteenth floor when he'd called the all-clear to the others.

Each of the floors had a window, offering a clear view of the sun as it slowly fell. This sixth floor of the Tower of Champions was quite different to the other floors they'd experienced. There was a time limit. Something told him that if the prince's father died at sunset and whatever ritual the goblins was performing were to happen, they would fail the floor and be pushed back to the Staging Room—or perhaps they would be forced to fight something far more powerful than the goblins.

And if we save him, does that mean we've cleared this floor?

That's what Xavier believed.

Clearing the floor, of course, wasn't an option. Not yet. They were simply here to gain levels. Farm. Howard strode over to the window and stared down at the prince. At his soldiers. He bit his lip and looked over his shoulder at Xavier.

The man had an indecipherable look on his face, but Howard figured he could read it. There was something they all knew, but none of them were saying.

If they cleared every floor of the goblin keep but the last, where the king was being held captive by the goblins, then headed back down the keep and through the Staging Room door—another trap-door, near the bottom of the keep—to refresh this floor, then the king would surely die.

It felt different now, farming a floor, when they knew the people on the floor were real. When he'd first learnt they were real, in his mind, he'd cursed the System for throwing him into these conflicts. Howard may have been a cop, someone who helped keep order, but he hadn't been a soldier. And here the System was, throwing them into conflicts that weren't their own.

He'd watched Xavier kill countless enemies—many of them human—and wondered if what they were doing was *right*. Those soldiers were fighting because they had to, weren't they? How could killing them be good? Simply because they were protecting Queen Alastea? Did saving a single life constitute taking so, so, so many?

And how could Xavier do it?

He'd come to the conclusion that the Endless Horde, and anyone who fought within it, were simply the enemy. He didn't know if he would go so far as to call them evil, but they were certainly taking orders from someone who was. If they surrendered, the fight would have ended.

They hadn't surrendered, and so the fight went on.

But this floor was different, wasn't it? Xavier intended to help Howard, Siobhan, and Justin gain as many levels as he could for them. Which meant farming this floor and the following floors countless times.

Which meant leaving the king to be sacrificed countless times, until Xavier deemed he was ready to clear the floor and no doubt get to the top of the leaderboard after doing so.

They'd done this before. They'd cleared several waves of the Endless Horde the first time they'd come to the fifth floor, then simply stepped back into the Staging Room. They'd abandoned the first Queen Alastea they'd met, from a different universe than the second one they'd met, and that woman had died. They hadn't known about the multiverse then—that every floor of the Tower of Champions led to somewhere that was *real*. That every time they stepped onto a floor, they created yet another universe.

God, the multiverse is a confusing place.

Howard took the lead, bounding up the spiral stairs to the next floor of the goblin keep. Bearded Menace cleaved through one goblin after another. Each swing took a head, an arm, or sank deep into one of the green bastards' chests.

He felt no remorse for killing the goblins, even if they were self-aware humanoids.

They're the enemy, about to sacrifice a king.

He embraced the thrill of the fight once more, relishing in his newfound power. With Xavier's help, he'd bought the most powerful weapon he could for his current class and attributes. These goblins were no match for him, Siobhan, and Justin. They hadn't needed Xavier's help once, and with his ability to tank, Howard had barely needed Siobhan's healing abilities.

They took out floor after floor until Howard strode up the stairs toward the nineteenth floor. On his way, he skimmed through the notifications he'd received.

Axe Mastery has reached Rank 15!
Axe Mastery has reached Rank 16!

Bulwark has taken a step forward on the path!
Bulwark is now a Rank 20 spell.
...
Martyr's Defence is now a Rank 18 spell.
...
Taunt is now a Rank 15 spell.
...
Backfire is now a Rank 15 spell.
One cannot walk backward on the path.

He couldn't help but bask in all the ranks. At the same time, he knew it wasn't enough. It hadn't taken them very long to make it to the penultimate floor of the goblin keep—maybe an hour—but he'd only gained two levels in that time.

We're going to need to do this a lot more times.

He thought about the king at the top of the tower. The man that was a real, living, breathing human being. Thought about sacrifice, and duty, and doing what needed to be done to keep stability, and order, even if sometimes what was needed was something dark, like killing an innocent person just because the System told you it was what was needed to survive. To become a Champion.

To farm this floor, we're going to have to do a dark deed. We're going to have to abandon that king.

Howard taunted the goblins on the nineteenth floor. There were more than there had been on the floors before it—at least two hundred—but they could take them. And they could take them *fast.*

Most of the goblins streamed toward him. To keep the fight manageable, he attracted them toward the doorway with his Taunt spell. That way, only so many goblins could come at them at once, hindered by the narrow arch.

He delivered death with one axe swing after another.

Though the archway was narrow, Justin flew over his head. The Airborne Duellist delivered death from above with his Air Strike spell, then swooped down and attacked at their heads—the goblins rarely looked up. Never expected him to be there. When his spell neared the end of its use, he flew back through the arch and stood behind Howard. If the goblins ever used their ranged spells on Justin, it was easy enough for Howard to use Martyr's Defence and take the damage on himself, though Justin was also trying to rank up his Magical and Physical Resistance skills, so that wasn't always required.

Justin's wings no longer resembled those of a baby duck, either.

The team made quick work of the penultimate floor.

When the last goblin died, Howard was breathing heavy. He leant against the stone wall of the keep and looked out of the window. They'd been at this for over an hour, and it looked as though the sun still had another half hour before it would set.

Plenty of time to spare, and that was without using the most powerful member of our party, not to mention not using the prince and his hundred soldiers. The floor seemed easy enough, if he were honest, though that made him wonder what surprises lay in store on the twentieth floor.

Justin stepped up to the final set of stairs. The teenager bit his lip.

"It's time to go," Howard said, keeping any hint of emotion from his voice. He looked over at Xavier, expecting the man to say the same thing.

The man's face was blank. His hood was down. He looked at the steps, then over at the window. "Not yet," Xavier said. "Siobhan, can you summon the prince and his soldiers up here?" The woman had practised her Summon spell a lot while they were on the fifth floor, stuck in that library.

Siobhan tilted her head to the side, looked as though she were about to say something, then nodded instead.

A bright light filled the room. The prince and his soldiers materialised in the middle of the keep's nineteenth floor. The prince had a look of confusion on his face, but it only lasted a moment. Howard imagined the man was used to pretending he knew what was happening.

The man looked around, seeming rather impressed by what they'd done.

Xavier held up a hand before the man spoke. "This is where we leave you."

"Leave us?" The prince stepped forward. "But my father, he's still in danger!"

Xavier looked at the ceiling, peering at it as though he could see through the floor. *Aura Sight.* A purple mist flowed from him, seeping upward, past the prince and the soldiers all with wide eyes. *Willpower Infusion.*

"The enemies on the final floor are about to fight each other. All but one will die. That final enemy will throw its weapon away and await you and your men to deliver its death and save your father from being sacrificed." Xavier lowered his gaze to the prince. "You must wait until my party and I have left. Watch us, from the window. Only then can you and your men move forward to the final floor and save your father."

The prince blinked, understanding dawning in his gaze. For

the first time since they'd been there, Howard realised the prince might know something of the multiverse—might know the consequences of having summoned Champions, just as Queen Alastea had.

"Thank you, Champion." The prince stepped up to Xavier. Took his hand. "Thank you."

Howard looked over at Xavier. Out of all of them, he'd imagined the man would be the first to sacrifice that king up there. Imagined he wouldn't have even considered an alternative, as they needed to farm these floors to get stronger. And that was more important, wasn't it?

In Howard's mind, there had been two options—clear the floor completely, or leave the king to die.

Xavier had found a third.

There's more to him than I thought.

Chapter 61
Cohorts

XAVIER WALKED INTO THE TAVERN AT THE BOTTOM OF THE Tower of Champions. His gaze panned around, taking in the different parties. There were currently ten parties in the tavern—more than he'd ever seen before. Warriors. Mages. Most parties had at least two of each. Only a couple of them wore equipment that hadn't been handed to them at the time of integration, though the majority had a single piece of new equipment—something they must have gotten after clearing the first floor.

He took in each of the faces but found he didn't recognise anyone here. His cohort had composed of five hundred people before they'd entered the first floor of the tower. That made him wonder how many of those Champions had survived.

It hasn't been nearly as long for them as it has for me and my party.

"Xavier." Sam waved at him as he stepped over to the bar. "Care for a drink?"

"Coffee. Make it strong."

"Alcoholic strong?" Sam raised an eyebrow.

Xavier shook his head. He wasn't in the mood for that kind of drink. He'd never been a huge drinker before the integration. Coffee had always been his vice of choice.

Sam nodded and poured him a cup. All the while, the barkeep hadn't taken his eyes off him. He was looking him up and down, taking in his new robes. "Something's changed."

Xavier had thought about how much he would tell Sam on his return. The man had told him he should be cautious. That he shouldn't be so trusting. Xavier knew far more about what the Greater Universe was like now, after how much time he'd spent on the fifth floor and all of the things he'd done there—he knew the man's words had been wise ones.

But he found he still trusted the man. To a certain degree.

I'll be honest with him. To a point.

He tilted his chin up, looked the man in the eye. "I'm E Grade."

Sam was mid-pour. He stopped. "What?"

Xavier leant on the bar. "I'd reveal my aura, but I fear it would be too painful for the rest of your clientele."

Sam continued pouring. The man usually had a fairly good poker face. He should, considering he was basically a spy. His face was a mess of emotions he couldn't control. He pushed the cup across the bar and looked like he needed to sit down. "That's impossible."

"You know what's on the fifth floor?"

Sam nodded numbly. "I do."

"I defeated it."

"What? You defeated what?"

Xavier sipped the coffee. "The Endless Horde. The one who ruled them." He paused. "A D Grade Denizen."

Sam stepped back. "You can't be serious." His eyes glazed over, as though he was looking at something. "I..." He shook his head. "Why can't I scan you?"

Xavier smirked. Before coming down here, after the other members of his party had headed to their rooms to sleep for the night—they needed far more rest than Xavier did; he still didn't feel tired after having reached E Grade—he'd spent a good while looking at items in the System Shop, until he'd found what he needed.

Something that could prevent others from scanning him.

He didn't know how powerful the item was. Already his own party weren't able to see his level when they tried to scan him. But he had to be able to block the scans from people of his own grade.

People like Sam.

Now he knew it worked.

"Oh, you won't be able to scan me," Xavier said. He remembered the first time he'd tried to scan Sam. The sharp pain he'd felt in his head.

He tried scanning him now.

???

Still too high. Guess I can't scan him either. But there was no stab of pain this time around. So that was a plus.

Sam poured himself a glass of something far stronger than coffee. He downed the drink in one, then poured another. He let out a long breath, staring off into the middle distance, just holding that second glass in his hand but not yet drinking from it.

Finally, his gaze returned to Xavier. "You killed a D Grade. You... you defeated the Endless Horde and *killed a D Grade?*"

The man's eyes were wide. Though he stared at Xavier, it didn't appear as though he were actually *looking* at him. His mouth had fallen open. He looked like a surprised fish.

"You killed a damned *D Grade?*" The man swore under his breath. "And you're telling the truth, aren't you? I mean, of course you are... What reason would you have to lie about such a thing? I told you to be careful who to trust. To keep things close, yet you're telling me this. Why? I still can't make a contract with you. My employer will know of this."

Sam kept shaking his head, mumbling something inaudible.

Xavier sipped his coffee. "I've thought about that. Had a lot of time to think, actually," he said, thinking, *over six weeks of it.* "I imagine your employer already knows what I'm capable of. I bet they're one of the people watching me." He didn't follow that up with the fact that he thought they were the weaker of the two presences he'd sensed. Not that it mattered—they were both well beyond his power. "If you're here looking for threats for them, well." He shrugged. "I'm already a known quantity."

He sipped his coffee again. Savoured it. God, he'd forgotten how good coffee tasted. He doubted caffeine really did anything for him anymore. He felt plenty of energy. But he still loved it all the same.

"Besides, I don't think that's what you're here for. You wouldn't have helped me otherwise." Xavier sat on a stool, turned and faced the other patrons, holding the ceramic coffee cup in both hands as though using it to warm them. He considered his next words carefully.

"You're the caretaker for this cohort, and something tells me we haven't been taking full advantage of your services. The last time we spoke, you said you couldn't make a contract with me yet. You've just said so again that you can't... but what if this contract wasn't to keep my secrets, but rather, do me a service?"

Sam frowned. His face had gone a little pale, but his colour was slowly returning. If this was him hiding his reaction as best he could, Xavier couldn't help but wonder how he was really feeling right now.

"What... kind of favour?"

Xavier motioned at the patrons. "These people need help, but I really don't have the time to help them myself, and I don't want to give up any of my party members for that cause. We all have too much to do, and we'll be returning to Earth. Very soon." He summoned a Minor Spirit Coin to his hand. He deftly made it play across the top of his fingers. "If I were to give you a large sum of money, would you be able to distribute it fairly between all the different parties that come into the tavern?"

Sam tilted his head to the side, his eyes glazing over again. "I can do that, yes. You want them all to be outfitted with equipment?"

"Yes," Xavier said. He almost sighed, then. He'd wanted to write a guidebook that could be disseminated out to the other Champions, too, but that unfortunately wasn't an option, as the System restricted information about different tower floors being written about or recorded in any way.

Another advantage those from integrated worlds had. They would have heard stories from their parents, mentors, or friends about the different floors. He imagined there was a strong oral tradition when it came to speaking about the tower.

He'd spoken to parties in this place before. Asked them to tell others what he'd told them. But he knew that wasn't *enough*. They didn't have to tell anyone anything if they didn't wish to. And there would be so many paths that simply didn't cross—that fact was clear, as he didn't recognise anyone in here from his last few times in the tavern.

He frowned. He didn't really trust any one of these Champions to give out the spirit coins. Even if he contracted them to do so, he didn't want to trap another Champion down here. But Sam was always here—that was simply part of his job as caretaker to this cohort.

A plan formed in his mind. A way that information could be better shared in this place. A way for the Champions of Earth to do... better than they were.

He wasn't worried about how long these Champions took to get to Earth. Not right now, anyway. Xavier wanted them to farm the floors, to linger here as long as they could. There were many things they needed to know—things he would regret not telling them, like that the people they encountered on the floors were *real*, and they should—if at all possible—be helped.

But not at the expense of their lives.

He would build an oral tradition of his own, and there was a way to ensure the Champions would pass on his words...

"But there will be some conditions."

Xavier outlined what he had in mind to Sam.

Sam would hand out money to each party that entered—and not just to one member of the party, but the individual members, so that none of them ripped off the other.

But before a party was given their spirit coins, they had to make a contract promising that they would return to the tavern every time they completed a floor and share everything they knew about the tower floors with other parties.

This made him wonder if there was a way to do this with more than just the members of his cohort. Before they entered the first floor, they'd had their orientation. The hologram had said roughly a million people from Earth had made it to the tower. Those people were split into different cohorts. And if the cohorts each had five hundred people, then there would be about two thousand of them.

He couldn't enter the taverns for those cohorts. Whenever he went down the stairs, no matter which staircase he chose, it always led to *this* tavern. But technically, he *could* talk to other cohorts. The hallway outside of his room in the tower appeared to go for miles.

Xavier might not be able to enter another cohort's tavern, but he could find other Champions, couldn't he? He wanted to outfit the members of his cohort with better equipment, but he certainly wouldn't be able to outfit *all* the Champions of Earth.

I still have over 10,000,000 Minor Spirit Coins. If I used 10,000,000, which is far more than I want to spend, that would be 100,000,000 Lesser Spirit Coins. Split between a million people, I'd only be able to hand out 100 Lesser Spirit Coins per person. Even if only half that many people had survived, I still wouldn't be able to give them much.

Not enough to make a difference.

"What is it?" Sam asked. "You went quiet."

Xavier flipped the Minor Spirit Coin he'd been playing with up into the air absently. Flip, catch, flip, catch. "I'm trying to see how I could scale this. I'm simply not rich enough to outfit everyone, but I know coin isn't the only important thing here. Even a little bit of knowledge will help the other cohorts."

On the fifth floor, he'd learnt that making contracts was a simple thing, even if he'd never done it before. "All right. I know how this will work."

Chapter 62
Contracts

Once Xavier concluded his conversation with Sam, he'd turned and faced the ten parties sitting down at the tables around the tavern. Some sat close together, drinking and talking loudly, others farther apart, huddled and whispering. One party sat at the far corner of the tavern, drinking with quiet determination. There were only three members of that party. He could guess what had happened to the fourth.

With all the Denizens—*adventurers*—in the tavern, weapons at their sides, drinks in hands, candles burning on thick wooden tables, the atmosphere screamed *fantasy tavern*. Xavier loved it.

He addressed them all, in a loud, booming voice. "Hello, fellow Champions!"

Some looked at him with open curiosity, some with open suspicion. Others looked angry or just blank. He remembered what had happened the last time he'd tried to talk to people in this place. The man who'd started a fight with him—one Xavier had finished, quite decisively.

He needed to get them all to listen to him, and he didn't feel like standing there and convincing them with some long spiel.

Perhaps, even though he kept having to counsel himself against arrogance, utilising a certain amount in this endeavour would be... prudent.

"Who the hell are you?" a heckler shouted from one of the more boisterous—*drunk*—tables.

Xavier stepped forward. His hands were together, hidden in his large sleeves. He raised his chin. "I am the most powerful, richest Denizen from Earth."

Silence followed his proclamation. The whole tavern holding its breath. Then one woman began laughing. A loud, shrill laugh. The rest of the tavern followed a moment later.

A man stood. The man didn't wear basic armour like the others. He wore full-plate armor. Xavier doubted he spent much on it. Instead of a sword at his belt, he wore a war hammer. The man was tall, maybe six-six, and built like a mountain. "Right. And I'm the King of England."

Xavier released a long sigh. "None of us have time for this. Earth is threatened by foreign invaders. It will need all of you at your best, which is why I'm offering you all 100,000 Lesser Spirit Coins each."

The big man had been walking toward him. He stopped. "That... that's a lot of money. You're serious?"

Well, that got them listening, he thought, before saying, "Yes, I'm serious. I'm sure you've all figured out the massive disadvantage Earth has here at the tower. I plan to change that, at least as much as I can. The first part of that is outfitting our entire cohort with superior weapons and armour. The second is imparting as much knowledge as I can to all of you. And not just us. Other cohorts.

"This money won't come for nothing. You'll each have to make a System Contract, outlining that you'll pass on the knowledge I give you, and any knowledge you have of the tower floors, onto two other Champions or full parties. You'll pass it on to one Champion or party from our cohort, and one Champion or party from another."

Xavier held up a hand as he saw some people about to ask

questions. "Before they can receive this information, they must make a contract as well."

"Sounds like some sort of chain email," someone muttered.

Xavier nodded. "It is something like that. We won't be able to offer money to members of other cohorts, so convincing them to make a contract will be the hard part for all of you." He flicked the Minor Spirit Coin he still had in his hand up into the air. "But I assure you, it will be worth your while."

Xavier detailed just about everything he knew about the different floors of the Tower of Champions to those ten parties in the room, then he handed over 5,000,000 Minor Spirit Coins to Sam once the man made a contract with the correct wording stipulated within it. The 5,000,000 Minor Spirit Coins would convert into 50,000,000 Lesser Spirit Coins. Split between five hundred people, it should go far.

There would even be plenty left over, considering how many Champions in the cohort had likely already died...

God, it felt wrong handing over that much money. It was more than he'd spent on his own equipment. He still had more than what he'd handed over left, but that didn't make it any easier.

It's an investment in the wellbeing of Earth, its stability, and the strength of its Denizens.

Xavier wasn't handing the money over to just *anyone*, after all. He was handing it over to Denizens who'd chosen to be Champions. People who'd chosen to fight for their world. People might choose Champion for selfish reasons in more established worlds than Earth, but no one on Earth had really known what any of it meant when they'd picked it.

Besides, the people in his own cohort, as far as he'd found out, had all come from the same geographical area. Everyone else in his party was from his city.

He'd offered the barkeep some compensation for dolling out

the money and contracts, but Sam had turned him down, saying he was happy to do it as part of his role as their caretaker and to garner goodwill with him.

Xavier saw no point in arguing. He'd spent enough coin as it was.

By the time he returned to the Staging Room, the other members his party were awake. The time limit they'd given themselves to level up before finishing off the last few floors didn't seem like it would be enough. Not at the rate his party was clearing the sixth floor, at least, so Xavier decided it was time to move on from that floor and onto the next.

First, however, he wished to experiment with his new spells. He had quite a few of them, and it would be a travesty if he didn't practice. Mentally, he went through each new spell and the different abilities that he'd acquired with his equipment.

Core Burn, Summon Otherworldly Spirit, Otherworldly Communion, Soul Shatter, Soul Puppet, Soul Step, Otherworld Phase, and Buffer.

Five new spells and three new imbued abilities to test out.

He was intrigued by all of them. Core Burn and Soul Step were near the top of his list to try out. Core Burn appeared to be exactly what he'd done to the Lord of the Endless Horde. He wondered how overpowered the spell was, but a part of him knew it couldn't be as strong as what he'd compelled the D Grade Denizen to do.

I won't simply be able to kill anyone I like with this spell. The System wouldn't hand me something like that, would it?

No. He doubted Core Burn would have even worked on the Lord of the Endless Horde. The only reason he'd been able to take that bastard out was because of that confluence of events. The man's emotional vulnerability. His arrogance. The cracking of his mental block...

It would be very, very difficult to make such a thing happen again.

But on enemies of a lower level? Well, if he could drain them of their Spirit Energy, at the very least he'd stop them from being able to cast spells. And if he did manage to burn their health as well...

It's like a Spirit Energy drain spell and a damage-over-time spell in one.

Summon Otherworldly Spirit and Otherworldly Communion were the two spells he was both most interested in learning about and most confused about. He didn't know what summoning a spirit from the Otherworld would do, nor did he know what insight he could gain with Otherworldly Communion. He could have tested these spells out earlier, but he'd been too busy overseeing the others' clearing of the sixth floor—not that they'd really needed his help.

He was glad he'd found a solution to the king being sacrificed at the top of that goblin keep. Farming floors of the Tower of Champions had far too many moral implications for his liking. If he could do it and reduce harm to those they were tasked with helping, if they happened to *be* tasked with helping anyone on a floor they came to, then he would do so.

"This will be our second-last time on the sixth floor," he told the others, who'd all gathered around him the moment he'd stepped into the Staging Room. "I already know how I'm going to clear the floor. A single usage of Soul Strike, area-of-effect, should be enough to destroy every goblin in that keep. If any floor boss remains alive at the top, I can Soul Step to the nearest dead enemy and kill them there."

Howard raised an eyebrow. "Yeah, that'll work."

"You'll clear the floor in a matter of seconds," Justin said. "I suppose you did the same for the fourth floor..."

Siobhan tucked a strand of hair behind her ear. "We really are holding you back, aren't we?"

Xavier shook his head. "No. You'll all be needed once we're back on Earth. You know that." Part of him couldn't help but agree with her words, however. If he wasn't bothering to wait and level them up, he'd already have cleared the tenth floor and be back on Earth.

I need to think of the bigger picture, don't I?

Besides, he'd be there by the end of the day. That was their plan, after all.

Not much longer now.

Chapter 63
Zombie Goblin

KILLING THESE GOBLINS FELT LIKE THE EASIEST THING IN THE Greater Universe, to the point where it was difficult to test his new abilities on them.

His Soul Shatter spell, which caused a burst of soul damage against an enemy, harnessing their own soul, had two paths: area-of-effect damage or single-target damage. As it was still only Rank 1, he could use either path.

When he cast it for the first time, he used it as an area-of-effect spell. It cleared the entire first floor of the keep. All one hundred goblins died in an instant.

Xavier had stepped into the room and cast it on the nearest goblin. Shards of what looked to be glass shot out from it in every direction. The glass wasn't corporeal—he could tell that much—and it didn't harm his party members. It tore through every other goblin in the large room, leaving their bodies untouched in that same eerie way that Soul Strike did.

"Well," Howard muttered, poking his head into the room from the doorway to the stairwell. "That was effective."

Xavier frowned. "Yes. It was." He stepped over the first few corpses, panning his vision about the room, then shook his head and sighed. "A little... *too* effective." He rubbed the back of his neck, contemplating his next move.

The Upgrade Quest came up instantly.

Soul Shatter – Rank 1
Upgrade Quest:
As you have now used this spell, you have begun your first step on the path to upgrading it to Rank 2.
Available paths:
Soul Shatter (area-of-effect) – Shatter an enemy's soul to detonate it and inflict soul damage to the target and nearby enemies. To upgrade, kill 200 enemies with Soul Shatter's area-of-effect path. Progress: 100/200
Soul Shatter (single-target) – Shatter an enemy's soul to detonate it and inflict soul damage to the enemy. To upgrade, kill 50 enemies with Soul Shatter's single-target path. Progress: 0/50
This spell is bound to your Otherworldly Reaper class. Gaining Rank 2 in this spell will not require you to forget another spell, and this spell cannot be forgotten while you remain in the Reaper line of classes.
One cannot walk backward on the path.

Good thing the spell requires two hundred kills for the area-of-effect path, otherwise I might have upgraded it by accident my first time using it...

Xavier, on reflex, harvested the souls of all the dead enemies around him. All but one—the soul he'd just shattered. That, he couldn't even detect anymore.

Justin stepped into the room, frowning. "What do you mean it was *too* effective? Are you really complaining about the fact that you took out the entire room with one spell?"

"Honestly, some people will just find anything to complain about," Siobhan said, the hint of a smirk playing on her lips.

"It makes it difficult to judge a spell's effectiveness if I can just..." Xavier snapped his fingers. "Kill everything with it. I'd need to fight stronger enemies to know which path is best."

"Area-of-effect or single-target?" Siobhan asked.

Xavier nodded. "I see the advantages of both." He sighed. "I think I'm leaning toward area-of-effect." He tilted his head to the side. "I think Soul Strike will always be my most effective weapon, and if I were facing a single strong enemy with many weaker enemies around it... I could target the strong enemy with Soul Shatter..."

"Which would then kill the enemies around it," Howard replied, "letting you harvest their souls and still damage the enemy in front of you. Then, you could use Soul Strike primarily on one enemy."

"Exactly. I also think I'll be facing more armies than single, strong enemies. At least in the near future."

"And those single strong enemies you do face certainly won't be D Grade," Howard said. "At least, not for a little while."

"We hope," Justin muttered.

Siobhan walked to the centre of the room, her purple robes trailing just above the ground as she stopped over the pristine goblin corpses. "It does *sound* like the best way to go, but maybe you should hold off deciding the path until you've tested your other new spells? You'll have better information then."

"Good idea." Xavier had been thinking of doing the same thing. While fighting the Endless Horde, he'd lacked the chance to take much time to make decisions on spells. He'd needed advantages as fast as possible. The shift from that to now was something to get used to.

He looked over at the stairs. "One floor down." He pushed forward. The others had cleared this floor twelve times the day before, getting faster and faster at it each time they went through. Not only because they grew stronger, but because their tactics improved. Which also meant Xavier knew every inch of this place —except for the final floor. He hadn't set foot up there yet.

The next spell he tried out was Core Burn.

He jogged up the stairs, taking four at a time, and reached the next room. When he stepped over the threshold the goblins let out little shouts and ran straight at him. Their swords and axes and spears slashed, chopped, and thrust into his robes and did... nothing.

"That tickles," he muttered. The smarter of the goblins realised their attacks were completely useless and began running away in wide-eyed terror.

Xavier cast Core Burn on one of the goblins that had remained behind. Instantly, its aura... exploded. It flared, brighter than anything of its level should have been able to. The little green beast stumbled backward, clutching its chest. Then the bright light was gone. Core Burn caused a chain reaction, eating at the goblin's health next.

Within seconds, it was dead.

Core Burn has taken a step forward on the path!
Core Burn is now a Rank 2 spell.
...
Core Burn is now a Rank 3 spell.
One cannot walk backward on the path.

Well, at least it's easy to rank up. At the moment.

The test didn't really tell him much, however. Honestly, he was glad the spell only had a single path. One less decision for him to make right now.

It seems there's a downside to being overpowered while testing new spells. These enemies are simply too weak for me to experiment on.

Xavier tilted his head at the goblin's corpse. The goblin, like the goblins on the floor below, looked as though it was unharmed. He could see the soul within the goblin, ready to be harvested. Instead of harvesting it, however, he cast Soul Puppet.

The goblin rose to its feet. Its movement was stilted. Eerie. As though it were a marionette.

A puppet indeed.

The spell gained an instant rank-up the moment he used it. Though unlike Core Burn, it only gained one rank.

The goblin just... stood there. Despite the spell's description, it certainly *looked* like a zombie. The spark inside its brain was gone —whatever spark a goblin had—and all that was left was its soul. A soul that Xavier commanded.

Xavier had become accustomed to controlling enemies with Willpower Infusion by using mental commands, so he did the same for Soul Puppet, sending it an instruction to run and attack the other goblins, who were huddled at the stairwell leading to the next floor. For whatever reason, though they were afraid of him, they hadn't gone upstairs.

The goblin snapped into action. Its head wrenched to the side, awkwardly turning before its body. Then it pivoted on the ball of its left foot and spun. It held a short sword in one hand and a shield in the other, but its arms were dangling by its side as though they had no bones in them.

Guard up.

The goblin raised its sword and shield, though it didn't look... quite right. Then it sprinted at the other goblins.

Siobhan came to stand next to him. She crossed her arms and raised her eyebrows. "Soul Puppet?"

Xavier nodded. "Soul Puppet."

"Looks a bit..." She tilted her head to the side, her face scrunched up in what she'd call stink-face if Xavier were doing it. "Um..."

"Weird?"

443

"I would have used the word *stupid*. But yeah, weird works too."

The other goblins seemed wary of the dead goblin running at them, something Xavier didn't blame them for. Though the little green beasties were true to form, just as cowardly as he remembered they were back when he'd first encountered them at his university.

So far, he was wondering what the advantage of a Soul Puppet was. The spell's cooldown had been fast enough—maybe five seconds. He supposed that was because his Spirit attribute was so damned high.

I guess the advantage is that I could make a whole damned army of the little bastards.

If the situation were different, he might wish to stand there and raise goblin after goblin until he had an overwhelming force. Each kill would grant him a new soldier.

I wonder how long they last if they aren't attacked. Seconds? Minutes? Hours? And how much of that is based on the strength of the soul that I use?

Xavier watched with great interest as the zombie goblin attacked the first goblin it reached. Its moves were jerky and strange. It attacked its enemy not just with its sword, but with its shield as well, as though trying to bash it to death. Not very sophisticated. It certainly didn't *look* like it was being controlled by a soul —nothing like how his soul apparitions attacked.

Maybe the soul has difficulty controlling a corporeal body?

The enemy goblin blocked a strike and counterattacked, slashing a wound into the zombie goblin's shoulder.

The zombie goblin was unperturbed. Didn't look hurt in the slightest. Its blood was no longer flowing, as its heart no longer pumped, so it barely bled from the wound.

It overpowered the other goblin. Not from skill, just by the very fact that it couldn't be harmed, only immobilised, and the enemy mustn't be used to fighting in such a way.

It didn't take long for the other nearby goblins to surge in and help. In moments, the zombie goblin had both its arms lopped off.

Its head followed soon after.

"It didn't do *too* badly," Justin said. "The spell's a bit creepy, though. Can you imagine an army of those things?"

Xavier grinned, a little sinisterly. "Yes. I can."

He gripped Charon's Scythe and activated its imbued ability, Soul Step, using it on the recently deceased goblin—not the zombie goblin, as that soul had deteriorated too much to be viable. Which meant he couldn't simply send his soul puppets wherever he wished then Soul Step to their location, using them as mobile teleportation platforms.

There goes that idea.

The world *shifted* around him. One moment he was standing by the doorway, Siobhan at his right, Justin at his left, and Howard behind him. The next, he was standing directly in front of the goblin his zombie had just slain, surrounded by other goblins.

Effective. I wonder if I can control which way I face next time?

Soul Step has a cooldown of 1 minute. It cannot be used for another 59 seconds.

He was disorientated, but only for a moment. He supposed he would get better at that the more he did it. It was a shame the imbued ability took a whole minute to refresh. As it wasn't a spell, he doubted he'd be able to reduce the cooldown on it.

Xavier couldn't help himself. He whirled around in a great sweeping strike with his brand-new scythe-staff. The blade sliced through the heads of six goblins with ease. The orientation of the blade, no longer at an angle against the haft, made the strike much more effective than his last weapon.

The heads thudded to the ground just before the bodies of their owners followed.

I could definitely get used to this.

The rest of the goblins on the second floor of the goblin keep, seeing no way out—as they presumably didn't want to head up the stairs to the next floor—came after him. He harvested the souls of those he'd slain and waited for the first goblin to reach him. Its axe slashed for his neck.

Xavier activated Otherworld Phase, the imbued connected to his Anointed Robes of Umbral.

The axeblade went straight *through* his neck, as though he were nothing but a ghost. The goblin's eyes widened in confusion. Xavier used Core Burn on the goblin, if for nothing more than to gain another rank.

Core Burn has taken a step forward on the path!
Core Burn is now a Rank 4 spell.
One cannot walk backward on the path.

He smiled.

Very good.

Soul Step and Otherworld Phase worked exactly how he'd expected them to. Though as he'd used them, he'd noticed something that hadn't been a part of their descriptions. An energy from within Charon's Scythe, then from within the Anointed Robes of Umbral, had been drained.

The items have their own Spirit Energy reserves...

Only a small portion of the energy in his equipment had been drained, but he funnelled some more into them all the same. He got the feeling that this wasn't something that would happen naturally, that he would need to remember to constantly refresh their reserves, lest he be unable to use one of his imbued abilities.

Speaking of...

At least a dozen goblins were surrounding him now, and so he used his final imbued ability, the one connected to his Dark Steel Bracer.

Buffer!

The goblins were rapidly pushed backward by an invisible

force, as though he were gripping each one of them with Heavy Telekinesis. They slid across the ground until they were twenty feet away from him in a circle, where they abruptly halted.

This could definitely come in handy too.

Xavier smiled, impressed with the spells and abilities he'd acquired since defeating the Lord of the Endless Horde. They would definitely add a level of versatility that he'd been lacking.

But he still had two more spells to try.

Chapter 64
A Spell with an Attitude Problem

XAVIER GAZED AT THE ENEMIES REMAINING ON THE SECOND floor of the goblin keep. Even with all his spell and ability experimentation he was still moving through the floor faster than the other members of his party had.

Once the imbued ability, Buffer, had ended, Xavier twirled his scythe-staff about him, lazily lopping off the heads and limbs of any goblins dumb enough to get within range. There was no difficulty to this, and so he took little enjoyment from the fight. He also didn't gain any Mastery Points from these kills—the enemies were simply too weak.

It was time for him to test Summon Otherworldly Spirit. He looked at the spell's description.

Summon Otherworldly Spirit – Rank 1
Summon Otherworldly Spirit is a legendary spell specific to the Otherworldly line of classes.
Summon Otherworldly Spirit is a spell that gives the Denizen the ability to call forth a spirit from the Otherworld.
One cannot walk backward on the path.

Yet. Just as I remembered. It barely says anything about what it actually does.

He'd theorised a few different possibilities, but there was no substitution for active experimentation.

Xavier cast the spell.

Everything around him froze. The goblins running about. A fly-like insect buzzing around one of the corpses. Nothing in the entire room was moving—not even Xavier, yet he could still see. Still think.

This isn't what I was expecting.

The world... shifted. Not in the same way as it had shifted when he'd used Soul Step. No, this was completely different. The colour from the room was leeched out. The already grey stone turned even greyer. The green of the goblins' skin and blood bled out and dulled. It was like the whole room was a freeze-frame in some black-and-white fantasy movie.

Were there any black-and-white fantasy movies? he wondered. *Not that it's important right now...*

A humming sounded somewhere. In his mind. In the room. Outside the keep. He wasn't sure where it was coming from. Though he didn't recognise the noise—it was unique, alien; other-worldly—he instinctively knew what it was trying to do.

It's calling forth a spirit.

You have successfully connected to the Otherworld.
What kind of Spirit do you wish to summon?

1. **Spirit of Protection**
2. **Spirit of Vengeance**
3. **Spirit of Time**

The cooldown for this spell varies significantly depending upon the spirit you summon.

Whoa. That's different.

Xavier tried to blink, then remembered he was currently frozen in time, unable to move his eyes. Before he decided on which option to choose, he wondered if there was any sort of time limit to this world-frozen thing he was currently experiencing. His mind worked quickly, what with his high Intelligence attribute, but being able to freeze time to think through a battle strategy? That seemed like a second hand benefit of this spell that he would most definitely take advantage of in the future.

Protection, vengeance, time... The options were quite interesting. First, he hadn't known he would *have* options. He could guess what the first two spirits might be capable of, but it was the third that intrigued him the most. What, exactly, would a Spirit of Time be capable of? Was time travel possible in the Greater Universe?

And would travelling through time simply create another alternate universe, like travelling to a floor of the tower does?

He dismissed that tangential thought. It didn't matter *how* it worked, only *if* it worked.

Xavier ruminated on his options. He wanted to test the Spirit of Time, but he worried about what the notification said at the end —that his cooldown would vary depending on which spirit he summoned.

How long, exactly, would he need to wait for the spell to cooldown? It could be anything from seconds, to weeks, to years for all he knew. The others had told him legends of some spells in the higher grades that took centuries to reach the ends of their cooldowns because of their immense power.

And to him, Spirit of Time sounded like the most powerful option.

I'll have to test that another time. Just in case.

Spirit of Vengeance, he also wasn't sure about using in this situation. Mostly because he didn't know how much control he would have over the summoned spirit. He wasn't worried about it attacking his party, but what if it went after all the enemies in the area? It might very well be strong enough to defeat every goblin in the keep. Then he would have cleared this floor well before he was ready too.

No. That's not an option I want to go with. I can't accidentally clear this floor.

He needed every single title he could get, even if those titles didn't seem as powerful anymore, in the long run—over a thousand tower floors—they would make a huge difference.

So, in lieu of not summoning anything at all, he decided to summon the Spirit of Protection.

The Spirit of Protection materialised before Xavier in a flash of bright light. Though the world around him had been bled of all colour, the spirit that appeared before him looked to comprise of every colour imaginable. Its brightness diminished from that of the sun on a clear day to a full moon's glow, allowing him to make out the spirit's details.

The ethereal creature looked more humanoid than Xavier had expected. It wore a glowing set of full-plate armour, though its face was hidden behind a dark cowl that wreathed its features in shadow despite the glow the rest of the spirit emanated. He couldn't tell what type of race the being might be—human, elf, demon, or something else entirely.

Am I even seeing its true form, or is it simply appearing as something I can recognise? Like angels often are said to appear, in ways human's can perceive, while their real forms would make us go mad?

The spirit cocked its head to the side. Though its eyes were not visible beneath its dark cowl, he knew it was staring at him. The room was still frozen, but in that frozen moment the spirit spoke, and the words echoed directly in Xavier's mind.

Why have you summoned me, Denizen? You are unharmed, and I do not sense anything that could pose danger toward you.

It can talk. The spirit can talk!

Do you think me a dim-witted fool? Of course I can talk!

Oh, crap. It can read my mind?

The spirit reared back, as though offended—or frustrated—by his thought.

All right, so it heard that too. Xavier, caught of guard, floundered for a moment before he settled on what he wanted to say to the spirit. *O powerful Spirit of Protection from the domain of the Otherworld,* he thought, trying to sound respectful. *I wish to learn about your abilities and the abilities of the other spirits that lurk within your realm.*

The Spirit of Protection floated in the air before him. It raised its head.

You waste my time, Denizen. I am not some minor spirit to be summoned on a whim. Give me instruction or dismiss me from this plane. Do not test my patience, or your ability to summon from the Otherworld will take far longer to rejuvenate.

Suddenly, Xavier saw the notification's text in a new light. The spell's cooldown wasn't dependent on the spirit he chose, but rather the individual spirit he summoned, which made him wonder if there were different spirits of protection, vengeance, and time.

Command me!

Xavier reined in the harsh thoughts he wished to have about the spirit, not wishing to have a long cooldown forced upon him.

I dismiss you, Spirit of Protection, and apologise for wasting your precious time.

The Spirit of Protection disappeared. Colour returned to the world in a flash. Slowly, and then all at once, Xavier Collins was returned to the flow of time.

"Impatient spirit," he muttered.

He willed the information for the cooldown to appear.

Summon Otherworldly Spirit currently has a cooldown of 10 hours. It cannot be used for another 9 hours and 57 seconds.

"Damned ghost."

"What are you muttering about?" Howard asked from the other side of the room.

Xavier didn't feel like actively dealing with the rest of the enemies on the floor. Instead, he cast Willpower Infusion. Purple mist drifted into the air and took control of the goblins. He sent them upstairs, to fight their allies, then walked over to the others.

"I just used Summon Otherworldly Spirit."

"But... nothing happened?" Justin said.

Xavier sighed. "Yes, well, the spirit said I was wasting its time."

"Wasting its time?" Siobhan replied. "The spirit talked to you? Why couldn't we see it? When exactly did this happen?"

Xavier raised a hand to forestall anymore of her questions from streaming out, then explained what had happened.

"And you just... dismissed the spirit?" Howard asked.

"Honestly? It really seemed offended by the fact that I had summoned it when I wasn't actually in danger." Xavier rubbed the back of his neck. "This is the first time I've had a spell with an attitude problem."

Siobhan smiled and shook her head. "That is pretty funny."

"It gave me a ten hour cooldown because it thought I was wasting its time."

"Siobhan is right. That is funny." Justin chuckled.

Even Howard had a grin on his face. "It sounds like it might be a powerful spell when you *actually* need it."

"Yeah. I guess. Like the other spells, it's just gonna be difficult to test unless I'm actually facing powerful enemies."

Several kill notifications popped up in his vision. He dismissed them. "I guess I shouldn't be complaining about being too powerful."

"No. You really shouldn't be," Siobhan said with a grin.

"You still have one more spell to test, don't you?" Howard asked.

"Otherworldly Communion." Xavier tilted his head to the side, put a hand to his chin. "Another spell with an incredibly vague description." Though he was a little frustrated that he hadn't been able to really *use* the Summon Otherworldly Spirit spell, he couldn't say he was disappointed with it. He wasn't even annoyed that the spirit he'd summoned had gotten angry with him. From the spirit's perspective, he was definitely wasting its time.

He had to wonder what exactly a spirit *did* with its time that it was so worried about it being wasted, however...

Even though it had only been a day since he'd faced the Lord of the Endless Horde, Xavier was chafing at how easy this floor was. He wanted another challenge. Something worthy of the spell he'd just tried to use. Something that wouldn't be deemed a waste of time.

Maybe protecting Earth will be more of a challenge than I've anticipated... though wishing for that wouldn't be a good thing.

As Otherworldly Communion didn't seem like a combat spell, Xavier turned from his party members and cast it right away.

The world froze again, bleeding of its colour, just as it had when he'd used the last spell.

You have successfully connected to the Otherworld.
What kind of insight do you wish to receive?

1. **Strategic insight**
2. **Personal insight**
3. **Sector insight**

The cooldown for this spell varies depending on the level of insight you receive. If you have a specific question you wish to gain insight on, hold it in your mind as you choose your option.

Xavier stared at the options in the frozen, greyed-out world, wondering what he should choose. He imagined strategic insight would be incredibly helpful to him in the middle of a difficult battle. Having the ability to freeze time, even if he couldn't move, and commune with the Otherworld to learn what his best path of attack might be...

Yeah, that could get me out of a tight spot in the future.

Personal insight was intriguing, too. Maybe he could learn about his abilities and what paths he should take with them. Could there be better options that he was missing out on? Would it know which way he should take Soul Shatter? Could it tell him what the spirits summoned with Summon Otherworldly Spirit were capable of?

Xavier would have bitten his lip in thought if he could.

The last option, sector insight, was admittedly the most intriguing to him. Information was something he lacked since the moment he was integrated into the Greater Universe. It was something his *whole planet* lacked. He thought of the Sector Travel Key he still had in his Storage Ring, and the Portal Stones. If he learnt more about the sector he resided in, maybe he could better decide where to go with that Sector Travel Key.

Even gaining an idea of the landscape around the sector, like who Earth's enemies might be, would be a huge boon.

So that was what Xavier chose to do. He selected the third option, sector insight.

Chapter 65
The Silver River Sector

A BRIGHT LIGHT FILLED THE STONE ROOM. COLOURS blossomed from this light, just as they had blossomed from the Spirit of Protection when he'd summoned it.

Who will I be communing with this time?

The brightness of the light dimmed until a figure could be seen. The figure was smaller than the last spirit he'd summoned. It looked humanoid and wore pristine white robes. Like the spirit before it, its features were obscured beneath a large hood.

Greeting, Denizen, the spirit's voice sounded within Xavier's mind. **What insight do you wish to receive?**

Xavier held his thoughts in. There was likely a way to distinguish the thoughts he wished it to hear from the ones he wished only for himself, but he didn't know how to do that yet.

I wish learn about the sector that my planet, Earth, inhabits.

He could have had a more specific question, like asking where he should go with his Sector Travel Key, but he wanted to get a lay of the land first. He also had no idea what type of limitations this spell had. Surely he couldn't simply learn *anything*?

The figure bobbed slowly up and down where it hovered. It nodded its head and spread its arms wide. Its hands were hidden beneath its voluminous sleeves. It looked like some holy monk about to spout the wisdom of the gods. Perhaps that wasn't too far off.

Xavier's vision went black. The world *shifted* around him, like he was in a rising elevator or on a roller coaster slowly inching to the top of its climb.

He sensed the drop coming before it did. It was a strange sensation, but he'd had a similar one before. His consciousness was being split from his body. This was something that he'd done on purpose, when using his Willpower Infusion spell.

Having it forced on him was not pleasant.

His consciousness... plummeted. It was as though he were travelling through space and time. A second or an hour or a million years could have gone by before he was stopped.

His mind could see, somehow, even though it didn't have eyes, and what he saw before him was a little blue planet, with a single moon revolving around it.

Earth. This... this is Earth.

Your world, Earth, is at the very edge of integrated space in your sector.

Xavier's consciousness plummeted again. He was moved through space faster than the speed of light until he was looking at a sea of stars, floating out in the nothing amongst them.

Earth is part of the Silver River sector. The Silver River sector's earliest integrated planet was 9,748 years ago. The slow but inevitable crawl of the System has integrated more than a quarter of the galaxy since then.

There are over 300 million viable planetary candidates for System integration within the Silver River sector, with over 75 million of those planets having already been integrated.

The Silver River sector is considered a young sector and, as such, has been the site of great upheaval. Since its integration, it has been purged

twice, with billions of Denizens from millions of planets being extinguished from existence.

The most powerful Denizen in the Silver River sector is Empress Larona, a C Grade known for her ability to see into the future.

The Silver River sector is in danger of another purge.

Xavier's consciousness violently snapped back into his body. He stumbled, the world suddenly no longer frozen, the spirit that had been hovering, cross-legged in the air before him, was gone.

He touched a hand to his head, feeling vertigo. With how damned high all his attributes were, he didn't think he'd ever be able to feel vertigo again.

Siobhan strode across the stone room and put a hand on his shoulder. "What is it? You used your other spell. What did you learn?"

Xavier shook his head. He'd thought Earth was the only thing that had been in danger. The only thing he needed to worry about. Apparently, he'd been wrong. "Our entire sector is at risk of being purged."

"Purged?" Howard said. "What does that mean?"

"That... doesn't sound good." Justin gripped the hilt of his sword, not that there was anything to fight right now.

Xavier explained to him what he'd seen—which, admittedly, wasn't a hell of lot—and then what he'd learnt about their sector.

"It's been purged twice before?" Siobhan asked. Her eyes were a little wide. "Who—*what* would do that?"

Xavier shook his head. "I've no idea. It didn't exactly provide much explanation."

He could sense the spell was on cooldown. He checked how long it would take to cast it again. Next time, he would ask for a more specific insight.

Otherworldly Communion currently has a

cooldown of 1 month. It cannot be used for another 29 days, 23 hours, and 57 minutes.

"Really?" Xavier swore under his breath.

"What?" Howard asked.

"The spell has a month-long cooldown! I felt like it barely gave me any information at all. At least no *context* for the information!" He sighed. "But I think I know who might." He shut his eyes and cast Willpower Infusion. A surge of purple mist flowed from him. He raised his arms as he felt the mist rise. He'd never used the spell on this many enemies before. He could use Soul Strike to kill all the goblins, but he didn't want to accidentally take out the floor boss.

He split his consciousness. Floor by floor, he felt the mist enter the goblins, take control of their weak minds. He commanded them to fight each other. Commanded them to die. A minute, maybe two, went by before every enemy but one remained. He harvested every available soul, bringing his soulkeeping reserve back to full.

"Tell the prince what he needs to know to save his father from being sacrificed, then get out of here," he said to Howard, then turned to Siobhan. "Teleport me down to the exit. I have someone I need to talk to."

Xavier burst into the tavern. A few heads looked up. He recognised many of them this time, after the contracts he'd set up and the many he'd handed away. He ignored them, looked at the barkeep, and strode across the tavern toward him. "What do you know about this sector being purged?"

Sam had been cleaning the bar, pristine as it was. He dropped the cloth he'd been using and stared at Xavier. There was recognition in his eyes. "Purged?"

"I've just learnt that the Silver River sector has been purged twice since it was first integrated into the System. Millions of planets extinguished. Billions of Denizens dead. And that the sector is threatened by *another* purge. You said the person you work for plays the long game. What game is that, exactly?"

"There are things that I can say, and things that I can't—"

Xavier shut his eyes. Sighed. "I've been patient with you. Honest with you. Now it's your turn to be honest with me." He remembered the name of the Denizen his insight had told him was the most powerful in the sector. Something clicked within his mind, the pieces coming together.

The presence that observed me... The person Sam is working for...

He stared at Sam, observing his expression closely, then uttered the name, "Empress Larona."

Sam's eyes widened. He rested a hand on the bar. Shook his head. "How'd you learn that name? Where did you hear about the purge?"

Xavier sat at one of the barstools. "You work for the most powerful Denizen in the sector. A C Grade."

Sam nodded slowly.

"What does she want from me?"

Sam bit his lip. Shut his eyes. Then he let out a long sigh and leant heavily on the bar, staring at Xavier. "For a hundred years, I've been looking for you. Sent from one instance of the Tower of Champions to the next. Again and again, I've seen Progenitors fail to live up to even the most meagre of expectations. Not a single one of them has been *enough*. Not a single one of them has been a *True* Progenitor." He shook his head again. "But you. You're not what I expected. You're like nothing I've ever seen. Something tells me you're like nothing *anyone* has ever seen. I'm still in shock about your grade. That you advanced to E Grade already. It's insane. If you were anyone else, I wouldn't believe you, but you're..."

The barkeep pulled an unlabelled bottle of dark liquid from beneath the counter. Two tumblers appeared as though from nowhere, hovering in the air. He let go of the bottle, but it didn't fall. Instead, it moved as though it were still being held by him, pouring its liquid into the glasses. Xavier had never seen the barkeep use telekinesis before.

One of the glasses came to rest in front of Xavier.

"Drink," said the barkeep.

And drink Xavier did. He downed the entire contents of glass. Slapped it back onto the counter. "You still haven't said what she wants from me. She's C Grade. She could crush me like a bug."

"I told you, she plays the long game."

Xavier pushed the glass forward. The bottle poured him more. "The long game. I've become strong enough to protect Earth, haven't I?"

"Yes, I think so. Though you getting to such a high level so quickly... it will have consequences you won't like."

Xavier frowned at that but moved past it for now. "But saving Earth, that's not going to be enough, is it?"

"Not even close."

Xavier grabbed his glass, downed it again. "The long game. She can't protect the sector, can she? As powerful as she is, she feels defenceless?"

Sam looked away. "There are things in the Greater Universe that are more powerful than you can imagine. Things that can wipe out entire planets with a snap of their fingers. Beings that can eat whole galaxies. Sectors as young as ours..." He sighed. "I shouldn't be telling you all this." He put a finger to his lower lip. "The System should be stopping me from telling you all this." He shrugged. "I guess you're more ready than I thought."

Xavier leant back on his stool. He considered having a third drink, but he knew that wouldn't actually help. Besides, the drink wasn't nearly strong enough to give him even the slightest buzz. "What am I supposed to do with this information?" The words came out in an angry growl. For a moment, he wasn't even sure why he was angry.

I just caught up. Got strong enough to protect Earth. And now I hear the whole damned sector is in trouble? How, exactly, does that responsibility fall onto me?

He shut his eyes. Thought of Queen Alastea. Of the Lord of the Endless Horde he'd just defeated.

I've already changed the fate of one sector... what's one more?

Except that sector was weak compared to this one. And how could he fight a threat that could purge millions of worlds?

"What do you *want* to do with the information?" Sam paced behind the bar. "Do you want to leave the sector? Because you can, you know. Maybe not yet, but in time, you'll be able to afford to do something like that."

Xavier was taken aback by the question. "What? Leave the sector? Why would I do that?"

"To avoid the threat," Sam said. "Other, older sectors are more established. Threats like these... don't happen. Many have a single ruler, or several strong rulers, who keep relative peace and stability. Our sector is splintered. Empress Larona is the most powerful, but she does not rule everything. If she did, your planet would be in a very different situation."

"I wouldn't need to save it from being destroyed or enslaved?" Xavier asked.

Sam chuckled darkly. "No, Xavier. You wouldn't be *able* to save it." He raised a hand, forestalling Xavier's next words. "Your people wouldn't be enslaved, but a ruler of her choosing would be installed. Someone who could guide your people. All of your people." He shrugged. "But making peace on an entire world can be difficult work, especially when they've been as fractured as the people of your world have, already a militaristic culture."

Xavier took in what Sam was saying. Empress Larona, were she in charge, would take over Earth? Rule it by proxy? How would that make her any different to the Lord of the Endless Horde?

He lowered his head in thought. The politics of the sector weren't his current concern. "I'm not going to flee the sector."

"Why not, now that you know it's in danger?"

"Because I wouldn't be able to take Earth with me."

Sam smiled. "You *are* who she's been looking for."

Chapter 66
Record Holder

Xavier returned to the Staging Room like a man on a mission, sprinting up the stairs with a sense of urgency he hadn't felt since his body had been degrading. It turned out what he wanted and what he needed were two very different things. He wanted to linger on the last few floors and give his friends more levels. He'd thought that was what they needed. Him to be there to help powerlevel them.

But he'd been distracted. Everything was feeling too easy, and that was a trap. Only a single day had passed since he'd returned to this place, but he *needed* to get back to Earth.

He no longer knew what to think about Sam. The man had treated him well, provided him with information—even if that information had never been entirely... complete. Maybe it shouldn't have been too shocking to learn that a powerful, C Grade Denizen would want to rule his planet if they had the chance.

He wondered what it would be like if he were in that situation. He was the most powerful Denizen from Earth—that he was absolutely sure of. Yet he'd never really contemplated *ruling* Earth.

But he needed them to listen to him, didn't he? Didn't he need Earth to be stable if he were going to help protect it? And Earth didn't only need protection from invaders, did it? Since the first humans crawled out of the mud, there hadn't been peace on Earth. Hadn't been one ruler able to provide order to the entire planet. There had always been war.

How would things change now, when killing another human gave them *Mastery Points*? When it actually made them *stronger*?

For too long, Xavier had been worrying about the outside threat, not the *inside* one.

The people of Earth need someone to rule it. I don't think I'm the best person for the job, but I'm the most powerful, which means I have a responsiblility to do something about it.

Don't I?

The others looked startled as he burst into the room. They'd been sitting on their loot boxes, speaking with one another. Howard was the first to stand. "What did you find out?"

Xavier strode past the man and headed straight for the doorway to the tower floors. "Honestly? Not a whole lot. The threat's real enough that the most powerful Denizen in our sector is worried. A C Grade empress who can see the future. Apparently, she's been looking for me to solve the problem."

"You?" Siobhan blurted.

Xavier was an inch away from grabbing the doorhandle. He turned. "I'm surprised too."

"I'm not," Siobhan said. Her face was red. Then again, her pale skin reddened easily. "I mean, consider what you've already achieved. If anyone could become strong enough..."

Xavier smiled, some of the tension released from his shoulders. Not all of it, but a little was better than none. "Glad you think so."

"When?" Justin asked. "When is this threat coming?"

"I have no idea," Xavier said. "But we can't linger here any longer. We're heading back to Earth. Then, on our return, I'm blasting through these floors as fast as possible. Alone." He grabbed the handle. "I'll need every title we can get."

He didn't say what else he was thinking. Yes, he would need them to be strong when they returned to Earth, but he didn't have time to be the one to *make* them strong. Not at the expense of his own development. Which meant the titles they were going to get over the next few floors—and the extra levels they'd just gained from farming this floor—were going to have to be enough.

"Are you all ready?" Xavier asked. When they got to the floor, the others wouldn't need to do anything, but they needed to all enter the floor at the same time.

"We're ready," Howard said.

"Then let's do this."

Xavier entered the sixth floor of the Tower of Champions.

He materialised atop the mountain, the tall stone goblin keep visible the moment he arrived.

Soul Strike!

He infused almost 2,000 souls into the spell. Energy flowed through him and out of Charon's Scythe. White lightning shot forth, the jagged bolts extinguishing all shadows from existence in the immediate area.

The soul apparitions materialised. Goblins, moving through the air as though they could fly, heading toward their own. The instant he saw it, Xavier couldn't help but realise he was using the souls of the very goblins that were in that keep—even if they were from an alternate reality, they were technically the same goblins.

I can make their own souls turn against them...

That kind of power was... intoxicating.

The floor boss—whatever it was, for Xavier had not bothered to set foot on the top floor of the goblin keep—died at the same time as every other enemy. He'd been prepared to Soul Step to the top of the keep to finish off the floor boss with a slash from Charon's Scythe, but he was glad that such a move wasn't necessary.

Xavier let out a breath as the notifications began to appear.

Congratulations! You have cleared the Sixth Floor of the Tower of Champions.
Party Member Contribution:
Party Member Contribution:
Xavier: 4,000/4,000 Kills.

Howard: 0/4,000 Kills.
Justin: 0/4,000 Kills.
Siobhan: 0/4,000 Kills.
No shared attributions apply on this floor.

Title Unlocked!
Sixth-Floor Climber: This title has been upgraded. You have cleared the Sixth Floor of the Tower of Champions and shall be rewarded.
You have received +12 to all stats!
Note: The title "Fifth-Floor Climber" has been stricken from your soul.

Title Unlocked!
Solo Tower Climber 6: This title has been upgraded. You have cleared a floor of the Tower of Champions by yourself. You are either very brave or very stupid for attempting such a feat. Know that whether this feat was achieved through sheer skill or unbridled luck, you shall be rewarded.
You have received +48 to all stats!
Note: The title "Solo Tower Climber 5" has been stricken from your soul.

Title Unlocked!
1ˢᵗ Sixth-Floor Climber: Out of Champions from five competing worlds, your party is the *first* to clear the Sixth Floor of the Tower of Champions within your instance.
You have received +30 to all stats!
Note: As you have a similar title, "1ˢᵗ Fifth-Floor Climber" has been combined with this title and shares its stats.

Title Unlocked!
Sixth Floor Ranked 1 – RECORD HOLDER
(Completion Time – 2 sec): Out of all the
Champions from all the worlds in the Greater
Universe who have completed the Sixth Floor
of the Tower of Champions in every possible
instance, you have completed it in the fastest
time.
This title is a Temporary Title. If your record
is edged out of first place, your title will be
turned into a normal top 100 title.
If your record is edged out of the top 100, your
title will be lost.
You have received +80 to all stats!
Note: As you have similar titles, each has been
combined with this title and shares their stats.
You may still view the previous titles and your
standing on the leaderboards, if you will it.

In 1 minute, you and your party will be
returned to the Staging Room.

Xavier's body shuddered. Another threshold had been passed. His Speed was now at 4,041. God, he felt *good*. He took a deep breath. He'd gained far more titles when he'd finished the last floor, but every title he'd just gotten here would help him.

"Time for the next floor." Xavier didn't wait for the countdown timer to finish. The gold he would get from the goblins here simply wouldn't be worth it for him. Not when he could *create* gold if he really wanted to.

He walked straight past a bewildered-looking prince and the man's soldiers. The prince—whom Xavier hadn't even bothered to learn the name of—tried to thank him as he passed, but he kept walking. He wasn't trying to be rude, he just had places to be.

In seconds, he was back in the Staging Room. He looked

around the place. The others were probably waiting for the count-down timer to reach its end before the System returned them here.

The loot boxes were in a circle. He didn't expect much from them. They barely gave him a single E Grade Mastery Point last time, despite the fact that he'd done something no one ever had before in defeating the Lord of the Endless Horde.

He looked at the record-breaking title.

I cleared that floor in two seconds. That's twice as fast as I cleared the fourth floor.

It was difficult to feel proud of his accomplishment this time around. The goblin keep had been... far too easy. His party could have completed the floor by themselves, without his help.

Xavier couldn't help but remember the difficulty he'd had on the first floor. When he'd almost died. But the first floor had only been difficult for him because he'd been moving through it so fast, trying to obtain a title. Now, it didn't matter how fast he moved through the floors. They were easy, no matter what titles he was able to gain.

I need another challenge, and I'm not going to face one until I'm back on Earth.

He walked over to his loot box, undid the latch, and threw it open.

You have gained 2 Mastery Points (E Grade).
You have gained 150,000 Lesser Spirit Coins.
You have received 2 Communication Stones.

Xavier frowned. He'd expected to gain more skill points. He still had two waiting to be used—none of the skills he'd found appealed to him right now, and he wasn't in need of any particular skill. If a challenge came up that he couldn't get through, then he would find an appropriate skill to help him.

Two Mastery Points, he supposed, were better than one. He was now 3 percent of the way toward his next level. God, that was moving slow. When he'd been pushing to Level 100, gaining levels had become incredibly easy.

As easy as slaughtering countless E Grade enemies...

He supposed he would come across E Grade enemies again soon enough.

More Minor Spirit Coins always helped.

It was the Communication Stones he was most interested in. The others arrived as he was staring down at them.

"What are those? More Portal Stones?" Siobhan asked.

Xavier shook his head. "Communication Stones." They'd appeared in his hand the moment he'd opened the loot box. They were blue crystals, each the size of a grape.

{Communication Stone – Restriction: Sector}
A Communication Stone has the ability to form a mental connection between two people, allowing them to communicate telepathically over distances both great and small. Once a connection is established, the stone can be used while inside spatial storage.
The power of this Communication Stone is restricted to a single sector and does not allow users to communicate with other sectors.
A Communication Stone is useless if it is not paired.

"Interesting," Xavier said, then told the others what it did.

Justin rubbed the back of his neck. "It sounds useful. But, back on Earth, wouldn't we be able to communicate with phones and radio?"

Siobhan shrugged. "Assuming those even exist. May I have a look at one?" Xavier handed her a stone. She examined it closely. "This will be far more effective tactically. Could you imagine being able to communicate with someone telepathically while in the room with another? You could easily communicate in secret."

"It would be good in a fight, too," Howard said. "A way to communicate without giving away anything to the enemy."

Xavier took back the Communication Stone when Siobhan offered it. "The fact it can work sector-wide is fantastic, too," he said, cocking his head to the side. "Makes me wonder who else has things like these. I guess it wouldn't work once someone stepped onto a tower floor, as that's a whole different *universe*."

The Communication Stone made him think of Sam. Did the man have one of these? A direct line to his empress? He looked at his party members. Should he give one of the stones to one of them? What about his mother, when he returned to Earth? Assuming he was even able to find her...

Maybe I'll be able to decide when I'm back on Earth. There could be someone there I need to communicate with.

He blinked, a realisation coming to him. "Do you think someone from Earth would be able to communicate with us here in the tower?" He began pacing, juggling the stones one-handed. "If they were able to communicate with us, we'd be able to know what was happening on Earth even while we're stuck here. We'd be able to come there prepared. We will have to return to the tower after our break on Earth, after all."

"It's definitely worth trying," Howard said. The man looked over his shoulder at the door to the next floor. "Are you going to push forward?"

"Get your loot first." Xavier nodded toward the boxes. "Then yes. Onward to the next floor."

Chapter 67
Forest City of Mithraela

XAVIER GRASPED THE DOORHANDLE, READY TO ENTER THE seventh floor of the Tower of Champions. He was a little worried that the System would force a break on him—like it did after he'd completed the third floor. Back then, he'd not been able to enter the next floor for ninety hours, as he'd passed the first Milestone.

That'd better not happen again.

A notification appeared as he touched the handle.

> **Congratulations! You have cleared the first six floors of the Tower of Champions! You have reached the second Milestone in the tower.**
> **As you have reached the second Milestone and are the leader of the pack, moving through the floors faster than anyone from the five different planets included in this instance of the Tower of Champions, you may choose whether or not to enforce a break at this point in the floors.**
> **If you enforce a break, you need not worry about losing your lead, as every Champion who reaches this Milestone will have to pause and**

reflect for the same amount of time before re-entering the tower.
If you do not enforce a break, be sure you are prepared for what comes next.
Your options are:

1. **0 hours between floors.**
2. **24 hours between floors.**
3. **90 hours between floors.**

Choose wisely.

Xavier raised his eyebrows as he read the notification. He sighed in relief. Without thinking about the options, he chose the first one. The other parties could take whatever breaks they needed. He wasn't about to slow down.

The seventh floor of the Tower of Champions was not what Xavier had been expecting. Though, if he were honest, he hadn't *known* what to expect.

The System dumped them in the middle of a magical forest with trees as tall as the skyscrapers back in Fronton, the city his university was in.

"Whoa," Justin said. The Airborne Duellist had a hand on the hilt of his sword as he took a step forward. "This is amazing!"

They stood in the middle of a small clearing. Ten large, standing stones surrounded them. He tapped the ground beneath his feet. Wood. There was a trapdoor just beneath the dirt. *This must be the Safe Zone, and that's the exit to the Staging Room.* There was a small barrier between them and the rest of the forest. Unlike on other floors, he was able to see through it.

Justin was right. The view was amazing.

The trees weren't only tall—they had houses built into them. Houses that looked like they'd been half-grown and half-made by humanoid hands. They were on raised platforms, with wooden supports attached to the massive trunks of the trees, allowing the houses to stretch out from the base of the trunks.

The buildings each had large windows and wrap-around balconies. It was dark in the forest, but candles burned in the houses. Narrow walkways connected one tree with another to the point where it looked as though whoever lived up there would never need to put their feet on the ground to get around the forest.

Xavier spotted shadows passing by the windows. Every one of those buildings was occupied.

"This place is quite something." Siobhan stepped over to one of the standing stones. "These remind me of Stonehenge, or some sort of druidic circle."

"I wonder what the System has in store for us here," Howard said. He narrowed his eyes at the buildings. "Seems like a peaceful place."

Xavier frowned. The man was right. He couldn't see any enemies around them. He'd be able to spot their auras, as they should be low-enough level that they weren't able to shield them yet.

"Let's find out." He walked out of the Safe Zone. The sound of the forest met his ears the moment he did. Night birds hooting in the trees. Small animals scampering through the underbrush. And the sound of chatter, coming from the windows of the buildings.

Welcome to the Seventh Floor of the Tower of Champions.

The Seventh Floor of the Tower of Champions is a test of your ability to escort and protect someone.

Princess Narella of the Forest City of Mithraela has sought your protection on her travels to the neighbouring realm of Galavantian, a human kingdom where a treaty of peace is to be signed between the four races of the world.

You and your party are tasked with protecting her on her journey to the neighbouring kingdom.

"An escort quest," Siobhan muttered. "That's different."

"We have to babysit someone through the forest?" Howard crossed his arms. "Sounds... easy."

Xavier frowned, realising he probably wasn't the best suited for this kind of mission. He hadn't bothered summoning Charon's Scythe, so he played with his Storage Ring, turning it around his fingers as he contemplated its contents.

Horns sounded. Xavier's head snapped up, his body tensing, coming to full attention, as though another wave were about to come—

But this wasn't the fifth floor. There were no more waves anymore. And these were not the horns of war, as he was used to; these were more like trumpets. He had no idea where they were coming from, but a moment later, a platform floated down from one of the treetop buildings.

A woman stood in the middle of the platform. An elf who wore the shining armour of a warrior. The armour was white, and there appeared to be some kind of ethereal glow about her.

Is that some sort of spell?

She wore no helm; instead, a crown adorned her head, her golden hair weaved around it, keeping it in place. Around her were an honour guard of ten elves. Five warriors, three archers, and two mages.

The elven queen somehow managed to look elegant even in her full-plate armour. "Champions." She greeted them with a regal nod. "I have summoned you for an important task."

She's summoned us for an escort?

It baffled Xavier that a *queen* of all people would need an escort through her own forest. Certainly she would be able to fight against any threats she found?

How far away is this other kingdom? And how long will it take me to get her there?

He much preferred the last floor. All he'd had to do to gain the record for that floor was kill a bunch of enemies using a single spell. This might prove more complicated. He imagined the record was still based on time.

At least I'm fast. I guess I could throw her over my shoulder and carry her.

He smirked as he imagined the regal princess's reaction to such treatment.

Xavier glanced out at the forest. That was when he noticed there was a barrier around the city he stood in. A barrier that was only visible when the light hit it at a certain angle. Maybe that was why he couldn't sense the auras of any of the beasts out there. There would certainly be a lot of them if this woman needed the protection of others.

This must be a very weak world. Or perhaps just a weak realm.

**Your escort quest starts in 1 minute.
Princess Narella must reach Galavantian in
two days' time.
If she does not reach Galavantian within the
time limit, the peace treaty will be
compromised.**

Xavier's forehead creased as he read the new notification. It had him worried. If he travelled all the way to Galavantian with the princess, how was he supposed to get back to the exit and the Staging Room door?

He'd been careful not to sacrifice the king's life at the top of the goblin keep on the last floor, now that he knew these people were *real* and not just fabrications created by the System. But this might be a little more difficult.

If it was a two-day journey by foot to this other kingdom, he would need to get her there fast, even if he didn't plan on clearing the floor at that moment. He didn't wish to just abandon the princess in the middle of the forest, after all.

Certainly not something a hero would do...

The princess pointed through the trees, kicking Xavier out of his thoughts. "The Galavantian Kingdom lies at the far edge of this forest. Though there is a safe route to the east, it is a circuitous one. I have just received news from my allies in the giant's court of a threat to the summit. An assassin has been sent by those who do not wish for peace in this world, an assassin sent to kill the king before the summit can begin."

Your escort quest starts in 35 seconds.

"If this assassin succeeds, war will once again break out between the four races. All chances at peace will be dashed. I have no way of communicating with the king's court and must journey through the most dangerous parts of the forest if I am to arrive on time to deliver this warning. Will the four of you help me in this journey?"

Xavier stepped forward. His hands were together in front of him, one finger tapping his Storage Ring, thinking about his Portal Stones, and trying to puzzle out how to do this. "We will protect you on this journey, Princess Narella. You have my word that you will arrive at the king's court in time to warn him."

Princess Narella raised her head. "Then we must leave at once. My guards will lead the way." She motioned them all forward through the trees.

I suppose I'll need to know how to get to this other kingdom before I can race over there...

For this run-through of the floor, he would let it play out normally. As the guards moved forward, the warriors moving to the front, and the archers and mages staying at the rear, Xavier came to walk beside the princess.

"Could you not simply send a guide and have us Champions traverse the forest in your stead while you take the safe route to

Galavantian? We could warn the king's court for you," Xavier said. Though he wouldn't do such a thing on this run-through, he did wonder if the princess's presence was even necessary.

"The king of Galavantian will be suspicious of any warning. I fear he will not trust this threat is real unless I am able to convince him, and he may only listen to one of royal blood." The princess said those last words with an apologetic smile.

"Of course, Your Highness. I promise I and my fellow Champions will see you through this journey safely." Xavier glanced behind him, up at the buildings in the trees. Noise still flowed out through the open windows. People chatting and laughing. He was certain one of those buildings, the largest of them, must have been an inn.

Part of him wished they could spend some more time in this place. Talk to the people. Learn about their lives. Grab a drink at the inn. Meet some crafters or blacksmiths. The universe was so much larger, so much more interesting than he'd ever known.

He'd spent weeks at Queen Alastea's castle, but he'd never had a spare moment to explore it.

That will change, one day.

His mind turned to the long-term threat he'd just learnt of. That his sector—the Silver River sector—was under threat of being purged. There were still thirty days until he could gain another insight from his Otherworldly Communion ability.

When the spell was ready to be used again, hopefully he would learn when this threat would come.

Please tell me it's a thousand years away...

Xavier, Howard, Siobhan, and Justin followed the princess's warriors as they led them through the city, toward the wild, untended parts of the forest, and through the barrier into the unknown.

Chapter 68
Escorting a Princess

Xavier did not want to spend two days in this place. He needed to know exactly how to get to the Kingdom of Galavantian, so he was willing to follow the princess's honour guards as they led the way, but he wasn't willing to make this take any longer than it needed to.

He was foolish to think he could blast through the last floors in a mere matter of hours. Foolish to think that some complication wouldn't arise. The difficulty level of this challenge might be well below him, but that didn't mean he could rush through it in seconds or minutes. At least not the first time around.

No point worrying about how long this will take, he told himself. *I just have to push through it.*

And so he did.

The forest was too overgrown, thick with trees and vines, for them to take horses or other kinds of mounts, which made traversal even more challenging. He used Charon's Scythe to clear the way before them. It could cut through more than just the vines and thick underbrush. He could clear trees from their path with one swift swing.

He didn't even need the scythe-staff for that. He could simply cast Heavy Telekinesis, but it felt better to keep his hands busy on this journey.

Though there were gaps, clear areas within the forest with nothing to impede their travel. This was where many of the dangers lay—the beasts that ambushed them from every side. Wolven much like the ones he'd encountered during the waves of the Endless Horde. Large silver bears that could shoot beams of energy from their chests. Flying monsters that looked almost like small dragons, capable of breathing fire from a distance of twenty yards.

Xavier found none of these dangers threatening. They were far too easy to kill. He left the fighting to the other members of his party. He hadn't been intending to give the others time to gain more levels and ranks, but there didn't seem to be a better way to go about this journey. He could make the honour guards and the princess sprint through the trees, but the guards, even though they were leading the way, didn't seem to have actually been through here before.

One of the archers would often scramble up a tree, their bow slung over their back, until they were high enough to see through the thick canopy and check the location of the sun and, when night had fallen, the orientation of the stars. Then they would keep on course or change direction if necessary.

All the while, Xavier noted landmarks. A large tree that was missing branches on one side partially blackened as though it had been struck by lightning; a dark cave with strange markings on the stone outside of it; an old brick well that the princess seemed baffled at, as supposedly this part of the forest had never been inhabited.

He burned these and other things into his mind so he would know his way the next time they came through, including the auras of the different beasts they encountered in the forest, so he could identify them from afar, all the while trying to puzzle out his first problem—how were they supposed to get back to the Staging Room door *and* allow the princess to reach Galavantian's court in time?

He knew the Portal Stones would be the answer on his second time through here. He had a plan for that. But the stones couldn't help him this time around. If he were to have left one of the stones by the Staging Room door to activate a portal when they reached their destination, then fast travel back from the neighbouring kingdom, how would he get the second Portal Stone *back*?

It couldn't be taken through the portal.

Maybe I should have left the others in the forest city.

He supposed there was still time for him to send them back, even if that looked strange to the princess and her honour guard. Xavier was confident he would be able to race back to the forest city and the Staging Room door fast enough to give the princess plenty of time to enter court *after* he and his party left, so they didn't accidentally complete this floor before they wanted to.

They were trekking through the night when this realisation came to him. He told the others. Howard, Siobhan, and Justin glanced at each other, eyebrows raised in slight confusion.

"What if we can't find our way?" Justin asked. "How will you know when we return?"

Siobhan perked up. "The Communication Stones."

Xavier nodded. "Exactly."

They were walking through a clear area of the forest, huddled close. The princess was in front of them, the archers and mages behind. Xavier sent out Soul Strikes whenever he needed to, clearing beasts from the immediate area so they wouldn't interrupt their conversation.

He took out the Communication Stones. He hadn't actually tested them before. He *willed* them to be connected—it only took a quick thought.

Communication Stones successfully paired.

He passed one of the stones to Siobhan.

[*I wonder if this will work...*] Siobhan's voice sounded in his mind with a quizzical tone.

[*Yes, it definitely worked,*] Xavier replied.

Siobhan's eyes widened and she smiled. [*I wonder how well we can control what thoughts we send through.*] She tilted her head to the side, her forehead creasing. [*Did you hear what I said about the elephant?*]

Xavier blinked. [*What elephant?*]

Siobhan nodded. [*It looks like we have to will the thoughts to each other—they need to be directed at the other or they won't send.*]

Xavier tested that theory.

I could use a cup of coffee right now, he thought to himself.

Nothing registered on Siobhan's face. He asked her, and she said she hadn't heard anything. He smiled conspiratorially.

"You two done with your private chat?" Howard asked with a smirk.

Siobhan nodded, her face slightly red. "Yeah, we're done."

"You guys should head back, then," Xavier said. "Let me know when you've returned to the forest city, and I'll let you know when I'm heading back."

Howard patted him on the shoulder. "Sounds good." He glanced around at the trees. "Hopefully we won't lose our way."

"In theory, we should have left a trail behind us," Siobhan said. "All we'll need to do is follow it back." She let out a sigh. "If I were able to summon my allies over longer distances, this wouldn't be an issue, would it? We could have left one of the Portal Stones by the Staging Room door, activated the portal when we got near enough to the Galavantian Kingdom, and have me, Howard and Justin head through. Then I could have summoned you back once you deactivated the portal."

Xavier had thought of that option earlier, then discarded it, knowing she wasn't ready. "You'll be able to do such things in the future. I'm sure of it." He bobbed his head toward the way they'd come. "You three should head back. And move fast. I'm going to... change the pace."

Howard looked curious. "What are you going to do?"

Xavier smiled. "Something drastic."

Xavier spoke with the princess, telling her a white lie.

"You have been summoned back to your realm? That's why the other Champions left?" Princess Narella had her hands folded in front of her, her chin raised, a regal, defiant look on her face. "You would abandon us in our time of need? I knew calling on Champions would be a risk—"

Xavier raised a hand, halting her next words. The woman's eyes widened, clearly not used to someone treating her in such a way. "I am not abandoning you. I will see you safely to your destination, and you will have plenty of time to spare. On one condition. You do not step into the safety of the Galavantian Kingdom until I return to your city. I shouldn't need very long." He cocked his head. "An hour should be more than enough time for my return."

The anger in the woman's eyes turned to confusion. "An hour? How could you only need an hour? It is impossible to traverse the length of the forest in that time!"

Xavier smiled. "When we reach Galavantian, you'll know more of what I'm capable of."

He called the guards to a halt. The warriors who were leading the group glanced at Princess Narella, looking for approval, not stopping until she nodded her approval.

"I am sorry about your forest, Your Highness, but it is the only way I'll manage to get you there with time enough for me to return."

"My... forest?" the princess asked.

Heavy Telekinesis!

The trees ahead of them were pushed back, flattened as though some horrendous hurricane had ravaged the land. The sky above became visible, the stars leading their way clear.

Xavier looked to one of the archers, the man who'd been up and down the trees, helping guide their way. "Which stars do I follow?"

The man took a step forward. One hand was wrapped around his bow, the other was free at his side. With his free hand, he pointed up at a star—the brightest one in the sky. "That is Ilnan. Our world's North Star." He pointed to another, less bright star in a cluster resembling a triangle. "That cluster is the Pyramid of Ishtu. The Western star." He cut the air with the flat of his palm between Ilnan and Ishtu. "We travel between the two, northwest, toward the human realm."

Xavier gazed up at the night sky. He couldn't help the feeling of awe that overtook him. This... this felt right. Navigating a forest on an alien world. Escorting a princess to another kingdom to stop an assassination...

He was living what he'd always read about.

He turned to face Princess Narella. "Do you trust me, Princess?"

The woman raised her chin. "I do not know if I have any other choice."

He shook his head. "You don't."

She stared at his hand. "Why must I take your hand?"

"Because we are about to travel much faster than you ever had."

No more would he wait for others to lead him. He'd thought of this option before and refused it, but he wanted to save this woman's world, even if it was simply one timeline in an infinite number of universes. These were the people in front of him. The ones he could see. They were not his enemy. If he were able to save them without risking the lives of those he cared for, then he would.

Princess Narella didn't take long to consider this. She took his hand. He pulled her in, then picked her up. The woman gasped but didn't protest. Internally, he couldn't help but find the humour in this moment, as he was holding her in what was commonly known as the princess carry.

"Onward, Your Highness."

He dashed through the forest, bounding from one tree to another. He hadn't tested whether he could Soul Step while holding another person, so he did that now. When he'd flattened the forest—destroying several *miles* worth of trees—he'd taken out a great many beasts. He felt their souls. Sensed their presence in the distance.

Soul Step!

The world shifted.

The princess remained in his arms, a wide-eyed look on her face. She clutched tighter to him. He kept bounding forward. Every minute, when the cooldown for the Soul Step imbued ability ended, he cast it again after sending out a Soul Strike to kill a far-off beast that he could sense the aura of.

Before dawn came, Xavier Collins and Princess Narella were standing at the edge of the great forest, looking over at a large, stone castle five times the size of Queen Alastea's. The castle was at the top of a tall rise, in a strongly defensible position.

They have the high ground.

He knew the way now. Knew exactly how to get to the Galavantian Kingdom. He looked at where the sun rose, and though the stars in the sky were no longer visible, he closed his eyes and knew where they'd been.

When I come next, I'll use the sun as a guide.

"King of Galavantian awaits your warning, Princess Narella, and you have a full day to spare."

The regal woman looked slightly flushed. She ran her hands down her armour, as though she subconsciously thought she was wearing a dress and was trying to smooth the lines. "Thank you for delivering me here safely, Champion Xavier." She smiled. "I believe you will be able to return to your summons in time. I will wait two full hours before I take another step. I am sure that will be plenty of time."

She looked to her side. A chair materialised out of nowhere. She sat, and the next moment a footstool materialised as well, and she put her feet up. When she raised her hand, a book appeared.

Xavier raised an eyebrow. *At least she'll be waiting in style.*

He said his goodbyes to the princess, then turned and headed back through the forest. He was a little worried that he hadn't heard from the other members of his party, so he contacted Siobhan as he ran.

Xavier and the other members of his party ended up reaching the forest city at the same time.

Chapter 69
A Purple, Shimmering Portal

XAVIER STEPPED BACK INTO THE STAGING ROOM, FEELING accomplished. There were an infinite number of universes. In many of those, he imagined Princess Narella had died while being escorted to the Galavantian Kingdom. Or that she hadn't reached the place in time. Hell, there might even be Champions who simply abandoned the woman in the forest to farm monsters.

All in all, he was finding the Tower of Champions to be... a rather cruel invention for anyone who actually summoned a Champion.

And that was why he endeavoured to still save the people who needed saving.

Queen Alastea, for the first time in trillions of iterations of that floor, was saved from her fate of dying at the hands of the Endless Horde. The king on the sixth floor, at the top of that goblin keep, had been saved over a dozen times by my party alone. And Princess Narella reached the Galavantian court with enough time to warn the king of the assassination attempt.

A part of him, not for the first time, wondered if he should feel guilty about the army he'd slaughtered on the third floor. He'd slaughtered the human side once, and the elven side twice. Killed over a thousand soldiers. Neither side of that fight, as far as he could tell, had been purely in the wrong.

They could no longer even remember why they were fighting.

He'd put aside any responsibility for those he'd killed there. He'd decided that he would do whatever was necessary to get strong enough to save his world. And now, it wasn't just his own world that was on his shoulders.

If his Otherworldly Communion spell could be believed—and unfortunately, he knew it should be—the whole damned Silver River sector was in danger.

And the person Sam served, Empress Larona, seemed to think Xavier would have some chance at stopping it from being purged.

Still, even with all that was at stake, he didn't need to completely lose his sense of right and wrong. He didn't need to abandon people in need just because it was expedient. If someone were the enemy, he would deal with them—he'd proven that with the Endless Horde—but if they weren't? He would do what he could to help.

As long as it doesn't stop me from reaching my goals.

"She got there safely, then?" Howard asked. The man was leaning against the wall, arms crossed at his chest, a curious look on his face.

Xavier lowered his head in a nod. "She did."

"That's amazing, Xavier," Siobhan said. "How do you plan to get the record for this floor?"

Xavier summoned the Portal Stones from his Storage Ring. He tossed them up in the air, juggling them briefly in one hand. "With these. Time to test them." He stopped juggling and willed their connection.

Portal Stone successfully paired.

He tossed one of the stones over to Justin. The teenager snatched it out of the air. "You want me to have the responsibility?"

Xavier shrugged. "At least for now. But other than me, you're the most mobile. You have the ability to fly, you have high Speed for your level. You can get places others can't. On this floor, I won't need you for that, but maybe you should get used to using the Portal Stone for the future."

Justin looked down at the stone, his thumb circling its top. "How do you activate it?"

"Good question." Xavier stared at his own Portal Stone. The Communication Stone he'd given Siobhan had worked instantly, only requiring a small amount of Spirit Energy when he'd paired it to its twin. He'd felt a bit of Spirit Energy leave him as he'd paired these stones as well.

He *willed* it to activate.

Do you wish to open twin portals?

"Maybe we should place these on the ground." Xavier put his on the floor and waited for Justin to do the same. They were standing on opposite sides of the Staging Room.

Yes, Xavier thought.

Spirit Energy flooded out of him. Not a great deal, considering his reserve, but it would have been a lot for someone of Justin's level.

Is Justin losing any, or is it just me because I activated them?

He wondered if the Portal Stones required more Spirit Energy depending on how far away they were from each other.

The stone rose from the ground, electricity sparking around its surface. It was shaking, vibrating in mid-air. When it rose to Xavier's head height, it stopped, frozen in place.

Thrum!

The rock exploded outward in a small shockwave of energy. A split second later, a purple, shimmering portal twice the height of Xavier hovered directly in front of him.

"Whoa." Xavier looked over to the portal's twin on the other side of the room.

"Awesome." Justin had a great big grin on his face. "This is unreal. I mean, I know you entered a portal back on the fifth floor, but this..."

"It feels different. *We* made this happen." Xavier raised a finger, touched it to the surface of the portal. Then he stepped straight through it. Suddenly, he was standing directly in front of Justin.

The Airborne Duellist took a stutter-step back, momentarily surprised, but he was still grinning. "That's awesome."

"Did you lose any Spirit Energy when you activated the portal?" Xavier asked, looming over the teenager.

"Not a bit."

"Good to know." There was no need to test it at a distance, then. If it required more Spirit Energy, he would have plenty. "Time to complete this floor."

The instant they materialised on the seventh floor of the Tower of Champions, surrounded by a circle of standing stones, in a fantastical elven forest with large, natural-looking treehouses, Xavier sprinted out of the town.

His Speed attribute was over four thousand points now. He couldn't help but smile as the trees zipped past him. Whenever he hit a difficult, thick patch of forest, he used Heavy Telekinesis to clear the area.

Running has reached Rank 53!

The notification came fairly quickly. He'd already gained a few ranks in the skill when he'd been running back from dropping off the princess the first time. He chuckled when it appeared, feeling a bump in his speed.

Another notification popped up a moment later.

Welcome to the Seventh Floor of the Tower of Champions.
The Seventh Floor of the Tower of Champions is a test of your ability to escort and protect someone.
Princess Narella of the Forest City of Mithraela has sought your protection on her travels to the neighbouring realm of Galavantian, a human kingdom where a treaty of peace is to be signed between the four races of the world.
You and your party are tasked with protecting her on her journey to the neighbouring kingdom.

Xavier glanced up at the sun, ensuring he was heading northwest. He sensed a far-off beast and sent a Soul Strike its way. The spell moved far faster than he did, the bolt of white lightning streaking through the sky. He didn't see the soul apparition materialise, but he got the kill notification and sensed the soul ready for him to harvest.

Instead of harvesting it, he used Soul Step, closing the distance in an instant.

I can do that every minute.

Another notification appeared.

Your escort quest starts in 1 minute.
Princess Narella must reach Galavantian in two days' time.
If she does not reach Galavantian within the time limit, the peace treaty will be compromised.

It hasn't even started yet. Good. The more distance I clear in this next minute, the better...

490

As he ran, leapt, and telekinetically flattened and flung trees, Xavier had a little bit of time to think.

Running has reached Rank 54!

He felt another slight bump in his Speed and wondered if he should have been practising his Running skill before trying to clear this floor. The ranks were coming surprisingly fast. He suspected that was because of how fast he could already run—like the skill was trying to catch up to his high attribute.

Further training in the skill would have garnered him even more points in his Speed attribute, after all, by boosting the percentage modifier. But, honestly, he didn't think that was necessary.

There was no way any other Denizen would have been as fast as he was while clearing this floor.

Unless they had the power to teleport at greater distances, with less cooldown...

He dismissed that thought. If that were the case, there wasn't really much he could do about it.

[*Princess Narella doesn't appear happy,*] Siobhan said in his mind, through the Communication Stones' link. [*I think she's going to take a minute of convincing.*]

[*Tell Justin to let her Identify the Portal Stone.*]

He'd wondered whether the princess would trust their plan, especially when they saw one of the Champions shoot off the second they were summoned.

Would she have even seen me? I probably got out of there too fast for her to spot.

Sprinting, bounding over trees, and flattening them when he needed to, Xavier continued to teleport as far as he could manage, Soul Stepping once per minute on his journey toward the Galavantian Kingdom.

Faster, he demanded of himself.

Running has reached Rank 55!

Keep pushing!

The Portal Stone was safely inside his Storage Ring. The sun showed him the way. He kept track of his teleports. He was glad he could Soul Step, but he also knew that every time he used it, another minute had passed. Which had him worried. He'd cleared the last floor in two seconds—this was the first time in a few floors that he wasn't absolutely sure that he would be able to break the record.

Should I try again? Rank up my Running skill? I can still deliver the princess here safely, just like I did the first time. I can portal her to the border as I'm already planning to, and run back...

Xavier frowned. There was no room for self-doubt. He was a True Progenitor. The fastest Denizen *ever* to reach E Grade. He had more titles than he knew what to do with.

There was no way anyone could have done this floor faster than him.

He grinned when he spotted the castle. It looked just as majestic as he remembered it. The moment he was in the clear—over the border the princess said they had to escort her to—he summoned the Portal Stone and tossed it on the ground. Justin already had his ready on the other side. According to Siobhan, Princess Narella was still dubious, impatiently waiting, tapping the floor with her armoured boot.

Xavier activated the portal. The stone rose, exploding in purple energy, until the shimmering pool was before him. He shook his head, staring in awe at the thing.

That's never gonna get old.

He'd been keeping track of his Spirit Energy when he activated the portal. It had only used a fraction more energy than the last time he'd activated it.

That bodes well. If it used considerably more at distance, how would I ever be able to use it from the other side of the sector?

Only a second passed before Princess Narella stepped through, a slight look of confusion on her face. Maybe once her realm and Galavantian were allied, they could set up more permanent fast travel between them.

Then this wouldn't be a problem.

That made him wonder about the possibilities back on Earth. The type of transport system they could set up...

The moment the royal elf stepped out of the portal, a stream of notifications appeared.

Xavier had finished the floor.

He skipped over all the notifications but one. He knew what they would say. He'd gotten the solo title despite Justin having placed the Portal Stone. Justin hadn't fought any beasts, or directly protected the princess, so the System hadn't recognised anything he'd done as a contribution.

Xavier skimmed down to the bottom.

Seventh Floor Ranked 1 – RECORD HOLDER (Completion Time – 14 mins 10 secs): Out of all the Champions from all the worlds in the Greater Universe who have completed the Sixth Floor of the Tower of Champions in every possible instance, you have completed it in the fastest time.

This title is a Temporary Title. If your record is edged out of first place, your title will be turned into a normal top 100 title.

If your record is edged out of the top 100, your title will be lost.

You have received +100 to all stats!

Note: As you have similar titles, each has been combined with this title and shares their stats. You may still view the previous titles and your standing on the leaderboards, if you will it.

In 1 minute, you and your party will be returned to the Staging Room.

Xavier sighed in relief.

Another record title earned. Only three more floors to go until we're on Earth.

Chapter 70
Sanctuary Seed

You have gained 3 Mastery Points (E Grade).
You have gained 200,000 Lesser Spirit Coins.
You have received a Sanctuary Seed.

THREE MASTERY POINTS?

His journey toward Level 101 was looking to be a long one. Xavier heaved a sigh. The Lesser Spirit Coins, at least, were slowly increasing, even if they weren't a great deal to him.

This amount of Lesser Spirit Coins will really help the other Champions once they reach this floor. Especially those in my cohort who already got a boost from the contract they signed.

He wondered how that was going. It had been over a day since he'd been down in the tavern. He didn't really want to have to talk to Sam right now.

"What's a Sanctuary Seed?" he mumbled. He turned to the others; their eyes glazed over as they looked at their notifications. The last three loot boxes he'd opened, he'd gotten an item that the others hadn't.

The Sector Travel Key, the Portal Stones, and the Communication Stones.

Now, he'd gotten a Sanctuary Seed. He quickly asked the others if they'd gotten one as well, but they'd shaken their heads.

Is this because I'm the number-one-record holder?

The Sanctuary Seed materialised in his hand. It was larger than a normal seed—about the size of a small rock—and oval-shaped. He turned it around in his hand, feeling its surface. It had glowing runes etched into it.

Curious, he used Identify on the item.

{Sanctuary Seed – E Grade}
The Sanctuary Seed can be planted in any terrain.
Once planted, it grows into a fortified dwelling. The appearance of this dwelling is dependent upon the environment in which it is planted.
The sanctuary that grows from this seed can be adapted and upgraded as needed, acquiring unique defensive and offensive capabilities and the ability to grow resources.
A telepathic link and portal nexus can be established with the Sanctuary Seed if certain conditions are met.
The Sanctuary Seed bonds with the soul of the Denizen who uses it. It will grow in strength with the user, but the user will suffer if the sanctuary is damaged or destroyed.

Identify has reached Rank 25!

"Damn," Xavier blurted. "That's awesome!"

"What's awesome?" Howard asked.

Xavier held up the Sanctuary Seed. "This."

"A... rock?" Siobhan smirked.

"It's a little more than just a rock." Xavier ran his thumb over the etchings. "It's a Sanctuary Seed. It can *grow* a fortress. This... this is going to really come in handy once we're back on Earth. And, somehow, it's E Grade."

"How the hell are you getting so many great items?" Justin looked at his open loot box, his expression forlorn. "I just got Mastery Points and spirit coins..."

Siobhan frowned. "Maybe we aren't getting extra items because of our contribution?"

"What contribution?" Justin asked.

Siobhan chuckled. "Exactly."

Howard nodded at Xavier. "And he's over here breaking records. Of course the System is going to single him out."

There was a pause after Howard said this, and Xavier could tell they were all thinking the same thing.

The System is watching...

"Where will you plant it?" Siobhan asked, breaking the tension. "It sounds like it could be really amazing. It must grow with the user, right?"

"I'm not sure. I guess we'll find a good place when we're back on Earth. Although, we won't be able to defend the sanctuary when we're in the tower... And yeah, it said it grows with the Denizen it's bound to. It also says the user will suffer if it's damaged or destroyed."

"Suffer?" Justin muttered. "That's, at the same time, not very specific and incredibly ominous."

Xavier examined the seed for another moment, wondering where such a thing could come from. He imagined what his fortress might look like. He couldn't help but hope it would be some sort of castle.

Who didn't want to live in a castle?

He was also curious about the defensive and offensive capabilities it could have.

I wonder how large I can make this thing. Maybe it will be able to help protect others while we're in the tower.

He imagined the fortress would be incredibly powerful compared with the Denizens and beasts on Earth right now.

They can't be very high-level if the invaders are only able to send Denizens a single level higher than the highest-level Denizen currently residing on Earth.

That thought made him shudder. He knew that whatever he faced back on Earth he could take. But he was worried what his appearance might cause. To learn the highest level of someone on Earth, the invaders had to send their own people through portals and hope they arrived alive. And apparently doing so was rather costly over such a distance—not only in the lives of their Denizens.

They would have to be pretty cruel to sacrifice their soldiers like that. Cruel, or really desperate.

The moment he started gaining a great deal of levels, he'd wondered what would happen when he returned to Earth. If one of the invaders discovered that Earth had an E Grade, they would be able to send E Grades too—Xavier would be able to demolish them, but he couldn't be everywhere at once.

They aren't going to learn my level. I'll make sure of that.

Xavier had acquired an item from the System store that made it almost impossible for someone of his own grade to identify him, which meant that *none* of the invaders, who would all be F Grade, would have any chance of doing so.

At least this Sanctuary Seed is something I'll manage to leave behind.

He deposited the seed into his Storage Ring. As he did, he looked at his hands. The modifications to his body from assimilating various properties weren't as obvious now that he'd advanced, but they still made him wonder about his future.

When he'd brought up his status information after advancing to E Grade, it had shown a question mark by his name. He didn't know what that meant. He hadn't discussed it with Sam. Knowing the barkeep, there wouldn't be anything he could say to Xavier anyway, what with the System's restrictions.

That question mark had stopped him from assimilating more properties after he'd defeated the Lord of the Endless Horde, despite his curiosity about their potential benefits.

I haven't faced anything I couldn't handle. Yet. I'll revisit that soon. *Besides, these titles are benefiting me more than I expected, especially after reaching E Grade. I thought it wouldn't make much difference, but I pushed through my Speed threshold again at the end of the last floor, and I should soon break my next Intelligence threshold, as it's currently sitting at 4,930.*

"Do you guys have anything you need to do before we move on to the next floor?" Xavier asked his party.

They each shook their heads. Though it often seemed he didn't need his party, as he could solo each floor, he was grateful for their presence.

Being able to communicate telepathically with Siobhan and having Justin place the other Portal Stone—it was the only reason I finished that floor so quickly. If I'd been truly alone, I would've had to stop and convince Princess Narella not to pursue me by myself, which would've wasted precious time.

Besides, without them, I never would've considered taking out the entire Endless Horde. They were the ones who planted that idea in my head.

He wandered over to the Staging Room door. Howard, Siobhan, and Justin did look a bit tired—they required more sleep than him, and they'd run all night through that forest the first time through the seventh floor—but they didn't complain about needing rest.

We're pushing hard until we're back on Earth. They understand that.

The eighth floor of the Tower of Champions was another easy one for Xavier to clear. They barely spent more than a few minutes there on their first time through to scope the place out. Much like the last few floors, there were people who needed his protection. Except there was no city, no fortress, no goblin keep to clear or princess to escort.

There was a desert wasteland. One filled with rawhide tents

and nomadic-looking people who mostly wielded spears or staves. The floor reminded him a little of the floor with the Endless Horde, except the enemies were all coming at once, and every single one of them was a beast.

The nomads called this occurrence a Beast Tide. On this world, they raged every ten years.

That's why their civilisation has never had a chance to flourish —the beasts wipe them out too fast.

He supposed the same thing happened on a sector-wide scale. The Silver River sector had been purged twice. Even if it had been over a thousand years since the last time that had happened, a thousand years—in the Greater Universe—apparently wasn't all that long.

Just like these Beast Tides were holding this world back, the purges were holding Xavier's whole sector back.

The notification told him the floor would be completed under two conditions. The first condition was the Beast Tide being destroyed in its entirety. The second condition was that, after the Beast Ride passed through the small encampment, 80 percent of the nomads had to survive. Enough to maintain their culture. Enough to push forward for another ten years.

There were one hundred nomads. Xavier wasn't going to let a single one of them die.

The System notification told him it would take a full half hour for the Beast Tide to pass through the area. Xavier had examined the area with his Aura Sight. He could see to the end of the beasts easily enough.

He cleared out the tide of beasts in a matter of minutes— mostly because he was rejuvenating his soulkeeping reserve and being careful not to kill every enemy—then left only one alive before heading back to the Staging Room.

The nomads bowed and prostrated themselves as he and his party passed. The second he left, they'd be able to deal with the final beast on their own.

When Xavier returned to the floor a second time, he cleared

the entire Beast Tide in three seconds and gained himself a record-holding title. Which meant that within five minutes of entering the eighth floor of the Tower of Champions, they'd already completed it.

That's more like it!

He skimmed over the titles. Felt the *thrum* as another threshold was met.

His head felt numb and lightheaded as his Intelligence was pushed over the 5,000-point threshold. Then it was like his mind was on overdrive.

God, this feeling... He would never tire of it.

If I'm this powerful now, how powerful will I be in a year? Ten? A hundred?

A thousand?

And how powerful were the truly strong Denizens in the Greater Universe?

He couldn't help but rub his hands together as he headed toward the loot box. The last few items he'd gotten had been amazing finds. Things that had either actively helped him on the floors, or would be incredibly useful to him in the future.

Xavier could only wonder about what he'd find next.

Chapter 71
Loot

Xavier felt a definite sense of déjà vu inside the Staging Room. He tilted his head from side to side, cracking his neck satisfyingly. The loot boxes sat at the centre of the room, just like they always did. He felt a thrill of excitement, staring at his.

He hadn't expected to be this excited about the loot boxes, not when he had plenty of Minor Spirit Coins in his Storage Ring, but it seemed as though the System was handing him the very things he might need in the future.

I wonder if what I'm receiving is available in the System Shop.

He hadn't been able to find a Sector Travel Key in the System Shop, after all. Apparently, they were quite rarely sold, and when they were found in the shop, they were quickly snatched up by those from more prominent sectors with far more coin than Xavier —which meant, even if he had found one in the System Shop, it would have been far outside of his price range.

Besides, he didn't know what to look for within the System Shop. He would have had to search for hours to come up with the items he'd received.

The others stepped toward their own loot boxes. They didn't look all that excited—they'd been getting the same old things,

Mastery Points, spirit coins, so he supposed it wasn't making a great deal of difference for them. But they did glance at him expectantly, waiting to discover what his next unique item was.

He knelt by the box, undid the latch, and threw open the lid. A smile swept onto his face as the notification popped up once again, hitting him with a rush of dopamine, no doubt.

You have gained 4 Mastery Points (E Grade).
You have gained 250,000 Lesser Spirit Coins.
You have received a Seed Garden.

Four more Mastery Points. One more than last time... At least I only have ninety left now.

He skipped past the Lesser Spirit Coins and moved onto the final item. The Seed Garden appeared in his hand. It looked remarkably similar to the Sanctuary Seed, except this was about half the size and bright green—almost like an actual seed. Except, of course, for the glowing runes etched into it. These glowed a pure white.

Xavier turned it around in his hand and used Identify on it.

{Seed Garden – ungraded}
The Seed Garden gives one the ability to grow a garden
within the Seed Sanctuary. Only Seed Sanctuaries at
Level 10 or higher, regardless of grade, can have a Seed
Garden attached to them.
The Seed Garden provides the perfect soil in which to
grow alchemical ingredients and crafting materials. It
also provides some basic starter plants when first
grown.

Identify has reached Rank 26!

Xavier frowned. A... garden? He supposed he could have

guessed what it did from the name alone. He couldn't help but feel a little disappointed. A garden wasn't nearly as exciting as the other items he'd received.

Maybe the System knows something I don't...

He supposed, in the future, being able to grow alchemical ingredients and crafting materials might be useful. It wasn't as though he could utilise those things himself, however—he didn't have the ability to make potions or craft weapons or armour, nor did he *want* that ability.

At least my Identify skill gained another rank.

Though that did beg the question. Could he gain such an ability, even though he wasn't a support class? His lifespan was significantly longer now that he was E Grade, and he planned to be around for a very, very long time... What kind of things would he pick up along the way?

The others looked over at him expectantly, staring at the seed in his hand.

"So, what did you get this time?" Siobhan asked. "That's not another Sanctuary Seed, is it?"

"It's called a Seed Garden." Xavier showed them the item and told them what he knew about it, struggling to keep the disappointment from of his voice.

"Nice," Siobhan said, and she actually sounded like she meant it.

"Is it?" Howard looked doubtful. Justin hadn't said a word.

Siobhan gestured toward the Seed Garden. "May I?"

Xavier shrugged and handed it over.

The Divine Beacon started pacing, holding up the seed. "I read about gardens in the tower library back at the castle. Apparently, before the castle was evacuated, there was a Royal Alchemist and a Royal Crafter. They created items for only the most prominent and powerful in the area. The items sold in the System Shop are *far* more expensive than ones sold by individuals, too. The way they mark it up has been said to be *criminal*, but also convenient."

"Queen Alastea didn't even have a System Shop in her queen-dom," Xavier said.

"No, she didn't. So where do you think her people got their weapons and armour? Their potions? From people who made them. There was a garden near the castle. One we never saw— must have been burned before we arrived." Siobhan waved a hand. "What I read was that settlements who have access to gardens like these are able to attract the best alchemists and crafters. And when you have those at hand, it becomes easier to outfit your people. Not to mention, an alchemist can brew far more than just health and mana potions."

"What else can they brew?" Xavier still wasn't sold on this. Wouldn't it be easier just to buy things from the shop? That was, he supposed, assuming they would even have access to the System Shop back on Earth...

I've definitely been spoiled here at the Tower of Champions.

"There are potions that can increase people's attributes for certain periods of time, not to mention ones that can increase the number of Mastery Points gained."

Xavier's eyebrows shot to the top of his forehead. "Really? They can do that?"

Siobhan shrugged. "That's what I read, at least." She handed the Seed Garden back to him.

He looked at the item with new eyes, beginning to see how useful it might be. "Will I need... a gardener?"

"Honestly? I'm not sure. Probably."

Xavier turned the seed around in his hand for a moment. Previously, when he'd been contemplating what his return to Earth might be like, he'd only ever really thought about fighting off invaders. Portals would have sprouted up all over the place. People needed his help. He couldn't imagine how many people might have died already.

But now, other things were entering his mind. Creating a fortress. Finding people to guard the place. Starting a garden, finding crafters and alchemists to utilise what it grew.

There was still the looming threat of the Silver River sector being purged. He was worried about that, but he had no idea how far away it was.

Empress Larona plays the long game.

That's what Sam had said about the woman that he worked for. The C Grade Denizen that was the most powerful person in this sector. A woman who was over a thousand years old.

What was the long game to her? How far away was this threat, really? Decades? Hundreds of years? More than that?

When I used Otherworldly Communion, I learnt that this sector was just shy of ten thousand years old, and it has been purged twice in that time. Twice in ten thousand years.

Who knew how far away this purge threat was and all the things he would need to do in that time? He kept telling himself he didn't want to rule Earth, but that didn't mean he couldn't *protect* it. And he knew for a fact that he wouldn't always *be* on Earth.

It's not only the Tower of Champions that will keep pulling me away until I clear all of its floors. There might not be much for me on Earth in terms of gaining more power. I'm going to have to move around the sector—that was why I got given a Sector Travel Key.

He wasn't going to leave Earth defenceless. He would need to leave something behind.

"All right." Xaiver deposited the Seed Garden into his Storage Ring. "Maybe this will come in handy." He was beginning to grow more and more excited for his return to Earth. For what he might do there, other than just fight. He glanced over at the door to the next floor. "Ready to go in again?"

Howard, Siobhan, and Justin each nodded their readiness.

"Hopefully this next floor will be as fast as the last," Howard said.

"I do wonder how everyone is doing," Siobhan replied. "Back on Earth."

Justin rubbed the back of his head. "I wanna know how long we'll get to be there."

"We'll find out. Really soon." Xavier stepped up to the door first.

They materialised in the middle of a stone chamber.

Floor number nine. No Safe Zone.

The chamber had high ceilings and braziers burning at short intervals along the wall. Behind them lay the door to the Staging Room. Ahead, there was only one exit.

Something roared in the distance.

Chapter 72

Dungeon

Xavier cocked his head, listening to the far-off roar. The sound echoed through the ancient-looking stone hallways.

Howard stepped forward, a hand on the haft of his double-bearded axe. "No notification appeared."

"They don't always," Justin said. "Only on certain floors. The first few floors never had any, remember?"

Xavier nodded. He walked over to the exit hallway. There wasn't a door, only an arch. The roar was still echoing, though it sounded even farther away now. "So, are we in some sort of maze?"

Siobhan shook her head. "No. This isn't a maze. Not exactly, anyway."

"What is it?"

The woman smiled. "It's a dungeon." She shrugged. "Or something like it."

"It reminds me of when we faced the Rat King, back on the second floor," Howard said. "Though not made of earth."

Xavier frowned. "Hopefully the walls don't move this time around." The second floor of the tower was the only floor that Xavier hadn't gained any sort of record for.

Siobhan nodded. "That... would not be good."

"Well, I suppose we should get moving." Xavier strode through the archway. He summoned Charon's Scythe to his hand. He liked his new weapon, but he was disappointed that he hadn't gotten a chance to use it in a real fight.

I wonder what we'll face at the end of this dungeon.

The second he stepped into the hallway, another roar sounded, louder than the last. Then beasts began bounding toward them. The hallway was so narrow that only one beast could fit in it at a time.

Except that these beasts could climb the wall and even cling to the ceiling.

"Spiders," Xavier muttered. "Why did it have to be spiders?"

He felt a cold shiver of animal fear run up his spine at the sight of the beasts. He wasn't *actually* afraid of them—he could kill them quite easily—but there was something, deeply rooted in his human DNA, that didn't like the sight of these creatures.

Xavier shoved those primal fears away. He'd sensed these beasts' auras well before he'd seen them, which meant they were incredibly weak.

Part of him wished the Tower of Champions scaled its difficulty toward him.

Be a bit harder to reap the rewards, then.

He used Core Burn on the nearest of the spiders and gained a rank as soon as the thing died. He didn't want to spend a great deal of time in this place, but he also didn't want to waste too many souls using Soul Strike. He'd tapped his soulkeeping reserve completely on that last floor and would need to replenish it before he smashed through this floor—which meant using Soul Shatter was still out of the question. He couldn't destroy the souls of the enemies he killed.

Besides, he still hadn't decided which way to go with Soul Shatter.

And Soul Strike's still in cooldown. I can't use it anyway.

But he had plenty of other spells to use. Heavy Telekinesis took care of the giant spiders well enough, crushing them into the stone walls of the dungeon. If he let the enemies get close, Charon's Scythe dealt with them with ease.

This is like a walk in the park. A dank, dark, creepy park filled with spiders trying to kill me even though they can't.

They pushed forward through the halls, quickly coming to a crossroads. Three directions in which to choose from.

"Should we mark the ways we go through?" Justin asked.

Xavier slashed a mark into the stone to the left, then turned down that way. He'd read something about mazes, and always turning the same way in one until you came upon a dead end. He figured it was the best approach.

He didn't *need* to mark the way to remember it, but it seemed wise all the same. They were about twenty steps down the hall, no hint of enemies in sight, when the ground shifted, as though an earthquake were rocking the entire structure.

"The ceiling isn't going to collapse on us, is it?" Howard asked. "I'm not sure if my Bulwark would do anything against that... I've never tested it."

Xavier frowned. *I'd survive that, wouldn't I?* But it wasn't the ceiling that collapsed—it was the ground beneath him. The solid stone turned into something akin to quicksand. He couldn't take a step—his feet were already stuck. He sank fast.

It reminded him of when he'd been trapped by the Rat King. Or when he'd been buried alive during a wave of the Endless Horde. He heard the others struggling.

Then the spiders came. The thuds of their large legs slapping the walls.

The perfect trap.

Being buried had always been a weakness for Xavier. Something that had gotten him into trouble in the past. Almost gotten him killed, or almost stopped him from saving his friends.

Except this wasn't a weakness anymore. And his friends? They weren't in any danger.

Heavy Telekinesis!

He pushed the spell in a circle around himself and the other members of the party, targeting only the spiders rushing toward them. He crushed them to the wall, killing over a dozen. Then he smoothly Soul Stepped to one of the corpses. The spider had died, crushed against the wall high near the ceiling, so he fell to the ground and landed in an easy crouch.

Xavier was about to help the others, but Siobhan had already summoned them out of their holes. Howard was slamming his double-bearded axe into the stone around Siobhan, freeing her from the trap, as she couldn't teleport herself out.

Within seconds, they were walking down the hall again.

Xavier couldn't help but chuckle and shake his head. "We've certainly come a long way."

Howard grunted. "This floor is definitely going to be a problem for those without the right skillset."

Siobhan sighed. "I still wish I could write up a manual for the floors. It's so lame that the System only lets that information out through word of mouth."

"Gatekeeping at its finest," Justin muttered. "But at least we don't have anything to worry about with this powerhouse at our side." He elbowed Xavier in the shoulder. "Seriously, I'm glad we decided to go with you on that first day when you told us you wanted to solo everything... I almost refused the idea."

Xavier glanced at him. "You did?"

Justin shrugged. "Well... yeah. After what I'd just been through back on Earth, when the System came, I figured I needed every advantage I could get. I didn't know how I'd manage that by standing on the sidelines, not getting any combat experience. But... I wanted to see what you could do before I made any decision."

Siobhan pursed her lips. "I felt the same. I remember, when we were waiting in the cabin, the Safe Zone back on the first floor..."

"We thought you'd died out there," Howard cut in. "I may have said... something about you being a damned fool."

Xavier snorted. "Well, wouldn't be the first time I've been called a fool since this all begin." He smirked. "Sam seems rather fond of calling me a System-damned fool."

"System-damned?" Howard asked with a raised eyebrow. "I'd hardly call you *damned* by the System. If anything, you've been blessed. The titles you've gained, the feats you've achieved. And the fact that the System is apparently *watching* you?"

"It's enough to make anyone jealous," Justin said with a chuckle. "You're the most powerful Denizen from Earth!"

"Jealous?" Howard frowned at the teenager. "You're actually jealous of what he has?"

Justin gave the man a sideways glance. "Of course. Aren't you?"

"No." Howard grunted. "Definitely not." He put a hand on Xavier's shoulder. "Xavier has the weight of the entire world on his shoulders. We will be there, to help defend Earth. To protect those who are weaker than us, but if we fail..." He was looking from Justin to Siobhan as he said this. "Then, in the grand scheme, it doesn't matter. But if *he* fails—"

"Earth is doomed," Siobhan whispered. Her gaze turned downward, as though the ground beneath them had suddenly become interesting. "And not only the Earth... maybe the entire sector."

"Exactly," Howard said. "I, for one, am not jealous of *that* kind of pressure. I want to protect Earth. Most of all, I want to protect my family. And I'll die in service of that if I have to. But..."

"You're glad it's not all hanging on you," Xavier said. He'd been quiet through what the man had been saying. But now, he had to speak. "It's a lot of pressure. But"—he smiled—"I think the pressure suits me." He lowered his head in thought. "Before all of this happened, I dreamt of living a different life. Of experiencing something *more*. Like..." He chuckled, shook his head. "It sounds foolish, and more than a little naive, but I felt as though I was *meant* for something more than what my life had been."

"Considering where we are, all we've been through, what you've achieved..." Siobhan smiled. "That doesn't sound all that foolish at all." She tucked a loose strand of red hair behind her ear. "Besides, you're not exactly alone in feeling that way. I liked my life, but this"—she waved a hand, as though trying to encompass the entire Greater Universe—"this is what's been going on, out beyond our solar system, since before life even evolved on Earth. I've got a feeling that somehow, in our collective unconscious, humans have always known they were bound for more than our world had to offer."

They turned a corner. Xavier idly slashed the wall, marking their direction, then crushed a half-dozen spiders that rushed toward them into the stone, making an unsettling *squishing* sound.

Siobhan blinked up at the dead beasts, then went on as though nothing had happened. "For millennia, we've had myths and legends of magical creatures, of gods, of higher causes. Of trials and journeys. We've had myths about *elves*, and many other creatures and races that we've since encountered. Races that have been around since before Earth ever was. How could it be possible that we knew of them when Earth had never been integrated before?"

The woman shrugged. "I don't have an answer as to the *how*, but it's clear we knew. And maybe that's why humans so rarely felt fulfilled. Maybe that's why we had so many wars... The Greater Universe is filled with conflict. Maybe we *felt* that—in our bones, in our *souls*—and have been preparing ourselves for it."

Xavier stared at Siobhan as they walked down another long, stone hallway. "You've been thinking about this a lot, haven't you?"

The Divine Beacon laughed. "Since the moment I saw a goblin. Maybe before that. And these status screens, resembling video games—it's all too familiar to be a coincidence."

The party went silent after her words, each seeming to be considering them on their own.

Xavier couldn't help but feel as though there was some truth in them.

Maybe that's why I gravitated toward fantasy novels, why I always wanted... more. Because all of this was out there, waiting for me, my destiny, in some ways, already written.

Even this dungeon, these giant spiders—it all seemed so familiar to him.

Didn't Frodo fight a bunch of giant spiders? Heading through a mountain?

Maybe Tolkien had some sort low-level, natural seer ability. The very thought made him laugh to himself, but after everything he'd seen... it might not be all that far-fetched.

We've come across plenty of elves, after all...

He shook away the thoughts. As interesting as they were to him, it didn't change what he needed to do.

They pushed forward through the dungeon's hallways, killing hundreds of spiders along the way. He wondered if he needed to kill *every* spider on this floor to clear it. That would be a pain. There was something strange about the dungeon's walls, something that had taken him far too long to realise—they were blocking his ability to read auras through them.

Usually, he'd be able to see an enemy's aura—if that enemy couldn't control their aura—through solid structures.

That wasn't so down here.

The party were met with several dead -ends. Xavier wasn't only marking the way with his blade, he was memorising their path in his mind. Memorisation, when he cared to put energy toward it, was a fairly easy thing for him to achieve. He would be able to navigate this dungeon with ease when it became time to fully clear the floor.

Finally, after navigating the dungeon at an unhurried pace for an hour or so, killing everything they passed, they'd mapped the entire area, covering every inch of it except for a final chamber Xavier refused to enter.

The chamber was open, no doors barring entry toward it. It was domelike, the stone blocks that made its walls curved up until they met at the ceiling, where a giant, intricate spiderweb loomed.

Inside that web, the massive form of the floor boss awaited them.

Chapter 73
Spider Queen

Xavier peered into the final chamber of the Tower of Champions' ninth floor, looking up at the floor boss.

"This seems easy enough," he muttered. He looked away from the chamber and at the others. "All right. Time to head back and refresh this floor." He smiled. "We're *almost* there. Almost to the tenth floor!"

Siobhan had a frown on her face. "Something feels too easy about this."

"Too easy?" Justin scratched at his nose. "Of course it's easy. How could it be hard with this powerhouse on our team." He nodded at Xavier.

Siobhan shook her head. "I'm not talking about the monsters—I'm talking about the dungeon. The walls don't shift and change like on the second floor. There's no one to protect... I just feel like there's something *more* here."

Howard ran a hand through his beard, a look of contemplation lining his face. "Maybe it just *feels* like it should be harder than it is? The sooner we refresh this floor, the sooner we get back to Earth. And that's something I very much want."

"That's something I want too," Xavier said. "But I don't think we should ignore what Siobhan is feeling." He stepped over to her. "What do you think we should do?"

Siobhan gestured toward the chamber. "I think you should step in there. I have a feeling some kind of trap will activate, and if it does, better to be aware of it now rather than on your final clear. And, if the floor boss attacks—"

"If?" Xavier raised an eyebrow at her.

Siobhan smirked. "Okay, *when* the floor boss attacks, it's not like it will be able to do any damage toward you."

"What kind of trap are you expecting?" Howard asked.

"I don't know." Siobhan shrugged. "That's why I think he should do this. If I'm wrong, we've only spent another minute or so here. No harm done."

Xavier saw the wisdom in her words, even if he didn't think there was anything to worry about. He already had his plan for this floor—sprint and teleport through every inch of the dungeon, killing the spiders as fast as he could until he reached the final chamber, then dispose of the floor boss. It wasn't a particularly sophisticated plan, but it didn't need to be when he was E Grade on a floor for low-end F Grades.

He wouldn't be able to clear the ninth floor as fast as he'd cleared many of the other floors, but he'd be able to clear it fast enough, he hoped, to get the number one record that he was after.

Still, as she said, there was no harm in stepping over that threshold and seeing if this floor had any tricks up its sleeve.

He laid a hand on Siobhan's shoulder. "You and the others stay in this hall." He glanced up at the spider. "I'm sure you'd be able to take on this thing as a team." He'd scanned the floor boss and found it to be called a Spider Queen—no surprise there. "But I don't want you guys taking any unnecessary risks.

The trio glanced at each other, but none of them argued.

Xavier deposited Charon's Scythe into his Storage Ring. He didn't want to kill this thing out of pure muscle memory. He could imagine what was about to happen next. The massive spider dropping straight to the ground, attacking him head-on, its pincers trying to grab at him—or its forelegs snapping down to try and puncture his chest.

Or maybe it will shoot its web at me, try and wrap me up in a cacoon before eating me...

That thought made him shudder.

Siobhan was right; the floor boss shouldn't be able to cause him any damage at all. Still, he couldn't help but feel a *little* trepidation. Back before the System, when he'd been nothing more than an average human, he'd... been afraid of spiders.

It was a completely irrational fear. He'd even researched the different common spiders that he sometimes encountered in his tiny apartment to ensure that none of them were venomous.

They were basically harmless. Could do nothing more to him than a small bite, which might sting and make him a bit itchy.

Yet still, he'd felt an unwarranted fear of them.

Looking up at the Spider Queen he knew couldn't harm him, he felt a shadow of that same irrational fear—even more irrational now, he supposed, after all the monstrous beasts he'd faced.

At least this spider won't be able to hide from me.

The instant Xavier stepped over the threshold, a screeching, booming voice sounded from above. It had a sort of high-pitched, cackling-crone quality to it.

"You dare enter my domain, foolish human!" The Spider Queen's entire body shuddered, making the intricate web it hid inside of vibrate. A purple glow suddenly suffused the web, as though a spell were about to be cast.

"Of course the giant spider can talk," Xavier muttered. "And of course it sounds like some lame movie villain, because why wouldn't it?" He couldn't help but be reminded of the Rat King.

The irrational fear he'd been feeling evaporated. He chuckled to himself with a shake of his head.

"Silence!" The Spider Queen's voice boomed. "You have made a grave mistake, human!"

The stone beneath him shifted. His feet sank into it, like they'd done before, in a different hallway. He could certainly see how this might strike fear into a normal party, but he couldn't get over how ridiculous this situation felt.

If this is the extent of the trap...

Siobhan's voice sounded within his mind through their bonded Communication Stones. [*Should I teleport you out of there?*]

[*No. Let's wait a little while. I've got a feeling this insect has something up one of its many sleeves. Not that it has sleeves...*]

Siobhan didn't reply with words. Instead, he felt a telepathic confirmation—like a mind nod.

The stone around him didn't become solid again until he'd sunk down to his waist. Looking down at the stone, he wondered if he could simply break out of it using the power of his Strength alone.

I bet if I really needed to, Charon's Scythe could cut through it.

He saw no point in testing this theory, however. When he came here on his final clear, the Spider Queen wouldn't even have time to trap him in the stone. And even if it did, he could kill it with ease trapped down here.

The Spider Queen's screeching voice boomed once more. "I summon all my children to meeeee!"

The web glowed ever more brightly, until the entire room was bathed in purple light.

Then... nothing happened. When no spiders appeared, the Spider Queen released a mournful, screeching wail. "You killed my babies! I will have my revenge!" Then flung itself down at Xavier.

Xavier smiled as the spider fell. [*Time to go,*] he communicated to Siobhan.

A white light enveloped him, and he was back in the hall.

Justin peeked his head into the chamber, then took a few steps back as the spider slammed into the ground. "Run back to the exit?" he said, looking askance at the beast.

Xavier grinned. "I'll be right behind you."

When they returned to the Staging Room, Xavier rubbed his hands together. "Siobhan, you're a genius."

Siobhan tilted her head to the side. "I am?" She blinked. "I mean, yes, of course I am." The woman nodded sagely.

Xavier chuckled. "This floor?" He jutted his thumb behind him at the door. "It's going to go *way* faster than I first thought."

Siobhan still looked a little confused.

"Didn't you hear what the Spider Queen said?" Xavier figured they would have caught on to his plan instantly, especially Siobhan, but none of them looked like they knew what he was talking about.

"There must have been some kind of noise-cancelling spell on the chamber," Howard said. "We didn't hear a word."

"After you stepped inside the chamber, a thin webbing blocked the doorway." Justin rested a hand on the hilt of his sword. "I didn't try, but I got the feeling it wouldn't be easy to cut through."

"Huh," Xavier said. "I didn't notice that."

"The webbing disappeared after I teleported you out," Siobhan replied.

Xavier nodded. "I can see how that room could be quite an effective trap. I'm glad you were able to teleport me out. Though I probably would have been able to break through the webbing." Despite his words, he felt a little doubtful about that for some reason.

"So... what did it *say*?" Justin asked.

"It said it would summon all its children to it, but when it tried, none of them came."

"All its children?" Siobhan's eyes lit up. "It was going to summon every remaining living spider from within the dungeon straight to it. But we killed them all, which means, when you go there next—"

"I can sprint straight to the final chamber, wait for the Spider

Queen to summon all the other beasts, then kill them all at once, making for a much faster clear."

"Hmm," Howard said. "We walked past that chamber a few times before we finally cleared the whole dungeon. I can imagine other Champions entering it before they cleared the other enemies. They'd be in for a shock."

"It'll be a while before any of the other parties reach this floor, but we'll make sure to let them know." Xavier had spent quite a bit of coin getting his information network in place. He was finding he was glad for it. Though he didn't plan to make another visit to the tavern until he was ready to clear the tenth floor.

He frowned. Something in his mind—an insight?—nudged him toward going sooner than that.

All right, he thought to himself. *I'll go after I clear the ninth floor, before stepping onto the tenth.*

He got a feeling there would be something different about the tenth floor. He'd learnt to trust these kinds of feelings.

"Well." Howard stepped over to the door. "What are we waiting for?" The man smiled, but it was strained, and Xavier couldn't help but feel his impatience.

He recalled the chat they'd had on the floor as they'd stalked through the dungeon's halls, when Howard had said he couldn't imagine being in Xavier's position, the weight of the entire planet Earth on his shoulders.

In a weird way, Xavier couldn't imagine what *Howard* was going through. He had the weight of his family. His kids. His wife. Two people he clearly loved more than anything.

People were dying back on Earth. Hell, they were dying in the tower. And while Xavier cared about every single loss—his mother maybe being among them—it was the protection of the Earth as a whole he was most concerned with.

Howard? He had only two people on his mind. If they died, it didn't matter how well the world as a whole fared; he would have failed.

Xavier squeezed the man's shoulder as he stepped up to the door. "I'll get you back to them. Real soon."

The former cop gave a sharp nod, his face impassive. He didn't say a word as they headed onto the tower floor.

Almost there, Xavier thought, readying himself for a fast clear.

Chapter 74
Planet-Wide

FOR THE SECOND TIME, XAVIER MATERIALISED ON THE TOWER of Champions' ninth floor. He'd felt a little foolish when he'd grabbed the doorhandle, assuming a sprinter's position, his scythe-staff still within his Storage Ring—he figured holding the weapon as he ran might slow him down, even if only by a small amount.

There were many hundreds of spiders within the dungeons, though Xavier hadn't kept an exact count, he *had* been able to significantly replenish his soulkeeping reserves. His Soul Strike spell had reached the end of its cooldown while they'd been exploring the dungeon on their first run-through.

He was as ready as he was ever going to be.

The instant Xavier arrived on the floor, he took off like a shot, leaving the others behind. There wasn't a Safe Zone on the ninth floor, but he wasn't worried about his friends. If any spider-beasts came to bother them, Howard's Bulwark spell would keep them at bay easily enough.

It wasn't as though they'd be spending much time here.

As he ran, he used Heavy Telekinesis to shove spiders out of the way. If one of the spiders was on the other end of a long hall-way, he'd kill it, then use the Soul Step imbued ability to teleport to the corpse.

God, I'm glad I don't have to go through all of these halls again.

He had barely any doubt that he would have lost out on the record if he had. Champion parties from other, long-integrated worlds would have already had knowledge of this floor. They would know about the Spider Queen summoning the rest of the beasts straight to it at the end, and though he doubted they could deal with the enemies as swiftly as he could, they could likely do it faster in one place—if they were sturdy and powerful enough—faster than he could going hall by hall.

Xavier left dozens of squished spiders in his wake as he skidded straight through the entryway to the final chamber, coming to a halt in the middle of it. He stood, a smile on his face, as he looked up at the beast.

"You dare enter my domain, foolish human!" The Spider Queen's voice was exactly as harsh and screechy as the first time around.

"Yes!" Xavier laughed. "I dare!"

The Spider Queen shook in what Xavier assumed must have been rage, said he made a grave mistake, then screeched, ear-splittingly loud, about summoning its children.

The web's purple glow brightened. And this time, the floor boss's spell worked.

The Spider Queen cackled, loudly and proudly, as it slowly lowered down from its large, purple web, down a single strong string. The spider was the most terrifying-looking beast that Xavier had ever seen, but his fear of it the first time he'd seen the thing had vanished completely the moment it had talked.

Now, he couldn't help but smile up at it.

Around him, many hundreds of large, eight-legged beasts appeared, making screeching noises of their own. Just like the first time he'd entered this place, Xavier had sunk straight down into the floor. He didn't bother to fight it, and he didn't kill the Spider Queen before it had happened—if he hadn't let the thing summon its children, this would be a failure, after all.

Xavier summoned Charon's Scythe into his hands, gripping it as he unleashed his spell.

Soul Strike!

Hundreds of bolts of pure white lightning shot forth from his weapon, making the chamber brighter than a sunny day.

Then the soul apparitions materialised. The translucent spiders launched themselves through the air at the real ones.

Once again, Xavier was glad he'd deactivated his kill notifications, as they would have flooded his vision, making it impossible to see around him.

None of the spiders ever even got a chance to strike him a single time before they were all dead, free of wounds, all around him.

Xavier drew in a deep breath as he harvested their souls. He looked up, just in time to see the Spider Queen—clearly dead—fall straight on top of him.

He couldn't teleport out of the way—not now that he'd harvested all of the souls. There was nowhere to teleport *to*.

The beast wouldn't really hurt him if it fell on him, but it would probably eventuate in him being covered in dead-monster goo. Even if the monster-goo would be all cleaned off by the System when he was teleported back to the Staging Room, it wasn't something he wished to experience.

He cast Heavy Telekinesis, throwing the massive beast into the chamber wall, crushing some of the spider corpses behind it and cringing at the sound that made.

Xavier straightened up and cut the stone around him as notifications began to appear in his vision.

He'd finished the ninth floor of the Tower of Champions.

A flood of power entered him as all of his stats were changed.

Now, it was time to figure out by how much. He grinned.

Xavier skipped over most of the notifications. The attribution for the floor was all for him, as always, and the other titles were always the same as every other floor.

It was only the final notification that he was really interested in reading.

Ninth Floor Ranked 1 – RECORD HOLDER (Completion Time – 2 mins 7 secs): Out of all the Champions from all the worlds in the Greater Universe who have completed the Ninth Floor of the Tower of Champions in every possible instance, you have completed it in the fastest time.
This title is a Temporary Title. If your record is edged out of first place, your title will be turned into a normal top 100 title.
If your record is edged out of the top 100, your title will be lost.
You have received +140 to all stats!
Note: As you have similar titles, each has been combined with this title and shares their stats. You may still view the previous titles and your standing on the leaderboards, if you will it.

Xavier let out a sigh of relief, then he smiled.

Two minutes and seven seconds wasn't too bad, especially considering he'd had to sprint through the hallways using his memorised map of the place and wait for the Spider Queen to summon all of its children.

He was still stuck in the stone the Spider Queen had trapped him in, but he deposited Chaon's Scythe into his Storage Ring, put his hands behind his head, and waited for the floor to end. He didn't bother placing the corpses of the dead spiders into his Storage Ring—they were simply far too low-level for him to provide much of any benefit.

Though Xavier was confident he had the ability to get the top record for every floor, he knew that it wasn't something guaranteed. There was no way for him to see what the record for a floor that he hadn't already gained a record for *was*, which meant he would never know what record he needed to beat. And even though he was incredibly strong, there might be others out there with abilities better suited toward a particular floor.

He tilted his head to the side for a moment in thought.

Is there a way to get that knowledge outside of the tower? Knowledge of what the best times on the leaderboard were?

When he brought up the leaderboard for floors he'd completed, he was able to see the records of other Champions. What if, somehow, when he was outside of the tower, he were able to contact previous record holders?

The information certainly wouldn't be able to be shared via text, which means I might have to talk to them in person, or at least through some sort of telepathic or video communication method.

He wondered what the odds of encountering a record holder in his own sector even were. There were only 100 spots for record holders to have on each floor, and yet there were countless sectors that had been around for far, far longer than Xavier's sector. There might be the occasional record holder out there. Ones who had the record for perhaps a single floor. But finding them sounded like quite the task.

He wouldn't even know where to begin.

Maybe there are information brokers out there, somewhere, in our sector, people who specialised in memorising things like this.

He shook the thoughts away. It wasn't something he could work on right now.

He basked in his victory, getting number 1 on yet another leaderboard, and waited for the countdown timer to run out.

When they returned to the Staging Room, the others congratulated Xavier. He couldn't help but smile. It was becoming expected that he would gain the number 1 title now, but that didn't mean it wasn't an achievement. He had to remind himself that just because he made it look easy didn't mean he wasn't accomplishing something that literally no one in the entire Greater Universe had.

At least in this reality, he thought.

He often forgot to consider the fact that the floors of *his* Tower of Champions weren't the same floors that Champions in the other, alternate universes that he visited through the tower had.

Their floors could be completely different...

It was a little mind-bending to think of things in that way. Something he knew he would be spending a long time wrapping his head around.

He rubbed his hands together as he looked over at the loot boxes. He honestly had no idea what to expect to gain from this floor. The items he'd gotten lately would go a long way toward helping him set up a base back on Earth.

Would the next item he found within the loot box be something to help that as well? Something that could enhance his Sanctuary Seed?

Only one way to find out.

Xavier walked over to his loot box. The other members of his party did the same. This was becoming a familiar ritual for them. Xavier was glad they'd been going through the last few floors much faster than the ones before them.

Only one more floor until we're back on Earth.

He knelt by the box, undid the latch, and threw the lid open in a dramatic gesture.

You have gained 5 Mastery Points (E Grade).
You have gained 275,000 Lesser Spirit Coins.
You have received a Portal Hub.

The Mastery Points he received, yet again, barely made a dent. But they were something. Step by step, he would get to Level 101.

Only eighty-five more points to go... Maybe that will be easier as I move up through the floors. There are 1,000 floors in this tower, after all.

That made him wonder what floor 1,000 would be like, and what grade he might be when he finally got there. Considering the strongest Denizen in this entire sector was C Grade, he didn't think that Champions who finished the tower could be much stronger than high E Grade—especially considering how big a deal a D Grade was back on the fifth floor.

The variance on the floors later down the line mustn't be as strong as between the first ten floors.

It might not take him as long as he thought to finish all these floors, especially considering the rate at which he was going.

The spirit coins, again, weren't all that much either.

He moved on to the unique item. He smiled at the name, long before he knew what the description actually was.

A Portal Hub sounded incredibly useful, however it ended up functioning. The item had materialised in his hand. It was shaped like a... coin? A thick one. It was rather weighty. If he had to guess, he'd say the little coin weighed about twenty kilos.

What kind of dense metal is this thing made of to weigh that much?

He examined it, turning it over in his hands. It had a single marking on one side. A circle, etched into the metal.

Is that supposed to be a portal?

He used his Identify skill on the item.

{Portal Hub – Restriction: Planet-wide – Upgradeable}
This Portal Hub connects a registered base to a planet-wide system of portals. For a price, it can open portals to other registered bases around a single planet.
Each planet will have its own registry of Portal Hubs.
A Base Leader can set their Portal Hub to open or private. If a Portal Hub is open, any other Portal Hub on the planet will have the ability to connect to it. If it is private, only accepted allies will be able to make a connection.

Identify has reached Rank 27!

Xavier smiled after reading the description. The Portal Hub sounded just as helpful as he'd imagined, though it did bring up a fair few questions.

For one, how did he make his base a *registered* base? What did that even mean? Would it receive some sort of official designation, given to it by the System?

And what, exactly, was a Base Leader?

Is that what I'll be when I plant my Sanctuary Seed?

That made him wonder what he might be called if he had *multiple* bases. It certainly seemed like something that would be inevitable in the long run.

Then there was the fact that this Portal Hub would be able to connect with *other* Portal Hubs around Earth.

What if my enemies have Portal Hubs?

And, last of all, it was *upgradeable*. Would he one day be able to connect with Portal Hubs on other worlds?

They were all good questions. Maybe Sam, down in the tavern, would be able to answer them. He'd decided he needed to visit the man before he entered the tenth floor, anyway.

Chapter 75

Leverage

Stepping into the tavern always felt like stepping into a different world. Xavier breathed in the smell of mead and ale and beer. Felt the warmth of the many fires burning. He closed his eyes and let it all settle over him for a moment.

Then he strode over to the bar. There were a few parties scattered at different tables. He noticed some of the Champions nudging at each other and gesturing toward them—and they weren't all people he recognised. Word about what he'd done must have gotten around. The money he'd given Sam had certainly gotten used, as almost every party within the place had on decent gear.

Well, that's a good sight to see.

A few of the men and women he passed nodded his way. He nodded back, feeling a little awkward doing so, and hoping none of them approached him. He wasn't totally against talking to them—he didn't keep to himself nearly as much as he used to—but he didn't have time for idle chitchat.

"How are you faring?" Sam asked.

Xavier was still a little frustrated with Sam after their last conversation. He didn't like the fact that his boss—the most powerful Denizen in the entire sector—would rule Earth if she could.

But he'd also had a bit of time to think about it, and part of him... understood better now why she might wish to do that.

Earth needs order.

Though he would never let a foreign invader be the one to give it that order. And he figured he had enough leverage over her right now to ensure that would never happen.

"We're about to enter the tenth floor," Xavier replied.

Sam raised an eyebrow. "Already?"

"I'll be honest, it feels like a long time coming." Xavier ran a hand through his hair and sighed. He glanced over at the other parties. Howard, Siobhan, and Justin would be down soon—they were only a few minutes behind him—to give out information about the last few floors.

Not that these people will need it any time soon.

"What brings you down here?" Sam asked.

Xavier rested a hand on the bar, tapping his fingers against the smooth wood. With his other hand, he summoned the Sanctuary Seed, Seed Garden, and Portal Hub, placing each side by side on the bar.

"I've got a few questions about these items."

"Whoa." Sam gave an incredulous chuckle. He gestured toward the Sanctuary Seed. "May I?" He had a great big grin on his face.

"As long as you don't steal it from me," Xavier said.

"Wouldn't dream of it." Sam snatched the item up and turned it around in his hand. His gaze slid from the Sanctuary Seed to the other items on the bar. "How'd you manage this? They can't all have been loot box rewards?"

Xavier remembered when he'd asked about the Sector Travel Key. Sam had told him that normally, a key like that was most *definitely* not a reward Champions would usually get this early on in the tower.

"These extra rewards... the System is preparing me, isn't it?"

Sam nodded. "It certainly seems that way. I've *never* seen someone rewarded by the System to this degree. Not in all my years."

Xavier touched a hand to his Storage Ring. Though he had a few questions about the items, there was something else he'd recently been thinking about. "When I go to Earth, invaders of one level higher than myself will be able to travel there."

Sam made a "hmm" noise and waited for him to say more.

"What happens to those Denizens when I get sent back to the tower?"

Sam frowned. "They remain there. If they leave your planet, then try to return while you're away, they'll be killed. Otherwise…"

"Otherwise they get to stay without any repercussions." Xavier sighed. "I was worried about that."

Sam placed the Sanctuary Seed back on the bar and locked eyes with him. "You need to be very careful on your return. Whatever you do, you cannot let the enemy know what level you are."

Xavier sighed. "I don't plan on leaving any of the enemies I encounter alive to report back, but… what if they're able to communicate telepathically? What if they somehow get a message off in the middle of a fight? They won't be able to scan me or feel my aura unless I drop it, but if they survive long enough to see how much power I wield, they'll know I must be a much higher level than I should be."

Sam rapped his knuckles on the bar in a constant rhythm and seemed to be gritting his teeth. He glanced to the side, as though checking if anyone was there. Xavier was getting used to this kind of behaviour from the man. He always looked a bit squirrely whenever he wanted to tell Xavier something he wasn't supposed to.

The barkeep leant forward over the bar. "There may be ways to block the types of communications you're talking about."

Xavier frowned. "Block communications?" That was new to him, but he supposed it made sense. It was both a good thing to hear in the context of what they were talking about, and a bit worrying. If *he* could gain this ability, wouldn't others be able to do the same? "And something like this might be available in the System Shop?"

Sam shrugged his shoulders and picked up a bottle of whiskey. He poured Xavier a glass and put it in front of him. "It's possible. Though something like that is liable to sell fast. And, honestly, most people who acquire such an item don't do so to sell it."

Xavier nodded. Now he worried he wouldn't be able to find this item, and even if he did, something that rare must be very expensive—likely outside of his price range.

I'll get Siobhan to have a look in the System Shop.

The door to the tavern opened just as he had that thought. Siobhan and the others stepped in. They nodded at him and Sam. Siobhan and Justin made their way to one of the parties sitting around the tavern, while Howard stopped by the bar to get drinks. When Howard stepped away, Xavier and Sam resumed their conversation.

"I have a question to ask you, Sam."

Sam chuckled. "You always seem to." He waved his hand in a circle. "What's this one?"

"Are you allowed to leave this tavern?"

"I am." Sam paused. "But not for long."

"Are you able to quit this job of being our caretaker?"

"Why, you trying to get rid of me?" Sam asked with a grin. Then he frowned. "You're not trying to get rid of me, are you?"

Xavier put up his hands. "No. Not at all. But..." He sighed. "I'm worried about Earth."

"Are you asking what I think you're asking?"

Xavier raised his chin. "Would you be able to travel to Earth? Help protect it while I'm in the tower? I'll be sent back there soon, but then the tower will just yank me back out again..."

Sam poured himself a drink. Took a hefty sip. "Few problems with that ask. One, I'm not supposed to provide that kind of help."

"While working at the tower," Xavier said. "But what if you *weren't* working at the tower anymore?" He took a sip of his own whiskey. "You're only working here to look for me, after all. And, well, you've found me now."

Sam frowned. "Part of my job is seeing how you do here. Through the *whole* of the tower. Not just the first ten floors."

"Part of your job is to earn my trust. I mean, isn't it? Why else would you warn me against being so trusting? Why else would you be upfront about what your empress would do with Earth if she could? I know what you're after—what your empress is after. The sector is in danger. You think I'm the solution to that."

Sam raised a finger. "That's above my pay grade. The one I serve, however—"

"I think you know what I mean, Sam. You want something from me. I want something from you."

"I can't travel to Earth. My level is too high. Besides, I'd need a portal."

"What level are you?"

Sam looked into his drink. "I'm not at liberty to share that information."

The barkeep tilted his head to the side. "But I suppose I would be able to travel to Earth soon enough. When you've gained, say, fifty levels..." The man winced, touched his jaw, as though he'd just felt some pain. He looked up at the ceiling.

The words "the System is Watching" suddenly entered Xavier's mind. It certainly seemed to have just punished Sam for that little slip.

"All right. And if I were to get high-enough level, would you travel to Earth? Protect it?"

Sam frowned. "I'm an envoy of my empress. If I travelled to Earth, I would be an invader, not someone there to *help*. Surely you understand that? The only way I'd even be able to get there is if she sent me. I don't have the kind of resources to make a trip like that myself... and you would need to be on Earth at the time for me to do it."

"No," Xavier said. "You can't come as an envoy. And I'd want System contract signed to that effect."

"You're asking for a lot here, and not really hearing that I'm saying I *can't* do this."

Xavier thought about what the empress wanted of him. Thought about how long she must have been at this long game of hers. With or without Sam, or the Empress's help, Xavier wanted to save his sector from whatever danger would one day befall it. When he'd heard of the danger, he'd already known that was what he would choose to do. To him, it wasn't even a choice at all. It was simply... his duty. He felt that in his bones. Felt it in his soul. He couldn't stand by while such a thing happened. He couldn't simply flee the sector and look for greener pastures, even if that might benefit him and keep him safe.

Keeping himself safe wasn't his primary goal.

"Talk to your empress, Sam. Tell her what I want, and why. I know what she wants from me, and if she's going to get it, she can't simply sit on the sidelines while my world gets invaded. And she can't take it over, either. Right now, Earth is my top priority."

Xavier still had questions. About the Sanctuary Seed, the Seed Garden, and the Portal Hub, but part of him wanted to turn around and walk out. Instead, he took a steadying breath, followed by a sip of his drink.

"Now, what can you tell me about these items?"

Chapter 76
Walking Before You Run

XAVIER TAPPED HIS FINGERS ON THE BAR AS HE WATCHED Sam. The barkeep picked up the Sanctuary Seed again, then held up the Seed Garden, then finally looked at the Portal Hub.

"Having all this..." Sam shook his head. "It's rather amazing, you know." He smiled, wistfully. "I've been doing this caretaker gig for a while. Seen a lot of Progenitors. Seen them strive, succeed, fail. Many of the Progenitors I've encountered haven't had to deal with invaders. You would think that would make them stronger. Safer. In a way, it did. But the ones who've had something to protect right away. The ones who've had massive amount of pressure on them..." He locked eyes with Xavier. "They've gone farther than I could have imagined." He placed the Portal Hub back on the bar, the little heavy coin making a loud *clink*. "But the higher they've risen, the farther they've fallen when they failed."

"That doesn't sound particularly motivating," Xavier muttered.

Sam shook his head. "You're going to be the exception." He nudged the Sanctuary Seed with a finger. "Possessing something like this so soon after your world has been integrated..." He bit his lip. There were still many things he clearly couldn't say.

Xavier sipped his drink, patiently waiting. He knew the man would get around those blocks if he could. It was much easier for him to do so when it wasn't about information regarding the tower itself.

"You've gained a lot of titles for being the first to do something," Sam said. He nodded at the items. "You're going to gain a lot more when you return to Earth."

Xavier smiled down at the items. He had wondered about that. A part of him imagined that the invaders would have already established strong bases in his world. Fortresses like whatever the Seed Sanctuary would grow for him. That they might have access to the System Shop, or to a Portal Hub like the one he'd just gained. But he supposed that all of the invaders on Earth would be quite low-level. Maybe they wouldn't be capable of doing such things?

I wonder how strong the people back on Earth have managed to become. How many levels they've managed to gain. It can't be much without the help of the Tower of Champions, all the advantages we've gotten...

Then again, he had no way of knowing that. He just assumed he was right. Though he couldn't imagine that any of them had spent six weeks in basically what amounted to a time chamber fighting increasingly higher-level enemies.

"This Portal Hub says it can be upgraded. Would I be able to use it to travel to other planets?"

Sam chuckled. "You really care nothing for the concept of walking before you run, do you?"

Xavier shrugged. "Running tends to get me where I want to go a lot faster."

"There isn't much I *need* to tell you about these items. For one, I've never actually used any of them myself. I've certainly seen what they've created, but I haven't been the one in charge of their operation."

"Huh. I suppose that makes sense," Xavier said. "You come from a well-established world. Why would you need things like this?"

"Oh, people from worlds like mine are familiar with these.

Don't get me wrong. It's difficult to establish footholds on other worlds without them, after all."

Xavier decided to ignore that. He still didn't exactly feel *good* about cultures who invaded other lands and took over. Though many humans from Earth certainly had a long history of doing exactly that...

Not what I'd like us to be known for.

Though he had to admit, after thinking on it for a bit following the last time he'd spoken to Sam, he certainly knew he'd been *very* naive. Protecting Earth wouldn't be as simple as making himself strong. He would need to make *Earth* strong. To do that, in the long run, he would need access to resources Earth didn't have. And if he wasn't able to get them through trade, he might have to resort to other means, else Earth would never be strong enough to hold its own without the threat of being taken over by other empires and conglomerates in the sector...

Though he still had trouble imagining himself invading other worlds. Right now, that certainly wasn't what he wanted to do with his life. He knew that sometimes, there simply weren't better options. But on the other hand, often people didn't realise what *all* of their options were, and they only took the obvious ones that were right in front of them.

That wasn't the person that Xavier wanted to be.

"What do you mean when you say you don't need to tell me much about these items?" Xavier asked.

Sam shrugged. "You'll be able to figure out plenty about them on your own. Some items have the ability to give the user quests, like when you have a spell that needs upgrading. I believe items like these would have such power."

"That does make sense." Xavier touched a finger to each of the items, returning them to his inventory. "I suppose you can't tell me anything about becoming a Base Leader, then?"

Sam shook his head. "No. Not yet, anyway."

Xavier sighed. He supposed he should have expected as much. It wasn't that he hadn't gotten *any* answers to his questions. He'd certainly learnt a thing or two from the man. But it was never quite as much as he wanted.

Is anything quite as much as we want? he mused.

He held his drink in hand, turned and leant backward on the bar, looking out at the other patrons. Howard, Siobhan, and Justin were holding court, taking turns to explain everything about the tower floors they'd just been through. The parties were staring at the three of them, their attention rapt. Justin was the one talking right now, using big, expressive gestures with his arms and hands. Xavier stopped for a moment and listened.

Turns out the kid's a good storyteller.

Xavier had often observed people who were good oral story-tellers, considering he was a big fan of stories himself. For a long time, he'd thought he would be a terrible writer because he wasn't good at telling stories to people. But he'd come to realise those were two very different skills. It was far easier—and probably always would be—for him to put words on the page rather than express them aloud.

Justin, however, appeared to be a natural oral storyteller. It made him wonder what the teenager's life had been like before the System had come down. He'd imagined him as quite serious, considering he was an Olympic-level athlete before all of this, but that didn't necessarily ring true.

Xavier glanced back at the barkeep. "Anything you can tell me about the tenth floor?" He didn't expect much of a response, but he figured a question was always worth asking.

Sam's face became expressionless. "Just... be ready. *You* won't have any trouble."

After those words, the barkeep stalked off and grabbed a broom. He stepped out from behind the bar and idly swept the ground—yet it was already perfectly clean.

Huh. That was a bit odd.

He frowned at the man, watching him sweep for a moment, listening to Justin talk about the eighth floor on the peripheral of his attention. He replayed the barkeep's words.

Why did he emphasise that I wouldn't have any trouble?

Xavier looked over at the members of his party. The tenth floor would have a Safe Zone, right? It was only floors three, six, and nine that didn't. But the way the man had spoken... it almost sounded like Xavier would be safe, but the others wouldn't be.

He still got the sense that there was something different about this next floor. Probably because he knew it would be his last before being sent back to Earth. He'd asked Sam how long he would have on Earth before. The man hadn't been able to answer.

I'll find out soon enough.

He had a few things on his mind now. One of them being the fact that the barkeep must be about Level 150. Xavier's levels hadn't moved since he'd come back from the fifth floor. He hadn't needed them to, to achieve his current goals. Now, he had another goal he wished to achieve.

Xavier was fairly confident that he would be able to convince Sam—or rather, Empress Larona—that the barkeep should come to Earth and help protect it. He knew it must be a very unusual proposition. Something that normally wouldn't be granted in a situation like this.

But these weren't exactly normal circumstances, were they?

I need to get myself to Level 150. As fast as I can.

Considering how few Mastery Points he'd been able to gain lately, he struggled to see how that would be possible, especially on Earth. Even when he came back to the tower...

He touched his Storage Ring, thinking about the Sector Travel Key, along with his Portal Stones, wondering if there was some-where within the Silver River sector he could travel. Somewhere that would help him achieve his goals.

I would need a pretty powerful insight to gain that kind of knowledge.

He smiled, thinking of one of his newly attained spells.

Otherworldly Communion.

He brought up the spell's cooldown.

Otherworldly Communion currently has a cooldown of 1 month. It cannot be used for another 27 days, 20 hours, and 32 minutes.

It's only been two days since the last time I cast it. I'm going to have to wait a while until I can use it again.

Xavier slowly sipped his drink as he drifted into thought.

The long game.

In the grand scheme, he supposed twenty-seven and a bit days wasn't all that long to wait for an answer to his problem. Besides, he might very well find the answer before then...

And wouldn't all of his spells' cooldowns refresh once he'd gained another level? If he got to Level 101, he would be able to use the spell a *lot* sooner. Unless these otherworldly spells worked differently.

When his drink was finished, he ordered another, contemplating the barkeep's words, wondering if his friends were truly in danger or not.

I'll talk to them about it. See what they think. Either way, I'm going to the tenth floor when this drink is done.

Chapter 77
Prepare Yourself

"YOU REALLY THINK WE HAVE SOMETHING TO WORRY ABOUT?" Justin asked.

They were sitting around a table of their own in the tavern. Xavier had taken a seat, nursing his whiskey as he'd listened to them tell the parties present all the details about the floors they'd just been through. When they reached the end, the three of them came to join him, and he'd told them of Sam's words, and that he hinted at a warning within them.

"I don't know." Xavier shrugged. "But we shouldn't take his words lightly. I don't think he would have said anything if it wasn't important."

Howard shook his head. "It doesn't matter. We need to go on that floor. We need to get home."

Xavier nodded slowly. "I hear you. But what if I went to the floor first, to scope it out?"

"You mean, without us?" Siobhan asked. She pursed her lips. "I'm not sure that's a great idea."

Xavier frowned at Siobhan. "Why wouldn't it be?" He looked at each of their faces. None of them seemed to like the idea of him going onto the floor before them. He hadn't realised it would be an

542

issue. "I'm not going to leave the three of you behind. I'd think you'd know that by now."

Justin rubbed the back of his head. "We don't think you would do that, it's just..." He glanced at Siobhan.

"We know nothing about the tenth floor. It's the final floor before Earth. A milestone. You've been saying you've got a weird feeling about this floor. Well, what if you're right and there is something... *different* about it? What if the floor locks you in, and it can only be done once? Do you know what that would mean for us?"

Xavier bit his lip. He did know what that would mean for them. As far as he knew, there was no way to enter a floor of the Tower of Champions one had already fully cleared. He couldn't go back and do any of the floors he'd just done. The only floor he and the others could enter was the tenth floor. Because Xavier had been doing all the heavy lifting, they were under-levelled for the floor they were up to. The extra titles they'd received for being in his party would no doubt make up for that, but it wasn't guaranteed.

Without him, they might not be *able* to complete the tenth floor.

"You're worried you'll get stuck."

Howard shrugged. "It's something we've considered before, but we know it would never actually happen—that you don't plan to leave us behind. Still, we want to be on that floor *with* you. I sincerely doubt we'd be in any real danger. And if we are, better to have you there with us."

Xavier leant back in his seat. He supposed he didn't really know what the danger of this floor was, or even if he'd understood Sam's words correctly. He was worried about his friends, about their safety, but he also trusted their judgement and their choices. If they wanted to come along, then he wasn't going to talk them out of it without a truly good reason. He sighed. "All right." He stood up from his chair. "Let's get going."

Howard grinned. He slapped the table as he stood. "Finally!" The man looked ready and eager.

Xavier wondered what it would be like on Earth. He hoped

that when they got there, Howard and the others would actually be able to find their loved ones. He had a feeling it wouldn't be easy.

Before they entered the floor, Siobhan had a look in the System Shop at Xavier's request. He didn't *really* think this would be the last time they could look in the shop before returning to Earth, but just in case it was, he wanted to see if he could get that communication blocking device Sam had mentioned.

"Did he happen to say what it was *called*?" Siobhan asked after standing at the System Shop's terminal for several minutes. "Because the search terms I'm using aren't coming up with anything relevant at all."

"No, he certainly didn't," Xavier said. He tapped his foot on the floor of the Staging Room, growing a little impatient after about ten minutes had passed.

Finally, Siobhan let out a great big sigh and pushed away from the pedestal. "Sorry. I'm not having any luck."

"That's all right." Xavier ran a hand through his hair. "Honestly, an item like that did sound a little too good to be true. It would probably be far too expensive."

Howard slapped him on the shoulder. "Maybe we'll be able to find what we need on Earth. Or maybe you'll get one in your next loot box." The man didn't sound overly confident about that, but there was a bit of enthusiasm in his voice anyway.

Xavier took the hint. "Yes, right. Let's go, then."

***

Xavier materialised in a completely white room, so white that he couldn't see where the floor met the walls. It reminded him of somewhere the System had sent him before, when he'd first been integrated.

This is strange.

He gazed around, but there was no sign of the other members of his party.

We've been separated?

That wasn't good. Not for the others.

He summoned Charon's Scythe to his hand, something he hadn't bothered doing before coming onto the floor. He didn't have a good feeling about this.

Welcome to the tenth floor of the Tower of Champions! Congratulations for making it this far!
The Tower of Champions is a true test of the might of Denizens from different worlds all over the Greater Universe. The tenth floor differs from other floors in the tower, as it pits you against other Champions in real time!

Xavier tilted his head to the side as he read through the notification, not liking where it was going one bit.

As this floor is not a test of how well you work together as a team, you have been separated from the other members of your party. Each member of your party is off in an identical room, receiving the same information as you. Do not worry about them, for it is your own life that is at stake!

Well, that's bloody ominous, Xavier thought.

No wonder he'd had a bad feeling about this floor. This must have been what Sam had tried warning him about.

Couldn't have been a little more specific in your warning, could you, Sam?

He sighed and kept reading the notification.

The challenge on this floor is called The Melee.

The Melee?

His mind went to the first challenge the System had given him when he'd decided to become a Champion, foolishly not realising the consequences—though he would make the same choice again if he had to relive it. He'd been forced to fight another person from Earth who'd chosen to fight for their world, and had chosen to be a Champion.

He still hated that the System had made every one of them do that. So many good people had died. Had been forced to kill.

Xavier hadn't fought. He'd only lived by chance—because the man he'd faced was too honourable for the System he'd found himself in.

That SEAL could have killed me with one squeeze of his trigger.

Was this tenth-floor challenge going to be something like that?

Soon, you will be thrown into an arena and matched up with eleven other Champions from around the Greater Universe who have been deemed most similar in skill to you. Though this is not a fight to the death, many do not survive the encounter. Unlike on other floors, Champions who've reached the tenth floor and join the Melee have the option to yield to the enemy. Though the System does not tolerate cowards, there are some instances where surrender is the most prudent choice a Denizen can make.

However, surrender has consequences. Though it is an option, it is a shameful one.

Xavier shook his head as he read through the text. He was finding it hard to believe that the System would let *anyone* surrender. Not after what he'd seen happen to that SEAL.

He was struck by lightning simply because he said he wouldn't fight. He hadn't even been given so much as a warning.

He still saw the man, sometimes, when he closed his eyes. That sacrifice, even though it hadn't been intentional, still sat with him.

If a Champion surrenders during this melee, they will be barred from the Tower of Champions, lose half their levels, and not be allowed to return to their home planet for a hundred years.

He blinked, tilting his head to the side as he read the consequences. It made him worry about the other members of his party. Being separated from them. This melee... He imagined it would be a fight to the death, right? Why else would people be given the option to surrender? Siobhan was the one he was most worried about. She was a *healer*. Then again, she did have her Divine Guardian spell, giving her the ability to summon a construct to her side whenever she needed it.

Will she be strong enough to survive this?

Justin was fast and had the ability to fly. Xavier imagined the teenager would be safe enough, especially since the System supposedly sets people up that are on a similar level of skill.

Howard, he knew, would *never* surrender. The man was simply too stubborn for that. More than anything that man wanted to get back to his family. Being barred from Earth for a hundred years... wasn't necessarily a death sentence. It wasn't even the worst thing that could happen to them. But for that man, it wouldn't be seen as an option at all.

Never in a million years could I imagine Howard abandoning his family.

There was no more text to read. Xavier paced around the white room, recalling Sam's words. You *won't have any trouble.*

Finally, after he'd paced back and forth five times, a notification appeared.

You are being sent to The Melee in 3 seconds. Prepare yourself!

Chapter 78
The Melee

You are being sent to The Melee in 3 seconds. Prepare yourself!

Prepare yourself? Siobhan gulped. *I'm not bloody prepared!*

She gripped her staff more tightly than she ever head. When she'd first been integrated into the System, she'd fully intended to go the route of a damage-dealing mage, but things had changed soon after she'd met Xavier. That man didn't need her dealing damage, and another path had become the one she wished to walk.

Now, she hoped that wouldn't be the death of her.

She supposed they'd been right about this floor—it *was* different to the other ones. Though she couldn't say she was *glad* she'd been right.

And it turns out it didn't matter whether we all entered the floor at the same time or not, because the damned System separated us anyway!

Siobhan was teleported out of the white room and into what looked to be a massive arena. The arena reminded her of pictures she'd seen of the Colosseum. A part of her gazed up at the amazing sight with wonder, mouth dropping open. Under other circumstances, she might think this turn of events was pretty damned cool. She might wonder if this arena had been inspired by the Colosseum somehow, or if whoever had designed the Colosseum had somehow dreamed of this, like how humans knew of elves and other races that existed in the Greater Universe before ever *seeing* any.

But right now, well... it certainly *wasn't* cool.

She'd tried using her Communication Stone to contact Xavier and see how he was, but it wasn't working. The System kept telling her he was out of range.

Where the hell has the System sent me?

She supposed talking to him right now wouldn't help anyway. Besides, he'd been fighting their battles every floor. Now, it was time to fight one of her own.

She found herself standing on a small platform. Around her was a transparent shield, similar to Howard's Bulwark spell. She took her eyes away from the arena and found that she wasn't alone. Including her own, there were a dozen other platforms.

The System had just thrown her into the damned Hunger Games.

In that moment, Siobhan tried to summon her Divine Guardian, but something was blocking her—perhaps she wouldn't be able to cast any spells until the shield dropped.

Other people began to materialise on the other platforms. Many of them were human, though some of them were elves. One was demonkin. And the last to appear was something she couldn't identify. She tried to scan the... whatever it was, but the System was blocking her from that ability. The creature was about four feet tall and looked like a cross between a goblin and... a moose? It had purple skin and antlers half as tall as itself.

Weird, she thought, wondering if the moose-goblin thought the same of her kind.

A notification appeared in front of her.

The Melee is a challenge of survival! You will be marked on your participation!

Marked on my participation? Does that mean we can't refuse to fight?

Considering her abilities, Siobhan was intending to cast Divine Guardian and Divine Beacon and try not to move away from the healing pillar. It would give her better magical and physical resistance on top of the healing it offered. As for her Divine Guardian, she wanted to keep the construct close. If it wasn't near her, it wouldn't be able to protect her very well. She also had nothing against the other Champions that appeared. She didn't *want* to fight them.

But she'd been in a situation like this before. Last time, she hadn't had the choice to surrender—she might have taken it, rather than taking another life. This time, even though she *could* surrender, the very thought of doing so didn't seem like a viable choice.

The Melee will begin in 5 seconds and last for 5 minutes. If you are alive and have not surrendered by the time the Melee ends, then you will have successfully cleared this floor.

Siobhan blinked, reading the text. It wasn't half as bad as she'd suspected it would be.

All I have to do is survive for five minutes? Well, that... that can't be too hard, right?

She watched as the seconds ticked down. The other people on their circular platforms gripped swords, hammers, axes. Staffs, bows, and one even had an odd, harpoon-looking thing.

Okay, maybe it's going to be a bit hard.

But at least the text didn't say anything about her *having* to fight, only that she would be marked on her participation. That didn't matter so much to her. If she cleared this floor, she would still get a first-clear title and the normal title she was used to. Survive... she could survive.

The timer reached zero.

Justin held his sword too tightly. He forced himself to loosen his grip. It was a bad habit of his, one he'd had for years. Whenever he wasn't confident about the outcome of a match, he would grip the hilt of his sword ever tighter.

He did what his coach had taught him to do in these situations, taking long, slow breaths in a box-breathing pattern, counting the seconds as he inhaled, pausing, then counting the seconds as he exhaled. Though something told him his coach hadn't had fighting in an intergalactic arena against alien races in mind when he'd taught him this technique.

Doesn't mean it isn't useful.

He looked at the other platforms, wondering if he would find the other members of his party standing atop them, but everyone he saw was a stranger. There were a few humans—roughly half of the Champions—but the rest were an assortment of different races. There were a few dwarves, a single elf, and what looked to be a female orc.

Seeing so many humans made him wonder how they'd managed to populate the Greater Universe so thoroughly. Siobhan said it had something to do with convergent evolution. Justin couldn't say he understood how that could happen.

Figuring that out isn't really a priority right now, Justin told himself. *Now come on, get it together.*

He didn't want to fight these people. He didn't want to *kill* these people. The notification simply said they had to survive for five minutes. That meant killing wasn't strictly necessary, right?

Could we beat the System, and have everyone not *fight?*

The thought made him give a small shake of the head. Something told him that would most certainly not be possible. The

System had never been that... forgiving, in his experience. He was surprised that it had given them the option of surrendering at all. And Champions who'd made it this far in the tower certainly weren't going to take it easy on others.

I'll defend myself, and I'll kill if I have to.

Justin was getting back to Earth, whatever the cost.

Howard found himself growling without even realising it. God, this was a mess. He hadn't dreamt that something like this would actually happen. That he would get separated from the others. From Xavier. He scoffed at the idea of surrendering. Of being barred from Earth. Of never being able to return to his family.

I'd sooner die than let that happen.

The haft of his axe, the Bearded Menace, felt natural in his hand. His shoulders were tense, and he relaxed them. Tense situations were something he was used to. He'd been a cop for years. Though his training hadn't exactly prepared him for everything that had happened after the integration.

When the notification came, telling him he had to survive for five minutes, he chuckled to himself.

Survive. That sounds easy enough.

Howard was a Shield Sentinel. A class built on Toughness. On tanking. He hefted up his tower shield, holding it in front of him. He didn't cast his Bulwark spell, not yet. That would limit his mobility.

He went through the spells he had at his disposal, thinking of which ones would be useful to him right now.

Bulwark. Definitely useful. Hell, I could probably hide out within it for the entire five minutes if I really needed to, especially if the other Champions are distracted fighting each other. Taunt. I'm not sure if taunting these bastards is the best thing I could do in this situation...

In combat, he was used to being the one out front, trying to bring the enemies toward him. That was, assuming Xavier wasn't in the mix. In which case, he basically didn't need to do anything.

Martyr's Defence. That definitely won't need to come up. Hold Ground will come in handy. Backfire, Toughness Infusion, Power Strike...

Howard grinned. He felt confident. Perhaps he should be feeling something else right now. He didn't want to fight these strangers. They'd done nothing to him. The only reason he was here was because the bloody System had put him here. But now that he was? Well, he would have to embrace it if he wished to succeed.

The time reached zero. The barrier around a dozen platforms in the arena disappeared, releasing the Champions.

The Melee had begun.

Howard glanced to his left and right at the closest Champions. He took a step back, toward the arena's wall. What surprised him the most was the fact that the second the timer reached zero, three different Champions instantly disappeared. His eyebrows rose to the top of his forehead as he saw that.

Are there really people out there who would just... give up?

One of the Champions to disappear had been a human to his left. A goblin stood at his right. Goblins, one of the races currently invading his home world. Howard gritted his teeth and charged the creature. The goblin had a staff, wore mage robes.

I didn't even know goblins could enter the Tower of Champions.

A dozen fireballs sprang into life. They formed a protective, rotating circle around the goblin. The little green creature took a step back. He had his staff raised in one hand, and his other hand was held palm facing out toward him. The universal sign for *I've no beef with you, but I'll fight you if I have to.*

Howard blinked. Considering all the goblins he'd killed back on the sixth floor, this reaction was the last thing he'd expected.

These people truly aren't my enemy. They've just been thrown into the exact same situation as me.

Howard backed off from the goblin. He heard rushing foot-steps behind him and instantly activated two of his spells—Bulwark and Hold Ground.

Thump.

He turned around to see a human warrior, wielding a heavy hammer, nursing his head after having run straight into his barrier.

The arena around him was the picture of chaos. Howard's eyes widened as he found that four Champions were lying dead on the ground. All of them were near another Champion at the far end. The Champion wore white robes and an odd mask that reminded Howard of a Japanese kabuki mask, only creepier. The Champion didn't have a weapon. Their hands were raised in what appeared to be a placating, *I'm unarmed*, gesture.

The dead bodies around the Champion clearly showed that even unarmed, this person was *very* dangerous.

Suddenly, five minutes felt like a very long time.

Thump.

The warrior's face was apple-red as he slammed his hammer into Howard's Bulwark.

Why so determined? Howard wondered.

Looking at the age of the warrior attacking him, he was about as young as Justin, which made sense. In fact, the majority of the Champions around him looked rather young—those he could tell the age of, at least. He was surely the oldest one there.

Humans on already integrated worlds get the System when they turn sixteen, the equivalent is likely the same for other races, which means I'm fighting a bunch of teenagers.

Just because they were teenagers didn't mean they weren't dangerous. As he watched the hammer-wielding warrior attack his Bulwark, he noticed there were two different types of Champions in the arena. Those happy to stand back and only fight when they needed to—like the goblin, or the white-robed, masked Champion. And those who wished to attack—like the warrior in front of him and those dead Champions around the other man.

As far as he could tell, every single one of these people was from an already integrated world. They would know several things that he didn't.

The System said something about being marked on our partici-pation. Do we get more rewards for killing others?

He looked at the kid in front of him, hearing the *thump, thump, thump* of his hammer, and wondered if killing was *really* something he wanted to do. He'd been keen on it at the start, at the sight of the goblin, but this felt different to a normal floor.

He glanced over at the goblin. An elf attacked the fire-wielding mage. Unlike Howard, this elf didn't back down when the goblin raised its hand. The elf lost the fight, and quite easily at that—he burned almost in an instant.

I thought the System threw us in with people on roughly the same level of skill?

That certainly didn't seem to be the case, not from what he'd seen.

Thump, thump, thump.

Howard swallowed. Killing teenagers wasn't exactly what he had in mind, but this kid packed quite the punch. His Bulwark spell certainly wasn't going to survive for much longer.

Thump.

The Bulwark burst, and the warrior rushed toward him.

Chapter 79
The White-Masked Figure

Howard's eyes widened as his Bulwark barrier burst at the might of the warrior's hammer strike. He cursed the System for putting him in this situation. For throwing him into an arena, forced to fight other Champions.

At least they aren't Champions from Earth...

He wasn't a fool. When his Bulwark spell had been up, he hadn't just stood there idly watching as it was ever more weakened by the hammer-wielding warrior attacking it. He'd been infusing Toughness Energy into his armour and into his shield to further strengthen them. He'd also activated two of his spells: Hold Ground and Backfire.

Howard might not be a focused damage dealer, but he packed a wallop when he wanted to. He might not have anything against any of the Denizens here, but he wasn't just going to stand by while they tried to kill him.

The warrior slammed his hammer into Howard's shield—he wanted to get an idea of the guy's level of strength.

BAM!

Holy crap.

Howard was pushed back a step. The Hold Ground spell shattered in an instant.

How strong is this guy?

Howard had never been pushed back so easily. He had a skill called Immovable, which helped him stay in one place. It paired perfectly with Hold Ground. And yet... it had done barely anything against that hammer strike. His shield had vibrated something fierce, the strength of the attack shaking his arm.

Who have I been thrown in this arena with?

He held his shield up high, despite the pain his arm was in from the initial strike, and took another hit.

BAM!

Howard gritted his teeth. The hammer-wielding warrior was too strong. At this rate, he was going to take out Howard's shield arm. That was simply something he couldn't let happen. He was starting to wonder what he'd gotten himself into. The System said it was making them face Champions of their own skill, but the Champions here... They seemed to vary quite considerably in power.

I can do this.

Howard took a third strike on his shield and could have sworn that the hammer *dented* it. This time, however, he hadn't been pushed backward. A moment before the hammer strike was to hit, he pushed forward, shortening the man's attack.

He's not a man, Howard couldn't help but think. *He's just a kid.*

Howard pushed that thought out of his mind.

He couldn't afford to think of this kid as just any, young teenager. This was the enemy. Someone who was trying to kill him. Nothing more than a threat that needed to be eliminated.

He slammed his double-bearded axe into the man's neck. At least, that's where he tried to slam it. The warrior was faster than Howard had expected. Somehow, he was already out of the way when the axe strike fell. He'd slipped away from Howard's attack as though he were as fast and nimble as Justin.

How could this kid be this fast?

Howard cursed himself.

Stop thinking of him as a kid! It's holding you back!

He wasn't sure why he was having so much difficulty with this. It wasn't as though he hadn't been in situations like this before, back when he'd been a cop. He'd had to deal with more than one violent teenager in his time, and he hadn't had any trouble subduing them.

Then again, it wasn't exactly as though subduing them was what he had on his agenda right now. If he focused on that, he surely wouldn't survive this fight.

He needed to go all out.

BAM!

Another hammer strike slammed into his tower shield, denting it a second time. Howard glanced around the arena, making sure there weren't any other Champions about to attack him. Then he looked the hammer-wielding warrior in the eye. "You really want to do this?" he snarled at the Champion. "Okay then, let's dance."

Howard came in. A horizontal slash, for the man's side. *Dodged.* An overhead, skull-splitting strike. *Dodged.*

He's too fast.

Howard growled and stepped back. He raised his shield, knowing he wasn't fast enough to get out of the way of the man's attack. His hammer strikes, though well and truly telegraphed, were too swift for Howard to get out of the way. Howard hadn't exactly spent many of his stat points on his Speed attribute, something that had never been an issue in the past. Howard was a tank, after all. He didn't *need* to be fast; he could just stand there and take it.

Which made him realise he'd been going about this fight all wrong. This Champion was strong, but that didn't mean he was strong enough to kill Howard in a single strike, even if he'd been able to dent his shield. That just wasn't going to happen.

But who takes a hit on purpose?

Someone with the Backfire skill.

Howard flung his shield out of the way a split second before the hammer was to fall onto it. The hammer strike slammed into

559

his abdomen instead. He'd braced himself for the hit, knowing where it would contact him. Even so, it winded him, and he heard —and felt—a *crack*. One or more of his ribs had definitely broken.

Now, Backfire wasn't the most powerful spell. It didn't actually do anything to prevent Howard from taking damage. But it *did* put half of any damage he took back on his enemy. And with Toughness being Howard's most powerful attribute, he could take a lot more damage than the average warrior.

The hammer wielder hissed in pain as the damage backfired onto him. The pain made the man falter, and it was time for Howard to sweep in and take advantage.

He activated Power Strike. His axe cleaved for the closest target—the man's arm.

His axe made contact. It didn't cut all the way through the arm. Didn't sever the limb like he might have expected. But it did break it. Made it entirely unusable—at least for the next few minutes when it would really count.

Howard didn't hesitate. He lunged forward and slammed his shield into the warrior's head. The warrior's head snapped backward. Howard followed that up with a swift kick to the man's chest. A kick that sent him flying backward. Howard might not be as strong as this kid, but that didn't mean he was weak.

The moment the kid slammed into the ground, Howard took a step back. He activated his Bulwark spell. The barrier sprang back up. He was glad he'd gotten his Toughness stat up so high, reducing the cooldown of the spell significantly. This whole time, he'd been working himself up to killing the young Champion he faced, but now maybe he wouldn't have to.

With his Bulwark up, Howard looked around the arena again, seeing how many of the other Champions were left.

The mysterious Denizen who wore the strange mask had even more corpses gathered about them. Strange how the other contenders kept running at the powerful Denizen.

The goblin mage stood proudly. Two corpses around him.

And that was it—those were the only Champions, besides the

hammer wielder—who remained. The rest were either dead, or they'd surrendered.

There were still a few minutes left until the floor ended. Howard watched as the hammer wielder stood. His hammer had fallen out of his hand. He took it back up and tried to hold it in both hands, but holding it with his right arm—the arm that Howard had injured—clearly hurt too much. He kept it in his left.

Don't attack again, kid. It won't end well for you.

The Champion stared at Howard. There was hatred in his eyes. An anger that burned bright. It made Howard wonder what his life had been like.

Suddenly, the warrior turned. He looked over at the white-masked figure.

"Don't do it," Howard muttered. "Just wait it out."

The Champion sprinted toward the powerful denizen. He held his massive hammer in a single hand.

Howard's eyes widened. Was the kid an idiot? Why would he go after someone who was clearly the most powerful Denizen here? It didn't make any sense to him.

The goblin mage took several steps back, its eyes wide with fear, watching what was happening.

The hammer-wielding warrior let out a war cry. The white-masked figure stood calmly, awaiting the attack. An overhead strike came for him.

White-Mask raised a single hand and stopped the hammer dead.

How strong is this Denizen?

Howard glanced at his dented shield, then looked back at the fight unfolding in front of him. White-Mask wrapped his fingers around the hammer head and—the hammer head cracked.

What the hell?

The hammer was shoved out of the way. White Mask gripped Hammer Wielder's head with his other hand.

It he going to crush his skull?

Howard stood rooted to the spot. He didn't like this. Not one bit.

A glowing silver light emanated from White-Mask's hand. Behind the mask, the figure's eyes glowed with the same silver light.

That's similar to Xavier's glow!

Howard had no idea what was happening. It didn't seem to be a damage-dealing spell.

Hammer-Wielder's entire body shuddered. He screamed in what must have been terrible agony as the silver light enveloped his head. Howard glared at White-Mask. Whoever that Champion was, they clearly had the power to give this man a swift death, or not kill him at all if they wished. Hammer-Wielder was by no means a threat to White-Mask, that was clear as day.

After a moment, the silver glow faded. The screaming stopped. Hammer-Wielder let out a pitiful whine.

He's still alive.

White-Mask cocked his head to the side and twisted his wrist.

Snap.

The warrior's neck broke. The kid fell to the ground, falling into one of the other corpses. Another one for the pile.

White-Mask let his arm drop, looking just as calm as he had before.

Howard swallowed. The worst was over, wasn't it? He was one of only three Champions left, and as powerful as White-Mask was, he'd only attacked those that had attacked him. Goblin-Mage didn't look as though they were about to attack anyone. He wondered if the System would intervene if all three of them just stood there.

Goblin-Mage was stepping backward. It still had that ring of fireballs rotating around it in a constant flow.

Then Goblin-Mage's posture shifted. They gripped their staff tighter. Their lips pulled back in a bestial snarl.

And they bolted forward, heading straight for White-Mask.

What... what the hell!?

"Oh," Howard uttered, as he finally realised what must be happening. With the shock of all that had been going on, it had taken him far too long to realise it, but now that he had, it was far too obvious. Other Champions kept running at the figure in the white mask, despite the Denizen's clear power, because they were being *taunted*—or at least, their minds were being influenced somehow.

This is not good.

Howard watched, unable to do a damned thing, as Goblin-Mage attacked White-Mask. They didn't attack like a mage should have. The goblin didn't need to run in close. That was the absolute worst thing for them to do. The goblin still flung fireballs toward their enemy, but the fireballs just slammed into the figure without seeming to bother them at all. Howard had seen a Denizen shrug off attacks like that.

Xavier could do that with ease...

Whoever this person was, they couldn't be as powerful as Xavier, could they? That didn't seem possible at all. Xavier was a damned E Grade Denizen already!

No. They aren't that strong. But they're far stronger than they should be for this floor.

Goblin-Mage came in close, and suffered from the same treatment that Hammer-Wielder had. In moments, they were just another corpse littered on the ground.

Howard looked at the countdown timer.

The Melee has 2 minutes and 21 seconds remaining.

He wasn't surprised not much time had passed, but he was *pissed.*

Is this the end of me?

He didn't want to surrender. Not if there was even the smallest chance that he could return to Earth. What good would he be, barred from his home planet for a hundred years? How could he be away from his family for that long? Things were different now, he knew. A hundred years wasn't a lifetime, not when a Denizen's lifespan could stretch into thousands of years as they grew in power, but he would never forgive himself if something happened to his wife and kids and he wasn't there to stop it. Not in a hundred years. Not in a *million* years.

Maybe his taunt spell won't work in me...

It was a foolish thought. Whoever White-Mask was, they were on a different level of power entirely to Howard. It would be a different story if Xavier were here.

But I'm not about to give up.

Howard prepared himself for it. He saw it coming. Knew what was about to happen. At first, it was just a single thought. A thought that sounded as though it came from his own mind.

Attack them. Kill them.

The thought was easy to shrug off. Then it became more insistent. More powerful. He kept telling himself the idea wasn't his own. Kept telling himself he didn't need to listen.

Then, suddenly, his mind shifted. He blinked. He wasn't standing in the arena anymore. He was standing in his living room back on Earth. And so was the figure in the White-Mask. In one hand, the figure held Howard's daughter's head. In the other hand, he held Howard's wife's head. At the figure's feet, his son lay on the ground, a foot at his throat.

"No!" Howard sprinted forward. His mind was filled with only one thing—the desire to protect his family and kill White-Mask. In the back of his mind, a voice whispered to him that this wasn't real. But how could he believe that voice over what his own eyes were showing him? How could he believe that voice when every other part of his mind urged him to attack? To protect?

He did not get in a single strike.

A hand was gripping his head. A silver light enveloped him. Then pain like he'd never felt before took over.

[*Let's see what we have here.*]

The voice sounded in his mind. It wasn't his own. He'd never heard the voice before. It was light, feminine, and filled with immense power. Suddenly Howard's entire mind was laid bare, and all that he was was revealed to the person—the woman—who held his head. His life flicked before his eyes, so fast he could barely make it out, until more recent memories, of the tower, of the floors, and—specifically—of Xavier, were shown.

[*Ahhh. Well, isn't this interesting?*]

The grip on Howard's head released. He fell to his knees. The pain... he still felt such immense pain. As though his very mind had been shattered, cracked into a thousand tiny pieces, and he didn't know how to put it back together.

"Do you wish to live, Howard of Earth?" The voice was no longer speaking in his mind. It was coming from behind the white mask. The woman had her head cocked. Her eyes retained their silver glow. "Do you wish to protect your family?"

Howard swallowed. "Yes," he said. Speaking was difficult. His shattered mind barely worked.

"What will you do to get back to them?"

"Anything." The word slipped out of his mouth before his mind could even catch up.

"Goooood," the woman crooned. "Very goood. We have very little time, Howard of Earth, but just enough for us to make a contract. Will you do that?"

Howard gritted his teeth. He could surrender, right now.

No. I can't abandon them.

"Yes."

The woman produced something from her Storage Ring. It materialised in her hand, and she passed it to him.

Howard didn't need to scan it to know what it was. He'd seen one—or rather, *two*—before.

A Communication Stone.

"Now," the woman said. "Let's make this quick."

Chapter 80
Easy Prey

Xavier raised an eyebrow as he looked around the arena. This place... It reminded him of the Colosseum in Rome. He would have thought the arena was beautiful, if not for the brutality of what it was used for.

He reread the message from the System.

The Melee is a challenge of survival! You will be marked on your participation!

He frowned, tilting his head to the side. He stood on a small, circular platform, one just big enough to fit his feet, really. There was a barrier around him. Something told him that even *he* wouldn't be able to break through that barrier, considering it had clearly been made by the System. There were eleven other identical platforms and barriers, with eleven other Champions standing upon them. If he'd read this correctly, the other Champions were from all around—not just their sector, but the Greater Universe. They could be from *anywhere*.

And though the System had said he would be placed with Champions of similar skill to his own, he had trouble believing that was true, or, well, even *possible*.

Yeah, that doesn't scream of arrogance or anything.

Xavier bit his lip. *Siobhan. Justin. Howard. What if they can't get through this alone? What if they can't survive without my help?"*

He had to push those worries from his mind. Sam had warned him, and he hadn't listened, but it wasn't as though they had a choice. They would have had to go through with this. If they had stalled for too long, the System would have forced them to do this floor. That was another thing Sam had told Xavier, back when he'd asked about the other Champions who refused to move forward on their floors.

The System liked giving consequences for inaction.

Which meant Xavier had a moral dilemma to sort out and barely any seconds left before the timer reached zero to come to a decision. He was trying to get number 1 on every single floor that he could. The challenge of this floor was fighting these other Champions, and if he was being marked on participation, wouldn't that mean he was marked more highly by, well, killing more of them?

If he wanted a chance to get the number 1 title for this floor, he should do what he always did—kill every single enemy before him as swiftly as possible.

But this was different to the other floors he'd been on.

They're just people like me. What if one of those Champions was Siobhan? Justin? Or Howard? What if they were just some innocent kid from a galaxy far, far away?

He bit his lip. None of these people were likely to be *innocent*. They would have all killed before to become Champions in the first place. But that fact alone didn't make any of these people his enemy. As many people as Xavier had killed through the different floors, like when he'd been facing the Endless Horde, slaughtering soldiers by the thousands, he'd still tried to protect the lives of those who deserved protecting.

Then again, maybe that was just something he was being naive about. Something he was applying his twenty-first century Earth logic to, just like when he thought he didn't want to invade other planets, even though it might be what he'd need to do in the future.

Will this floor even have a top 100 leaderboard? Is seems so different to the other floors. This scenario isn't something that can be replicated, because the Champions will always be different Champions, meaning the challenge will never be the same.

Xavier sighed. One second left on the countdown timer. One second for him to decide what to do here.

He thought of the operative word in the notification. *Participation.* That could mean a lot of things.

Arturous Lothbrokian gripped his chains tightly. The tenth floor. He'd been looking forward to this one. He couldn't wait to be pitted against Champions from all over the Greater Universe. Couldn't wait to prove that he, Arturous, was their better.

He held his head high and blinked, looking around at the other contenders, trying to appear disinterested.

They don't really look like much, do they?

His instincts told him to use his Identify skill on them, but he knew that was futile. Identify didn't work on the tenth floor. *Everyone* knew that. He scoffed to himself. *Some of these idiots might not know that. They could be from some backwater baby planet that's just been integrated into the System.*

He gripped his chains more tightly as his gaze swept from one Champion to the next, then it paused on a man in dark robes, holding some sort of scythe-looking thing. *That's an odd poleaxe.* He tilted his head to the side, examining the man's face. He was human, like Arturous, but he was most certainly older than System age. *At least* five winters older. The only explanation for that was...

Arturous chuckled to himself. *Easy prey.* He'd actually encountered one. New blood. The Greater Universe was so unimaginably large, the frontier of the System so far away from Arturous's sector, that he hadn't imagined he would encounter new blood even in ten thousand years.

And yet, here one stands before me. This is going to be fun.

The countdown reached zero. Arturous's chains were wrapped around his fists. His mother had looked down on his combat style.

She called it *savage*. Said it relied too heavily on being in close quarters. Arturous, like all from his family, chose his fighting style at the age of five. He'd been given many options by his mother, father, and his dedicated trainer, Rainolt. Rainolt had been the one who'd presented the chains to him. Arturous had been captivated by them.

On occasion, Arturous had wondered if his mother had been right. Wondered if he'd made some sort of mistake in his choice. There were many things he hadn't known before he'd gained the System. All the training he'd been able to undertake was *before* he'd gained the System and his actual skills and spells, and he finally had the opportunity to gain levels.

The more enlightened planets really should get the System at an earlier age, especially those from families like mine. It's only fair, considering we're superior.

He'd been telling his mother to inform the System of this since he was eight—he hadn't wanted to wait *eight more years*. She'd always just brushed him off.

He raised his fists. His mother had been right about one thing. His fighting style *was* savage. But it turned out that's exactly the way he liked it.

When the barrier around his platform and every other platform disappeared, Arturous activated Shadow Step, a spell that let him teleport into his enemy's shadow. He was going straight after the new blood.

He appeared just behind the man, but something wasn't right. A purple mist flowed outward from the dark-robed figure. A mist that he recognised. *Willpower Energy.* He scoffed internally, going in for a punch. There was no way that Willpower Energy alone would be strong enough to overtake his powerful mind—

It seeped into him. Through his nose. Through his mouth. Through his *eyes*.

This is rather unpleasant!

He threw up all of his mental barriers. He'd been trained in the art of meditation. Trained in the art of blocking unwanted thoughts. Trained in blocking unwanted control, even, as it was proven if one used Willpower Energy on someone who hadn't yet been integrated at System age, having them try and fight it off gave a boost in their stats, even if only marginal.

His barriers were shattered. It felt as though they hadn't been there at all, and suddenly, his body froze in place, his fists and chains an inch from striking the man's back.

All he could do was blink and look around, as he'd received a mental command to *stop*. What he saw terrified him.

His parents had warned him about what becoming a Champion could mean. Told him it might be too rich for his blood. He'd ignored them, of course, as he often did. He wanted to experience the Tower of Champions. He was from an elite family. His parents were B Grade, for System's sake.

Yet maybe they'd been right.

Every single one of the other contenders had frozen in place alongside him. The man in the dark robes glanced about. He had a somewhat bored expression on his face, an air of disinterest so perfect there was no way it could be crafted. He sighed, as though being here at all were a herculean task, then he hiked up his robes slightly and sat cross-legged in the middle of the arena, muttering something about hoping this would be considered full participation.

Then he just... waited.

Arturous's eyes widened the more he stared at the man. He did some mental math, trying to figure out how it could be possible for someone to do what this man was doing. Controlling *one* other Champion of an equivalent level—that *might* be possible for a second or two. Maybe longer, if the Champion doing the controlling were particularly gifted, but this? How could he expect to control someone for *five minutes*?

And it wasn't just *one* of them he controlled. It was *all* of them. Eleven Champions, all who'd made it to the tenth floor, all who'd been matched up with him, Arturous Lothbrokian, so they must have at least a decent level of power...

Yet this man was controlling all of them and showing not even a hint of mental strain.

Th-that's impossible! Who in the Greater Universe is this monster!?

Arturous stood there, absolutely frozen and completely unable to move. A simple command of *stop* had been enough to make him just... stop. A fear began to grow in his chest. One he'd never felt before. He'd done everything right. He'd been training on each floor again and again and again before clearing them, gaining as many levels as he possibly could from them—or so he thought.

He'd been in this damned tower for *months*.

Maybe I should surrender. If I surrender, I'll be barred from my home, lose half my levels, but I'll still be alive. Besides, in the grand scheme, one hundred years really isn't that long.

It wasn't as though he'd be the first in his family to flunk out of the Tower of Champions. Kulrous, one of his older brothers—like, *really* old, the guy was over two hundred years old when Arturous was born—apparently only made it to the tenth floor, too.

I really shouldn't have made fun of him so much for that. I was a fool. I should have listened to my mother.

That was a lesson he wouldn't forget. And a hundred years away from his home planet... well, it wasn't as though they didn't own multiple planets in their sector. He'd still have access to the family's bank account. He'd be able to live in luxury. Maybe take a break from levelling for a few years to recover from this trauma...

It wouldn't be cowardly. This man is a monster.

Arturous willed himself to surrender, but... the System wasn't responding! Something was stopping him from communicating with it properly!

Oh no... he's not letting us surrender! He's going to kill us all!

Xavier rested Charon's Scythe along his legs and looked at the other contenders. One of them, the kid with chains wrapped around his fists, had actually been close to punching him in the back. He could have slipped the attack, or whirled around and blocked it, but he was impressed by the kid's swift teleportation and Speed attribute.

Higher than Justin's, that's for sure.

He tapped his fingers on the haft of his scythe-staff. The worry about his friends hadn't left him, but he was no longer worried about killing these people. Controlling every single one of them so thoroughly? Making it impossible for them to attack him, or anyone else? That *had* to gain him full marks for participation, right?

And it means they'll all survive this. Really, I'm doing them a service.

Besides, maybe he could gain something from this. There was still over four and a half minutes left, after all.

Xavier cleared his throat. "Can any of you tell me about the next floors of the tower?"

Chapter 81
Grave Robbing

Justin didn't like this one bit. The barrier around him came down. He took a step backward. It wasn't that he was worried about killing these people—maybe he *should* be worried about that, but he wasn't. He'd do what do what he needed to do to survive, just as he had been doing since the System arrived on Earth and changed everything.

No, what he was worried about was *losing*.

I want to get back to Earth. Want to find my mother... and I want to protect everyone.

There was something else that he wanted, too. If he were completely honest with himself, he didn't want to be separated from his party. He'd become close with them. Especially with Siobhan and Howard, as the three of them spent so much time together while Xavier was off doing his thing.

And he didn't want to be separated from Xavier.

The world... *everything*... had changed so damned dramatically. Before the System had come, he'd thought he'd had pretty much everything figured out. He was an Olympic athlete at the age of sixteen! That was quite a feat. He knew he'd get a scholarship to the college he wanted to go to. He knew he wanted to study to be an engineer. His path was laid out for him...

Then it had all changed.

Xavier could singlehandedly save Earth. Anyone who stands by his side is going to be protected. Become powerful. Rich, even.

He wanted that security; after all, he'd seen being taken from place to place by the Tower of Champions. He wanted to get in on the ground floor. Be part of the new elite, the new protectors of Earth.

We'll be like the Avengers. Protecting our world from alien threats. It's going to be awesome.

A few seconds after the barrier had come down, three different contenders disappeared.

What the hell? They've surrendered already?

That was the last thing he'd been expecting. Justin had to assume that the majority of Champions who made it here were from already integrated worlds, because most worlds in the Greater Universe had been integrated for hundreds, thousands, millions, some even *billions* of years, so statistically, there would simply be far more integrated worlds than non-integrated worlds, right?

Did some Champions enter the tower already knowing they would surrender when they got to this point? Were they too cowardly to deal with this challenge? He had trouble imagining that, considering what the first challenge that a Champion had to go through was—fighting another person from their own world who also wished to be a Champion.

He swallowed. Maybe this fight was even more dangerous than that one had been.

Of course it's more dangerous. That was before any of us got integrated. Before we got our classes, spells, skills, levels...

One of the closest Champions next to him attacked. They sprinted toward Justin. It was a warrior, wearing full armour similar to the full-plate that Howard wore. He even had a tower shield and an axe like Howard did, though he lacked a beard.

He looks so young. As young as I am.

Justin didn't hesitate. He used Slip Dodge to get out of the way, activated Winged Flight, then sent an Air Strike straight into the man's flank. The ranged attack took his enemy by surprise. It didn't move him—if he were a tank, he'd be damned tough—but it did make the man falter.

He's slow, just like Howard is slow. I can work with that.

Justin used his peripheral vision to ensure there were no other threats nearby, then he went in for the kill.

He turned off the part of his brain that worried about whether he *should* be killing—that was no longer useful to him, he'd discovered that pretty fast after the System had come down.

It's a new reality. Kill or be killed. If I'm threatened, I'm not going to use half measures.

His strikes were fast, precise. The warrior, supposedly a tank, had been foolish to rush him. Justin was now within the man's Bulwark radius—which meant he couldn't activate the spell and keep him outside of it. Justin had sparred with Howard enough times to know how to get around his tricks. This warrior might not have the exact same moves and spells, but it was close enough.

Justin's sword was long and slender. It made it through the gaps in the other man's armour. The slit under his arm. Into his neck. And finally, straight through the slit in the man's helm and through one of his eyes. A kill notification came up. Justin dismissed it and looked at the rest of the battlefield.

He blinked. Three Champions, not including the one he'd just fought, were already dead. The rest were... were they frozen?

In the centre of the arena, a woman with striking purple eyes and long, purple hair stood. She was clearly a mage—even her robes were purple. She had a smirk on her face, and she was... well, she was *beautiful*.

Not the time to think about that, Justin!

In one hand, the woman held a staff, raised high. Her other hand was also raised but empty, palm facing outward. The other contenders—the ones who remained alive—had all appeared to try and attack her. And they weren't frozen, exactly. They were... moving in slow motion.

Very slow motion. So slow that at first, he'd only thought they were frozen. Justin stepped away from the man he'd just killed—the teenager, someone of his own age. For a moment, he'd been surprised that all of the Champions around him were so young—for it wasn't only the one he'd fought and defeated who was—but then he realised why.

People are integrated at age sixteen, just like I was, or some sort of equivalent age depending on their world or race. Of course they're all my age. It makes the most sense.

And yet here this woman was, who looked just about as young as he was—though held herself as though she were older—exhibiting an immense amount of power and control, not to mention enjoyment. She was smiling in his direction in a way that gave him butterflies in his stomach. 'Cause he was, um, afraid.

Yeah, that's why.

Justin bit his lip. Not even a full minute had passed yet. He didn't really know what he should do in that moment except stand there. The mage clearly had some sort of localised time manipulation, which, admittedly, was incredibly cool. Justin folded his wings behind him—they had a much longer duration these days—and glanced around the arena. There were enough stands to fit thousands upon thousands of people, yet every single seat was empty. He tilted his head to the side.

This was once a real place, wasn't it?

The woman cleared her throat. "What, are you just going to stand there?"

Justin blinked at her. She had that same, self-satisfied smile on her face. She looked as smug as he might after winning a fencing match. "Well..." He gestured toward all of the frozen Champions, and then at the dead ones on the ground. "Seemed like the wise thing to do, considering how all of these ended up."

"You figured the best thing you could do was to do nothing?" She raised an eyebrow.

"Where are you from?" Justin asked. He was glad the System

was translating their languages. The mage might be human, but that didn't mean she spoke anything even close to English.

"I'm not sure I should answer that."

Justin sheathed his sword. Every instinct in his body and mind told him that wasn't a good idea, but he did it anyway. Sometimes you just have to take a chance. Something told him that if this woman wanted to kill every Champion here, she could do it with ease, and his sword being drawn wouldn't do a thing to stop it.

He knelt by the corpse of the warrior he'd just killed and pulled the man's Storage Ring right off his finger.

"You're grave-robbing the poor fellow?"

Justin grunted—a habit he'd probably learnt from Howard—and stood up, turning the ring in his hand. "Well, it's not much use to him anymore." He nudged the corpse with a foot. "And this isn't exactly what I'd call a *grave*."

"The spoils of war are often ill-gotten rewards."

Justin frowned at the woman. "That's an interesting way to see things, especially considering..." He gestured toward the arena, trying to encompass the entire Greater Universe at large. "Everything."

The woman tilted her chin up. "Where are *you* from?"

Justin considered his next words. He brushed a small patch of the arena's dirt with his foot, kicking away a few pebbles, then sat cross-legged on the ground.

"By all means, get comfortable."

He watched as one of the Champions the woman had frozen inched a little closer to her. It was an orc—a race he wasn't sure he'd seen before, and only really knew from *Lord of the Rings* and video games.

Is there any harm in telling her where I'm from?

"I'm from a newly integrated world."

The woman's eyes widened briefly. Her smile slipped, then suddenly became more vibrant. "Really? You're at the Edge?" She took a step forward. "That's fantastic! I've always wanted to see the Edge, but travelling that far..."

The spark of excitement in her eyes and her smile betrayed her age. She was definitely a teenager, just like him, even if she could pass for older.

Justin checked the timer. Three and a half minutes left. This melee, so far, wasn't at all what he'd expected. A fight to the death? Check and completed, without taking a single scratch. Talking to a pretty girl who could probably crush him with a single spell? That hadn't been a part of his expectations.

Looks like I'll be getting back to Earth after all. He'd been a little worried there. But not so much anymore.

"You must be from somewhere where the System is already established?"

The mage nodded vigorously, her purple hair bobbing around her face as she did. "My sector has been integrated for... a billion years?" She shook her head. "Something like that. I mean, that's basically *forever*!"

"Your sector... a *billion* years? The history of my people doesn't stretch back a fraction that far! Not even the dinosaurs were alive back then..." He'd known this was possible, of course, but actually meeting someone from a world that had not only been around for so long but had been inhabited by intelligent life for just as long? It felt... well, *insane*! "A billion years..."

The woman tilted her head to the side. "You know my sector's still considered young by many of the older ones, right?" She smirked.

"Honestly, that just boggles my mind," he replied. "Why do you want to travel to the Edge?" He'd never heard it called that before, but he liked the way it sounded. "Something tells me it's safer where you are, somewhere that's... established."

"I want to see the frontier! I want to experience something *new*. You must still have wars." She shook her head. "It's such a strange thing to even contemplate."

"You... don't have wars?" Justin scratched the back of his neck. "I thought the System was all about pushing conflict?"

The woman shook her head and gave a sigh. "It is, but that

doesn't mean you have to give in to it." She waved a hand at the arena, at what was happening. "There are... ways around the System, if you know how to manipulate it." She tilted her head forward. "Many ways. My sector is peaceful..." She paused, now having a sad look about her. "Not all are. Most aren't... but mine is, because of the one who rules it. I suppose I wouldn't need to go to the Edge to see war."

Justin frowned. Ways around the System? What did that even mean? That simply didn't seem like something that could be possible. How, exactly, could one get around the System? It was powerful enough to change entire *galaxies*, to bend them toward its will.

"How?"

The woman smiled sadly. "The System is watching. Besides, I can't go spilling these secrets. Not while I'm under contract. My family are... very tight-lipped about their abilities and knowledge. It's rather unfair, really. For others."

"Ways around the System," Justin muttered. The words stuck with him. How could they not? If there were ways to circumvent the System restrictions... what exactly could that *mean*? The System was what was stopping them from being back on Earth permanently right now. What if they somehow found a way to travel to Earth whenever they wished?

"I can see I've put a few ideas in your head," the woman said.

Justin nodded. "A few."

The woman walked over to him. Perhaps he should have been afraid of the powerful Champion, but he was used to being around power after having spent so much time around Xavier, and though he didn't exactly trust this woman, he didn't feel as though she were a threat to him.

She sat a few feet across from him on the dirt floor of the arena. "We only have a couple of minutes left. Tell me about your world?"

Chapter 82
A Dangerous Game

THE MOMENT THE BARRIER DISAPPEARED, SIOBHAN RAN. She turned and sprinted away from the circle of Champions. The last thing she wanted was to get mixed up in the initial frenzy she was sure was about to happen. She remembered watching the *Hunger Games*. Being in the thick of things, where death could come in an instant, wasn't where she wanted to be.

As she ran, she summoned her Divine Guardian. A purple puddle of light materialised on the ground, quickly forming into her construct as it rose, becoming solid. She ran and got behind it, hiding and not feeling ashamed even in the slightest.

The construct was a walking suit of full-plate armour, far taller and broader than herself. When she'd first summoned it, it had been seven feet tall. As she'd ranked up the ability, it had grown a few inches. Regrettably, she hadn't had a chance to train with it as much as she'd liked.

When she looked back at the middle of the arena, two of the other Champions were already dead, and four were missing.

Six left, including myself. And how can four be missing? What, were they obliterated or something?

She glanced around the arena, wondering if they'd simply moved as she had. Then she looked up. Ever since Justin had gotten wings, she'd kept reminding herself to look up for enemies. They were rarely above her, but when they were, she was glad for the habit.

All clear up there too.

Then it came to her—they'd... surrendered?

She supposed she couldn't blame them. Surrendering was certainly an option for her, but it wasn't one she wanted to consider. Though out of all the members of her party, she had a Communication Stone. A direct line of contact with Xavier—even if it currently didn't work right now because she was out of range—would certainly work if she surrendered and was sent to another world within her sector.

Siobhan bit her lip.

That's a last resort. A very, very last resort. I don't want to be away from everyone for a hundred years. Besides, how would I even be able to survive out there on my own? What if I was sent to a hostile world where everything was at a higher level than me and also wanted me dead? I'd be so doomed.

She didn't waste any time. The remaining Champions in the middle were all focused on each other and blessedly *not* on her. She wondered if it was obvious that she was a support class, and that they were ignoring her because she didn't look like a threat— not that she thought she *was* a threat.

Divine Beacon!

She rarely got to use her Divine Beacon spell. It had the draw- back of needing to remain in a single place, but right now she didn't want to be moved. A puddle of white light—similar to the purple puddle that had formed into her Divine Guardian—had materi- alised. The pillar shot upward out from it, growing to five feet in height. That pillar's height was also the length of its radius, which meant she was under its protection as long as she didn't step out of the dim aura it provided to the area.

Siobhan glanced at the timer. Only ten seconds had gone by. She watched the other Champions. Another of them disappeared after taking a sword slash to their shoulder, one that sliced straight through their armour. The woman must have surrendered when she realised she was outmatched.

That's a dangerous game, that is.

There were only five Champions in the centre of the arena now. Siobhan eyed each of them in turn, trying to discern their level of threat, wishing she could scan them, though she knew that knowing their level wouldn't necessarily tell her how powerful they were. She wondered what she would do if one came rushing at her. She simply wasn't an offensive fighter. The only real offense she had was her construct. And, well, she could *bonk* them on the head with her staff, but that wasn't going to do much of anything.

Another Champion died. One of the elves. He'd been slain by a powerful-looking man with glowing red eyes. The mage had robes the red of blood and wielded strange magic. From a flick of his staff, a violent red slash cut down yet another Champion—one that hadn't even been *facing* him.

He's just killing indiscriminately.

That made her wonder what the other members of her party might be doing. Would Xavier destroy everyone in his path, or would he let the other Champions live? He'd been kind in these last few floors, saving people wherever he could, so she was leaning toward the latter. Still, she knew the man was capable of the former if he wished it.

The remaining few Champions noticed the red-robed mage's power and aggression. They glanced at each other. Short nods were exchanged—all of this happening within the space of a second— and the three of them rushed their enemy. One of them—a woman in full-plate armour wielding a long spear—took a violent slash across her chest. The slash seemed to ignore her armour somehow, as it wasn't damaged at all, but blood seeped through it, and she'd clearly taken a lot of damage, as she looked like she would fall straight to her knees.

She wasn't dead, however.

Instincts Siobhan had honed on the battlefield kicked in in that moment. The last thing she wanted was for the red-robed mage to survive. *That bastard would just turn on me and kill me in a second.* The same might be true for the warriors, but Siobhan had to take a chance.

She raised her staff, power coursing through it, a glowing white pulsing at the staff's crystal head.

She healed the woman.

The woman's eyes opened wide, her brow shooting up her forehead. A heal in the arena must have been the last thing she imagined receiving. The other Champions all glanced at the woman. The ones rushing the red-robed mage didn't pause in their assault. They went straight for him. But Red-Robes himself stared directly at Siobhan, holding her eyes, his own still burning red, rage evident within them.

Oh, wonderful. Now I have the homicidal maniac's attention. Great job, Siobhan. Let's just piss off the most powerful Champion here.

Red-Robes raised his staff, aiming it toward *her.* He flicked it forward, one of his trademark slash spells heading her way.

The spear wielder, whom Siobhan would henceforth dub Spear Maiden, saw the attack coming. The woman gritted her teeth and *dove in front of it.*

Huh.

Siobhan healed the woman instantly.

Spear Maiden just took a hit for me—put all her trust in me. Something tells me she can't take more than one of those.

The other two warriors reached the man. The first, a hammer wielder, slammed her hammer straight for Red-Robes' head.

Red-Robes flashed away in a pulse of red light, then reappeared somewhere else in the arena.

Just outside Siobhan's Divine Beacon's radius.

Sick 'em, Siobhan thought, sending a mental command to her Divine Guardian. The massive construct stepped forward, far more nimble than anything that size and weight had a right to be.

Another *flick* of Red-Robes staff brought a slash hurtling toward her. The Divine Guardian ate the damage. Siobhan could feel how much damage it took. Unfortunately, though she could heal everyone else, she couldn't heal her Divine Guardian—only the beacon had an effect on it.

Sorry, construct, but you're not the best of protectors, are you? She supposed she wasn't being entirely fair. She'd always considered the Divine Guardian a last resort, and she hadn't had much of a chance to get its ranks up all that high, though she knew its strength was directly related to her stats. *If I get out of this, I promise I'll use you more.*

Siobhan had a connection with the Divine Guardian, one that made her instantly know exactly how much damage the thing took. That one strike had brought its health down to 15 percent. There was no way it was going to survive another hit, and though the bulky construct was nimble, it wasn't fast enough to avoid Red-Robes magical slashes—they were too fast, with seemingly no way to block them.

It's a shame my construct doesn't have a shield, though I'm not even sure how much good that would do.

Siobhan stepped behind the five-foot pillar of light. Something told her it wouldn't be much of a defence, but what else could she do?

My party is supposed to be here to protect me! That was the only reason I felt comfortable taking on a support class in the first place!

In video games, Siobhan had never liked playing a support class, mostly because the majority of her male friends always *assumed* that she would be the healer. That alone made her despise doing it. But the other members of her party... They hadn't asked her to do this, and being able to heal in real life versus being able to heal in a video game? Two very different things.

Now, she was filled with fear and regret.

Her Divine Guardian slammed its sword down toward Red-Robes's head, who slipped away from the strike with ease. Siobhan's first thought was that a mage didn't have the right to move that fast. Then she remembered that Xavier was a mage, and the old video game and tabletop roleplaying rules she was used to didn't exactly apply here.

There was a flash of red light. A slash slammed into the construct. It didn't bleed—constructs had no blood. When a slash had struck Spear Maiden, it hadn't cut through her armour—it had skipped over that and went straight for her flesh. Whatever spell this was, it seemed to have the powerful ability of completely ignoring physical protections.

As the construct's armour *was* its flesh, the slash cut straight through the Divine Guardian's torso. It was split in two. As it died, it turned back into a purple goo, melting to the ground, then disappearing into nothing. Siobhan's defender had died.

Red-Robes gave her a sinister grin. He looked kind of insane. Someone who only cared about winning, and seemed to have forgotten that they'd all been thrown into the exact same boat here.

The man raised his staff. Siobhan was well aware that she didn't have a high Toughness attribute, so she didn't have nearly as much health as a warrior like the Spear Maiden likely did. Her Willpower was decent, which would lend her some Magical Resistance, but considering her Divine Guardian had taken 85 percent damage with *one* strike, she knew she'd not be able to survive this.

So she ran toward him, her staff raised, ready to give this bastard a serious bonk on the head, knowing it was futile—there was no way she'd be able to reach him in time. When this match had started, she'd separated herself from the other Champions, backing away until she was on the far side of the arena, which meant the warriors—like Spear Maiden—were too far away to do her any good.

Then again...

She glanced over at Spear Maiden. The woman had fully healed once more, thanks to Siobhan's spell, and it was already proven she was strong enough to take one of these hits.

I've healed her twice now, and she jumped in front of an attack for me, what if...

Todd Herzman

Siobhan cast her Summon spell—a spell that only worked on *allies*—targeting Spear Maiden.

She targeted the other two contenders as well.

We're allies in our fight against this man, after all.

White light flashed around all of them. A split second later, Spear Maiden appeared in front of Siobhan. She took Red-Robes' spell, releasing a hiss of pain. Siobhan cast her healing spell on the woman.

The other two contenders had been enveloped in light. Those, she'd summoned not to her, but to the red-robed mage. She willed them to appear on either side of him, hoping that he wouldn't simply be able to teleport out of the way like he had before.

Red-Robes had enough time to widen his eyes in shock, but no more. Apparently, he'd had his full focus on Siobhan, unworried about the other contenders as they'd been too far away from him, and none of them ranged fighters.

A hammer crushed his skull. A sword pierced his side. The man cried out in desperate agony, but Siobhan felt nothing for him.

It didn't take him long to die.

Red-Robes slumped to the ground. The two warriors who'd killed him looking down at the body impassively.

Spear Maiden was breathing heavily in front of Siobhan. Siobhan checked the cooldown on her Divine Guardian and cursed under her breath—she wouldn't be able to summon it before the arena's countdown timer ended. The warrior in front of her turned around. Siobhan swallowed.

Is she going to turn on me now?

The Hunger Games had been one of Siobhan's favourite movies—she'd enjoyed the book too, but she'd watched the movie far more times. Whenever she saw the tributes making alliances with one another, she'd always wondered how trust could be possible between them. How they could ever turn their backs when they knew they'd all have to murder each other later. How could an alliance be possible at all when one was in that situation?

"Are you going to kill me?" Siobhan asked.

The four remaining Champions—Siobhan, Spear Maiden, the hammer wielder, and the final warrior, a man who carried sword and shield, looking much like a classic knight might—all stood in a circle facing one another.

The man drew Siobhan's interest for a moment. She hadn't gotten a good look at him before this.

He's... old? He had grey hair. A grey beard. Even *wrinkles*. There was no way this man could be from an already integrated world. The others—the two female warriors—were both young. Teenagers, just like Justin. *System age*.

It was the man who spoke first. "The System notification said nothing about killing each other."

Siobhan blinked. She brought the notification up in her mind.

The Melee will begin in 5 seconds and last for 5 minutes. If you are alive and have not surrendered by the time the Melee ends, then you will have successfully cleared this floor.

"All it says is we must be alive by the end of it," said Spear Maiden. She glanced at the others. "Though we are marked on our participation." She looked over at the dead mage. "I think we've managed enough."

The hammer wielder nodded. "This isn't like the first challenge, when we were pitted against another Champion from our own worlds. The System does not *force* us to kill; it simply rewards us on what we do." She gestured toward the dead Champions. "Most do not see it that way, however. They see what must be a fight, and they kill without thought."

Spear Maiden nodded. "That's only something that should be reserved for true enemies." She looked Siobhan in the eye. "It might be different if we met on the battlefield."

"Then I pray we never do," Siobhan replied.

Spear Maiden smiled warmly in response, and the four Champions from different worlds and sectors around the Greater Universe stood in a loose circle about one another, inside the radius of the Divine Beacon, waiting for the timer to reach its end.

Chapter 83
You Have Been Warned

XAVIER, STILL SITTING CROSS-LEGGED AT THE CENTRE OF THE arena, his Willpower Infusion spell working on every single one of the eleven contenders around him, tried to wear a disarming smile. He wasn't the most charismatic person around, so he didn't know how well he was managing.

"Can any of you tell me about the next floors of the tower?"

He'd commanded each of them to *stop,* and so right now he realised they couldn't actually speak. He adjusted the command, allowing them to move but not attack him—or, for that matter, each other.

Xavier had been careful when he decided to do this. Julian Myers, the Navy SEAL who'd sacrificed his life, had wanted to take the peaceful way out of that first challenge, and the System had killed him for it. But this was different. The options of surrender had been given, and the System had merely told them that they needed to remain *alive*—it hadn't said they needed to *kill.*

"Y-you're not going to kill us?" the guy with the chains wrapped around his fists said. He'd been the one who'd teleported directly behind Xavier at the start of the match.

He's definitely got some power behind him, at least for a normal Champion who's gotten this far in the tower.

Xavier supposed he didn't really know what *normal* was, all he had to compare with were the other Champions in his party, and the ones in his cohort, and none of them were even close to reaching this floor yet.

"If I wanted to kill you, you'd all be dead."

The other Champions glanced around at each other. All of them wore wary expressions, none of them seeming particularly trusting. Xavier couldn't blame them. He felt nice and relaxed, but that was because he was the one in control.

Xavier raised a hand. Several of them flinched. He sighed and shook his head. The hand was supposed to be placating, not threatening. "I hereby swear on the System that I'm not going to kill any of you unless you somehow threaten my life. We can even make a contract on that if you'd like, though as there's only a few minutes left…"

"I believe you," said a mage in blue robes.

One thing Xavier noticed was that only a few of the Champions had visible auras—the rest had theirs hidden. Xavier had since learnt that one could get items that would help hide their aura before they had the ability to. He wondered if that was what was happening here, as many of these Champions would have come into the tower with money, considering they'd come from established worlds unlike himself. If they were high-enough level that they'd already learnt Aura Control? Well, that was an interesting fact, too, as he was pretty sure most didn't do that until they were at a much higher level, as they needed to discover their Spirit Core to manage it.

"The man's right. If he wanted to kill us, he would have. And this challenge… has never needed to be to the death." The mage tilted his head to the side. His eyes glowed blue. "Besides, I can tell when someone is lying."

Xavier blinked. *He can tell when someone is lying? That's an interesting ability.* He could see how that would come in handy. He nodded his head at the man in thanks.

"And why should I trust *your* word on that?" Chain-Fist asked with a quirked eyebrow.

Blue-Robes offered up a simple shrug. "You really don't have to. It doesn't bother me one bit. But since he's spared all of our lives, I figure we owe him something in return, don't you?"

Chain-Fist blinked. Then a smile split his face. "I'm so glad I don't have to surrender!" He smashed his fists together. They made an awful, metal-crunching sound. "My brother is never going to hear the end of this. He never even made it past the tenth floor." He walked over to Xavier and sat across from him. The fear that the teenager had felt a moment before seemed to have disappeared, though if Xavier looked closely enough, he thought he could see a hint of it in his eyes. "You must be a Progenitor!"

A few eyes widened. It seemed as though many of the other Champions mustn't have figured that out.

I suppose Progenitors—let alone True Progenitors—must be incredibly rare.

"I am." He didn't feel the need to offer up that he was a *True* Progenitor, or that he'd made it to E Grade already. It seemed wise to keep that to himself. "Now, what can you tell me about the next floors?"

Chain-Fist shook his head in wonder. He opened his mouth to speak when something stopped him. Instead of saying words, he... *choked*, gripping his throat. Xavier was reminded of when he'd seen the barkeep, Sam, trying to tell him something he wasn't allowed to. The System had always stopped him. Prevented him from doing so.

"What's happening?" said another Champion, an elven woman wearing white robes. In her hand was a gnarled staff that looked like nothing more than a fallen branch, but it was clearly an item of far more power than that. "You said you wouldn't harm us."

"The System." Blue-Robes looked up at the sky above them. His eyes glowed blue once more. "It's watching." He closed his eyes. "I... I can feel it."

Champions from different worlds are forbidden from sharing information about the Tower of Champions whilst in the Tower of Champions. You have been warned.

Xavier swore under his breath. He stood up, the words hovering before his eyes, and stared up at the sky. "Really?" He gestured upward. "That's what you're going with?"

Chain-Fist was still gripping his throat. Though he wasn't choking anymore, his breathing was still raspy.

Blue-Robes stared at Xavier. "It is not wise to speak in such a way to the System, Progenitor." He tilted his head to the side. "You must be careful."

Xavier kicked a pebble. It soared all the way to the edge of the arena and slammed into the stone wall that surrounded them, turning to dust on impact. "The System refuses to tell me *anything*." He looked at Blue-Robes, at Chain-Fist, and all the other gathered contenders that were currently in his control. "You don't understand the advantage you have, being from established worlds. My people are going in blind."

Blue-Robes, his head still cocked to the side, smirked. "The advantage we have? I wonder why one such as you even wishes for information on the floors." He waved his hand toward Xavier. "You are a Progenitor, and, considering what you've done to the eleven of us... you don't need any more help. Progenitors have access to titles that no one from an established world could ever gain, and if they harness that... Tell me, are you in the lead for your instance of the Tower of Champions?"

Xavier nodded, almost surprised that the System hadn't stopped him.

"Do you know how difficult such a feat is?" He put a hand to his chest. "I've been training since I could stand, well before I had access to the System. I've been tutored by powerful experts on the Tower of Champions. I've been given every possible advantage one can find on an established world, and so have the other members of my party." His forehead creased in concern at word of his party. "We have managed to keep the lead on only half of the ten floors, despite all of that. If you knew the families we came from... And yet here you come, out of nowhere, not knowing a thing about the System, or the tower, and you have shown us how terribly weak we are in comparison."

Xavier conceded the man's point with a short nod. "I need to be strong. My world is being invaded."

"Hmm. Indeed. What sector are you from, Progenitor?"

Chain-Fist released his throat. "Should we really be talking to him? The System..." His eyes were wide in fear. "It certainly doesn't seem to *want* us to."

Blue-Robes raised his chin, looking down his nose at the other man. "It is wise to fear the System, but remember to read what it is actually telling you. We are not divulging tower secrets here."

"This is not how I expected this floor to go," Chain-Fist muttered.

"Then you don't know your history." Blue-Robes sighed. "The tenth floor of the tower is where many Denizens from far afield have spoken. It brings Champions from all over the Greater Universe together in one place. Many think it is only to fight, but there are other things to be gained."

"Participation..." Xavier muttered. The System hadn't said what participation *was*. He'd thought it would be foolish to tell them where he was from. Maybe he was wrong about that. They still didn't know his level, *couldn't* know his level. And mentioning his sector wasn't the same as mentioning his planet. There were no doubt countless worlds in his galaxy that had been recently integrated into the System. He was only from one of many. "I'm from the Silver River sector."

Blue-Robes lowered his head. "I am from the Blue Heart sector."

Chain-Fist looked unsure, but he no longer looked quite as afraid as he had a moment ago. "Dragon Scale."

Another Champion stepped forward. An elven woman. "The Great."

"The Great?" Xavier raised an eyebrow at her. "Your sector is called 'The Great Sector'?"

The woman shrugged. "I was not the one who named it."

Chain-Fist chuckled. Shook his head. "I've never heard of any of these sectors! Sometimes I forget how big the Greater Universe truly is..."

The others mentioned their sectors. No two Champions had originated from the same one. The time was slowly ticking by, and something told Xavier he wasn't going to gain any useful information from this encounter, but he was gaining something else important. He may have been the one who'd stopped the others from fighting, but to his eyes, it looked like they didn't want to fight each other at all. At least, most of them. Some had anger burning in their eyes.

There wasn't always just a simple, black-and-white choice. Fight, die, surrender... There were other options. Less obvious options. And if he were less powerful, he was certain, more *difficult* options.

He lowered his head in contemplation, listening on the peripheral to what the others were saying, comparing their experiences, mentioning how old, strong, or important their sectors were—apparently Chain-Fist had parents who were B Grade, that took Xavier by surprise, though he wasn't sure why.

When he returned to Earth, perhaps he should take this mindset with him—that fighting wasn't necessarily the only answer to the problem of invaders. Oh, that didn't mean he would tolerate them on his world. Didn't mean he wouldn't kill the enemy wherever he found them.

He knew for a fact that it might be too dangerous to keep an enemy alive, as it would risk the invaders finding out his level and sending higher-level Denizens to Earth in return...

But still, maybe there wasn't only one solution to every problem. And maybe—in time, when he became strong enough—there might be alliances to be made, ways to ensure Earth's safety in the Silver River sector, and the Greater Universe at large.

Alliances won't stop what's coming to our sector. The threat my Otherworldly Communion spell showed me. But maybe if I have help from others, like Sam's empress, I can find ways to level up even faster, become even stronger...

Xavier watched the timer, which he'd placed in the top-right corner of his vision, as it ticked down to zero.

The tenth floor had been nothing like he'd expected.

I just hope the others survived this.

Chapter 84
24 Allen Grove Street

There were no record titles for the tenth floor. The notification stated it the moment it appeared, so at least he didn't need to worry that he hadn't gained one.

There were, however, something called Participation Points. He stared at the notifications for a moment. He got his normal titles for this floor. Solo and first clear—that made him wonder, did everyone get a solo title for the tenth floor? It wasn't as though they were permitted to go in with their party...

Xavier shrugged off the question. It wasn't important right now.

You have received 100 Participation Points! This is the full number of points that any single Champion can receive from the tenth floor of the Tower of Champions. You will be able to spend these points once you are back in the Staging Room.

What, exactly, will I be able to spend those points on?

He was no longer standing in the arena the System had transported him back to that white room, where it had first taken him when he'd entered his floor. It was slightly disorientating, being back here, but he was more than used to the System teleporting him all over the place.

Though he didn't receive a record title for this floor—something he was rather disappointed about, considering he'd been doing so well with them—he got something else.

Title Unlocked!
Tenth Floor (Tower Milestone): You have completed the dreaded tenth floor of the Tower of Champions. The tenth floor is unique in the tower, as Champions do not have the ability to go through the floor more than once.
More Champions die on the tenth floor than through floors one and nine combined, and many surrender, not having the courage to face other Champions and risk their own deaths. Good job on not being one of them!
You have received +50 to all stats!

Fifty points? To all stats? That's more than I would have gotten for a record title!

Reading through the title, thinking back to the arena, the eleven other Champions that he'd faced, the opportunity to surrender... He had to wonder how many Champions from Earth would make it through this floor. Considering how easy the floor had been for him—he hadn't needed to fight at all—it made it difficult to imagine so many Champions died on this floor.

Then again, of *course* it was easy for him. A True Progenitor.

I might be even more than that...

He frowned. He still struggled to imagine how someone could surrender after making it this far. Could they really abandon their world for a hundred years?

He wouldn't judge. If dying was the only other option, he

didn't think there was anything wrong with doing whatever else you could to survive.

It wasn't long before he was teleported back to the Staging Room. When he arrived there, he glanced around, looking for the others, but none of them had arrived. He was just standing there alone. Xavier ran a hand through his hair.

How could they not be here? The tenth floor was timed. They should have all completed it at the same time, shouldn't they?

That was when he noticed there was something different about the Staging Room. It wasn't exactly how they'd left it. For instance, there were no doors. The exit that took him back to the staircase, that led down to the hallway to his room and down to the tavern instance, wasn't there. Turning around, he found that the door to the next floor of the Tower of Champions wasn't there either.

That's not good.

He just stood there for a long moment, wondering if his entire party were dead and thinking about the consequences of that. Would he be able to find their families when he returned to Earth? To protect them in their stead? He lowered his head.

They can't all have lost. Is this my fault for not letting them train? For taking all of the kills on every floor? For pushing them through the tower too fast than they needed to go?

"We all just wanted to get back to Earth so quickly..." he whispered to the empty room.

The air in the Staging Room seemed to shift. "Where are the others?"

The voice came from behind him. Xavier turned, saw Siobhan standing there, a crinkle in her forehead, worry in her eyes.

"You're alive!" Xavier stepped forward and enveloped the redhead in a hug.

"Of course I'm alive," Siobhan said, returning the embrace with a squeeze before they parted. "Why would you expect a support class to fail in an arena? We're basically unstoppable."

Xavier chuckled. He didn't even feel embarrassed for hugging her, which, under other circumstances, he might have.

I can reap souls, teleport, move things with my mind, and control the will of others, and I'm still awkward in these situations? Yeah, that's going to have to change.

His chuckle cut off abruptly. "I don't know where the others are." He ran a hand through his hair again. "I'm sure... I'm sure they'll be along shortly. How did you make it through?"

Siobhan folded her arms. "I'll wait until the others are here. I don't want to have to tell you all twice."

Neither said what they were both no doubt thinking—that the others might never return. That Howard and Justin could have surrendered. Or worse, died.

Howard would never surrender. He would do anything to get back to his family.

It felt like an age had passed by the time Justin finally arrived. He had a great big grin on his face—hardly what Xavier would have expected, considering he could only imagine what the kid must have gone through.

"You made it!" Siobhan wrapped the teenager in a hug, then held him at arms' length, beaming.

"I did! So did you! God, that was... exhilarating. And, well..." He blushed. Why would he be blushing? Because of Siobhan's hug? "I think I have a crush."

"What?" Xavier spluttered. "You came out of the Melee with a *crush?*"

"You should have seen her." Justin stared off into space with a stupid grin plastered on his face. "So beautiful. So... *powerful.*" He frowned, looking around. "Where's Howard?"

"He hasn't shown up yet," Xavier said. A second later, Justin's eyes shifted to somewhere behind Xavier. He turned around and found the former cop standing there, looking bereft.

Something is wrong. How could there be something wrong if he made it back?

"Howard!" Siobhan ran over to the old cop. "You made it!" She threw her arms up in the air and spun in an excited circle. "We *all* made it! Our entire party is going back to Earth!"

Justin laughed. He slapped Howard on the shoulder. "I knew we'd all make it through." He paused. "Okay, if I'm honest, I had my doubts there for a minute... but we did it!"

Howard's forehead was creased, his eyes looked sad... He brought up his head and stared at Xavier.

Xavier stepped over to the man. The excitement and good mood seemed to dim as Justin and Siobhan noticed the man's expression, that he wasn't celebrating like they were. Xavier got a terrible feeling in the pit of his stomach. "Howard? What is it?"

Howard's gaze slipped downward, as though he were struggling to maintain eye contact with Xavier. No, this was more than that. This was *shame*.

"Whatever you had to do to survive, it's okay. Whoever you had to kill—"

"I didn't kill anyone." Howard's voice was quiet, barely above a whisper.

"I don't understand," Siobhan said. "What's got you feeling this way?"

"I had to do something terrible to survive." Howard's gaze was locked on the floor now, as though a tremendous weight were pulling it downward. "And I don't know what the consequences will be." He shook his head. A tear streamed down his face.

Xavier put a hand on the man's shoulder. "Whatever it is, we're in this together. We can fix this."

"She wants to come to Earth."

Xavier blinked. "She?"

Howard held out his hand. A moment later, something appeared inside of it. A stone... and not just any stone. A Communication Stone.

"How...?" Xavier was confused. "How did you get that? And who is *she*? Who are you talking about?"

"She controlled me. Made me want to fight her. Then..." Howard placed a hand on his head. "She sifted through my mind. Broke it up. Looked through my memories until she set eyes on you."

Xavier still didn't understand what the man could have done wrong here. "Wait... was she from our sector?"

Howard shook his head. "No. She was from very, very far away. She said..." He swallowed. "She said if I wanted to live, I had to make a contract with her."

"A contract?" Siobhan's face paled. "She forced you to make a deal? What kind of deal? Why didn't you fight it?"

"She killed everyone else. Without any trouble whatsoever. Her power... was on an entirely different level to my own. There was nothing I could do. If I'd surrendered..."

"You wouldn't have been able to come back to Earth. Not for a hundred years. You wouldn't have been able to return to your family."

Howard dipped his head in shame. "You *have* to kill me."

Xavier stumbled backward. "Wh-what?"

"You can't be serious!" Justin blurted, at the same time as Siobhan said, "We're not going to kill you!"

Howard bit his lip. "I didn't know. I didn't *know* what the contract would be when I agreed! I just didn't want to surrender... A hundred years away from Earth... You don't know my wife's name, my daughter's name, my son's... How could you protect them if you don't know who they *are* or how to *find* them? So I *couldn't* surrender. I had to get back here! So I went along with it for as long as I could. I read through the contract. Trying to find... to find a loophole. Something that I could use to get out of it, or if... if signing the contract risked Earth, then I *would* surrender, for I knew it wouldn't be worth it." The man thrust the Communication Stone toward Xavier. "Take this. That's... that's part of the contract. I have to give this to you, then I have to set something up when I return to Earth, something that will allow her to pinpoint our location. That's why you have to kill me, Xavier. Because whoever this woman is, bringing her to Earth... It's too much of a risk."

Xavier stared down at the Communication Stone in the man's hand. "This doesn't make sense, Howard."

Howard's frown deepened. "I know. I shouldn't have signed! But don't you understand? It was the only way to get back here! Their names. My wife, her name is Kelly Jacobs. Our daughter's name is Rebecca. Our son's name is Michael. We lived in West Fronton, on Allen Grove Street—24 Allen Grove Street. A small, two-bedroom house with an ancient pick-up truck on the lawn and roses flanking the front door. My wife, she liked gardening, we have a vegetable patch in the backyard. Rebecca..."

"Howard, stop."

Howard shook his head. "I need to tell you. Everything about them. Kelly, she's beautiful. Her eyes are the colour of sapphires. Her hair is light brown. Her freckles make her look younger than she is. Rebecca—"

"Howard!" Xavier gripped the man's shoulders so tightly that he felt something give in. He loosened his grip as the man's eyes finally came up to meet his. "I'm not going to kill you."

Howard was about to talk.

Xavier raised a hand and continued, "No, Howard, I'm not going to let that happen. Our whole party will be getting back to Earth, and you don't need to tell us everything about your family because you're going to be able to find them yourself!"

Xavier sighed. "The woman who made you sign this contract, she could have put *anything* in it. She could have sworn you to secrecy, but she didn't. She saw through your memories. Saw the type of person you really are. That means she would have known that the second you returned, you would have spilled everything about what happened to me. So why didn't she swear you to secrecy in the contract?"

"I..." Howard trailed off. "I don't know. But it doesn't matter. I won't simply lose levels or stats or the System if I don't fulfil the contract, Xavier. It's death-locked. If, when I don't return to Earth, I fail to do as she asks within twenty-four hours... I'll die. And when I get back there... see my family... dying is going to be the last thing I'll want to do. I don't think I'll be strong enough to resist this if they're by my side. So you have to kill me *now*. I *refuse* to betray you. To betray Earth." He thrust the Communication Stone forward.

"The woman," Xavier asked. "Did she tell you her name?"

"Adranial," Howard said. "She told me her name was Adranial."

"I'm not going to let you die, Howard." Xavier finally looked down at the Communication Stone in the man's hand. He took it from him. "Let's see what this Adranial wants."

Chapter 85
This Isn't How You Make Friends

Xavier stared at the communication stone for a long moment. Everything had been going so well. The tenth floor of the Tower of Champions, the last floor before they finally got to return to Earth, had been easy—he hadn't even needed to kill anyone. It had been a piece of cake.

At least for him.

Justin, Siobhan, they'd come out of the arena without so much as a scratch.

But now Howard...

Xavier had told the man he wouldn't kill him, that they would find a way to save him and prevent anything bad from happening to Earth in the process, but he was worried. Worried he'd been wrong.

The contract let him tell the truth to us. Someone as powerful as whoever this Adranial was must know that was a foolish thing to do. They could have asked for anything in the contract, couldn't they? All Howard needed to be was willing to sign, even if willing *wasn't really the right word.*

This was bad.

After he'd taken the stone from Howard, he'd had the man

describe everything that had happened. Had him describe Adranial as well.

A white-robed, white-masked figure who didn't so much as wield a weapon yet caused everyone to attack her and took them down with ease. Also someone with the ability to read people's thoughts and sift through their memories...

Inviting someone like that to Earth... honestly, he didn't doubt that he would be able to defeat her. But odds were she came from an established, *powerful* planet. Who knew what kind of backing she had? If she were outside the Silver River sector, then her backer could be more powerful than the empress.

Stop worrying. Take this one step at a time.

Xavier needed to stop getting lost in his thoughts. Needed to stop delaying action. It might be okay to do that here, in the Staging Room, his break between floors, but very soon—once they'd opened their loot boxes and had some time to look in the System Shop—they would return to Earth.

The notification had appeared a few minutes after Howard's return. A countdown timer, ticking down from two hours to when they would be teleported back to Earth. It also explained that they were not permitted to exit the Staging Room.

Which means I can't go to the tavern and inform other Champions of the challenge that lies in wait for them on the tenth floor. There will be no way for me to warn my cohort, or countless other cohorts of Champions from Earth.

It was a difficult pill to swallow.

Howard sat in the far corner of the Staging Room. The big man, usually so stoic, only really showing emotion whenever he talked about his family, looked terrible. Alone. Depressed. His knees were tucked up to his chest.

He hated seeing the man look so... pitiful.

He thinks he's betrayed me, betrayed Earth, but he hasn't. Coming here, it was the only way he'd be sure that we would know who his family was, that we might know how to find them—and protect them.

Howard had offered to sacrifice his life, and Xavier just hoped it wouldn't come to that.

Now or never.

[*Adranial, this is Xavier Collins from Earth, and you have made a terrible mistake.*]

There was a long pause after his message had been sent. When he'd gone to do it, he'd had to *will* which Communication Stone he wished to use, as he now possessed two different ones. After a minute had passed, he shook the stone, as though that would help it work.

[*Xavier Collins.*] The voice was cool, *milky*, self-assured confidence leaking from it. A young woman—she must have been only sixteen—yet she sounded older. [*It is such a pleasure to speak with you. My ancestor will be proud that I've made contact so soon.*]

[*A pleasure? You forced my friend into making a contract with you.*]

[*Oh, surely you can't blame me for that. I had to make use of him somehow—it was either that or killing him for Mastery Points, not to mention Participation Points. Killing and contracts are a part of life in the Greater Universe that you will have to get used to. Yes, yes, I've heard of those peaceful sectors out there in the Greater Universe. They may sound warm and fuzzy, but it would curdle your blood to hear how they got there in the first place. There is no peace without a war first, Xavier Collins.*]

Xavier didn't like the way she kept repeating his name, saying it slowly, emphasising each syllable.

[*Is that what you wish to bring to Earth, Adranial? War?*]

[*There's only so much I'm allowed to tell you, Xavier Collins. I'm bound by contracts of my own. But I promise you this: I mean you no harm—besides, I do not believe there would be any way for me to harm you, do you?*]

Again, there she was, emphasising words, putting a lot of power in *I* when she explained *she* didn't want to harm him.

[*Who is this ancestor you mentioned?*]

[*Tsk, tsk, Xavier Collins, tsk, tsk. Don't you know you need to offer a little something before I'm willing to give? You haven't even taken me to dinner, and you want to ply me for all my secrets? Asking about my family? Isn't that a little personal? Really, manners isn't something you learn out there on the Edge, is it?*]

Xavier blinked. This woman, the way she talked, it sounded as though this was all a joke to her. [*You knew Howard would tell me about the contract, didn't you?*]

[*I know a great many things... That was, however, something I'd merely guessed would happen. Or rather, something I'd hoped for.*]

Xavier was getting frustrated with this conversation. This woman hadn't divulged a single bit of information about herself. [*What do you want with me? And why do you want to come to Earth?*]

[*You are a curiosity, Xavier Collins of Earth. A powerful curiosity. I have been tasked with befriending you, and it is a task that I plan to take seriously.*]

Xavier's frustration turned to anger. [*Befriending me? After what you did to Howard? You must be insane!*]

[*Insane... No, despite what some of my tutors have said, rumours of me being insane are highly exaggerated. I am merely eccentric.*] There was a pause. [*Are you going to kill him?*]

Xavier blinked. He looked over at Howard. The man hadn't moved from his spot in the corner. His mind was no doubt elsewhere, thinking of his family, hoping he would be able to see them. Xavier wondered if he should tell the woman the full truth. That he didn't know what he was going to do. If Howard didn't do as the woman asked within twenty-four hours of returning to Earth, he'd be a dead man anyway.

[*Get him out of the contract,*] Xavier demanded.

[*Hmm. No. Try again.*]

Xavier sighed. [*This isn't how you make friends, Adranial.*]

[*My mother always told me I came off a little... prickly. Something she said would only worsen once I gained the System.*]

Xavier shut his eyes, touched his head. Was he getting a stress headache? He figured he'd be free of those, considering his massively high Toughness attribute, but apparently this woman—this bloody *teenager*—brought them out in him.

What's the worst that could happen if I brought her to Earth?

He almost hated having the thought. Would he really risk Earth over the fate of a single person? Howard was important to him, sure, but how could he put the value of one life over so many others?

Howard himself asked me to kill him. He would understand.

He cursed under his breath. When reading fantasy novels, he'd always enjoyed when characters faced dilemmas such as this. When they'd had to stare down a decision and choose a path when there was no right one. Some of those characters would choose to kill Howard. They would call that the *hard path* and do *what needed to be done.* But Xavier thought he knew better than them. Killing Howard wasn't the hard path. In this situation, it was the easiest solution possible.

But it wasn't the only one by far.

And a realisation came to Xavier—one he should have known. [*You're from a very powerful family, Adranial, aren't you?*]

[*Well, I don't like to brag...*] There was nothing but humour in her words, telling him that she very much *did* like to brag.

Xavier was becoming sure of a few things. First, that one of the powerful presences he'd felt observing him was Empress Larona, and that she was the weaker of the two. And second, that the other powerful presence—the first one he'd felt, the one that had made him feel like nothing more than a speck of dust—wasn't going to stop at just *looking* at him. It was clear now that he'd put the pieces together.

Adranial had said her ancestor would be pleased that she was in contact with him, but how could her ancestor know anything about him? Hadn't she only just learnt of him from sifting through Howard's memories?

Xavier bit his lip.

Whoever that presence was, he was able to circumvent the System, able to spy on me in the Tower of Champions. Something like that shouldn't be possible, but it was. And why was this woman looking through the memories of everyone in that arena? On the off chance she'd find a reason to make a contract? No. She was on a mission. If whoever her powerful ancestor was could observe him while he was inside the Tower of Champions, could he also somehow... alter the Tower of Champions?

That would be impossible, wouldn't it? But hadn't Xavier made it a matter of course to do the impossible?

Could he—or she—have somehow forced the arena match-up between Howard and Adranial?

He must be insane for even thinking in this way, but this just didn't feel like a coincidence.

This would be the perfect time to gain some wisdom from the otherworld with my communion spell. If only I could use the damned thing.

[*Xavier? Don't tell me you've gotten all shy? Don't you want to talk to me anymore?*]

Xavier put all his thoughts together and came to a conclusion. Whether this woman was who he thought she was or not, she was clearly someone close to power. Before Xavier had even returned to Earth, this woman knew what level he was—she must *know* that he was E Grade, if she had access to Howard's memories.

Her contract with Howard wasn't the only way that she could mess with him. Wasn't the only way that she could make trouble for him.

She could get this information out. I don't doubt that she would have the means to contact the worlds and factions currently invading Earth and let them know what my level is. They could send E Grade enemies to Earth the moment I returned. There would be no way for me to hide my level...

He tapped his fingers against the Communication Stone resting in his left palm.

I need to make a contract with her myself. Something that prevents her from ruining Earth with her knowledge.

It was only then that another realisation dawned on him, and he identified the Communication Stone he was holding.

{Communication Stone – Restriction: None}
A Communication Stone has the ability to form a mental connection with two people, allowing them to communicate telepathically over distances both great and small. Once a connection is established, the stone can be used while inside spatial storage.
The power of this Communication Stone bears no restrictions.
A Communication Stone is useless if it is not paired.

The Communication Stone wasn't restricted to a single sector —it wasn't restricted at all.

Where in the Greater Universe is this woman?

Chapter 86
Keep Your Friends Close, and Your Enemies Closer

[*I was wondering when you'd come to this conclusion, Xavier Collins.*]

[*If you truly want to befriend me, you have no other choice.*]

Xavier had just outlined his wishes, stating that for Adranial to come to Earth, she must make a contract with him. At first, he'd worried a contract would not be possible over a Communication Stone, but according to Adranial, making contracts over long distances was one of the functions a Communication Stone had. He didn't ask her why his Identify skill hadn't told him that—he assumed it was because it wasn't a high enough rank to reveal everything about an item he was examining.

Which means there may very well be more things I've identified that I don't know as much about as I thought.

[*Oh, let me assure you, there is always a choice. Choices are about the only thing we have in this universe. The problem is we can never take back the choices we make. One cannot walk backward on the path, as the System is so fond of reminding us.*] The woman paused. [*I'm glad you didn't kill your friend.*]

Her voice sounded different than it had before, lacking the self-assured confidence and humour that had practically been dripping off of it. If he didn't know any better, he'd say he heard some sincerity in it.

[*Like you care what happens to Howard. He told me what you did—that you taunted everyone in that arena and made them attack you. You didn't have to do that. You were powerful enough to survive the arena without killing. I'm sure of it.*]

[*Interesting. From the memories I saw of you, I did wonder about your sense of morality. There is a difference between doing what I did—killing total strangers in a situation where their deaths are only to my advantage—and killing a friend. Yes, you are correct in asserting that I care nothing for Howard's life, not because I am callous, but because there are trillions of lives in the Greater Universe that are simply of no consequence to me. How could they be? But it would be different if it were the life of someone I trusted. Did you know that I've been training with my party since the moment I could walk? On my world, we know a little about how cohorts are formed, and so we take everyone who was born on the same day on the same year and have them train in the same classes. I, of course, had my tutors outside of that. But this comradery—it forms a bond. A strong bond. I would feel much pain if I were to have to kill one of them, and I would not take it lightly.*]

Xavier took a moment to digest the woman's words. He felt like he was learning something more about the Greater Universe the more they talked. [*You... were testing me, weren't you? There were other ways you could have made that contract with Howard. You just wanted to see what I would do. How I would react. And something tells me you could find your own way to Earth without his help.*]

[*Ding, ding, Xavier Collins. Ding, ding. You're absolutely right. There are many ways I could have gone about this. I'll sign your contract, as long as it is to my liking. And in doing so, I will release Howard from his.*]

Xavier blinked. [*Just like that? What's the catch?*]

[*Ah, my dear Xavier, that comes later. You'll have to wait.*]

Am I making a terrible mistake?

Xavier looked at Howard once more and thought of Earth. This all seemed a little too easy. There must be a thousand variables he hadn't thought of. Things he didn't even know to think of. But if this Adranial would truly sign a contract with him, then he had to do it, didn't he? How else was he going to hide who he was from the invaders in his sector? He thought through the contract he wished for her to sign, then sent it though.

XAVIER COLLINS has sent a System Contract to ADRANIAL ------

Xavier tilted his head to the side. The woman's last name was blocked. Interesting.

Contract details:
XAVIER COLLINS agrees to provide ADRA-NIAL ------ with coordinates to planet Earth in the Silver River sector and provide her with safe harbour as long as she does not pose a threat to him or the people of Earth.
ADRANIAL ------ agrees not to harm a single Denizen from Earth unless there are exceptional circumstances and harming them is only in self-defence. This self-defence clause, however, does not include being allowed to defend herself against the members of XAVIER COLLINS'S party—

There was an interruption, the text cutting out. Adranial's voice rang in his mind. [*That basically says any members of your party can attack me and I can't do a damned thing in response. Now, now, that doesn't seem fair, does it?*]

Xavier bit his lip. [*Neither is the corner you've put me in to get this, Adranial. Besides, we've agreed to give you safe harbour, remember?*]

[*You've agreed to give me safe harbour. It says nothing about your party members. Which means there's nothing stopping them attacking me at all, especially the one who may just have a grudge against me.*]

[*And whose fault would that be?*] Xavier paused. Sighed to himself. [*Fine. I'll change that line.*]

ADRANIAL ------ agrees not to harm a single Denizen from Earth unless there are exceptional circumstances and harming them is only in self-defence.
ADRANIAL ------ agrees not to share information about Earth, its defences, or the level of its Denizens—in particular XAVIER COLLINS—with anyone XAVIER COLLINS has not permitted her to share said information with.

[*That last one's a little bit strict, isn't it?*]
[*That last one is non-negotiable.*]

ADRANIAL ------ is not allowed to harvest any of Earth's resources without strict permission from XAVIER COLLINS.
ADRANIAL ------ is not permitted to bring anyone with her to Earth.

[*I can't bring my party?*] Adranial replied. Xavier could practically hear the pout in her voice. [*They're like family to me, Xavier Collins, and they would be a great help against the invaders you're about to face.*]

Xavier tapped his fingers against the Communication Stone in his palm. He already wondered if he was making a terrible mistake in bringing this woman to Earth in the first place. Did he really want to have to worry about her party, as well?

There's nothing stopping her from sharing information about me with them right now and instructing her party members to sabotage Earth by releasing that information to the invaders if something happens to her. Maybe I'd be better off securing a contract with them as well...

This was beginning to feel far outside of his control. Adding more elements into play.

If she has a Communication Stone that has no restrictions within the entire Greater Universe, she probably has more like this. She could already have told countless people.

Now, he knew he was starting to sound a little paranoid, but he couldn't help it. Besides, it was hardly paranoia when people were actually out to get him—or at least, paying close attention to him.

Two incredibly powerful Denizens already know who I am and what I'm capable of. I felt them, watching me again, after I defeated the Endless Horde. If they wanted Earth to fall, there wouldn't be anything I could do at this stage to stop them.

This is the only way forward—the only way to break the contract currently holding sway over Howard's life.

Xavier looked at the countdown timer. He'd already spent more time on this than he would have liked. Over half an hour of the two hours he had before they returned to Earth.

[*Fine,*] he told Adranial. [*I'll cut your party into the deal, but they'll be under the same restrictions as you, and I'm adding another clause to the contract.*]

[*Are you now?*] There was an interesting lilt to her voice; it almost sounded as though she were impressed. If she were who Xavier *thought* she was, the descendant of that powerful Denizen that had looked in on him, the Denizen that had probably held the top spot on all the floors before Xavier stepped into the tower, then she probably wasn't used to being spoken to in this way by someone outside her family.

[*If you or your party members do anything to piss me off, I get to ban you from Earth, and you still don't get to talk about me or my planet.*]

Another long pause followed his words, which made him

wonder if she was conferring with someone. Her party, or perhaps the ancestor she'd mentioned.

[*You may be interested to know, Xavier Collins, that I do not care how your world fairs in the Greater Universe, nor am I going there because I think the world itself is particularly special, though if I do, and I quote, "piss you off" enough to have you throw me out of it, then I will have already failed in my duty, and being barred from a backwater baby planet on the Edge will be the least of my worries.*]

Xavier couldn't help but smirk. He was beginning to wonder... Maybe there *was* more truth than lie in this Adranial's words. Maybe she *did* intend to befriend him, and if that were the case... what advantages could he get out of having such a knowledgeable Denizen and her party of Champions on Earth? Opposing Champions might not be able to share information about the tower *within* the tower, but outside of it?

That could very well be a different story altogether. And he had no doubt that, however strong this woman and her party were, he would still be able to defeat her if it ever came to a fight—not that the contract should allow such a thing. She would not have anywhere near the same number of titles as he possessed.

Though who knows what her ultimate motives are...

He couldn't help but be reminded of that old adage: keep your friends close, and your enemies closer. Choosing this course of action would definitely have him adhering to that, whichever she turned out to be in the end.

Xavier spent the next little while putting contracts together for the other members of Adranial's party. He'd tried to stipulate a clause that would require them to provide information to him and his people, but Adranial had shut that down pretty fast. Apparently, she had contracts of her own already in place that she had to adhere to, and many of them had to do with the sharing—or rather, with the *restriction* of sharing—information.

The whole negotiation—for lack of a better term—had taken longer than he'd hoped to sort out, but when it was done, the final line of the contract between himself and Adranial being to free Howard from his contract, Xavier watched as Howard got a faraway look, blinking off into space. The big man stood, his armour clinking loudly as he did so, his double-bearded axe sent swinging where it hung from his belt, and he looked over at Xavier.

"You... you did it. You freed me from the contract!" The man's eyes widened. "What—what did you give her?"

Chapter 87
Item Brokers

Xavier stood in the Tower of Champions' Staging Room, the doors gone, the loot boxes waiting for their recipients to open them, the other three members of his party staring at him in anticipation.

He stared over at Howard. "I'm letting her come to Earth." He paused. "Along with her party."

"Are you insane?" Howard asked.

"That... doesn't seem like a good idea," Justin said.

"Let's hear him out." Siobhan stepped in front of them. "Xavier wouldn't make a decision like this without having a good reason." She looked at him. "You have a good reason, don't you?"

It was the only way I could save Howard, Xavier wanted to say. It was the main reason he'd done it, after all, but they knew that. He could already see the guilt in Howard's eyes. The man thought this was his fault, but Xavier knew better.

There were consequences of Xavier being who he was. Attention from powerful Denizens in the Greater Universe. Empress Larona, and now this mysterious ancestor of Adranial's. Xavier had thought hard on this and come to the conclusion that there simply couldn't be any other explanation as to how Howard ended up in that arena with Adranial other than it having been set up.

Maybe he was stretching. Maybe it was more than a little self-centred to think in this way, but he was sure that it was the truth. Sure in his bones.

And so he told all of that to them. He knew that if he didn't, Howard would bear the weight of all of this. Yes, he could have surrendered, but Xavier didn't blame him in the slightest for what he'd done.

"You could have killed me," Howard said at the end. "Perhaps you *should* have. This is dangerous, Xavier. You don't know what they want."

Xavier smiled. "Everything has been dangerous since the System integrated. I figured we might as well lean into it—the only way out is through, after all."

The others wanted to keep talking about it, but Xavier stopped them. They had other things they needed to do.

Like open their loot boxes and spend their Participation Points.

Xavier walked over to his loot box and knelt in front of it, a motion that was giving him an intense feeling of Deja vu. He flipped off the latch and swung the lip open. His heartbeat quickened in the split second between the lid coming open and the notification appearing.

The last item he'd gained was a Portal Hub, something he imagined would come in very handy, so he was eager to find out what he received next. He knew he was lucky—knew he was getting better items than perhaps any other Champion on an equivalent floor, and he wanted to savour it.

You have gained 6 Mastery Points (E Grade).
You have gained 300,000 Lesser Spirit Coins.
You have received a Portal Block.

Xavier tilted his head to the side. The Mastery Points and spirit coins were another drop in the bucket, one he wasn't concerned about quantifying at this stage, but the Portal Block was interesting.

A long iron rod with a spherical crystal top had materialised in his hand when the notification had appeared. He turned it around, examining it with his eyes before using his skill. It almost looked like some sort of weapon, though he doubted it would be a very effective one. The rod was about four feet long, the sphere at its head roughly the size of a large apple. At the other end was a spike.

Why do I get the feeling I'm supposed to jam this in the ground?
He used Identify on the item.

{Portal Block – Radius: 5 Miles – Upgradeable}
A Portal Block is an item which is defensive in nature, giving the user the ability to block all unauthorised portals within the defined radius.

Well, I can certainly see how that would come in handy.
It made him wonder if Queen Alastea had had one of these at her castle. The Endless Horde's portals had been a fair distance away from the castle itself, which Xavier had always thought was so the enemy could amass their armies.

Why didn't he ever wonder why the portals weren't simply opened behind a fortress's walls? Wouldn't that be the perfect way to get through defences?

Xavier held the Portal Block in his hand, hefting it up and down. He was glad to have it, but its very existence made him worry. If something like this existed, and it was a difficult item for someone of a low level to acquire, that meant that right now the chances of there being any defences like it on Earth were slim to none.

I'm almost back there.
He found he was sick of thinking how close he was to returning to Earth. Even the hour and fifteen minutes or so they had remaining on the countdown timer was too long.

The others got basic items once more. Attribute Tokens and the like. They were getting more of those than he was, but it didn't bother him—they needed it more than he did, after all. Besides, he could probably purchase them at a later date. He knew the number of attributes one could gain from tokens was limited as well.

They must have had a nice boost from that last floor, gaining the solo title. Not to mention that milestone title. Everyone who gets through the tenth floor will get that.

His forehead creased, thinking of that. Was he annoyed that he didn't get any unique titles from that floor? As if he wasn't spoiled for titles as it was? He shook his head and chuckled.

Yep. I've definitely been spoiled.

He couldn't wait to get back to Earth. He was curious to find out what normal titles there were for him to get, or if there would be titles for taking out invaders. What if there were invasion generals? Would he get something special for being the first on Earth to take one out?

I'm getting ahead of myself.

"So," Xavier said, looking over at the others, "how do we spend these Participation Points, and what exactly do we get for them?" He blinked. "You know what, I forgot to ask—how many do each of you have?"

Justin rubbed the back of his neck and looked sheepishly down. "I got about sixty-five."

"Sixty-five?" Xavier raised an eyebrow. "That's pretty good... Wait, weren't you just chatting up a girl?"

"I wasn't chatting up—I mean, okay, maybe a *little*." The teenager's face flushed beet-red. "But... I also had to kill someone."

"You did?" Siobhan blinked.

Justin shrugged. "Kill or be killed."

Xavier frowned. There wasn't a hint of emotion in Justin's voice. Though, if Xavier had to kill someone on his floor, he supposed there'd be no reason in regretting it. He was standing there, looking out from an incredibly privileged position. He was strong enough that restraining the others in his arena didn't risk his own life. If there'd been a chance of them hurting him, or the System had required it, he would have killed everyone in that arena.

This new reality has certainly changed me. How many thousands of people did I kill when facing the Endless Horde? Would it really have been any different?

Howard cleared his throat. "I only got twenty-five points. I fought one man—a boy, really. No offense, Justin, but sixteen... just feels so young to me. Though I did not kill him. Then that Adranial... well, I guess the System doesn't look too kindly on the type of failure I experienced."

"It's not your fault who you came up against," Xavier said, "or that you weren't strong enough to fight them."

"No," Siobhan said, a little strongly. "It is his fault. It's all our faults."

Everyone looked at her.

The skin around her eyes wrinkled. "We've been lucky, riding on your coattails, Xavier. Very lucky. You've been able to carry us through nine floors, but you can't carry us forever. That floor... that proved it. I only survived out of sheer luck, because of the people I was matched up with. Something like this... can't happen again. We need to be stronger. You won't always be there to protect us. If this floor taught us anything, it was surely that."

Xavier nodded. "I know." He looked at each of them. "I've been taking the lead, and I haven't been doing it perfectly. I haven't been taking the three of you into consideration enough, despite all the help you've given me. That's going to change from now on."

"Should we... split the party?" Justin asked. "When we return here for the eleventh floor? I mean, Xavier doesn't *really* need us, does he?"

"No," Xavier said. "We're not going to split the party. The three of you can still benefit from the first-clear title. But that doesn't mean we'll be doing things in the same way as before." He paused. "How many points did you get, Siobhan?"

"Ninety," Siobhan stated.

The others all looked at her. Xavier couldn't help but be a little stunned. "Ninety? That's... *amazing*. How'd you manage that?"

"I... healed one of the other Champions there. Kept her alive.

Helped them take out this mage who..." She shook her head, her hair falling into her eyes, then tucked it back behind her ear. "I guess the System has a different idea of participation than we might have thought."

Xavier nodded. He couldn't help but be surprised by how well she'd done, which he supposed wasn't fair. But, out of all his party members, she'd been the one he was worried about the most.

And I was worried about Howard the least...

"I received one hundred Participation Points," Xavier said.

Justin chuckled. "Well, of course you did. You're *Xavier*."

Xavier smirked at that. None of them looked surprised—they had surely been expecting that eventuality. He rubbed his hands together. "All right. Let's figure this out." He walked over to the pedestal that held the System Shop's terminal, figuring this must be where they'd be spending their points.

When he accessed the interface, a notification popped up.

Congratulations on completing the tenth floor of the Tower of Champions! You have acquired your first Participation Points. Every item you look at will now have its value in both spirit coins and Participation Points.

That sounds promising.

The last item they'd been looking for in the System Shop had been something that blocked an enemy's ability to communicate. Sam had informed him of the item's existence, but unfortunately, he hadn't told him what the item was, which made finding it very difficult.

I wish I could access some sort of item broker, or research assistant... someone that can help me find the things that I need. An item broker would be good, if such a thing exists—they would be able to search the shop for me. Something tells me items appear and disappear from the shop all the time, what with trillions of people having access to it.

He tapped the base of the pedestal with his fingers and frowned.

Maybe I can already access this?

He searched the System Shop for the word *broker* in hopes that he was right. He pumped his fist into the air as he saw the top results.

"Yes!" he exclaimed. The others raised their eyebrows at him. Siobhan opened her mouth, as though about to ask a question, Xavier waved her off, stuck in focus mode.

He felt a little foolish, not having looked for this before, but it was difficult to know what he didn't know. For instance, he hadn't even realised there was a category for services in the store.

There weren't as many options as he might have assumed an entire universe worth of Denizens would have, but when he prompted the System for more information, it told him that services could only be bought from the nearest four planets because he was from a planet still experiencing its first five years post-integration.

He blinked. Nearest four planets... There were five different worlds—including Earth—competing in this instance of the Tower of Champions. It was those other worlds' Champions he had to keep ahead of to gain first-clear titles, and who knew what else later down the track. They were worlds that were within his sector.

It makes sense that they would be the closest worlds, which means I can only purchase services from those worlds that we're competing against.

It made him wonder if the worlds he competed against were also those that were invading his planet.

Would they even want to sell their services to me?

There were different tiers of Item Brokers, and most of them had unique specialties—weapons and armour acquisition, defensive item acquisition, base building acquisition, different resources, even down to special types of crafting items, and so on. He wasn't exactly sure what category the item he wanted would be in.

Security? Espionage?

Some of the Item Brokers had *general* as their specialisation, which he found rather humorous. Specialising in generalising always sounded like some sort of oxymoron. He selected Tier 1, General Item Brokers, and gawked momentarily at the price of their services.

"Are you kidding me?" he muttered. Just to have them *search* for an item, it would cost a minimum of 1,000,000 Minor Spirit Coins. It wasn't that he couldn't afford that sum—he certainly could—but it seemed like an exorbitant amount of money just for someone to locate an item and buy it on your behalf, not even including the price of the item itself.

And that it was in Minor Spirit Coins and not Lesser Spirit Coins made him wonder if someone under E Grade would even be able to use this service. That would be a hell of a lot of Lesser Spirit Coins...

That's just ridiculous... but, then again, I've no idea how to find this item myself.

He bit his lip and continued tapping his fingers against the pedestal, something that the other Champions kept giving him slightly frustrated glances at.

They can deal with it.

He sighed and selected the services of one of the cheaper Item Brokers. A menu of selections came up, showing him different time frames for item acquisition.

The first few time frames were in the span of *years*, though they did specify that items could be found before the end of the time allocation depending upon the work load of the Item Broker—which hadn't been given a name by the System, only a seemingly randomly generated signifier of $R2D25E$.

Would people really select the century options? A hundred years seems like a long time to wait for someone to find you an item, even if some Denizens' lifespans are unimaginably long... right?

Though the price for the Item Broker had initially said 1,000,000 Minor Spirit Coins, it appeared that was for the one-week delivery. There were significant discounts for longer periods of time.

But for shorter periods, like the hour timeframe Xavier had been hoping for, there were high markups.

"Ten *million* Minor Spirit Coins?" Xavier swore under his breath. It looked as though he wouldn't be able to get this item before returning to Earth, and that was before he even knew how much the item *cost!*

I only have about 5,000,000 Minor Spirit Coins left after handing over so many to Sam to help fill out those contracts...

Then he looked at how many Participation Points he'd need for the service, and his jaw dropped.

He only needed fifty.

Chapter 88
Ding!

Xavier couldn't look past this opportunity. He needed to act now. There was only an hour and ten minutes left before they would be returned to Earth, and though he couldn't wait to get back there, he was pretty darn sure he wouldn't be able to access the System Shop when he got there.

He selected the one-hour option and found he had two choices —he could either give the Item Broker his budget for the item itself, and the broker would purchase the item instantly on his behalf, or he could put a hold on the item. A Tier 1 item broker apparently had the ability to put a ten-minute hold on an item being purchased, which hid the item from other users of the System Shop for that duration.

As Xavier had no idea how much the item would cost, either in spirit coins or in Participation Points, he chose the latter option, which happened to cost the exact same amount.

That means if I can't afford to purchase this, then I've just wasted fifty of my Participation Points, which seem to be far more valuable than I'd previously realised.

Xavier put in a description of the item that he wanted, then purchased the service.

Then he spent a good minute wracking his brain for other

useful items he might be able to use when they returned to Earth. He had a Seed Sanctuary, a Seed Garden, a Portal Hub, Portal Stones, and a Portal Block. All of these things would be incredibly useful when he returned. Not to mention the Communication Stones he had—something he'd looked up in the store, too, and they were currently way outside of his price range, at least if he hoped to afford the item from the Item Broker.

It was a lot easier getting items from loot boxes than it was getting them from the System Shop, that was for sure...

Maybe I could use my Participation Points for some more Communication Stones. If I have enough for each member of my party, I'll always be able to keep in contact with them, and the stones that were world-restricted were much cheaper than sector-restricted...

He pushed that thought aside. There was a chance he would need every single Participation Point that he had for the purchase of the item he wanted. It was too important to risk.

This item will help Earth's safety, stopping enemy invaders from getting word back to their people about what level I am. I need this more than I need more Communication Stones.

He sighed. He also needed it more than he needed a smithy, which was another item he'd just thought of—somewhere for a skilled blacksmith to work. He imagined adding that to his Seed Sanctuary would be very advantageous. There was probably an item that could *grow* what he needed.

Instead of worrying about what other items he might be currently missing out on, Xavier sat down, cross-legged on the floor, and did something he hadn't had the time nor the inclination to do in a while.

He created more spirit coins, and with his Spirit attribute being as high as it was, he was a little astounded by just how many he was able to create.

In a single batch, he could create 1,580 Lesser Spirit Coins, or 158 Minor Spirit Coins. He actually had an option as to which one he could choose. He, of course, chose Minor Spirit Coins. The amount became a *little* disappointing when he changed it to those, but he couldn't complain.

His Spirit Energy reserve was, well, for lack of a better phrase, a *crap ton*. Each batch took him about a second to create, and his E Grade Spirit Energy was 79,100 points when full.

Previously, when he'd been F Grade, he'd needed to use 500 points of Spirit Energy to create one batch of spirit coins. Now, it only took him 50 points of Spirit Energy to achieve the same task.

Which meant he could create 1,582 batches of 158 Minor Spirit Coins in less than twenty-six minutes, which gave him just shy of two hundred and fifty thousand Minor Spirit Coins. His Spirit Energy regeneration, while not perfect, was incredibly powerful, which meant for the entire time he sat there he never had to stop creating coins—his reserve regenerated as he created them, though it didn't regenerate quite as fast as he was expending it, so it would *eventually* run out.

Piles of coins kept appearing in front of him, over and over. He touched the piles, deposited them into his Storage Ring, and repeated the process over and over.

The others ignored him. They knew when he needed to focus, and they always respected that. He could hear them chatting amongst themselves, but their words never penetrated his mind, as focused as he was. He didn't need to be so laser-focused on creating spirit coins. The last time he'd been steadily doing this, it had been while they'd all been sitting in the bar, but he was contemplating how exactly currency worked in the Greater Universe. Or rather, how the economy worked.

How could spirit coins be worth much of anything if one could simply create them? It was a question he'd had before, and one he didn't really have an answer to.

Xavier had been keeping track of how much time was passing as he accumulated more and more spirit coins. He was both eagerly awaiting the response from the Item Broker, and dreading it in case he couldn't afford what he'd ordered. Participation Points, he'd discovered, were non-transferable. He wasn't about to take the

Participation Points away from the other members of his party—he'd stopped taking their winnings away from them a few floors ago—but he just hoped using half of what he had would pay off.

Time, he thought. *Time equals money, literally.*

He wondered if it was some kind of metaphor. The universe will give you anything you want as long as you put in enough time. It sounded like a rather naive idea. He supposed it only worked if one stayed alive long enough to benefit from it.

Ding!

The noise sounded in his mind, making him open his eyes and frown. It had only been about forty-five minutes, but he'd been able to create 426,000 Minor Spirit Coins in that time.

Hopefully that would make a dent.

Your order from Item Broker R2D25E is complete! The item is awaiting your purchasing decision. You have 10 minutes to purchase the item before it goes back on the market.

Xavier had been standing rather close to the System Shop's terminal. He sprang up and slapped his hand against it. Ten minutes was plenty of time right now, but he wondered what would happen if he got one of those notifications while he was in the middle of a massive battle, or far away fighting vicious, magical monkeys in some jungle.

I guess that's where having a Portal Stone linked to a Portal Hub could really come in handy, assuming it works that way...

He brought up the interface. There was a little red bubble near the top right corner. Xavier couldn't help but chuckle when he saw it. It reminded him of Facebook, or any of the social media apps he'd ever used back on Earth, as though the Greater Universe had been taking UI advice from Mark Zuckerberg.

Or maybe it's actually the other way around...

He selected the button, which opened the very same notification he'd just read, then took him to the item he wanted to purchase.

> **{Subspace Communications Area Blackout Array – Radius: 5 Miles – Upgradeable}**
> *The Subspace Communications Area Blackout Array (or SCABA) gives the user the ability to set up an array that radiates interference up to the noted radius. The array requires multiple insertion points for it to be activated.*
> *SCABA is an equal opportunity blackout device, meaning it blacks out all subspace or telepathic communication within the affected area, whether from friend or foe.*

Xavier frowned. The last thing he'd wanted was to blackout his own communications. He could see how that could get him into trouble. It was interesting that it noted it blacked out telepathic communication as well as subspace communication. From Xavier's sci-fi knowledge—which, admittedly, was from *fictional sources—* he assumed that communication through subspace was instantaneous even when it was with someone light years away.

That's how Communication Stones must work, if they are sector, and even Greater Universe, wide.

But telepathic communication? That seemed like something else entirely.

There was a countdown timer beneath the item.

You have 9 minutes and 34 seconds to purchase this item. Thanks for using Item Broker R2D25E's services! If you're satisfied with this user's service, come back for a 25% discount on your next acquisition! Or recommend them to a friend!

Xavier blinked. Even interstellar Item Brokers gave discounts. Good to know. He tapped his foot on the floor of the Staging Room. The item was upgradeable, maybe that meant that if he strengthened it, eventually it would allow his own Communication Stone, or those of his allies, to work within the designated blackout area?

Either way, this was an incredibly important purchase.

Finally, he looked at the price.

This item costs 15,555,555 Minor Spirit Coins.

Xavier swore under his breath. That was three times what he had. He blinked and looked at how many Participation Points he would need for the item.

This item costs 80 Participation Points.

Xavier shut his eyes and sighed. He didn't have enough. He couldn't bloody well *afford* it. Then he blinked. What if he combined his Participation Points and Minor Spirit Coins?

Was there a way to... split the payment?

He prompted the System Shop to give him that option. When it did, he sighed again, this time in relief. He had enough.

Just enough.

Buying this item would leave him with no Participation Points left and only 125,480 Minor Spirit Coins.

Perhaps it wasn't wise to spend almost every bit of his money on this one item just before returning to Earth. He had no idea what they would need to do when they returned.

But he did it anyway. He could always create or earn more spirit coins—what he *couldn't* undo was the invaders' home worlds' learning of his true power. Learning that he was E Grade.

The item appeared on the ground before him. Usually items he purchased would end up in his hands, but this one had more components than he'd expected. He should have guessed that it would, as the description had said it had multiple insertion points.

The item looked similar to his Portal Block, but the rods were a little bit shorter, roughly three feet long, and the spherical crystals at their ends was smaller too, roughly the size of a golf ball.

"What's that?" Howard asked.

Xavier smiled. He'd been quiet for almost an hour now, focusing on this, and gathering more spirit coins—which he was glad he'd done, or he wouldn't have been able to afford this at all.

"This is going to help word of how strong I am never leave Earth."

He chatted with the others for a little while, letting his reserve of Spirit Energy regenerate back to its fullest—he didn't want to return to Earth and have it be empty, even if it was tempting to create some more money.

There was an air of excitement about the group. The others hadn't purchased much. Siobhan had mostly gotten health potions that could be used by F Grade Denizens. They didn't know what they would be returning to, and even though she could heal, she wanted to distribute them to those they encountered.

"We have no idea if they even have access to health potions back on Earth," Siobhan said. "There's certainly no chance they will have a System Shop. If Queen Alastea's castle didn't have one set up, I doubt anyone back on Earth will. They may have alchemists creating them, but who knows how organised it will be."

"The invaders might have access to the System Shop," Justin muttered.

Siobhan shook her head. "No, I don't think that they will."

"We don't have to speculate for much longer," Xavier said, looking at the timer in the top-right corner of his vision.

It was almost at zero.

Siobhan smiled. Justin rubbed his hands together, then placed one of them on the hilt of his sword. Howard got this intense expression on his face that made him look very serious. Xavier wondered if that was the face he wore back when he was a cop.

Xavier summoned Charon's Scythe to his hand and looked down at himself.

The System had integrated Earth into the Greater Universe less than two weeks earlier in Earth time. He and his party had experienced more of that time than anyone else, being on the fifth floor for as long as they had been.

Less than two weeks, and he felt like a completely different person. Less than two weeks, and he was now the most powerful Denizen from Earth, with the weight of the entire world on his shoulders.

And now, they were finally returning home.

How much could have changed back on Earth in that time?

Accidental Champion continues
in Accidental Champion 3**!**

Thank you for reading Accidental Champion 2

We hope you enjoyed it as much as we enjoyed bringing it to you. We just wanted to take a moment to encourage you to review the book. Follow this link: Accidental Champion 2 to be directed to the book's Amazon product page to leave your review.

Every review helps further the author's reach and, ultimately, helps them continue writing fantastic books for us all to enjoy.

ALSO IN SERIES:

Accidental Champion
Accidental Champion 2
Accidental Champion 3

Want to discuss our books with other readers and even the authors?

JOIN THE AETHON DISCORD!

You can also join our non-spam mailing list by visiting www. subscribepage.com/AethonReadersGroup and never miss out on future releases. You'll also receive three full books completely Free as our thanks to you.

Don't forget to follow us on socials to never miss a new release!

Facebook | Instagram | Twitter | Website

Looking for more great LitRPG & Progression Fantasy?

Check out our new releases!

Betrayed by his guild... Left for dead... He must become stronger than they ever imagined. *Ever since Arwin was summoned as a child, all he has known is war. And now, to claim the demon queen's life and end the war, he has to sacrifice himself. But, as he deals the final blow, the Hero of Mankind is betrayed. Caught in a magical explosion thought to end him, Arwin awakens a month later to find that everyone has already moved on. His [Hero] class has changed to a unique blacksmith Class called [The Living Forge] that is empowered by consuming magical items, but some of his old passive [Titles] remain, giving him the power to forge his new future exactly the way he wants to. Arwin isn't going to settle for anything less than completely surpassing the powers he wielded as the Hero. After all, you are what you eat – and Arwin's diet just became legendary.* **Don't miss the next epic LitRPG Saga from Actus, bestselling author of Return of the Runebound Professor. With nearly 7-million views on Royal Road, this definitive edition is perfect for fans of Seth Ring, Jonathan Brooks, Michael Chatfield and lovers of all things Progression Fantasy and Crafting. About the Series:** *Features a healthy mix of crafting and combat, a strong-to-stronger MC, power progression, a detailed magic system, item enchantment, smithing, unforgettable characters, and much more!*

Get Rise of the Living Forge Now!

A magical new world. An ancient power. A chance to be a Hero. *Danny Kendrick was a down-on-his luck performer who always struggled to find his place. He certainly never wanted to be a hero. He just hoped to earn a living doing what he loved. That all changes when he pisses off the wrong guy and gets transported to another world. Stuck in a fantasy realm straight out of a Renaissance Fair, Danny quickly discovers that there's more to life. Like magic, axe-wielding brutes, super hot elf assassins, and a talking screen that won't leave him alone. He'll need to adapt fast, turn on the charm, and get stronger if he hopes to survive this dangerous new world. But he has a knack for trouble. Gifted what seems like an innocent ancient lute after making a questionable deal with a Hag, Danny becomes the target of mysterious factions who seek to claim its power. It's up to him, Screenie, and his new barbaric friend, Curr, to uncover the truth and become the heroes nobody knew they needed. And maybe, just maybe, Danny will finally find a place where he belongs.* **Don't miss the start of this isekai LitRPG Adventure filled with epic fantasy action, unforgettable characters, loveable companions, unlikely heroes, a detailed System, power progression, and plenty of laughs.** *From the minds of USA Today bestselling and Award-winning duo Rhett C Bruno & Jaime Castle,* An Expected Hero *is perfect for fans of* Dungeon Crawler Carl, Kings of the Wyld, *and* This Trilogy is Broken!

Get An Unexpected Hero now!

638

Order Now!

(Tap or Scan)

He has a year left to live… unless he gains the power to kill the Gods first. *Each year, the Nightlords choose a new Emperor to rule Yohuachanca. Delicious food graces his palate. The realm's most beautiful women fill his vast palace. Four priestesses counsel him in all matters. The life of an emperor is good, luxurious, and short… For at the year's end, he is sacrificed to the Nightlords under the light of the Scarlet Moon. Iztac is the piss-poor orphan chosen to be this year's emperor. A sacrifice bound for the altar. But the Nightlords have made a mistake this time. For Iztac is a sorcerer, whose soul journeys into the secret underworld to plunder the secret spells of the dead. There, in the darkness, hides the power to drag the Nightlords off their throne. He has a year to find it, or perish for good. Iztac may not be the first emperor, but he* will *be the last.* **Don't miss this action-packed Progression Fantasy saga with a unique spin from Maxime J. Durand, bestselling author of Vainqueur the Dragon, The Perfect Run, and Apocalypse Tamer.**

Get The Last Emperor Now!

For all our LitRPG books, visit our website.